"PRIM? I TAKE OFFENSE, SIR!"

One night of wine and fifteen years of resentment bubbled up in her.

"Prim? *PRIM?*" she said furiously, stamping her foot. "You vulgar, uppity, disrespectful—
"I'll show you 'prim'!"

She took his face in her hands and kissed him. The shock of it took his breath away. She insisted until he yielded, then tried to back away, realizing with horror what she'd done. He circled her slim waist with a strong arm, pressing her body to his. "Don't shy away. I won't hurt you," he whispered.

"I'm not afraid—I don't think," she responded uncertainly.

"You want me to stop?"

"No. Kiss me again before you leave."

"If I kiss you again, I won't be leaving."

BENEATH THE COOL EXTERIOR BURNED AN EVERLASTING FLAME

Books by Valerie Vayle

LADY OF FIRE
SEAFLAME

SEAFLAME

VALERIE VAYLE

A DELL BOOK

Published by
Dell Publishing Co., Inc.
1 Dag Hammarskjold Plaza
New York, New York 10017

Dell ® TM 681510, Dell Publishing Co., Inc.

ISBN: 0-440-17693-X

Printed in the United States of America

First printing—October 1980

For Larry
and
Tycho Brahe

Why not?

Prologue:

POINTS OF DEPARTURE

An opulent tropical moon lighted their way.

Desperate, greedy men, their swarthy skins gleaming in the moonlight, they rowed small boats cautiously into the concealed Tortuga bay, empty now of the lumbering men-o'-war that had been there earlier. That was why these furtive derelicts of humanity had come. The French buccaneers who inhabited this tiny island were gone, having sailed that morning to ravage the rest of the Caribbean, and the silent raiders came now to plunder what the buccaneers had left behind: jewels, gold plate, silks, spices—whatever spoils they might get their grasping hands on. And there would be human bounty as well. Women for rape and children to sell as slaves.

They pulled their flat boats high on the beach, the wooden bottoms hissing against the fine sand. As they checked the daggers and pistols at their waists one man crouched in the sand and struck flint to tinder. A wisp of fire flickered, died, flamed back, and grew. One by one the raiders stuck torches into the feeble glow and the oil-soaked rags exploded into garish orange. The men passed the light from torch to torch, then filed silently through the undergrowth toward the small village.

Both children were sleeping soundly when hell erupted around them. The rude structure that was their home had primitive wooden poles for walls and a packed earth floor, but the children slept on velvet covers. In the corner was a carved mahogany coffer, jewels and ropes of fat, waxy pearls spilling carelessly from it. On a rough-hewn shelf above there were gold plates and goblets encrusted with sapphires. A cloisonné vase, worth a king's ransom anywhere in Europe, was simply a water jug here.

The mother, a dark-haired woman whose extraordinary beauty was miraculously unmarred by the desperately hard life she'd lived, was asleep on a pallet by the door of the hut. Suddenly the steamy night air was full of shouts and pistol shots. The woman was instantly alert—she was no stranger to midnight alarms and danger from men who wanted what was not theirs. She gently shook the children awake and whispered urgent instructions. "Hide in the jungle and don't come out for anyone but me. No sounds!"

The older girl, a sable-haired replica of her mother, put a thin arm around her younger sister. "Gen, we have to hide now," she whispered, then quickly clamped a hand over the fair child's mouth. "No, Gen, don't cry."

The mother opened a soft leather flap that covered the window at the back of the hut and helped the older girl climb out. With eight-year-old agility, the girl clambered out the tiny opening and reached back to help lift her younger sister through. The mother brushed a light kiss to each sleep-confused face as the children disappeared. "Quickly!" she urged them away.

Sudden light glared from the open door behind her and the woman spun around, hastily dropping the window flap. A dirty behemoth with greasy hair and rotting teeth stood leering at the door. "A pretty piece, ain't ye," he said in a voice slimy with lust.

The woman tossed back her raven-black hair defiantly. "I'm spoken for," she said sarcastically. An echo of gutter French tinted her speech. "Get out, *bâtard*!"

Grinning horribly, the man moved toward her. "I like spirited wenches," he said. A trail of spittle glistened on his matted beard.

The woman stood perfectly still as he came closer,

then she ducked her head and dodged to the right. The raider, though large and clumsy, was fast. He reached out a hammy fist and yanked her back, dragged her out the door and into the clearing in the center of the group of huts, shouting to his comrades.

The village was in chaos—huts had been fired and the thatched, palm leaf roofs burned brightly, casting an insane orange glow over the scene. Women screamed, children cried, and an elderly man who hadn't gone with the rest held a broken arm at his side and retched. The woman, trained by life in the arts of misdirection, did not look back toward the hut and the lush jungle behind where her children were hiding.

Her captor pressed his filthy face close to hers and muttered an obscenity. His breath stank of corruption and decay. She tried to strike him, but he wrenched her arm around and flung her to the ground. Falling on her, nearly crushing breath from her body, he writhed in animal ecstasy. Gritting her strong white teeth against the useless cry for help that welled in her soul, the woman flailed her arms in seeming helplessness. But in a moment she felt the worn handle of the dagger the man carried. Fixing her grip firmly, she drew back her hand and then, with all her strength, plunged the dagger into his fleshy side.

He reared up, bellowing with pain and surprise. She slashed at him again, and again. Blood spurted from his neck and with a gurgling cry he clutched at his throat and rolled away. Splattered with her captor's blood, the woman leaped to her feet and ran. She had gone but a few steps when another strong hand clamped her arm. "Ye gone and killed me matey, slut!" her new assailant accused. A weasily, wiry man with an elaborate moustache, he had a terrible strength and she could feel his fingers biting bruises into her arm.

She heard a thin, breathy cry and from the corner of her eye she saw another of the raiders stepping out of the jungle. Torch held high in one hand, he pushed two children ahead of him. The dark girl held her small, shapely head high, reflections of her mother's defiance flashing. The younger, the fair-haired one called Gen, was dry-eyed with carefully controlled terror. She walked stiffly, hugging herself with thin, trembling arms and casting anxious glances at her sister as if for direction.

The mother made a move toward them. *"Mes enfants!"* she cried.

The man holding her arm jerked her back. "Not no more, they ain't."

"I've killed a man tonight," the woman said with venom, "and I'll kill anyone else who puts his filthy paws on my babes."

The man slapped her—hard. She reeled back and he pursued her, striking again and again. The orange glow at the edge of her vision faltered, faded to gray, then black. The circle of light and consciousness was closing. She fell to her hands and knees and tried to crawl away. In the narrow tunnel of her vision she could see her beloved children ahead of her, two of them—then four, then two—blending, overlapping, tilting. She struggled forward and could taste blood in her mouth.

Her elbows gave out and she fell forward. She held out her arms to them. "My treasures—" she whispered through cracked and bleeding lips.

The last thing she saw was the little girl as she broke away crying, "Mama!"

Then the circle closed. Relentless, merciful darkness wrapped itself around her, blotting out pain, fear, everything. . . .

Two weeks later, at the slave market in Port Royal, Jamaica, a well-dressed Englishwoman talked to the auctioneer. "I need a kitchen maid of good health," she told him. Something deep in her stirred guiltily, but after all, the slaves were dark-skinned people who spoke strange sullen languages and God seemed to intend them to work for white Christians.

The slave seller led her into a large, dirty, fenced area. Manacled to the posts were slaves—old and young, men and women as well as children. Mrs. Anne Faunton, the buyer, looked about, pity and disgust mixing in her heart as she surveyed the wretches. Suddenly she saw something out of place. A group of children huddled in the corner of the vast pen, their dark heads bowed in pain and hunger. But among them was one that was different. "That child is white!" Mrs. Faunton said.

The auctioneer shrugged his unconcern. "They was two of 'em. Just one left now. I don't supply 'em, ma'am, I just sell 'em."

Mrs. Faunton pushed past him, knelt in front of the child, cupped the dirty chin, and raised the girl's face. She was encrusted with dirt and long-dry tears had etched rivulets in the filth. Her hair hung in blood-caked strands and her eyes were weary and dull. "What is your name, child?"

The little girl looked at her blankly for a long time, then said very softly, "Genevieve?" A look of confusion passed over her features as if she were surprised at the name—for her name was now the only part of her past that remained in her memory.

At the same time, half a world away, it was an hour before what would never quite be dawn. A murky, slate-colored French sky dribbled sullen sleet on the solitary traveler. Wearing a massive, sodden cloak that covered all save his upper face and the horse's head and legs, he looked from a distance like some grimly determined nightfiend plodding home after an exhausting Sabbat. The dark animal beneath him could have been an extension of his demon form—hooved, tailed, hairy. Lightning flashed and sizzled, making a grotesque silhouette of man and beast. Thunder bellowed, rumbled, and answered itself into oblivion.

The sleet thickened to the consistency of grease-glob-uled gravy.

There was no path, no beacon, no joy. When lightning flared closer, it revealed a thin, wet, middle-aged man on a rangy mare, not a black demon seeking the gates of a homey hell. The man was past youth, but not past hope. He patted the leggy mare under the folds of the cloak where the thick wool kept her neck warm. "We have done this before, *ma belle*, do you recall? But that time we spurred to the wind and ran for all we were worth. This time the danger, though still pursuant, is not quite so keen on our trail. We move at a safer pace this time. Time marches, does it not, and we are no longer so young as we were that time, *ma belle*."

There was a dissatisfied mew under the cloak, then the weight on the man's lap shifted. "I'm hungry, Matthew," the child said sleepily as he stuck his face out in the sleet.

"A few more hours, then food and warmth and a new home."

"I like the home I *had*," the child answered, withdrawing his face from the cold so that he spoke in cloaked tones from beneath his wool tent.

"I know," the man told him softly, "and I am sorry. But this must be done. Do you still have the ring?"

"Yes, here on this chain." A hand stuck out, holding an engraved signet ring. "Matthew, will I ever see my real family?"

"Maybe in heaven. Go back to sleep. When you wake all will be well." *I hope,* the man added to himself as the mare plodded on through the icy rain.

Part One

WIDOW'S EMBARKMENT

1

"Ship ahoy! Starboard bow!" the sailor called down from the crow's nest. No one actually stopped their work to look, but there was an instant air of quickened alertness among both crew and the isolated knots of passengers on deck. Genevieve Faunton shaded her eyes with a properly gloved hand and looked out to sea, squinting into the sunsketched horizon. But she could see nothing but flat blue miles of sea. At twenty years of age, she was a small, deliberately neat woman clad in chocolate-colored linen, unadorned with either lace or jewels. Instead of the tortured curls that were still fashionable, her thick brown hair was confined to a long braid which twisted into a plump figure eight at the nape of her neck. Her appearance suggested iron bands of good sense imprisoning something vital and rare.

At her side was frothy Mrs. Faunton. Genevieve hoped she hadn't heard the warning that there was another ship in the area. It would alarm the older woman and she thrived on alarm. The only thing she did better was love pity. There was no permutation of pity and condescending affection that Genevieve hadn't been subjected to in the past fifteen years—since the day she was "born" at the slave market, five years old and possessing only tattered clothing and a dim sense of her Christian name.

Mrs. Faunton passed a delicate lace handkerchief over her face and sighed. "I do so wish John could have made this trip with us," she said, foaming with delicious regret.

Of all the people in the world, only John could have made this trip any duller than it already is,

Genevieve thought, but gave no outward sign of dis-
agreement. John Faunton was the older woman's only
son—or had been until an attack of measles had taken
him to his reward. He had also been, for a mercifully
short time the previous year, Genevieve's husband.
John had been in school in England for most of the
years that his family lived in the Caribbean and upon
his return had developed an overwhelming affection
for his parents' ward.

Mrs. Faunton had taken to her rooms in tears when
he declared his intention to marry Genevieve. She had
emerged later saying, ever so bravely, that she thought
it was "too, too wonderful" that her son wanted to
marry "poor, dear little Genevieve." The arrange-
ments were made without too much consideration of
whether Genevieve wished to marry or not. The fact
that Genevieve had also spent the week weeping was
taken as evidence of normal virgin timidity.

As a husband, John had been everything Genevieve
had feared. Servile and domineering by turns, he
meant to extract at least a semblance of love from his
wife at any cost. Somewhere between his lachrymose
pleas and black-edged threats, Genevieve had learned
to despise him and strengthened her already well-
developed sense of reserve. In the privacy of her own
mind, she dreamed on about the mystery of her past,
oblivious to the storm of John's emotions swirling
around her. When John died, spotty and feverish,
raving his warped love to the end, Genevieve donned
mourning, secretly smiling behind her black veil. His
funeral was the most festive occasion of her life, but
this too she concealed and it was remarked in Mrs.
Faunton's circle how very, very brave poor, dear
Genevieve was being.

"She still approaching?" The shouted question took
Genevieve by surprise. The captain stood behind her
bellowing up at the boy in the crow's nest.

"Yessir!"

"Well, dammit boy, what colors is she flying?"

"Colors? Whatever is happening?" Mrs. Faunton twittered and fluttered her fan.

"Nothing. Don't worry," Genevieve soothed. "Perhaps you would be more comfortable in the cabin. It's very hot here in the sun—"

But Mrs. Faunton wasn't going to be deflected from a scene this easily. "It is another ship, isn't it? Oh me, oh dear, you don't suppose—you don't think that it's—"

"Pirates?" A mellow male voice cut in. Robert St. Justine, fellow traveler and lazily amused observer of life, had joined the women at the rail.

Genevieve thought she detected a note of hope in his voice. As bored as *she* was with this seemingly endless voyage, a handsome young man like him must be feeling the boredom even more keenly. He looked the sort of rich rakehell whose natural habitat was gambling dens and questionable salons, though to be fair, his behavior toward her had been courteous—almost negligently courteous.

"Pirates!" Mrs. Faunton fairly screamed. "I knew it! I knew it! We'll all be murdered! Oh dear, my jewels! I've got to hide them. Quickly, Genevieve—"

Genevieve cast a resigned look at heaven, then shot a quick glare at Robert St. Justine before leading the older woman away. Robert watched them go, wondering idly why the plain brown wren of a girl was traveling with the nearly hysterical woman. Was she a paid companion? She had that look—basically attractive young woman dressing and acting a denial of her appearance. But no, he'd been introduced to them earlier and he seemed to recall that they shared the same last name. Mother and daughter? No. No resemblance. Their somber clothing seemed to indicate mourning—mourning, or just very poor taste. Pity. The girl could be pretty.

Genevieve was back in a few moments. "Why did

you tell her that?" she demanded. "Was it just to give me something to do, or do you think it might really be pirates?"

Robert was astonished at her self-assured tone. He'd categorized her as a pleasant enough little dormouse and here she was, chiding him. "Do you *want* it to be pirates?" he asked.

"What a perfectly outlandish thing to say, Sir," Genevieve answered.

He looked at her more closely. Was this genuine outrage or did he detect a thin film of mockery in her reply? "You haven't answered me," he said.

She was rescued from response by the quartermaster striding to within a foot of her, cupping his hands about his mouth and shouting up, "What flag does she fly, lad?"

Genevieve, slightly staggered by the proximity and volume of the question, reeled to one side. She caught a glimpse of light glaring off something in the crow's nest—a spyglass, doubtless.

"English, Sir," the boy shouted down.

Robert cocked an eyebrow at Genevieve, noting the relieved sag of her shoulders. "I shouldn't relax yet, Miss—Madame?" She gave him a tight-lipped smile that lent no response to his fumbling inquiry as to her marital status. "I wouldn't relax yet," he repeated. "Notice how they're angling in toward our bow so we can't fire on them. They could still be pirates."

"You don't appear overconcerned, Sir."

"Be the biggest excitement of this trip. You act none too alarmed yourself. Five quid says it's a pirate ship."

Genevieve caught herself about to take the wager, before remembering that well-bred young ladies did not gamble. Not even with charming, frivolous—a glance at his clothes—*rich* young gentlemen. She contented herself with the insinuation of a scoffing laugh and leaned on the rail. Seaspray stung her face as she watched the dark brigantine breasting the foamy seas.

"She's moving slowly, taking in the situation," Robert said, leaning on the rail with her and staring at the lurking vessel with a fascinated frown. "Sails are furled, she's waiting."

The sleek, unidentified vessel was nudging the wind, bucking the sea and quite effectively lining up at a point directly in front of the merchantman *John Cooke* and its staring passengers. The dark brigantine hovered, motionless, still too far away to show more more than her flag and adumbral bow. Genevieve found herself clutching the rail with paralyzed fingers. Salt spray on her lips—why was that so familiar? Salt spray and billowing white sails above her neat brown hair. *I have done this before. . . .*

The crew and several passengers gathered, locked in silence, as the brigantine lurked and lolled, debating possibilities. "They're lowering the British flag!" cried the cabin boy in the crow's nest. "They're raising— they're raising the—" his voice was now soprano with the passage from excitement to fear.

Sails burst open on the brig, unfurling in a flood of wind-billowed ebony canvas.

The wind filled the black sails, propelling the trim ship forward at an incredible speed. Raven-draped, it seemed to be clad in mourning for its soon-to-be prey. Even more horrifying, from her flagline flew one of the many banners traders called the Bloody Colors or Jolly Roger—in this case a snow-white banner emblazoned with a winged black skeleton wielding a gory sword. "My God!" shrieked a sailor. "It's the *Black Angel!*"

"You see?" Robert said. "Had you taken up my wager I'd be five pounds richer this very moment." But his flipness had a thinly serrated edge of fear.

"Tis just as well you did not win it. They'd be taking it away from you in another hour, anyway." Genevieve matched his tone.

His mouth fell open. "So the little wren has talons!

Best fly belowdecks, Miss. Or is it Madame? We will probably be boarded soon and I understand the process is not pretty."

But the sight of the attacking ship exerted a hypnotism like a snake's gaze on Genevieve and she stayed where she was as the black ship swooped in for the kill. It was coming straight at them now. Sun gleamed off the bow. "Why is she so shiny in front?" Genevieve asked, suddenly losing her icy demeanor.

"Probably an iron-sheathed hull under the paint. They've removed that notorious figurehead for ramming, I see. There's an odd rumor about the *Black Angel*. People claim her captain is—"

The sailors shoved them roughly to one side and applied themselves to slitting open canvas bags with long daggers. Sand gushed, whispering, from the bags. "Why are they doing that?" Genevieve asked. "They're throwing sand all over the decks."

"You don't want to know," Robert said with awesome control.

Genevieve whirled to face a bare-chested sailor. "What are you doing?"

"Sanding the decks so when she boards us we don't slip in the blood."

Sand. Blood. Something rang fleeting recognition in Genevieve's throbbing mind and was instantly gone, leaving behind the clotting taste of foul, fractured memory that led to nothing but fear. Robert St. Justine saw her shiver and put an arm around her narrow shoulders, all his jovial bantering gone. She did not feel it. The black ship filled her line of vision through the slick, tarred cross-roping the crew was stringing down from the shrouds and ratlines. It would give boarding pirates no grip but a futilely slick one that would drop them to the sea before they could land. Genevieve gulped, faltered, and forgot herself far enough to seize hold of Robert. His eyes widened with this unexpected turn of events. "Say, this isn't going badly at all," he mumbled. "Bring on the pirates." Then, more seriously, "We better go below."

She lifted her head. "We? Aren't you going to stay up here and fight with the crew?"

"Why? What has the crew of the *Black Angel* ever done to me?" he asked with indolent surprise.

His fear was of the immediate danger, but hers was of the strange shadowy childhood ghosts that were beginning to emerge—not the looming pirates.

Looming? God! The black ship was upon them! There was no need to extricate herself from Robert's arms. The splintering collision did that for her. She was lifted as though by a mighty hand and flung to one side. Barrels tore loose from their lashing and rolled with her.

Sand and sea spattered the decks. Sailors toppled end over end to the turquoise and emerald seas that leapt hungrily below. Men swore, wood groaned and buckled; rigging split and came snaking down like vengeful vipers, bloodying all in its path. From below-decks came the screams of terrified women and the lowing of panicked cattle. Horses whinnied, hens cackled deliriously.

Even before Genevieve regained her footing, the clang of steel on steel filled the air. Buccaneers had slashed their way through the torn, tarred rope meant to repel them and were swarming onto the crippled decks of the *John Cooke*. Saber met rapier and shattered the lighter weapon; cutlass clashed with its kind; scimitar met antique claymore and exposed its weaknesses. Pistols exploded on their owners nearly as often as on their foes. The pirates had come prepared. With handguns slow to load and fire, the boarding party had hung half a dozen primed pistols from each belt, ready at a moment's notice for firing.

The cannon on the *John Cooke* were stationary, mechanical monsters locked in place and unable to fire in any direction except straight out. The *Black Angel*, existing only as a seagoing bird of prey, bore light swivel cannon, three of which sent massive roundshot into the bowels of the *John Cooke*, making her sag despondently in the water. Genevieve flailed her arms in search of something solid to hold onto as the ship listed sickeningly. Other swivel guns were cranked back on their haunches, muzzles up, to belch forth chainshot which ripped and tore through the shrouds and sails.

Rigging and acres of canvas sank to the sanguine decks, imprisoning Genevieve and a score of others. She fumbled in the sudden, stifling dark and felt a body next to her—but it was merely that—a body. No head. A deep pit of nausea tunneled in her stomach, making her retch.

She crawled through hot, sticky blood on her hands and knees. She had to get away from the nightmare corpse—anywhere! Just away! She placed her hand on something sharp and cold. She jerked back. Knife? Sword? She grasped it and found it to be a heavy cutlass. Not sure why she did so, she dragged it along as she crawled. Above the canvas she heard the appalling din of battle.

There was no opening, no direction or escape from the oppressive sails. Even the concept of up and down had become murky in the steamy half-darkness. At last she stabbed the cutlass through the canvas and was amazed at the ease with which it sliced the ponderous material. The ship pitched again. It seemed she could hear water slapping wood closer than it should have been.

She stumbled, striking head and arm. Blood started to trickle on her arm, but she pressed resolute fingers to the cut and fought her way through the rent in the canvas. Where were Mrs. Faunton and the Colonel? And the jesting Mr. St. Justine? She glanced about wildly.

The *John Cooke* was riding low in the water, listing to port. Strangled gurgles in the wood told her that it was only a matter of time before the ship sank.

The *Black Angel* rose above them, undaunted by the bone-crushing, timber-shattering collision. Genevieve stared up at the figurehead of the pirate ship, removed from the prow and lashed high in the masts to avoid damage in the collision.

It was a larger-than-life-size figure of a voluptuous, naked woman. One knee was slightly up, back arched to jut out her pelvis and breasts. Unbound waves of carved raven hair fell to her hips. Massive black, spread wings were rooted on her shoulders. One arm was at her side, the other up, holding a sword. The wooden woman's face was a masterpiece of the wood-carver's art, scarlet-lipped, black-eyed, serenely self-confident, lushly sexual, and menacing in a brazen, bewitching way. Robert St. Justine had not been exaggerating when he referred to it as "that notorious figurehead." It shamed and fascinated Genevieve and she had to force herself to look away.

And none too soon. A hefty brigand with mud-colored hair lunged for her. She leaped to one side, hampered by her long skirts, now heavy with bloody sand. She turned to flee, but the man caught her, lifting her off her feet. Death chanted in her ears—a mad symphony of last screams, curses, and banging swords. She twisted and shrieked futilely, then remembered the cutlass. She was too close to use it for stabbing, but when she brought it up behind the brigand's back and smacked the flat of it across the side of his head, it made an effective club. He staggered, swore in Gaelic, and released her. Genevieve picked up her damp, gritty skirts and bolted.

"Mrs. Faunton! Mrs. Faunton! Colonel! Mr. St. Justine—Robert!"

She did not know why she called for the dashing Englishman. Perhaps because he had been the last civilized person she had talked to before this foul nightmare began, perhaps because he had been kind and clever and she could not bear to think of him as one of the gory corpses with half-faces in the downed rigging.

Someone raced toward her, someone she did not recognize as a crewman—a tall, grizzled man in blue trousers and filthy white shirt. Savage with unthinking fear, she raised the heavy cutlass with both hands in a threatening pose. He hesitated a moment, but continued closer. An enemy, then. Genevieve cried out, swung the cutlass with all her strength and cried out again in greater horror as her flashing blade went through his arm—through sleeve, flesh, and sinew as if all were custard. Blood geysered and the man, with the cool acceptance of utter shock, turned slowly and looked down at his nearly severed limb.

She had not realized her own power, nor that of the weapon. She had never willingly harmed anyone or anything, not even the nasty lizards that had forever been dropping from ceilings in Jamaica. Something in her had snapped for a moment and she had inflicted grievous harm on another human. Horrified, she turned away and tried to run, stumbling over flaming hunks of fallen masts and disemboweled barrels. Blood, oil, rum, and sand made a disgusting pudding that sucked at her feet with vampiric noises.

She saw a shot that narrowly missed her drop the captain of the *John Cooke* in a neatly uniformed bundle. A horse from the hold had freed itself and rearing away from flaming timbers, dashed wildly through the melee to disappear, skidding and screaming, over the edge and into the impervious sea. Smoke, acrid and oily, billowed around her, gagging her. *Flames and a dead man.* Where had she seen all this before? Why was there an oppressive sense of *déjà vu* about this insane violence?

The ship was burning, sparks flaring to full-fledged flames and devouring everything in sight. Genevieve pushed her dirty, half-loosened hair out of her eyes and swayed, drunk from weariness, pain, and shock. Women were being slung over broad, sweating shoulders and carried to the pirate ship. Horses and cows were being herded across, some panicking and missing the short leap.

The *John Cooke* sat lower in the waves. *We've lost and everyone's dead or dying.* She released the cutlass and sank dizzily to the deck. Voices buzzed in and out of her head like annoyed insects. "That's it, bo'sun, we got them flames out."

"Got that worst hole patched?"

"—necessary, you know. When they saw she was sinking they come over real quick."

"Carpenter! Get to the leak on the second deck!"

Hammering, nailing. The shrill female screams and animals' complaints had died out. Someone poked Genevieve rudely. "Hey, we missed one. Here's a woman."

"Dead?"

"Naw, don't think so. Don't even look hurt much. Heft her over, Tommy."

Heat and solidity under her limp body. Weariness. Rolling colors and great silliness.

Then nothing.

London 1701

"And in summing up—"

The piracy trial of Isabelle Angeline Marie LeBeau Ninon Meddows, *née* Charron-Giraud, was nearly at an end. The defendant, a buxom black-haired woman none the worse for wear, in fact rather improved for it, sat irreverently picking at her cuticles with the handle of her ivory and bird-of-paradise feather fan.

Like many another wealthy prisoner, neither her health nor her wardrobe had suffered from a stay in jail. The source of this wealth was the matter under judicial consideration.

The attorneys, flocked like starlings around her,

might have been discussing the possibility of rain for all the interest she showed. Piracy was a hanging offense, but it didn't appear to affect the weathering beauty. Her prettily plump, slightly lined throat was in grave danger and she gave no sign of caring in the least. Only the closest observers noticed the beads of sweat on her icy forehead, the clammy palms sliding on the fan handle, the barely perceptible tremor to her knees.

There was no doubt about which way the verdict would go. The tea leaves had settled; the dice had landed. The madly colorful sands had run out in the defendant's timeglass of life. The reputations of the witnesses were impeccable, the jury untouchable, the judge unbribable. She knew—she had tried. Her defense counsel, though not the man she had requested, had gone above and beyond the call of money and loyalty in trying to save her.

It was hopeless.

The bewigged, myopic judge cleared his throat and addressed a courtroom pillar. "Members of the jury, I wish you to take ample time deliberating this case of Isabelle Angeline Marie—Marie—" he stumbled over his words and recovered in the same drone with few noticing his lack. "This case, this—ah—lady pleads—"

"Not guilty. Not guilty!" A defiant male voice called out. It rang through the packed courtroom like the clarion call of some clear, utterly sincere if slightly self-righteous bell. Isabelle Meddows gave nothing away, merely sat straighter as the trembling traces of a satisfied smile formed at the corners of her ripe scarlet lips.

The judge fumbled for his ear trumpet, missed, and sent it scuttling along the floor to the refuge of the witness stand, where it testified to his ineptness. "Er? What is this disturbance?" he demanded of a nearby banner stand which he took to be the defense attorney.

A young man elbowed his way through the crowd. Brown-haired, smoke-eyed, the pleasant stereotype of everyone's brother back home, he insistently made his way to the front of the courtroom. "My Lord, I am Jean-Michael Vavasour, an attorney, and I have important evidence in favor of the defendant."

"Evidence? Evidence, my good man?" the judge roared at an empty chair. "This trial has dragged on far too long as it is! Nay, there will be no more evidence! The jury is being sent out to deliberate!"

"There be no need to discuss it, M'lud, we have the verdict already," the foreman said. It did not take a seer to know what he was going to say next.

The young man who had casually taken the name "Vavasour" only seconds before sighed quietly. "The evidence—" he attempted again.

"For the last time, no new evidence is admissible!" the judge bellowed at the chastened chair. Onlookers were suddenly quiet, trying to soak in this and the fact that the young man was wearing not one but two beautifully matched Toledo rapiers.

"My Lord Judge, this intolerable imitation of so-called justice forces me to do something much against my wishes."

The woman Isabelle, with an almost nonchalant flick of her braceleted wrist, caught the second Toledo blade as it flashed through the thick air of the courtroom. The first was already aloft in the quick hands of the renegade lawyer who, half her age and deceptively innocent looking, had encircled an opposing lawyer's neck with his arm and was urging the man toward the doorway by slicing the buttons off his brocade vest with the tip of the rapier.

The woman was at his back in an instant, guarding him as they moved toward the sliding double doors. When a barrister stepped too close she poked him with her weapon, not enough to draw blood, merely a warning jab that let him feel cold, grim steel pressing his ribs. The barrister withdrew.

There was trouble near the door; the prosecution lawyer deliberately stumbled, drawing a dagger from his trouser waistband. Jean-Michael "Vavasour" was trapped between him and the crowd. Isabelle coolly wounded the dagger-wielder while her companion hastened back the crowd. People pressed them, cries of "goddamned pirates!" resounding through the room. A spectator drew a sword and violence flared.

Swords ringed them, pricked them. The oddly matched pair dueled their way to the door, still managing to drag the prosecution attorney with them as a shield. A rapier came up, struck a blow against the heavy signet ring Jean-Michael wore, causing his weapon to spin from his grip. Isabelle never missed a stride. She thrust her rapier into his hand and drew a "witch-sticker" from her bosom and a primed pistol from her skirts. Thus armed, they backed outside, bolted the door, and threw the opposing attorney into a watering trough.

Jean-Michael had brought two strapping geldings with him, but as Isabelle reached for their reins, she saw him leaping at the heads of two sleek roan mares, racers born and bred. He was astraddle one, nudging the other toward her in an instant. Thus mounted, they fled, leaving a chorus of muffled exclamations behind them.

The doors burst open. "After them!" Roan mares in the lead, a shrieking pack came hurtling down the crowded streets behind them, upsetting applecarts, terrorizing curs and giving sailors something to write home about. The pack blasted around corners, skidding on cobblestones and firing random shots at the two riders ahead. But the roan mares were Eastern stock and desert-raised—running was in their rich blood. The distance between prey and pack increased.

Still, the sustained strain was grievous. Even the roans were wheezing by the time Jean-Michael whisked them into a dark livery stable where all but two horses had been carefully rented out ahead of time. He flung two glittering doubloons to the urchin who exchanged horses with them. "That's a good boy —now burst that keg as I asked!"

Astride two sturdy cobs, Jean-Michael and the woman dug in their heels and wheeled out of the stable. The urchin bolted the doors behind them and raced into the street with the end of a rope in his hand. It connected to a stout barrel tottering in a window above. As the yapping pack of hunters clattered up the street and shouted at the sight of their quarry, the urchin gave the rope a solid yank and ran.

The barrel crashed to the cobblestones, releasing a wave of melted lard. The charging horses could not stop. They hit the slime and went skating crazily, long legs scrabbling in all directions until their riders went end over end. By now the pair everyone sought had nearly gained the crest of the hill. One of the men sliding madly in the muck managed to kneel and take aim. He balanced his long pistol on his wrist, squinted, and squeezed the trigger. The recoil sent him sprawling in the lard, but not before he saw one of the horses on the hill stand straight up on its hind legs and fall over backwards.

Jean-Michael reined in his horse and turned. The black-haired woman was faster. She had already regained her footing and was reaching out her hand. He caught it, pulling as she put her foot in the stirrup on his and vaulted up. The side of her face was blue with bruises, but she said nothing. He urged the horse on, over the peak of the hill.

Later, having doubled back, they boarded a ferry and crossed the Thames. On the other side a flower girl waited with a buggy, and a seedy bonnet and cloak for the woman. The young lawyer had already discarded his coat, mussed his hair, loosened his collar, and rolled up his sleeves. The flower girl giggled and coyly threw dirt at him to aid his disguise, then clamored for a much-deserved kiss. He complied, then tried to assist the buxom pirate woman into the buggy. She calmly pushed him to one side, kicked off her dainty, buckled shoes, and climbed in unaided. Once seated, she peeled off her silk stockings, loosed her abundant raven tresses, and yanked the bonnet lower to hide her face. The young man disentangled himself from the amorous violet vendor and climbed aboard.

Eyes locked in silent combat. They each took a rein, neither relinquishing control until they had driven quite some time in silence, giving the unfortunate buggy horse conflicting directions at every turn. At last the woman gave him the other rein, sank down comfortably in the seat, and pulled the disreputable hat over her face to shield it from the sun. As they left the city, the only sound was the clop of the buggy mare's hooves and the chirping of birds.

With a firm push from a little pink-nailed index finger, the woman moved the bonnet back. Her dark, mischievous feminine eyes in a hedge of charcoal lashes twinkled up at the young lawyer.

"Christ, Freddie," Sabelle said with a throaty laugh, "I was beginning to think you'd never get there!"

2

Genevieve awoke, not to the brutal fumbling of a rapist, but to the careful ministrations of an old Negro doctor. She jerked upright, nearly upsetting the basin of pinkish water. "Lady, please lie down again so I can bind de arm," he said simply, bending his grizzled head over the steaming cloths in the basin. Genevieve obeyed, letting him finish cleaning the lumpy cut. He wrapped it with a minimum of fuss, and moved away to dump the basin into a chamberpot. Genevieve glanced about her, thinking she had gone mad. This was no ship! Or was it? She was in a rosewood-paneled room, all parquetry inlaid and scalloped with gilt edges and grinning golden gargoyles.

She sat up, suddenly aware of how dirty she was with sweat, blood, and black soot, her hair hanging in limp wisps from its formerly tidy bun. She was on a neat pallet on a marble-tiled floor. A desk floated in and out of her field of vision and she realized she had not yet the strength to focus. "Lay you down, Lady. De captain come soon," the doctor said.

"The pirate captain? What would a pirate captain want with me?" she asked. He only shrugged. "I'll be poor sport!" Genevieve cried defiantly. "I'm dirty and plain!"

"What you think captain care about dat?" the doctor asked, shaking his head as if he were in the presence of a lunatic. He kept shaking his head as he left the room. She heard a bolt drawn behind him. *No, no, no, NO! No swine is going to rape me! I'll kill him— I'll kill myself before he touches me! Being handled by John was bad enough, I'll never let some filthy privateer do it! Me, of all women. Plain, plain me!*

There were pretty women on the ship, why won't the captain take them?

Rape and slaughter. Black hair. A woman with black hair like the shocking figurehead of the *Black Angel*. What were these ghost images flitting bizarrely through her mind? Genevieve rubbed her eyes, pursuing the taunting spectres. *The black-haired woman . . . there were men after her . . . blood and screams and. . . .*

It was gone. She had exorcised the ghost for the moment. Pain. Dizziness. Genevieve went on hands and knees, clawing at the intricate wood paneling until she could stand. The desk still seemed to float. She realized vaguely that she was still on a ship, surely in the captain's cabin and half out of her mind with fear.

She reminded herself that she was not one of those silly fainting women. She must be calm—breathe deeply, slowly. Yes, that was better. She could see things a little more clearly now.

She took one step, then another, and ran into the desk. She stumbled and fell over it. *Rape.* They were going to rape and torture her, make her tell who the rich passengers were. *Rob, kill. The heady scent of a steamy jungle night.*

"No! Go away!" she sobbed, flailing at the invisible demons that haunted her. She slid to her knees, groping for a drawer in the desk. Paper, money, jewels, ink bottles, a letter opener. That was it, a letter opener. She gripped it to her breast. They were not going to use her unless they enjoyed romancing dead women. But perhaps she could take one of them first. Hysteria, she thought flatly. Was she going over the crumbling edge of sanity?

The ship pitched, throwing her on the floor and rolling her across the captain's cabin. She struck a heavy piece of furniture and lay still, gulping sustenance. It must have been dusk, for the cabin was eerie with elongated shadows stacked upon one another. The doctor had left a lit lantern swinging from the wall.

Lights flaring in the night. Orange counterpoint to watery moonlight. Deep, drunken male voices.

Genevieve squeezed her eyes shut trying to force away the frightful waking dreams.

"Evenin', Cap'n Meddows," a voice outside the door said. Genevieve sat, scrambled and fell as the cabin door banged open. Useless. She was useless. She clutched the dagger as heeled boots swaggered across the marble-tiled floor, clicking to a halt near her head. Swaying like an Eastern fakir on hashish, Genevieve forced back tattered brown hair and propped herself on unsteady elbows.

Boots. Red knee-high boots of rich Moroccan leather; butter-soft, saber-scarred boots, laced up the inside. Cavalier boots encasing a well-shaped ankle and calf. Diamond buckles at the knees of too-well-worn trousers of dusty, indeterminate hue hugged slim, well-muscled thighs. Hips—there was something odd about the hips. And the heavy linen shirt with its faded blood and powder stains, lace dripping from cuffs—it did not fit properly, there was a pronounced swell beneath it.

Genevieve gaped, trying to look beyond the splattered rapier, the powder-burnt pistols hanging from a thick belt of Moorish design. Trousers, boots, and a hand holding a pouch of heavy gold. She forced herself to look farther, past the lace jabot of the once-gorgeous shirt, past the ruined magnificence of the brocade vest, past the mass of coal-black hair curling about shapely shoulder and soft bosom. Past the flamboyant plume of a captain's tricorn.

Genevieve stared straight up and found her astonished gaze pooled in the glittering black eyes of a wholly beautiful, wholly dangerous—woman!

"T'was a closer call than you're tellin' me, wasn't it, boy?"

The young man's eyes met Sabelle's. "Yes, it was, as a matter of fact. They hung Kidd today, did you know? He was allowed no attorneys, no counsel, not even law books. The government's cracking down on piracy, Sabelle. The aristocrats who hire the privateers will get away with a slap on the wrists, but scapegoats like you and Kidd will be strung up all across England."

"Poor ol' Kidd, he weren't never a dyed-in-the-wool pirate anyway. You saved me life, Freddie."

There was a wry silence as the barmaid refilled their tankards, then the lawyer put an elbow on the table and glared at the female swashbuckler. "Will you stop calling me that? My name, as you damned well know, is Jean-Michael and all my English friends call me Michael. You and your disreputable sea-going friends are the only people who call me Freddie. God! The very sound of the name makes me think of those years at sea as a cabin boy. I get queasy just remembering."

"I know you never took to it, but the name fit when I found you just a wee mite on the slave docks in Port Royal. Christ! The times I've spent in that hellhole lookin' for me own babes and *you're* all I turned up!" The affectionate tone in her voice belied the harshness of the words.

"Wee mite? Hell, I was twelve years old. I'd lived with nice people and gone to school until I was pressganged. You make it sound like I was a puking infant and you plucked me out of a woven basket."

Sabelle wasn't impressed with this rhetoric. "That was in France where you lived, weren't it?"

He cocked an eyebrow at her. "Well, nice *Spanish* couples don't name their sons Jean-Michael."

Sarcasm was wasted on her. "I suppose now that you're tryin' to be some sorta swell I should mend my ways, eh?"

He fingered the handle of his pewter tankard, a griffin rampant on a chimera's back. "The only direction in which you should mend your ways is to avoid England from now on. The war on piracy is spreading through Britain."

Sabelle put her feet up on the bench next to him. "Bet that courtroom business cooked your goose with the authorities."

"I'll get out of it."

"Ahhh, still doing secret work for the government? O' course, I hear rumors time to time, but—"

"So, what are your plans now?" he asked with a spurious smile that made her throw her hands up in despair at digging any deeper into his ways. Sabelle shook her head fondly and bellowed for more rum.

"*Sacre merde*, boy, me plans are to get back to me ship the *Nightbird* and go about conducting business same as usual—but not in British waters, that's damned sure! Why don't you come on along? Hell, I'll even fix the votes so's you're elected quartermaster."

Surrounded by the darkly glowing wood that matched his hair, the young man could have been a ship's figurehead. Then he lifted his head, showing amused gray eyes and more of a grin than most ship's carvings sported. "Sabelle, you know I hate the sea. I've sworn to never step foot aboard another ship as long as I live."

"How are you gonna cross the Channel? Walk? So you *was* a cabin boy and got wounded and knocked about—you're older now, we'll get you a good job on the ship and—"

"I didn't spend all those years at the University just to help me count loot on a pirate ship, Belle. I'm through with all that. I've got to establish a law practice." Michael waved off the fluttering barwench who was trying to refill his tankard. Sabelle had, of course, bribed the girl, but it was doing little good. Michael firmly turned his empty tankard face down, pewter rim resting unevenly on the scarred oak table with its ancient stains and dagger cuts. He met Sabelle's gaze evenly. "No. I am not returning to the sea, and you are not getting me drunk so that I'll stupidly agree to your little plots. I've got to go, Sabelle. My friends will be wondering why I've taken an unscheduled vacation."

"You mean it, don't you?" she asked, drooping as much as a brilliantly plumaged bird-of-paradise could droop.

"Yes. On top of all else, my friend from the University, Robert St. Justine, should be returning from the Caribbean any day and his family's asked me to meet him at the docks. I can't afford to offend them. They're brim full of wills and documents for a young lawyer to shuffle around and get paid generously for— and I *do* like getting paid! So, I really must go." He stood.

After a moment's pause Sabelle gathered her neat little pink-nailed feet under her ripe form and stood as well. "You've been a good friend, Freddie—er, Michael. Hell, you're Freddie to me! I'll send a messenger ahead to me crew. A fishin' boat'll take me to the *Nightbird*. So go on, boy, you've done more'n enough for me already. Get back to your lawbooks and flower girls."

She tried to shake his hand, but Michael enveloped her in a hug. She laughed, ruffling his hair. "Get away now, you young rake, before I go forgettin' me age and disgracin' the twain o' us."

"We'll see each other again, Sabelle. We always do," he said with grinning certainty.

"Get along with you now!" She gave him a kiss on the cheek and a whack on the rump. As she watched through the open shutters, Sabelle saw Michael pat the old bay nag he had brought. Then he passed it up and hopped nimbly on the back of a prancing black barb that someone had unwisely left in the yard. He clucked to the horse and trotted off in a shower of gravel.

"Quit piracy, me arse," Sabelle said with admiration. "He's just switched it to land, that's all."

Genevieve pushed her hair back out of her eyes and stared at the exotic vision before her. A woman? But the doctor had referred to Captain Meddows. *My wits have become addled,* Genevieve thought. She fought the temptation to close her eyes and drift back into unconsciousness. As she struggled to her feet she heard a throaty laugh that tickled a memory she could not grasp. She tried to form a question, but so many queries jostled for position that she merely sputtered, "Wh . . . what!"

The woman laughed again. "So, you're not dying after all, my fine lady. I heard how fierce you were during the attack and had to meet you. You damn near killed one of my men. I don't like that unless you're ready to take his place in the riggings." A taut thread of sarcasm laced through her words.

"Are *you* Captain Meddows?" Genevieve asked incredulously. The room seemed to lurch around her and she groped for support.

"Captain Evonne Meddows," the woman said and took a belligerent stance, hands on hips. "My, but you're the nervy one. *I'm* the one to ask questions and you'll be answering them or I'll have your tongue on a pewter plate. Who are *you?*"

Genevieve felt the blood drain from her face. Tongue on a pewter plate. A simple vulgarity—but why did it seem familiar? No, not familiar. She had never known the sort of individual who would say a thing like that—had she?

Flames, pistol shots, a leather flap hanging crookedly at a window.

The image flickered at the back of her mind, not quite memory, not quite imagination. She blinked it back, gulped nervously, and twined her fingers together so tightly it hurt. The pain brought her back to the moment. "I'm—" she hesitated, strangely unsure of just who she was.

"Tis a good start," the other woman said. "Now, move your pretty lips into the next word or I'll have it flayed out of you." She leaned against the inlaid wood edge of the massive captain's desk.

A bearded man lying in the dirt, blood gushing from his throat.

Genevieve passed a trembling hand across her forehead. What was happening? Strange images from nowhere were assailing her senses. "I'm Genevieve Faunton," she finally said.

"Married?" the other woman asked sharply.

"Widowed."

Screams. Scraps of burning palm leaves drifting through the night air.

"Too bad. No doting husband to pay ransom."

"Ransom?" Genevieve asked numbly.

"What do you think kept you alive?" Captain Meddows asked harshly. "You've got to be worth something to somebody. Those clothes are ugly as hell, but they must have cost a pretty penny."

The woman's attitude irritated Genevieve back to her senses. "My clothes were not ugly—until I had the misfortune to meet up with *you*," she said, grabbing a handful of tattered skirt and displaying a scorched hole as big as her hand. "If you think I'm going to bring you a handsome ransom, you had better go ahead and kill me right now—*if* you think you can!" She still held the dagger like letter opener in her left hand and she brandished it awkwardly.

Captain Meddows started to lunge toward her, but instantly caught Genevieve's motion and stopped. She stared for a second, smiled broadly, then bent over laughing.

Gen, we have to hide. A child's whisper in the dark. Shadowed half-memories flickered through Genevieve's mind.

"You're not much good at this," the woman said,

still chuckling. "But mayhaps there's more to you than I thought. Try putting it in your other hand and brace your feet better."

Genevieve almost obeyed, but felt an unfamiliar emotion well up and threaten to spill over. Hot tears burned against her eyelids. "Look, I'm not worth anything to anyone and you needn't mock me. It's hard enough not knowing who you are or where you belong without the unwarranted cruelty of strangers as well." The minute the words were out of her mouth, Genevieve regretted this outburst of old secret woes. What had come over her?

Captain Meddows stopped laughing and gazed at her strangely. There was no pity in her look, but there was bright-eyed curiosity. "Are you just feeling sorry for yourself or what?"

"I never feel sorry for myself," Genevieve said, untruthfully, for she had never felt *more* self-pity than she did at this moment.

"Then what do you mean—not knowing where you belong?"

The words sounded silly—pretentious and stagey—in another's mouth. Genevieve felt a need to justify herself and wondered vaguely why she felt that way. "It's just that I have no family, no purpose, no future, and now—now this!" She made a mad gesture that took in the woman, the ship, a pointless lifetime. She dropped the dagger and it clattered to the floor, unnoticed by either of them. She covered her face with her hands. "I'm—I'm unwell—"

"Sit down before you faint," the dark-haired woman ordered in a softer tone than she'd used before.

No, don't cry, Gen. A small child's hand over her mouth.

Genevieve felt her knees weakening and she reluctantly lowered herself onto a cushioned bench by the door. There was a long silence. The other woman paced the room, the diamond buckles at the knees of her trousered legs flashing wickedly in the candlelight.

She gnawed thoughtfully on a scarlet-painted finger-nail, asked Genevieve's age, and was answered. Once again she paced and turned, eyebrows arched in a half-formed question, but she did not speak again.

Genevieve tried to pull her thoughts into a pattern. For some reason this trousered beauty was interested in her hysterical outburst. Why? Genevieve felt only shame. Certainly the workings of her confused mind could be of no interest to such a creature and yet—? Was she going to be killed? Had she inadvertently said something that had sealed her fate?

Finally the captain yanked another chair forward, turned it around and sat down straddling it. She crossed shapely arms across the back, rested her chin on them and smiled. This close Genevieve could smell the exotic scent of jungle flowers the woman seemed to exude—the nightblooming smell of something white and waxy. "You're going to tell me all about yourself," she declared.

"Why?"

"Because I said so! Where's your home?" Captain Meddows asked.

The fetid smell of thin green porridge and death.

Genevieve took a deep breath of the floral scent around her and forced the eerie, unwanted images back. "I have no home," she said defiantly.

"*Merveilleux!* Who are you traveling with?"

"You, apparently! I *was* with my in-laws. I don't know if they're even alive now."

"Silly butterfly sort of a woman and old man with a moustache?"

"Yes." In other circumstances she would have smiled at the characterization of the Fauntons.

"They're alive. Got them down in the hold. Not very healthy place to stay for long, but they'll be brought up when I've got answers to my questions."

Chains chafing wrists and ankles.

Genevieve shrugged in defeat. Why endanger the

Fauntons? It wasn't as if she had any worthwhile
secrets to withhold. The only mysteries in her life had
been forever veiled from her *own* consciousness. "Very
well, ask your questions, but tell me, please—there was
a young man on board our ship. What of him?"

"A passenger? I don't think any of them were killed.
Only my crew got their guts spilled. Now," the captain
said, getting down to the business of her questioning,
"where are you going?" While waiting for the answer
she got up and strode to the door, shouted an unintelligible order and stood back as a servant brought in a
steaming bowl of water and set it down.

"We were on our way to England, to a little town
on the Scottish border where the Fauntons' family
home is." Genevieve watched in astonishment as her
questioner rummaged in a drawer, pulled out a bar of
soap and then, with complete immodesty, stripped off
her vest and shirt and began to wash her face, arms,
and neck. "Why are you going to England?" she asked
between splashes.

Genevieve was speechless. She had never seen anyone naked except herself, and this woman peeled off
her soiled finery as if there were nothing at all strange
about doing so. She had full, high breasts, a tiny waist,
and ivory silk skin—except where the faint pink
shadows of long-healed lash marks crisscrossed her
back. It took little imagination to see that this woman
was the inspiration for the figurehead of her ship. The
superb figure, waterfall of raven hair, and coldly sen-
suous ruby lips—all that was lacking were the wings.

"I said, why are you going to England," the half-
naked vision said as she crossed the room and searched
unselfconsciously through another drawer.

Genevieve was trying very hard not to be shocked,
in fact a part of her was somewhat envious of that sort
of uninhibited freedom from the conventions that
Genevieve had wrapped around her own life. "I'm
going to England because my husband's father has

retired and is returning to his family home there. I'm going along because—because there is no alternative. I had no choice."

The other woman pulled out a sea-green taffeta blouse trimmed with acres of silver lace and slipped into it with slithering grace. "Why not stay with your own people—or are they in England too?"

My treasures!

"I have no family." Genevieve shivered as the unbidden words echoed in the dark, doorless corridors of her mind. "I don't even know who they were. Why are you doing this? What possible concern can my private life be to you?"

"Remember, I'm asking, you're answering."

Genevieve put her fists to her temples. "Well, I'm tired of answering. I've hurt my arm, my clothes are rags, my head is about to crack open, and my mouth tastes like an old bird's nest. I need a drink of water and some sleep."

The woman laughed again, clearly delighted with this outburst. "I might even like you. *C'est bien.* I'll reunite you with your loving companions," she said. "We'll talk more later."

Genevieve opened her mouth to protest, but the door had already closed behind her captor. She sat there stunned for a moment. Whatever had happened to her dull, orderly life? Only this morning she had foolishly wished something interesting would happen once in a while. Well, something *had* and she wasn't prepared for it.

Get up, dear. I'm taking you home.

The words came from nowhere—out of the thick, dark miasma that was Genevieve's forgotten childhood. Who had said that? Why was her erratic memory throwing it back to her now? The questions that had crowded her mind only an hour ago had multiplied tenfold and she had no answers at all.

There was one thing she *did* know. She wasn't afraid of this woman Meddows though by all rights she ought to be. In a strange way she was almost drawn to her—an opposite pole of blunt, natural authority. Power and color and determination draped her like a cloak—and that fascinated Genevieve.

Jean-Michael's luggage was on the front veranda of Althea Pasteau's stylish Stuart mansion in London when his purloined barb came clattering up the glazed brick drive. He reined in at the foot of the stairs, leaned forward, chin in hand. Althea herself emerged in a minute, the pinnacle of eccentric fashion, from her watered silk ballgown (inappropriate in mid-morning, but quite becoming) to her gilt-edged monocle. Michael regarded her with a trace of exasperation. "Married him, didn't you?" he asked.

Trim, long, blond Althea, on the wrong side of thirty-seven and well on the road to becoming a *grande dame* no matter how she fought it, gave a helpless shrug. "I admit he's jealous, but he makes up for it. He simply wouldn't believe there was anything innocent in letting a young man stay at my house."

"No wonder, there *wasn't*."

She cocked a fan at him. "Only between marriages, dear boy. He simply packed for you and firmly set everything out here a week ago. I come out and dust your bags every day with surpassing loyalty."

He had to laugh, no matter how hard he struggled to keep a stern face. "Althea! You are completely and utterly incorrigible!"

She handed up two valises and a creased portmanteau, not huffing at all under their weight. "The Dowager St. Justine has been sending you frantic notes about drawing up a lease or something. Perhaps you could stay with them until your friend Robert returns. I truly am sorry, Michael."

"About what? I've been trying to move out for three years! You went into a snit every time I mentioned it. Couldn't stand to lose someone who regularly let you cheat at whist."

"I never," she declared, buckling bags to his saddle.

"—and bridge and chess and—"

"It is not physically possible to cheat at chess."

"Althea, you'd cheat at hide-and-seek if you could think of a way."

"There are *several* ways," she said firmly, tugging at his stirrup. He leaned over and tolerated a perfunctory peck on the cheek. "Off with you, dear boy. I shall expect you on holidays and every third Sunday of the month for dinner and—"

"Althea—"

"—and you will write when you can and eat your vegetables and stay away from chambermaids with the pox, is that clear? And no more of this rescuing female pirates in flamboyantly illegal ways."

"How did you know about that?"

"I read your mail. It's in the top bag. Certain peoples *very* high up in the government are furious with you. Of course, I'm not one to bandy monarchs' names about."

He kissed the top of her elegant blond head. "Thank you, my would-be watchdog-guardian angel. Go back to the house, I can tell you're dying for a smoke."

The fleet black barb pranced down the carriage path. *The King was furious?* Michael groaned. He'd overdone it again!

3

Genevieve had a great deal to think about that night, but her thoughts seemed to run about aimlessly like frightened animals darting through darkness. She had been captured by pirates, Mrs. Faunton was wailing in her ear, the Colonel was snoring raucously, and passing pirates were making frequent unkind comments on Genevieve's sex and untidy state of being. She looked and felt like a bundle of used scrub rags. Scullery rejects. They were confined with another family in a tiny cubicle that must have normally served as a storeroom of some sort and there was practically no air. Mrs. Faunton tried to smear some of the grime off Genevieve's face and only made it worse. "Oh, my dear," she lamented in the sugary, whiny voice that had been grating on Genevieve's ears for fifteen years, "You look almost like a blackamoor."

Better than looking dead, Genevieve thought sourly. "Have you seen Mr. St. Justine?" she asked her mother-in-law.

"Oh, that rich young man? He was slightly injured, but he's somewhere nearby. It isn't at all like you to inquire about a gentleman, Genevieve."

The Colonel, suddenly awake, said, "Can't spend her entire life grieving for John, you know. Girl's got a life ahead of her. Get married again. Cousin Ffolkes's boy George, I was thinking. Wrote to Ffolkes. Approves entirely. Fine boy, George."

George! Before she would marry George, Genevieve would have them open John's crypt and cast her down alongside him into eternal darkness. George was the essence of John's flaws deepened and widened, especially the cruel streak.

"Yes, that's the thing to do. Genevieve dear, you can't spend the rest of your young life tied to us," Mrs. Faunton said.

Panic gagged and held Genevieve speechless. First pirates, then the maddening snip of visions and shattered memories plaguing her all day, and now this! Nowhere to go, no one to hide behind. Bride of George or eternal companion to the Fauntons. Either alternative gave her a stifling sense of suffocation. *I would rather die than face the future they have planned for me.*

Mrs. Faunton and the Colonel fell asleep soon, comfortable in settling Genevieve's fate between them. She sat, back to the damp wooden wall, staring out at nothing. A pinpoint of light soon swelled and grew, revealing itself at last to be a whale-fat lamp in the hands of a lovely young mulatto woman. "Gen Faunton?" she asked with the soft accent of the islands.

"Yes?"

"Cap'n Meddows, she sent you this."

"This" was a bucket of cold, clear water and a hairbrush. "Cap'n say tomorrow you and others go through your bags and find yourselves some clean clothes."

"Why—thank you. I'm afraid I don't have any money to tip you—"

The mulatto's velvet-brown eyes flared up with gold sparks. "Tip me? *Tip* me? I no servant—I best damned gunner's mate in Caribe!"

"Oh—I'm sorry. I've never heard of a ship with women on board, much less as crew members and captain."

"Betcha we de only one ever. Not to let servant business happen again, Lady," the dark beauty said and padded off on swift bare feet into the black hold of the ship. After a moment's pause Genevieve realized the woman had left her a lantern. Thank God—she hated the dark. She removed the shredded bodice of her dress, then the filthy, scorched skirt, loosened her petticoats, and opened the neck of her chemise, sponging herself down with pieces of her skirt dipped in cold water. Neck, arms, face—ahh, that was so much better. She unbound her snarled hair and brushed it, fifty long strokes that made it feel silky and almost clean.

It was impossible to put her dress back on in the shape it was in, but she knew Mrs. Faunton would be shocked, so she began to smooth her rags with an eye toward gingerly crawling back into them.

Suddenly the lithe black woman loomed up above her again, startling Genevieve so that she dropped her bunched skirt.

"Sassy gent with saber cut asking for you. Gave a good bribe. Come on." She seized Genevieve by the wrist and yanked her to her feet.

"But I'm in my undergarments!"

"Dat don't distress sassy gents none. Scurry now."

Genevieve, lantern, underwear and all, was dragged halfway across the hold, protesting all the way. "Lady, when dis much gold involved, I deliver promised goods, so no more whine. Go," the mulatto said.

Genevieve was unceremoniously dumped on Robert St. Justine, who eyed her with a mixture of humor and lechery. "I wanted to assure myself of your well-being, not ravish you, but if you're going to make midnight visits in your shift—"

"How can you jest at a time like this?"

Stubble-chinned, wounded, dirty, he gazed at her from one clear greenish eye and one blackened, swollen one and said, "What do you mean, a time like this? I'm having the adventure of a lifetime and so are you! So what if conditions are less than sanitary and we haven't been allowed to choose our bunkmates. We're alive, life is exciting, and if we keep our wits about us, it'll all be a grand tale to tell our friends when we get home."

Genevieve, having no friends and no home she considered her own, was stung by this. "There's an un-complimentary term for a person who refuses to face the grim, sober facts," she said coldly.

"Yes, but there must be a worse one for people who keep their noses to the grindstone and do their best to dredge up all that is dull, brutal, or terrifying. Here I am alone—or nearly so—in the dark with a half-dressed female of—ah, obvious charms, let us say—and I'm arguing philosophies. It seems rather—oh—God—" he clutched at his bandaged arm with a stricken grimace.

Genevieve knelt over him, catching his shoulders in an effort to steady him. "Does it hurt? What can I do, Robert? I mean, Mr. St. Justine? Relax. Here, let me look at it." She laid him down, efficiently undoing the bandage and carefully probing the cut. It hardly looked fatal but he was carrying on vehemently as if this were his last moment on earth. "Mr. St. Justine, it looks fine. I don't see any infection or torn muscles—maybe it's caught a touch of fever."

"Fever?" he echoed brightly, then sagged. "Fever, that's it. I'm hot. Hot! Burning up. Delirious. Swimming in the cursed depths of oblivion."

"For a man swimming in the cursed depths of oblivion, you've maintained your vocabulary remarkably well."

He managed to shift his head onto her lap. His one unbruised eye opened up at her. "It's the curse of a good education. I was taught to always get the predicate in the proper place even when fading for the last time."

"I'll see to it that you fade for sure if you don't get your face off my leg and cease this deplorable act."

"It's not an act. I really am hot. And mad with fear." He caught her hand and placed it on his fore-head.

"From what little I know of you, Mr. St. Justine, the only thing you're madly frightened of is not getting to the gaming tables on time." Genevieve was surprised at her own spunk, but she was tired and her resistance was worn down to a nub. There was no more courtesy left in her soul, no more tempered, lady-like grace and charm. She quite frankly wished the whole world would go to hell—except Robert. He was charming in a vulgar way, and his caressing grip on her arm was far more pleasant than it should have been. She was too weary to be shocked when he moved closer and drew her to him.

What surprised her was not that he kissed her, but that she did not slap his charming, black-and-blue face for doing so. Wounded or not, Robert St. Justine never passed by an open deck of cards or a half-dressed woman who had cleaned up nicely, especially out of that stuffy wren's gown and old-fashioned hair-do. Her light brown hair floated about her milky shoulders—better shoulders than a man would have expected, seeing her earlier in that drab garb.

Genevieve found that he did not kiss at all like John, the only man she had ever kissed. In fact, John was the only man she had ever known aside from Mrs. Faunton's dear, stuffy old spouse. John had mingled brute lust with fumbling inadequacy. Robert, however, was careful and skillful and drew back when she'd just begun to like it. "No," he said sadly, "you're much too nice. For all I know, you might be married and you're going to run and tell your husband."

"Widowed," she whispered in a vague voice she hardly recognized as her own.

"I'm sorry."

"*I'm* not." What was she saying? Had she lost her mind, sitting here with most of her clothes gone!

Robert twined his fingers through her fine hair. "My best friend wouldn't believe I was letting you go, but I am. Wouldn't be much fun with my arm like this anyway and those big eyes of yours telling me you don't know what I'm talking about. It appears, dear little Mrs. Faunton, that at this late stage of the game I have developed an unwanted sense of honor. But try me tomorrow night. I expect to be fully recovered by then."

She took the lantern and fled into the musty shadows of the black pirate ship.

Early the next morning the passengers of the captured vessel were invited on deck. "They're going to throw us overboard! I just know it!" Mrs. Faunton cried.

"Nonsense!" the Colonel snorted.

Genevieve tried to cover herself as best she could with the tattered remnants of her dress and joined the rest of them on deck. They found that the reason they had been summoned was entirely innocent, even somewhat considerate. Their belongings, captured earlier, had been dumped into a vast heap on deck, pawed through for valuables and left for reclamation. It was all a hopeless jumble, but Genevieve's garments, being the plainest of the lot, had been left by the greedy pirates. There were only, it seemed, a few women in the crew, and the men didn't particularly want to take Genevieve's unadorned dresses home to their lady loves.

She managed to locate three dresses and several petticoats that had neither sea-water stains nor blood on them and felt she had done well. The mulatto woman, who Genevieve had discovered was named Xantha, took one of them from her, examined it, and announced, "You cut de neck outta dis, run some pretty ribbon in de sleeves—it be fit to work in de kitchen. Dis way—faugh!" Genevieve looked at her and smiled. Xantha was wearing rainbow hues that would have made eyes water at half a mile.

When, at last, they had gone through everything and stood clutching bundles of clothing, Captain Meddows appeared and told the captives that they would be putting in at Barbados in a few days. Most of the passengers from the *John Cooke* would be allowed to disembark. They would be put off on a deserted beach, and it would be up to them to find their way to civilization.

"It's a small enough place," Robert said, having made his way to Genevieve's side. "You won't have any trouble. You'll be able to get another ship to England within the year, I should think."

"Us? What about you?" Genevieve asked.

"Oh, I won't be released," he said cheerfully. "I get to go straight home."

"I don't understand. They'd have to go a bit out of their way to deliver you to your doorstep and as charming as you are, I can't quite believe the captain is *that* enamored of you."

"Strange as it may seem, it is not my charm that interests the 'lady'—perhaps an ill-advised term—it is my money, or rather my grandmother's. She's got positively tons of it."

"But how did someone like Captain Meddows know that?" Genevieve asked.

"Why, I *told* her. You don't think *I* wanted to spend a year lounging around Barbados, do you? Nasty place —all hurricanes and mosquitoes."

Genevieve spent the rest of the day trying very hard *not* to think about the prospect of spending a year on Barbados with hurricanes, mosquitoes, and the Fauntons—a year followed by the equally dismal future as Mrs. George Ffolkes. If only she had a rich grandmother to ransom *her*.

She could not sleep that night and after several hours of tossing uncomfortably and listening to Mrs. Faunton's maddeningly irregular snoring, she dressed and went up on deck. She half expected someone to stop her, but no one seemed the least interested in her wanderings. A few sleepy pirates were above, scanning the black-on-black horizon, and in a far corner some men sat on the polished wood deck playing at dice by the light of an oil lamp.

She avoided them and found a dark place where she could stand unnoticed. It was a heady feeling—the freedom and the lonely roll of the night sea. The sails overhead flapped softly in the light wind and there was a steady lap of sea against ship. As she became accustomed to the darkness, the stars seemed to become ever brighter. She took a deep breath of the night air, rich with the scent of sea-spray, and the fragrance of myriad spices oozing from the hold.

"Have you ever been at sea?" a voice asked. Captain Meddows, stealthily as a satisfied cat, had joined her at the rail.

"Yes," Genevieve answered automatically, then realized with something of a shock what she had said. "I mean, no. I don't think so. You see, I have no memory of my childhood. I was purchased at a slave market when I was five or so and before that—I know nothing, recall nothing." *Whatever has come over me,* she thought ruefully, *pouring out my silly little confidences to this woman. It must be the sea air and the starlight going to my head.*

"What about your name? How did you get that?" Captain Meddows asked, sounding genuinely interested.

"I believe it's my true name. Mrs. Faunton says that's what I told her the day she bought me."

"Genevieve—" the other woman said thoughtfully and repeated it slowly. "Genevieve—Gen—"

Genevieve spun around. "Gen? Why did you say that?"

Don't cry, Gen. A ghostly sliver of a memory pierced Genevieve.

"I have some good rum in my cabin. Join me?" Although phrased as a polite question, the tone was that of an order. Genevieve followed obediently.

The captain's cabin was in the aftercastle and there were diamond-paned windows along the back wall with a cushioned bench running underneath. Genevieve sat down there and watched the stars' images flutter in the irregular glass panes while the captain poured rum into silver tankards. She handed one to

Genevieve, then sat sideways at the other end of the bench, with her knees pulled up to her chin. There was a strange, almost girlish, vulnerability in the pose. "I was born on an island called Tortuga—" she said, and watched Genevieve carefully.

"Why are you telling me this?" Genevieve asked.

But the woman ignored the question. "My name is Evonne Meddows—"

"Yes, I know—"

"Evonne Meddows. Evonne—"

"I know!" Genevieve took a burning sip of rum. No reason to be upset. If this woman wanted to sit about in the middle of the night repeating her name to a stranger, well—

"I had a sister—younger than myself. My father was a pirate."

Genevieve was feeling distinctly uncomfortable. She half rose. "You don't have to tell me th—"

"One day my father went out to sea—"

White sails, shrinking into the clouds at the horizon.

"—and that night raiders from another island came to ours. It was a hot night, very late—my sister and I were sleeping—"

"Torches!" Genevieve whispered the word and recoiled from the sound of her own voice. She jumped to her feet, spilling the golden rum on the floor.

Evonne Meddows grasped her arm and pulled her back down. A look of triumph and a little sadness bathed her face. "Yes, there were torches, Gen. Torches and pistols. Our mother woke us and helped us climb out the window, but she didn't—couldn't—follow. We crawled through the jungle—"

The scent of damp, fecund earth and overripe jungle fruit.

Genevieve put her hands to her ears. "Please! Don't tell me this! I don't want to know—"

"You already know!" Evonne said brutally. "We hid behind a rotted log and a man caught us—" she went on relentlessly.

Yellow hair, matted and foul. A still-smoking pistol in his hand.

Genevieve bent over, sickened by the visions in her mind. "Stop! Stop!"

"—and he took us back to the clearing. Mama was there. She tried to come to us, but another man grabbed her and hit her—"

NO! NO! DON'T HURT MY MOTHER!

"She fell and tried still to reach us. She fainted and they beat her and raped her. Four or five of them—"

"STOP!" Genevieve was screaming now, and Evonne was holding her, forcing her hands away from her ears.

"—and they made us watch and said it would happen to us if we weren't good. Gen, our mother's name was—her name was—" Suddenly she released her hold.

"Sabelle!" Genevieve sobbed. "Our mother's name was Sabelle!"

Evonne wrapped her arms tenderly around her. "Yes, Gen," she said, her own voice thick with emotion and tears beading her thick lashes, "Our mother's name *was* Sabelle."

It was dawn before Genevieve staggered back to the tiny cramped cabin she shared with the Fauntons. It had been the longest night of her life. At first Evonne had simply let her cry out her shock. She had left the cabin while Genevieve, half-conscious under the tidal waves of memory, faced her past, her heritage which was unlike the romantic dreams she'd invented over the years. It had all come back to her with searing, blinding clarity. The swaggering father the other men had called Willie, who was often gone, but always returned with silk, coffers of jewels, and once, a whole box of elegant dressmaker's dolls clad in the height of French fashion.

The girls had undressed and redressed them and made them extra hats of leaves and bits of jungle vines. She recalled playing games on the floor of the hut, drawing lines in the dirt and using egg-sized jewels as men.

She remembered her mother as well, a buxom beauty with masses of raven hair, sparkling eyes, and a cheerful, uninhibited manner. A woman who spoke the language of the world with equal doses of slum French, bawdy English, and Caribbean patois. The mother who had lovingly called them her "treasures" and tried to save them from their fate.

Finally Evonne had returned to her cabin with a plate of stew and bread and made Genevieve return to the present. "How did you know who I was?" Genevieve asked her.

"I didn't *know*. I noted, of course, that you had my sister's name and coloring and there was something oddly familiar about you, but that meant nothing. When you said that you'd been at a slave market and didn't remember before that, I started to wonder if it was possible. I thought if I told you about *my* past, you might recognize something—and you did."

"What of the others? Our mother and father?" Genevieve asked. She was hoarse and weary and still felt that she was merely moving mechanically through a dream.

Evonne shrugged. "Our father is dead and good riddance. I met him once—he'd forgotten all about us. Killed a couple of years ago in a brawl in Port Royal, I heard."

"And Mother?"

"I have no idea. She was tough as a sailor's conscience though. If she lived through that night on Tortuga, I imagine she got on."

"Do you think she's still alive?"

"Possible. What difference would it make? She wouldn't remember us either."

"Yes, she would! Oh, yes, she would. She loved us, she wouldn't have forgotten."

"Love!" Evonne sneered. "You lily-livered sap. That's something in stories."

"No, It's real," Genevieve said with determination.

"What do you know of it? You've seen nothing of the world but your own backyard. Have you ever loved anyone?" she asked brutally.

Genevieve touched her sister's hand. "Yes. I loved you—and Mama."

Evonne turned away, aimlessly sorted maps on the wide desk. "That's silly," she mumbled. "Get out of here. I've got duties to attend to and I've lost a whole night's sleep as it is."

Genevieve rose shakily. So love was a taboo topic. But there were so many questions. "Evonne," she asked gently, "where have you been all these years?"

"Everywhere. A planter bought me and I worked in the fields until I was thirteen. Then the planter's son took a liking to me. Brought me into the house, dressed me up and taught me to talk like he did. Teachers and everything during the day and his private perversions at night. I hated him."

"What happened?"

"We parted ways," Evonne said, the sneering sarcasm back in her voice. "I left with fifty lashes and the clothes on my back, and he got to keep the dagger scar across his face and one ear. I went to sea as a captain's whore and when the old boy died I took over his ship. I had to maroon half the crew—the half who wouldn't take orders from a woman—but I kept the ship . . ." her voice trailed off.

Genevieve was tempted to say something, whether "I'm sorry" or "congratulations" she didn't know, but one glance at Evonne's defiant look told her she had better say nothing. She picked up her plate and mug and went to the door. "I'll take these back," she said and left without looking back.

And now, as the sun rose and cast feeble pink light on the ship, Genevieve was back with the woman who had raised her, owned her, and heaped her with unwanted pity for most of her life. "Genevieve! Where have you been?" Mrs. Faunton said. "It was most inconsiderate of you to just disappear like that, or did that horrible woman—?"

"What horrible woman?" Genevieve asked.

"That captain. The disgraceful creature in man's trousers. I just wouldn't have believed such brazen, wanton—"

Genevieve turned on her tormentor. "She is my sister," she said calmly.

"Why would you say a foolish thing like that? I declare! The sun and shock has affected your mind. Of course, you always were delicate, poor dear."

"I am *not* a 'poor dear'! You have never understood that, have you? Please stop fussing over me and let me rest."

"Well!" Mrs. Faunton sniffed emphatically. "I can only say I hope we get to England before too long. When you're happily settled in with cousin George you'll come to your senses."

Genevieve burrowed into the pile of covers that served as rude pallet and covered her head. She either slept or pretended to sleep most of the day, her mind in a whirl at first, but finally her thoughts began to stick to one another and form into patterns. For one thing, certain fantasies were well and thoroughly dead now. Genevieve had often helped herself get from day to dreary day by imagining that she was actually the daughter of a fine lady and a rich gentleman who would someday rescue her from her fate. She had never known what she was, but now she knew that she couldn't even be what she had hoped and imagined she was.

She was the daughter of pirates, the sister of a pirate and yet, rather than lamenting her lost fantasies, she felt relieved of their burden. Now she *knew* who she was!

At dusk the mulatto Xantha came in and told the women to get their things together as they would be getting to Barbados shortly. "Tie silly ugly dresses in sheet, Missy Gen," she said.

"Xantha, where is Ev—Captain Meddows? I need to see her."

"She on deck, but she got de snake tongue. Takin' off de heads left and right. Not to go near her."

"Genevieve, whatever are you thinking of?" Mrs. Faunton asked. "If you irritate that unspeakable hussy, you might jeopardize all of us."

But Genevieve had already gone. She found Evonne standing at the wheel, barking orders at a crew who knew enough to cringe and obey. "If you don't have that sail patched in five minutes I'll sew it myself with your filthy guts! And get that cook up here. The slop he's been feeding us isn't fit for sick dogs!"

"Evonne, I have to talk to you," Genevieve said.

There was a communal gasp among the bystanders. Imagine this snip of a girl talking that way to the captain!

"I haven't time now. Get your things together," Evonne snapped.

"I don't need to. I'm not getting off at Barbados," Genevieve replied.

Evonne waved an imperative hand at the crew and they instantly slunk off. "Just what are you planning then?" she asked coldly when everyone was out of earshot.

"I want to stay on board with you. You go everywhere and I want to find our mother."

"That's ridiculous. I've not got room to cart along someone like you. You're useless."

"I'm useless now, but I'll learn to earn my way. Look, Evonne, you owe me something."

Evonne swirled to face her furiously. "I owe you *nothing!*"

Genevieve's anger matched hers. "Oh yes, you do. You gave me back my childhood, my heritage. I didn't *want* it . . . I had blocked it out of my mind and you forced it on me. I'm not the same person I was yesterday and it's your doing. *You* are responsible for my being who I am today."

Genevieve took a deep breath and plunged on. "I can't ever go back to being drab, obedient, 'poor little Genevieve,' letting my life be shaped and molded by people who have only a vague, kindly pity for me. I don't like or want pity any more than you do. Certainly you can understand that. I will prove my worth to you. Just let me stay on board as far as England. If you still want to put me off there, I won't say a thing."

Evonne shaded her eyes, looked out to sea as if she hadn't even heard Genevieve.

Genevieve was almost breathless with the effort of making her will prevail for once in her life. "I won't talk to you of love, I promise. And I won't let my own desire to find our mother interfere with your plans. Just let me prove myself—please!"

She stood then, holding her breath, waiting. There was nothing else she could say. She had to rely now on Evonne's judgment and the affection that Evonne would probably never admit. A muscle fluttered under the smooth, tanned skin of the older woman's jaw. Finally she turned back. "Only until we get to England."

Genevieve wanted to embrace her, but held back and contented herself with a slight smile. "Thank you," she said.

"But," Evonne went on as if she hadn't heard, "you will be a working member of the crew, not a passenger. I'll work you harder than I've ever worked anyone and you'll get no special treatment. And you'll not call me Evonne!"

"Yes, Captain Meddows," Genevieve said, blissfully unaware of what was in store for her.

4

Genevieve returned to the cabin and packed her things as if to disembark. She didn't wish to let Mrs. Faunton suspect anything was amiss until the last possible moment. When finally they stood on deck and orders were given for the passengers to climb down the ropes and into the small boat that would take them, Genevieve took Mrs. Faunton's hand and said, "Wait a moment. Mrs. Faunton, you and the Colonel have been kind to me in your way and I don't want you to think I'm ungrateful, but—"

"That's sweet of you dear, but let us talk about it later. I'm so afraid we might not get on the boat—"

She turned to go, but Genevieve held her back. "I'm not going with you. I haven't time to explain, nor do I think you would understand, but—"

"That woman cannot keep you on this vessel!" Mrs. Faunton exclaimed.

"No, I assure you, I'm staying of my own free will. Now, please hurry."

"But—" Mrs. Faunton looked around frantically for someone to protest to, then slowly she began to realize just what Genevieve had said. "Of your own free will?" she asked, anger beginning to cloud her dumpling face.

"I thank you for everything, but there is nothing else to say."

"I beg your pardon, but there is a great deal more to say!" Mrs. Faunton said. "Am I to understand this is the payment I get for all the years I cared for you? Treated you like my own daughter—you! An orphan of God-knows-what background. Now you dare to *choose* a life like this when you have been brought up with the finest of education and social graces. I even allowed you to marry my son!" she said, making it sound as if the marriage had been the ultimate favor she could bestow.

"Please, this will do neither of us any good," Genevieve said. She was trying so hard to keep her temper that it was almost a physical pain.

"Well, I daresay I shall have to tell the Colonel he was right. He told me that breeding will win out! I suppose you have proved *that*! I took you in because I pitied you and look how you turn on me—"

"Did it ever occur to you that I didn't want pity?" Genevieve said, her voice rising in spite of her resolve.

"Well, you certainly shan't have mine anymore! Thank the good Lord that John did not live to endure this mortification."

"Damn John!" Genevieve said loudly.

Mrs. Faunton gasped in shock. "I should have known! I should have known that you can't make a lady of a child of the gutter!"

Genevieve was far more shocked. "Is that really what you have thought of me all these years?" she whispered. "Was I just an experiment to prove the Colonel wrong? A project? A hobby to fill your idle days? How you must have felt when your foul, unspeakable son wanted to marry me!"

Mrs. Faunton glared at her for a moment, then said coldly, "Stand back, young woman. You are in my way. I believe these are mine by rights!" She bent, huffing with indignation, and picked up Genevieve's bundle of clothing that sat on the deck between them. "I paid for these items and I should rather throw them into the sea than think you were wearing them."

Genevieve was so angry and hurt she could hardly keep her balance. It seemed the world was spinning in confusion. In a sudden, unreasoning need to make a grand gesture, no matter how senseless, Genevieve grasped the neck of her dress and gave a strong yank. It ripped down the front. One more violent tear and she stepped out of a heap of rags and handed them roughly to Mrs. Faunton. "Throw this in the sea then! And these!" she said, taking off her shoes and flinging them to the deck. "I suppose you would like the underwear as well!" she said and put her hands to the neckline of her shift.

"My God!" Mrs. Faunton exclaimed. "This is the most frightful—!" She turned and fled to the rail where a sailor managed to help her over the edge without once taking his eyes from Genevieve.

Genevieve stood rigid and trembling in her shift for a moment, aware that she had indeed made a terrible display of herself. There was a stunned silence on the ship, broken only by the raucous laughter of circling gulls and the gentle ripple of wind in sails. She turned with what slight dignity she could muster and found herself face to face with Robert St. Justine.

"Good show," he drawled.

She slapped him briskly and marched to her cabin.

Once alone, she gave in to the sobs that had been rising in knots inside her. How could she have so misjudged for all those years the feeling the Fauntons had for her. She had been floundering in guilt about depriving them of her company and daughterly affection and all the while they had considered her only a charity case whose doubtful birth would one day disgrace them. Well, they had the proof they had waited for all those years. It didn't bear thinking about!

The door was flung open with a crash. Evonne stood there, hands in tight fists on hips, feet planted firmly and sparks of black anger lighting her eyes. "I hope those are the last public hysterics you plan to have."

Genevieve sat up very straight, brushed the tears from her face and said, "Yes!"

"Good, because that sort of thing will not be tolerated on this vessel. You will be fully dressed on deck and remain so. Your private problems will be dealt with in private, not with the deck of my ship as your stage. Now, put some clothes on," she said, tossing a bundle of rough brown garments at Genevieve. "There are six four-hour watches a day. You, like everyone else, are on duty for four hours and off for four, day in and day out. As a new crew member you will spend one watch per day in the shrouds."

"Doing what?"

"Learning to climb them and stay alive. You will rotate duties on the other two watches. Before we get to London you will have done everything that has to be done on a ship and you will damned well do it all right. Now, put your clothes on, the next watch starts in five minutes."

Genevieve spent the next four hours clinging precariously to a rope, twenty dizzying feet above the deck. She had no idea how splintery ropes were nor how sick she could feel that far up from the motion of the vessel. Once Evonne passed by underneath, looked up and warned, "You throw up and you'll clean it up yourself, get five lashes and go back up there for double watch!"

Eventually the first watch was over and Genevieve crawled back down, every muscle in her body burning and aching. She got to her cabin just as Evonne got there. "What do you think you're doing?" the captain asked.

"Sleeping for four hours, Evonne," she said.

"Crew members do not address me by my first name and you're not sleeping in here. Crew members don't get their own cabins. There are hammocks below. Go down and see if you can find an empty one."

Bone-weary and perched on the frazzled end of fatigue, Genevieve descended into the depths of the ship and found that there were indeed hammocks— rough hemp cradles suspended only scant inches from one another in a low-ceilinged hold far below water level. There was no fresh air and only one feeble light from a lantern at the far end. She struggled between rows of snoring bodies until finally she found an empty hammock. She managed to get into it on the second try and gave only a fleeting moment's consideration for the conditions before falling soundly asleep.

In what seemed like only seconds, Xantha was shaking her. "Not to sleep past watch, Missy."

From then on things got worse. During her next watch Genevieve learned to tie a variety of knots. Her "teacher" was a Portuguese sailor with astonishingly bad breath and a very short temper. He explained the knots in quick spates of Portuguese, then waited impatiently for Genevieve to repeat what she'd been shown. When she got it wrong or was too slow (which was almost every time at first) he brutally slapped her hands and screamed what could only be curses. At the end of four devastating hours Genevieve's hands were red and raw. Tears of pain were coursing unnoticed down her cheeks.

But she knew how to tie knots.

Her next watch started at noon, after a short sleep on the damp, slimy floor of the hold since there was no empty hammock available. This time she was assigned to scrubbing the deck. First she got sand, then a little water and some rags with which to scour the wooden deck. Then more water and sand and a metal scraper. As she finished each little patch she had to haul a heavy bucket of sea water up and rinse the sand off. It was beyond any doubt the hardest physical work she had ever done. The sand took the skin off her hands and knees, the sun beat down on her back until she felt nearly roasted. Just as she felt she could not go on for another moment without suffering a sunstroke, a bell sounded the end of the watch and once again she crawled into a hammock.

Xantha woke her again, saying, "Dis time you got easy job."

"Easy job—you mean like painting the whole ship," Genevieve groaned.

"You back in shrouds again, remember?"

This time, perching in the rigging sounded good. Only a day earlier it had seemed the most awful punishment in the world, but tonight it seemed a gift from heaven. She dragged her aching body up the ropes and managed to maintain her balance while napping. But it didn't last long. "You're learning to climb, not sleep!" Evonne called from the twilight deck below. "Get up there to the crow's nest."

"But that's clear up—"

"You have your orders!"

Genevieve looked up at her objective. There was a woman up there already, a short, plump redhead with strongly muscled arms and an engaging grin. Laboriously Genevieve climbed. Her feet kept slipping and her abused hands throbbed agonizingly at the very touch of the rough rope. "Don't ever look down!" the redhead shouted encouragingly. "Here, work your way to the right then straight up."

Genevieve followed the instructions and eventually found herself at the very top. The sails billowed and flapped beneath her and she felt queasy at the panorama of never-ending blue-black ocean and sky surrounding her. The other woman introduced herself as Kate and Genevieve passed a pleasant half hour talking with her.

She learned that there were about seventy men and ten women on the ship. "Don't you worry 'bout the men doin' anything ter ye," Kate assured her. "There's a strict code of how to behave on this ship and they all know it's death to touch yer while we're under sail. But in port—look out! You could sleep belly to belly wid them here and nary a mad moment, but in port they're on their own and Captain Meddows don't have no hold over 'em."

Genevieve realized with a start that she hadn't even considered that aspect of life on a pirate ship. She'd been so tired that she hadn't even taken note of the sex of the individuals she was sleeping in the same room with. She'd been negligently naive and would have to keep in mind that she was no longer living among the ladies and gentlemen of drawing room and piano concert society.

She was glad that she hadn't really known what she was getting into; it might have made her decision to stay aboard more difficult. She had pictured herself working, of course, but never having done an hour's real work in her entire life, she hadn't had the slightest idea what it was like.

A call came up from the almost-dark below. "I want to see you at the top of *that* mast in half an hour," Evonne shouted at her, pointing to the opposite end of the ship. "And don't set foot on deck."

"She's trying to kill me!" Genevieve lamented.

"Long as you act like it might work, she'll keep tryin'," Kate informed her and Genevieve could sense the truth in this statement. She nearly slipped three times as she made her way through the ropes and sails, but once she achieved her objective she found that she was quite proud of herself. She started down and got a sharp slap in the face with a sail corner and nearly fainted, but when the watch was over she reached the deck with a look of triumph.

"Took you twice as long as I gave you," Evonne said. "You'll do that until you can make it quick."

I suppose that's praise of sorts, Genevieve thought.

She stumbled across the heaving deck and ran into Robert St. Justine. "Dear Lord, what have we here?" he said.

"Oh, Mr. St. Justine," Genevieve said, sweeping a mock curtsey, "I do hope you're enjoying the trip. We do try to please our passengers." She was gratified to see a look of complete surprise on his handsome face.

"What *are* you doing!" he finally managed to say.

"I'm learning to be a pirate," Genevieve said matter-of-factly.

"And I thought you'd been in your cabin having the vapors all this time. How wonderful! You actually *wear* these clothes or are you taking them out to be burned someplace?"

Genevieve looked down at herself. Brown baggy trousers tied up at the knees with strips of rag, bare legs and feet, and a shapeless, once-yellow shirt with the right sleeve torn from shoulder to wrist and flapping in the wind. "Yes, I suppose you've been out of touch with the latest fashions from France or you would recognize that this is what all the ladies are wearing this year," she answered in a flip tone to hide her very real embarrassment.

He was bent over double, laughing. "I wouldn't have believed it!" he said. "Is this the same dowdy, sour little widow I met a week ago? A true wonder! Do clean yourself up and dine with me later, and you can tell me all about this game you're playing."

Suddenly Genevieve felt weary and dirty and hungry. "It's not a game and no, I'm not the same 'sour little widow' you met last week."

"I'm sorry," he said more seriously. "I meant no offense. I'm just so surprised at the change in you. Please—do dine with me."

"I can't. I am entitled to four desperate hours of sleep right now and I'm using precious minutes of it talking. Then I have to go back to work."

"But you have to eat sometime! It might as well be with me."

"Perhaps another time," she said, walking away. She was vaguely aware that she was being rude and resolved to apologize later.

"Got Missy easy job dis time," Xantha said when she next dragged her from her restless dreams.

"Don't you ever sleep? Last time you had an 'easy job' for me I nearly killed myself climbing from one end of the ship to the other."

"Faugh! Nothin' to dat! But I *really* got easy job. Get your body outta der now."

This time she was right. The watch periods were

measured in half-hour intervals and someone had to sit and monitor the sand glasses. That was all. Every time the sand ran out, a bell had to be rung—one bell the first time, two the next and so on until the four hours, or eight bells, had passed. Except for turning the glass and ringing the bell, there was nothing to do. It seemed like a virtual holiday.

Voluptuous Xantha, apparently off duty, came to join Genevieve toward the end of her watch. "You got invite to eat wid de cap'n and sassy gent after watch."

"I do? But Xantha, I'm so dirty and smelly I can hardly stand to get near *myself*! I can't dine with Mr. St. Justine."

"Got de answer to dat, too," Xantha assured her and disappeared, returning in a moment with a bucket of hot water, a brush, and an armload of clothing. "I watch de sand go, you wash!" she ordered, and Genevieve obeyed with alacrity. "Now strip off dem rags. I got some things don't fit me, you can have. Look here."

She waited until Genevieve reluctantly shed the last bit of clothing, the shift she'd threatened to give Mrs. Faunton several days before and had been wearing bunched under her clothing since then. Xantha, bangles glittering against her flawless chocolate skin, took a long look at blushing, naked Genevieve. "Why Missy, you got a body'd make God himself drool. Why you keep it hidden so long? Dose bosoms could take prizes. I got just de thing."

She pulled a length of gold fabric from the bundle she'd dropped on the floor. It was long and narrow and she propped the middle over Genevieve's head, crisscrossed it over her breasts, pushing them up alarmingly, and tied it behind her neck. Then she flung her a pair of brown velvet trousers.

Genevieve was so glad to have anything to put on that she slipped into the trousers quickly. They fit snugly—too snugly. "Xantha, I can't wear these! They aren't even decent!"

"Dat de whole idea, Gen Faunton. You got a lotta decent to get rid of. Been altogether too decent for a long time. Pretty soon you be old and crinkley and too late to be anything else." She rummaged through her treasure trove of clothes and came up with a blouse with a plunging neckline to go over the gold halter. She draped some jewels on Genevieve and tied her hair up with a bright, peacock-blue scarf. She stood back to admire her handiwork. "Dat better," she announced.

Genevieve sighed. She felt like—well, like the sort of woman she'd only heard referred to in discreet whispers, but Xantha meant well and she had to admit that the outrageous outfit was a distinct improvement over her last attire. "Thank you, Xantha. It's very generous of you to loan me these things of yours."

"Dey ain't loaned, dey ain't even mine. Was my share of de loot from dat ship you was on. Dey's yours now, Missy, 'cept for de emeralds. Oh-ho, watch dat sand!"

It hadn't occurred to Genevieve that Evonne would wish to dress up for Robert St. Justine. She was surprised to find her attired as if for a court ball. Evonne had a scarlet silk gown with full skirts and snowy white lace outlining an incredibly low neckline. She wore huge square-cut rubies in her ears and her raven hair was pulled up at the sides and cascaded down her back in billowing curls. She had a touch of rouge on her lips and kohl on her eyes. She was quite devastatingly beautiful and seemed surrounded by an aura of electric sexuality.

Robert managed to tear his gaze from Evonne's spectacular bosom long enough to greet Genevieve and cast a quick, appraising glance at her before going back to his fascinated contemplation of the older woman. He seemed unaware of the change in Genevieve, and it was no wonder. But Genevieve felt a

sharp twinge of jealousy just the same. "Good evening, Captain," Genevieve said respectfully.

"No, Gen. Not 'Captain'! We're sisters tonight,"
Evonne replied. "Will you have some rum?" She rose
from her chair to serve Genevieve, who noted that in
deference to the small space in the cabin Evonne had
forsaken the full petticoats that normally went under
such a dress. In fact, from the way the silky fabric
draped itself to her shapely hips and thighs, it seemed
she had forsaken any undergarments.

"Your mouth is open," Genevieve said coldly to
Robert, who was still staring at Evonne.

"I—us, what? Oh, yes—" he mumbled.

Genevieve seated herself and listened to the conversation between her sister and Robert. They talked
knowledgeably and brightly about affairs of the Caribbean, shipping, European politics, and other matters
about which Genevieve was lamentably ignorant. She
wondered, too, how Evonne managed to sound both
intelligent and flirtatious at the same time. Genevieve
had *many* lessons to learn.

Dinner was served with crystal goblets, fine china
plates, and gold-handled forks and spoons, but ship's
food was ship's food and even an intimate dinner in
the captain's cabin had to draw on available supplies.
Thus, a woven silver serving basket lined with pris-
tine Belgian linen contained weevily biscuits, and the
soup course was thickened pea soup which, though
strained, still contained unthinkable bits of foreign
matter. There was fairly edible cheese and generous
portions of fresh fish, but Genevieve made no distinction between good and bad. She'd had practically
nothing to eat in the last day. She was starving and
gulped down everything that was put before her,
washing it down with something called "flip," a
cooked, sugared mixture of beer and whiskey.

When dinner was done Robert said, "Now, Captain
Meddows, tell me about my fate."

Evonne smiled seductively. "Your fate? I have no

idea. I intend to exchange you for as much money as possible at the first opportunity. After that, your fate is your problem. I shall send along one of my men to your grandmother and when he comes back with the ransom, I'll bid you farewell."

"One of your men? Good Heavens, there's not a man on board who could get near the tradesmen's entrance without being arrested. They would stick out a bit in my neighborhood. Why don't you go yourself?"

"Nay, there's a price on my head. I dare not set foot on English soil. We'll lay at anchor off Rye."

"And what is to prevent my grandmother from simply having your man hauled off to Newgate when he presents his demand?"

"Why, the fact that we have you, of course. She wouldn't risk endangering you."

Robert stretched his long legs out and tented his fingers thoughtfully. "I don't think you quite have a grasp of my grandmother's attitude toward me—or rather, her attitude toward parting with money. She'll expect to haggle, and I don't believe that she would even condescend to discuss the matter with some rough sailor."

Evonne's patience was wearing thin. "Since you seem to be managing your own kidnapping so well, why don't you tell me what you have in mind."

"I think you should send a lady of quality to her— a lady whose own family is being held and with whom Grandmama can lament their mutual misfortune."

Evonne stared at him blankly for a moment, then a slow smile spread across her face. She and Robert, of one accord, turned and gazed thoughtfully at Genevieve. "I *think* I know just the lady," Evonne said.

"Are you talking about *me*?" Genevieve asked sleepily. The meal, the flip, the hours of work had taken their toll and she was hardly able to stay awake, much less follow the conversation.

"Yes, dear little sister, we are," Evonne said. "You said you would make yourself useful if I took you on and I believe Mr. St. Justine has just shown us *how* useful you can be."

She strolled over and sat herself on Robert's lap. "I wonder what other clever things you can come up with," she purred as she ran a scarlet-nailed finger along the line of his jaw.

Genevieve stood up and cleared her throat.

Evonne glanced over her shoulder, "Oh, Gen—don't you go back on watch soon?"

"Thank you for dinner," Genevieve said. But Evonne was too busy kissing Robert to pay any attention.

5

London!

Genevieve was pop-eyed as a baby lemur. "Xantha, what's the building over there? Xantha, what do they call that hairstyle and how would I look in it? Isn't that a charming little starched lace hat?"

The imperturbable gunner's mate leading Genevieve and both horses kept walking. "De building's St. Paul's Church, de hairstyle's new to me. De hat's a Fontange from France—named after one of de Sun King's concubines."

"Xantha, they don't call them concubines, they call them royal mistresses."

"Faugh! Whore's a whore, little ninny. Not to matter none what de high 'n mighty call dem. Hurry now, girl. Quit starin'."

"You seem to forget I've never been in a big city before. I'm not as 'citified' as some people I know."

She and Xantha grinned at each other, then Genevieve was off again. "Did you see that! I've never seen hair that shade of yellow! Everybody seems to have wigs or powdered hair. I think it looks silly; it must be unsanitary."

"Wid de way you been livin' on de ship, you call dis unsanitary?" Xantha laughed.

Genevieve supposed Xantha was right. Life on board the ship had been a distinct assault on her sensibilities, yet her lot had not been quite so hard after Robert and Evonne hatched their plot to make use of her. Evonne decided that she could not play the role of "fine lady" very well if she was deeply tanned with weather-beaten hands, so she had been allowed less strenuous duties. Not easier, just less damaging:

hours in the galley and sitting over the damnably boring sandglasses as well as one memorable night on a cold deck catching rainwater for the cook to use in place of the slimy, abominable liquid in the water casks.

"Here's where we get you cleaned up," Xantha announced, turning up a cobbled walk to a public bath house.

Genevieve, still struggling with her luggage and long skirts, stopped and looked. "Oh, no! I can't go in there. Pirates and *whores* frequent public baths!"

"White girl one of dose things. Inside, in, in!"

"Hot potatoes! Git yer hot potatoes!" bellowed a street urchin. Genevieve fumbled for a coin, empty stomach yearning for food, but Xantha yanked her away, insisting potatoes caused "body wind" and weren't safe to eat—at least not for one's companions when the "wind" began. Xantha put it in far cruder terms which sent Genevieve, scarlet-cheeked, scuttling into the bath house's women's quarters.

Xantha started stripping Genevieve down to her chemise and held out a small bundle of muslin and lace. "Brought you spare shift, knew dem rags fall apart in water. Then we lace you up tight in low new-fashion gown and you look grand."

Genevieve shed her underwear behind the sanctuary of a large bathing blanket and wriggled into the other woman's spare shift. "You know perfectly well I'm not buying any of those indecent gowns."

"You not sweat none when you popped some buttons 'round Robert, eh, little Lady Puritan? Come along now to water. And bring money, fool, not to trust bath attendants wid nothin' but trash. Come, come, get you clean, den off to dressmaker lady Robert say fancies up all his ladies on such short notice."

"It doesn't sound like a very reputable place."

"Ha, you forgettin' again, Missy Priss. *Black Angel* no floatin' church neither. In!" And Genevieve was flung into the steamy water, where she was subjected

to a fierce shampooing and scrubbing and dousing
with some disagreeable-smelling liquid meant to an-
nihilate any small creatures picked up aboard ship.
She rinsed it off, nearly gagging at the fumes, then
shampooed again, wadded her hair in a towel, and
climbed out. Xantha had her reasonably dried and
dressed and out on the street in fifteen minutes. "Need
haircut first. Take you to ol' Lucy. She do you right."

Thus it was that Genevieve was soon sitting in a
sleazy back room of a wigmaker watching clumps of
her spongy, split brown and sun-bleached hair cascade
to the floor. The muscular brown Delilah patted her
from time to time and told her in the kindest of
voices not to cry, only the best would remain. Genevieve, more prone to kick than cry, glowered at everyone within range and ground her teeth.

When at last she was presented with a mirror,
Genevieve was stunned almost beyond words. "You've
cut it all off! I look like a boy!" she cried, fingering
the short, soft curls.

"Any boy got shape like you be in bad trouble,"
Xantha scoffed. "Look nice to me. All gonna go under
wig most times you go out anyways. Don't look like
wild island pony no more."

Genevieve turned her head examining herself from
several angles. Now that the preliminary shock was
wearing off, she had to admit she rather liked it. She
had never seen a woman with short hair, but it did
look nice in a shocking sort of way.

Next they were off to the front of the shop where
they selected two wigs and then they moved on to the
dressmaker's where several too-brightly clad young
ladies of improbable virtue explained the fundamen-
tals of face-painting to her while a huffing, buxom
matron with flaming orange hair took her measure-
ments.

Genevieve kept asking in a small firm voice that
went unheeded in the melee, for dove grays and black.
From time to time she caught glimpses in the mirrors

of Xantha fingering a bolt of lush green velvet or crimson brocade or sapphire moire. She had a suspicion that Xantha was undoing her work behind her back, demanding lower necklines, stiffer, showier petticoats, and richer fabrics. "After all, you a lady now," the chocolate-hued beauty would retort every time Genevieve began sputtering her objections. "Gots to look rich, but not too flashy. Go in der like school teacher in browns and grays, dey step on you like carpet. Heel marks all over de face you get. Xantha know best. Xantha get you gorgeous. Find Gen some men, too."

"Gen doesn't want any men!"

"Gen lucky to get *horses* de way she look dis morning. What kinda man was dat husband—blind priest? Never mind. Get you fancy, find young rakes like Robert."

At the mention of the name, the portly seamstress went off on a loving enumeration of Master Robert's last few mistresses. Genevieve listened carefully to catch every last deliciously shocking syllable. Apparently Robert and a good friend of his knew no social distinctions when it came to women and had sent a good many to Madame Sophy to be properly attired. Genevieve was wonderfully scandalized and lapped up each gossipy morsel like manna from heaven. Robert was "rich as Croesus" and his university friend was a chronic horse thief "with manners like a duke and taste in clothes that a king would envy."

"Gotta go to inn to get us rooms," Xantha announced abruptly. "When clothes ready we go to fancy hotel. Gonna take 'bout a week. We got dat long to bruise some manners into Henry, make a footman of him. Den we get lookin' like lady and maid and we go to hotel. Hurry, child," she ordered.

Genevieve shook her head with a smile. People weren't going to be fooled for a moment as to who was the servant and who was the employer. They had only to look at Xantha lording it over the world at large to know that Lady Faunton-Ffolkes was a "ninny white girl" and nothing short of a miracle would change that.

Fortunately for Genevieve, a miracle was right around the corner at the nearest den of friendly vice. The miracle had manners like a duke and was a chronic horse thief. And she would meet him a week later in the ornate home of the St. Justine's.

Elegantly clothed, elaborately coiffed and attended by a surly bo'sun's mate primed to act as footman, Genevieve presented herself at the front door of the St. Justines' London town house. She waited for her "servant" to implement the lion's-head door-knocker. When he failed to do so, she was forced to delicately apply the silver point of her parasol to his ribs.

"Watcha do that fer, ya bitch!" he said.

"Henry! Have you forgotten *all* your manners? You are supposed to knock at the door so I don't soil my gloves," Genevieve reminded him patiently.

Henry muttered further obscenities about the probable origins of both Genevieve *and* her gloves and knocked at the door with such vicious enthusiasm that the carpenter had to be called in later.

Genevieve smiled placidly when the door opened to reveal a portly, superior servant in gold-festooned livery. Genevieve had to choke back a giggle. Robert hadn't warned her that the family colors were yellow and white, and the sight of a large, molting canary of a man unnerved her. "Lady Faunton-Ffolkes to call upon the Dowager Duchess St. Justine," Henry parroted the lesson he'd been repeating all morning.

The canary bowed. "Please enter, Milady. I shall inform the Dowager."

Henry, forgetting his manners yet again, made a move to precede Genevieve, but her parasol point brought him back in line. "*You* will wait in the carriage," she said.

The canary had flitted, or as close as he could come

to it, to parts unknown, leaving Genevieve to bask in
the opulence of the entry hall. It was the size and
general aspect of a generously endowed museum. A
full two stories high, there were twin staircases winding up either side of the room and joining to form a
balcony that could easily have accommodated the
population of a medium-size village. The walls were
covered with lemon silk and the ceiling was a masterpiece of ostentatious plasterwork. Cupids, flowers, baskets of fruit vied for space with artistically draped
nymphs, unicorns, urns, and Grecian gods.

Genevieve couldn't conceive of the sort of money it
required to live in such splendor and money usually
meant power. Suddenly the full force of what she was
doing struck her. This wasn't just an entertaining
game—she was about to irrevocably involve herself in
a serious and dangerous crime. It had seemed like a
lark on the ship. Robert was so amusing about it all;
Evonne had treated it like the most commonplace of
business; and she had fallen right in with them because the prospect of playing lady relieved her of some
of the more distasteful of ship's chores. But standing
here in an entry hall that could dwarf a queen and
probably had, she was aware of a horrible inferiority
and breathtaking danger.

How could she hope to convince anyone she was
a real lady? She nervously brushed a speck of lint
from her moss-green moire gown and lightly touched
her cheek with a kid-gloved finger to check that the
tiny star-shaped beauty patch was still in place. At
least she was properly dressed from the top of her
fancy powdered wig to the ruffled hem of her petticoats. In addition to the new clothing, Xantha had
provided her with a discreet strand of black pearls
that positively screamed of wealth—and presumably
breeding.

Her hands were trembling and her knees felt like
custard. She seated herself in a chair by the door that
could easily have served as a throne for an Eastern

potentate. *Compose yourself*, she scolded mentally. *It's too late now to turn back.*

"Harumph!"

The canary was back. "The Dowager Duchess will receive you, Milady, but she is in family conference at the moment. She begs you to take your ease in the morning room and she will join you in a moment."

Genevieve was not prepared to do any more of this nerve-shattering waiting. Better to just get it over with. "Kindly inform the Duchess that I am here on grave business concerning the safety of a member of the family and it is imperative that I speak to her at her earliest convenience."

The canary's eyebrows went up slightly. "Very well, Milady." He was back this time rather quickly. "If you will follow me to the library, Milady?" He escorted her to a pair of enormous double doors and swung them open with the air of a man officially opening an exposition.

Genevieve stepped through as briskly and confidently as she could. It was, not surprisingly, a huge room. Bookcases lined the walls and disappeared into the gloom at the top of the darkened room. Though it was broad daylight outside, the heavy maroon drapes had been pulled and the room was illuminated only by candlelight, giving a feeling of oppressive secrecy. There was a long marquetry table down the center and there were several people sitting around it arranging stacks of papers and documents. As she stood there, they turned one by one and looked at her expectantly.

The pale, hawkish old woman at the head of the table was obviously the Dowager Duchess. To her left was a man who was Robert with age and a paunch added. That had to be his father. Across the table was a thin, washed-out-looking middle-aged woman dressed entirely in beige. She gave the impression, in fact, that her blood was probably beige. There was another man, apparently a clerk, who was moving around

the table, gathering the papers into neat stacks and
checking signatures, mumbling "yes, ah, yes," to himself in approval. He completed his job and disappeared.

"Lady Faunton-Ffolkes," the canary intoned.

The Dowager Duchess waved a dismissive hand.
"Very well, Bert."

Genevieve thought for a moment that the Duchess
had called him "bird" and was immeasurably cheered.

"Faunton-Ffolkes?" the Dowager said. "I'm not familiar with the name? Well, come in child. Will you
take tea? Bert!" she bellowed at the retreating figure.
The beige lady cringed. "Bert! Bring tea and some of
those honeyed biscuits and some watercress sandwiches."

Genevieve couldn't see how this woman could be
concerned with honeyed biscuits and watercress sandwiches when she knew that a family member's safety
was in jeopardy. There was certainly something about
these people she didn't understand. The family members rose from the table, and Genevieve suddenly realized that the dim candlelight had prevented her from
noticing that there was someone else in the room. A
young man who had draped himself casually against
the mantel of the fireplace at the far end of the room
strode forward now.

No relative, Genevieve thought, comparing him to
Robert. The features were totally different, the coloring changed. There was a strong hint of auburn in his
hair and his eyes were gray, not greenish like Robert's.
A little taller than Robert, a little less cocky—and yet
he was no servant. There was something indescribably
refined, well-bred about his features. A sort of innate
self-assurance that was both fascinating and a little
frightening. "Lady Faunton-Ffolkes, will you take a
seat?" he said, and with a light touch of fingertips to
her elbow guided her to a sofa grouping by the fireplace. She could feel the warmth of his hand through

her sleeve and was oddly disappointed when it was removed.

The Dowager Duchess crossed the room in a rustle of starched petticoats and layers of crisp new silk, Robert's father lending his arm and providing an escort. She sank into a bronze chair of nouveau Oriental design and joined her sticklike fingertips forming a bejeweled steeple. "I understand you are here to discuss the safety of a member of our family. This is interesting indeed as we were discussing just that shortly before your arrival."

The young man at Genevieve's side remained silent though Genevieve could feel his gaze on her. Robert's father stood and cleared his throat. "We are a small family, Lady Faunton-Ffolkes, as you can see—only my mother, my wife, my son Robert, and myself," he droned along as if he were teaching a class in a very dull subject. But Genevieve was hardly listening. She was interested in the fact that the other young man in the room, being treated as though he were part of the family, was obviously not. Then who was he?

"We therefore presume that you are here with news of Robert," the Dowager concluded, apparently well-practiced at interrupting her son.

They waited now, for her to take up her part. She disliked the inquisitive eyes of the young man evaluating her. "This is so delicate a subject, I do not know how to attempt it. Perhaps in private?" She produced a filmy lace handkerchief and balled it up in her fist as if nervous (which was true) and took a few tentative swabs at her eyes as if bravely trying not to cry (this being blatantly untrue).

"Nonsense!" the Dowager barked. "Michael is like one of the family."

The young man decided to speak for himself. "Milady, I am Michael Clermont, a junior member of the family's law firm and therefore highly interested in anything you might have to say." Was there a tiny

ripple of sarcasm in the word "might"? Genevieve
noted that everyone glanced at him, but said nothing.
Apparently he was welcome to speak up in family
gatherings such as this.

But wasn't he extraordinarily well-tailored for a
struggling young lawyer? Heavy, exquisitely fitted coat,
brocade vest, elegant silk cravat—Genevieve tried to
force tears into eyes that remained as dry as the sands
of the Sahara at high noon. She trained her brown
gaze on the Dowager's impressive nose. "I hardly know
. . . well, the merchantman *John Cooke* coming from
the Caribbean . . . was taken by privateers. . . .

The beige woman gasped. "Robert—?"

"He is unharmed," Genevieve hastened to assure
her, "but he is being held for ransom."

"Ransom!" the Dowager fairly shrieked. "Ransom!"

"Please calm yourself, Mother," Robert's father said
lethargically. Only he seemed remote from concern for
either Robert or the family money.

The handsome young solicitor drew forward a delicate chair and sat down next to Genevieve. His physical proximity seemed somehow dangerous to her, as if
he could see through the sham more easily at close
range. "Lady Faunton-Ffolkes, may I inquire as to
just where you come into this? Where did you get
your information?"

Genevieve looked at him warily. He didn't seem
alarmed, merely curious and businesslike. She had
been counting on everyone's emotional upheaval to
cover any mistakes she might make. "I was traveling
on the *John Cooke*. I too, have someone on board."
They don't have to know it's the captain, she thought.
"I was released in order to inform my own people and
the Dowager Duchess of the situation."

"What about this ransom?" Michael Clermont
asked.

"Ransom—!" the Dowager echoed despairingly.

He cast her a quick glance of respectful irritation.
"How much is the ransom?"

Genevieve looked down demurely at her gloved hands. "A hundred thousand pounds," she said softly.

"A HUNDRED THOUSAND POUNDS!" the Dowager screamed.

"Now, Mother, calm yourself," Robert's father said mildly.

"That's utter nonsense! Young lady, you can tell those unspeakable villains that I won't pay a farthing over ten thousand," the Dowager said in a slightly lower tone.

Dear God, I had no idea it would be like this. We might as well be haggling over the price of a pumpkin, Genevieve thought wildly. She glanced at the young lawyer. He had his hand over his mouth and was coughing ostentatiously, the light catching on his signet ring. *Is he laughing at her or at me?* Genevieve wondered.

The old lady had risen and was angrily banging the head of her silver and walnut cane on a marble table top. "I shan't give in to such an outrageous demand—"

"But what of dear Robert?" her daughter-in-law, the beige lady, was asking in weepy tones.

"Fie with Robert! He's forever getting himself into these scrapes—"

"But Robert's *never* been kidnapped and you can hardly think he did it on purpose!"

"I shouldn't be surprised if he had. I well recall the time he and one of his school friends got sent down for stealing the Dean's horse—"

"Ah-hum," the young lawyer cut in nervously. "I think we should keep to the matter at hand. We must get the ransom details straightened out."

"Details, my foot!" the Dowager blared. "Lady Faunton-Ffolkes, you tell those ruffians they'll get ten thousand pounds for my disreputable grandson and nary a farthing more!"

"But Mother—" the beige lady pleaded.

"Ten thousand pounds and—" a great whack of her silver-headed cane on the table with each word—

"Not," Whack! "One," Whack! "Farthing," Whack! "More!" WHACK! WHACK! WHACK!

"Well, if you feel that way about it—" Genevieve mumbled in a tiny voice. *Good Heavens, what have Evonne and Robert done to me, dropping me into the steely lap of society?* For a hundred thousand pounds Robert's grandmother plainly didn't care if they mailed her his toes and upper molars. The determined old female warhorse meant exactly what she said.

She could strangle Evonne! What was all that talk of hysterical, helpless families and rich old bawds dying to save the heir's life? Evonne had let her waltz into this lioness's den without any instructions to follow should the lioness refuse to act according to plan. But showing her fear would do no good, neither would arguing or attempting to reason with her. She must remain genteel, helpless, sweet. She sat forward in her chair. "I shall tell them of your position," she said softly.

The cane was emphatically flourished at her. "Please do, and take my word for it, young lady—don't pay what they're asking of you, either. Devil those brigands down to the bottom figure. Never let them get the upper hand. For the Lord's sake, Eloise, stop sniveling. They won't harm him. For each mark on the boy I'll lop off another hundred quid. Now let this poor young woman go home. Can't you see she's terrified for the sake of her own family?"

Genevieve was terrified all right, but not for her *own* family. She made her exit, Robert's father silently accompanying her to the door. She was relieved when the dowager intercepted the young lawyer at the door, saving her from who-knew-what. She might fool the rest of these people, but something about him made her want to keep him at loaded musket's length.

Michael did not trust her and it annoyed him. He excused himself as quickly as possible, but was too slow, her carriage was nothing more than a rumble of wheels far in the distance. *The young lady is lying,* he thought.

Lady Faunton-Ffolkes. He went to sleep that night turning the name over and over in his mind. The next day he rose early and went to the city offices to spend the morning dredging through musty ledgers. He found Fauntons, he found Ffolkeses, he eventually found a Faunton-Ffolkes, but the latter combination had died out a quarter of a century ago and in the West Indies at that.

Choice A, she was descended from a missing heir to the Caribbean planter who had died a quarter of a century before in a slave uprising. Choice B, she was a liar and had made up the name. But if so, where did that leave him? He ran a dusty hand through his hair, replaced the last ledger, and paid the clerk for the use of the information. Out in the misty London afternoon, now frowning with every step, he wandered along wet cobblestones forgetting to turn his collar up against the damp chill. If she was lying, what did it prove? She was too well-bred to be involved with pirates—he knew a good deal more about pirates than most of his friends would ever suspect. If anything, she seemed to him to be convent-bred: the niceties of phrasing, the subtle ways, the restrained manners.

Perhaps she was truly some minor member of the aristocracy and merely shielding her name—but why? A lark? No, the girl looked frightened. She certainly wasn't doing this for the fun of it. No. The young woman was no aristocrat. She lacked the nose-in-the-clouds, blue-blooded, haughty self-righteousness of the upper class. Perhaps she had married into it. No, that didn't work either. People who acquired nobility were even worse than those who were born into it. Mistress Whoever-She-Was lacked the true, dyed-in-the-wool, snobbish bearing that should have gone with her name. Oh, she carried offended dignity well enough, but there was insecurity beneath it.

Nice-looking female, though. Good skin, clear, with a golden tinge that spoke of—that spoke of the sun— despite light dustings of rice powder. He stopped in the middle of the sidewalk, letting two loudly inviting whores, a disappointed pickpocket and a cripple fairly run him over.

Sun. No lady of quality let sunlight touch her face.

"So, she *isn't* a lady!" he said aloud.

"None of 'em are, laddie," said the cripple, who had regained his balance and strode off without trace of his former limp.

Michael Clermont dug his hands deeper in his pockets for warmth and hurried back to the hitching post. He took the wrong horse: for the first time in years it was by accident.

"—and when I told the man your message, he simply said he would report it to the captain of the pirate ship," Genevieve said. It was her second visit to the St. Justines' and more nervewracking than the first.

"So this representative had no authority? This man who called upon you at your hotel—" Michael Clermont asked. Robert's father sat elegantly unconcerned in a chair across the room, and the beige mother was nervously picking apart a paper fan. The Dowager said nothing, content apparently to let her legal advisor ask the questions for the time being. Only Genevieve was not content with this arrangement. One did not look at a lady the way this impudent lawyer was looking at her now. She had the stripped-to-the-stays feeling that he was capable of calling her bluff at any second and only avoided doing so for some strange, private reason of his own.

"Odd that he should have waited several days to contact you," he said thoughtfully. "What do you suppose accounts for the delay?"

I'd like to know that too, Genevieve thought. *That foul Henry must have gotten lost somewhere*. But she smiled with sweet confusion and meekly said, "I cannot imagine, Sir. Tis truly wondrously unexplainable, is it not?" She disliked this Michael Clermont, but at the same time found herself regarding him as an intriguing member of the opposite sex. Strange—the wine she'd shared with the St. Justines must have affected her more deeply than she'd thought. He had a manner both enticing and aloof, a smooth, attractive exterior drawn tightly over things that were none of her—or anyone else's—business. She caught his eyes on her and blushed. She noted that he seemed to be regarding her keenly, almost pityingly. Pity! She found herself experiencing the Evonne-like reaction of wanting to box his ears. What an unladylike thing to think.

"What sort of man was this?" Michael asked.

"Oh, Sir. A terrible man! All hairy and unkempt—with a very strange accent," she shot back.

He smiled slightly as if she had passed some sort of test. "A typical pirate type, would you say?"

"I'm hardly experienced enough in such matters to say," she parried.

"Not experienced, but very, very clever, I should say." He spoke in a quiet tone that did not carry beyond her.

"What did you say!" the Dowager demanded.

"I was just sympathizing with Lady Faunton-Ffolkes on the distress this situation must be causing her," he replied dryly.

He was completely unnerving her, and she could not wait to be away from him. She tried to make her excuses and leave, pleading distress for the welfare of her poor relatives "on board that dreadful brig," but to her tooth-grinding annoyance the lawyer invited her to stay longer and said that he would be happy to see her back to her place of temporary residence.

Trapped. She was trapped. And this Michael was the enemy—not Robert's nervous mother, nor his non-chalant father, nor even the fanatically frugal Duchess with her complaints about taxes, kidnapping fees, and having great big pennies wrung out of her poor, threadbare hide. No. The foe was this expensively tailored, brown-haired gentleman, hardly older than herself and too poised to be an ordinary junior partner in a law firm, no matter how prestigious the senior partners might be. Genevieve was not what she appeared to be and she knew instinctively that he wasn't either. What's more, in some careful, tactful way he was trying to spring a trap on her.

So she played elaborate word games with him, dodging insinuations, weaving through dagger-quick innuendos, bowing and swaying through every verbal pitfall he lay before her with painstaking good grace. Michael was so polished, so chivalrous, she could not catch him in the act. At last she insisted that she must leave, again pressing wrist to supposedly fevered brow. The lawyer not only insisted on sending her on her way in the St. Justine carriage, but invited himself along as well. So she ended up being handed into an overdecorated carriage like the lady she claimed to be.

"Now, I did not wish to alarm the family, but is Robert truly safe?" Michael asked. His personal concept of the situation was Robert with dice and doubloons on the deck of the ship winning the very trousers off the crew, but he kept a sober face and pressed Genevieve's hand as he said it. What sort of noblewoman referred to a pirate ship as a "brig"? If she knew enough to call it a brigantine, she'd spent some time at sea—getting that suntan. Her little hand shook in his, her palm clammy with cold sweat. Afraid. She was scared half to death and was doing a pretty good job of not showing it. But Michael had been involved in enough intrigue and had enough good scares to recognize the most subtle symptoms in others.

"Yes, he's quite safe—as long as his family pays the ransom," Genevieve said stiffly, like a sleepwalker, her words floating tonelessly on the sultry air. Her heavy dress rustled furtively as she tried to move away from him without any overt fleeing gestures. Still he imprisoned her hand in a grip hard as iron, but much more pleasant.

"Some proof would be helpful. Definite proof that he is alive and in good health," he insisted.

She withdrew haughtily. "Sir! You have my word as a lady!"

"Ahhh, but my dear Lady Faunton-Ffolkes, I was

thinking only that someone else might be deceiving you. Mayhaps he has even been murdered since you last laid eyes on him. I have heard much of this *Black Angel* even here in London. Tell me, is it true she's lateen-rigged and has a shocking figurehead?"

Genevieve neatly skirted the incriminating issue. "She has a disgusting figurehead, tis true, but I have no idea what you mean by lateen-rigged."

A pretty dodge, rather a verbal sword dance ensuing between them. One led, one backtracked, both moved to the side and slathered good manners over the obvious jabs and thrusts. Genevieve was frightened and yet thrilled. Her life with the Fauntons had been sedentary to a killing degree and she was ashamed to find herself now appreciating every little danger, each minuscule thrill. She cherished the excitement and disliked herself for it. It was as if she had spent most of her life in a cocoon and was only now breaking free and fanning her wings to try them for a first flight. She was needed by Evonne and the crew; she was playing with life and death and leading a merry chase. It was intoxicating. She wanted to run far beyond the reach of lawyers and dowagers and the noose—and yet in a twisted way, her life at last had meaning.

"You shiver, Milady. Are you frightened?" Michael put the traveling cloak lying on the carriage seat around her shoulders.

Genevieve thought that kind of thing had gone out with full-circle farthingale skirts and wimples. She eyed him suspiciously. "You take such interest in a poor, panicked—"

"Nonsense. You seem like a perfectly feisty, red-blooded female with more than average sense. I choose not to believe you are either a poor, panicked woman or a fragile vessel of piratical tidings. I would back you against the pirates any day. Any brigand foolish enough to face you surely paid for it with half a life."

She said nothing, but wondered how he knew. But

of course he couldn't. Merely a neatly turned phrase that was coincidentally true.

"Furthermore," he continued in a disrespectfully friendly manner, as if addressing an equal, "I think this problem can be simplified if we but put our heads together, Madame, and pool our resources. Perhaps we could meet for dinner tomorrow night?"

Genevieve narrowed her eyes, trying to decide whether he was thinking seduction or subterfuge. Probably both. She knew him to be a versatile opponent and that Evonne would be furious, but she fluttered her fan to cover a cold, glad smile reserved for confronting the foe and picked up the invisible gauntlet. "I believe, Sir," she said to the first man who had ever accredited her with intelligence, "that it might be arranged. Come to the Chadwick Arms Hotel tomorrow night at eight. We shall dine in my rooms."

"Crazy in head," Xantha repeated, lacing Genevieve into her stays. "Could have had St. Justine. What need for tricky lawyer fellow and putting Xantha in maid clothes?"

"You're right. I'm risking my neck and there's no reason to do this and I might let something slip," Genevieve admitted, feeling flowered silk and whalebone close in on her.

"But handsome man, eh?"

"Marvelous eyes, polished manners, and I don't trust him worth a brass farthing. He suspects me. But Xantha—I've never had a handsome man ask me to dinner—except Robert on the ship, and he didn't even notice I was there," she said, still smarting over the memory of that night.

"If he ask you to dinner, why we de ones throwing de feast, woman?"

"Why are you complaining? We didn't have to cook it or even arrange it."

"No, but I gotta lurk around and let you out of de stays after he leave—if he not done it for you, dis slippery solicitor person. Rather trust de Debbil. No wig tonight—dat for goin' out. Which dress?"

The heavy oaken bed with its ceiling-high posters and gold-fringed coverlets was covered with dresses—all her hastily stitched or purloined finery laid out. "The black damask, you think?"

Xantha placed stubborn hands on her hips. "Bury dat!" she replied, lip curling in disgust.

"The brown taffeta is nicer."

"No more black and brown. Sometin' bright."

"I'm not wearing that buttercup thing."

Xantha rummaged serenely, shoving Genevieve to one side. At last she strode over to the massive Jacobean wardrobe and wrested it open. "De green velvet with green moire under. No arguments. Suck your gut back in—must lace you tighter."

"Tightening it won't give me a figure like Evonne's."

"Tightening it not give *God* a figure like Cap'n. No breathin'."

Over the shift, stays, and five petticoats went the sea-green moire bodice and underskirt, yards of the skirt flowing out in rustling acres of mint. Xantha shoved and pushed Genevieve's figure into the proper proportions while Genevieve howled with self-pity. The moire was scalloped with delicate hairpin lace of the same hue, frothy rows and flounces of it. When she looked in the pier glass she was pleased at the tiny waist, but shocked at the shamefully low neckline. "Not this low. No, no, no," she said, tugging at it.

Xantha slapped her hands away. "Have to be cause de gown dips low. Up with your arms, up, up."

Babylike, helpless in the face of so adamant an instructor, Genevieve obeyed. Yard upon yard of jade green brocade velvet dropped over her. She stood still while the mulatto beauty smoothed things into place, slipping silk loops over the tiny fabric-covered buttons along the back. "Pull low, show nice little pale shoulders and top of de pretty bosoms. Get shift lace over neck of overgown. There, gives nice ruffle. Hold!

Got green Persian slippers in wrong size, but we get dem on you anyway. Got white silk stockings on? Uh-huh—uh-huh, like dis. Good. Now sit and not to wrinkle while Xantha hang up things."

Released at last, Genevieve stared at herself in the mirror. The woman who gazed back at her was exquisite! Poised, divinely dressed, and coiffed to the last curl and flounce. How could she have worried about short hair? It looked lovely. As she stared, her friend wound a fat jade choker about her neck and slipped dangling diamond earrings through her pierced lobes. "Oh, Xantha," she breathed in almost religious rapture. "You've made me almost beautiful!"

She felt the beginnings of tears for years of plainness and emptiness, but Xantha immediately cut them off. "Almost beautiful? *Almost*? Have your heart in soup tureen for dat! Plain damned gorgeous, girl! Xantha not do bad work—make you goddess."

"But I don't really look like this. I was like a bare canvas you painted on. Tomorrow the colors will all wash off in the rain."

Xantha hung the last gown and folded a lace shawl on a tall, armless chair upholstered in topaz kidskin. "Not paint on nothin'—only worked with what you had, silly ninny. Pretty, pretty thing. Dat man gone to come in door and eat you up with spoon, just yum, yum, yum."

"I'm not sure that's what I want," Genevieve said. Xantha looked at her, a skeptical smile lurking at the corners of her mouth.

They hurried into the main room, lit candles, and fussed with the silverware. When there was a knock at the door, Xantha meandered over, a striking figure in her stark black servant's gown and scarlet turban. There was a lazy grace to her walk, a becoming sway that spoke of exotic paths in torrid jungles.

The doorman handed her a calling card on a silver salver. "Jean-Michael Clermont, Attorney at Law." Jean-Michael. So he was French. She had wondered whether Clermont was English or French. "Where your manners?" Xantha scolded. She turned to the doorman and handed him a coin. "Send dat boy in—fast."

Michael was in impeccable form, having brought with him to the Chadwick Arms flowers, wine, and someone else's horse. The flowers were because they were a pleasant, impersonal gift and his next door neighbor grew nice ones; the wine because he didn't trust anyone's taste but his own and his last mistress's husband had been a wine merchant; and the horse because he fancied a gray, having not ridden one for at least two weeks and it had been unattended. He was immaculate in heavy brown velvet and cream linen, hair tied back and unpowdered, as usual. He bowed neatly, then laid the fragile yellow tearoses in Genevieve's arms. She received them with doe-soft eyes and her mouth in a soundless "Oh. . . ."

"What is it? Is something wrong?" Michael asked.

"I've never had anyone give me flowers before," she said in a small, vulnerable voice. Xantha shoved the doorman out and followed him.

Michael said, "You're incredibly lovely. Green suits you, Lady Faunton-Ffolkes. With those flowers you look like a painting. Shall I pour?"

Why did his voice waver like that? Had she let something slip? Was he making fun of her—calling her lovely? She recalled the jade reflection in the mirror as she tugged at the bell-pull to signal for dinner. No, he wasn't mocking. She no longer looked like the humble little purchased daughter. She squared her shoulders and let him seat her at the table. What beautiful manners he had. What beautiful eyes. Now if he could just keep away from the business that had brought them together. . . .

In the end, it was she who brought up business. When she had invited him to dinner, she had expected the worst, but he was being such a complete and utter gentleman, she wondered how she could have thought ill of him. But there were still memories of their first meetings and the little voices that had shouted to her: this is the dangerous one. This is the Foe.

But when the food was gone and they had retired to chairs by the fire with old champagne and quiet, evasive chatting, she wondered if her initial aversion to him had been chiefly the product of an overactive imagination—or years of sexual repression boiling to the surface.

She had wondered what it was about men that Xantha and Evonne knew that made them so different. The knowledge affected their language, posture, walk —even the lives they led. Genevieve's sheltered life had allowed little contact with the opposite sex. What was it that made Evonne and Xantha take frequent forays into the erotic side of life?

Wine-loosened, a little sad for the past, and very glad she had escaped it, she refilled their glasses and thought how nice it might be to kiss this young man. Robert had taught her that kissing could be more enjoyable than she'd ever suspected. But he was the enemy, remember? She reminded herself halfheartedly. Don't let anything slip. Act stupid about ships. Shed counterfeit tears about relatives aboard the *Black Angel,* and let him pat her hand sympathetically. He was fishing for clues again. Genevieve put on her best fawn-faced expression of innocence. Among his general rambling (for he had consumed as much wine as she and both of them were too relaxed and easily amused), she heard him say, "a surprise, getting a ransom notice from such a prim, straight-laced lady with her lips buttoned together. Closer to a shock, really. You're a different person now."

One night of wine and fifteen years of resentment bubbled up in her. "Prim? Buttoned lips? I take offense, Sir."

"I mean no offense, only that . . ."

She stood, facing him where he leaned, silhouetted at the fireplace mantel. "You certainly *did* mean offense. You're one of those rollicking university people I've heard about, all ale and whores and silly pranks played on the don. Anyone different from your free, loose world is an easy satire for your sort."

He did not back down under her temper, but flared. "I have already apologized once, Milady. But in truth, I have found you a pleasant companion this evening, not at all the stiff-spined prig you were that first day. I far prefer you this evening."

"Prig? PRIG?" she said furiously, stamping her foot in its tiny, hurting slipper. "You vulgar, uppity, disrespectful—I'll show you 'prig,' you obnoxious—" She took his face in her hands and kissed him. The shock of it took his breath away. She insisted until he yielded, then tried to back away, realizing with horror what she'd done.

But it wasn't that easy to change her mind. He circled her slim waist with a strong arm, pressing her body to his. "Don't shy away. I won't hurt you," he whispered.

"I'm not afraid—I don't think," she responded uncertainly. He lowered his head to her neck, mouth seeking the gentle pulse line along the side of her throat. John had never done that. John had rolled his body onto hers and back off and that was all. Michael was holding her as one held a rare, precious possession. She had been native stoneware to John, but if Michael wished to treat her like bone china, bone china she would be. It was pleasing and lovely to let herself be spoiled and caressed so slowly and carefully, long, hot kisses scorching her throat and on down the low neckline of her jade green gown. "Oh—" she sighed distantly.

"You want me to stop?"

Even a gentleman in romance, she thought. "No. It feels nice. Kiss me again before you leave."

"If I kiss you again, I won't *be* leaving."

She slid her finger up to his thick dark chestnut hair and pulled. In a moment his warm, wet mouth opened on hers. Genevieve felt her toes curl, and it had nothing to do with the discomfort of borrowed slippers. She fastened her arms about his neck and returned the kiss, touching his tongue with hers, quivering as he ran practiced hands lightly over her body. It was longer than she'd thought a kiss could be. Head fuzzy with wine and the first awakenings of desire, she hung on his neck and let him touch her, let him rouse both of them beyond the stopping point.

She wondered if he could feel her stays as well as she could feel his buttons. Both were digging cruelly into her ribs, causing nagging discomfort among her pleasures. As if reading her mind, he said, "We'll abolish the stays." *Christ,* she thought, absently quoting Evonne to herself. *Christ and bedamn! He even romances like a lawyer!* He scooped her up effortlessly and unerringly found his way to the bedroom. Things were getting fuzzier and much more wonderful—soft, scented candlelight near the massive four-postered bed—he was undoing all those tiny green buttons down her back while she sat in his lap, shivering with pleasure as he kissed each new inch of skin he exposed.

It never occurred to her to stop. She had thrown all caution to the winds of change and was too dizzy with wine and sensual excess to gain control over her body. Her body. All those years she had kept it hidden under drab grays and browns, shapeless gowns a mourning sparrow might have worn. No more sparrows. Tonight she was a peacock. Her velvet dress was on the floor. When Michael bent to retrieve it, she lay back against heaped pillows and coverlets and said, "No. Leave it, Michael. Please." She held her arms out to him.

But there was more to be unfastened. Genevieve felt him patiently unfastening her here and there, kissing, caressing as he did so. "Well," he inquired at last, "am I supposed to sit here in my suit all night?"

She sat up, hugging herself. The only garment left

on her was a lace and muslin shift, short and gauzy, not nearly enough of a guard against the cool night air—and his eyes.

"Are you a virgin?" he asked.

"No, worse—a widow who couldn't stand the sight of her husband," she admitted.

He took her into his arms tenderly. "Did he hurt you?"

"No, I d-don't think so, not really. But he was horrible and hungry-acting and prayed before and after. I must be drunk or I wouldn't be telling you this."

"Chérie, the only praying I'll do in bed with you is to ask for more," he told her. He smiled as if at a joke.

"What—?"

"I can't call you 'Lady-Faunton-Ffolkes' in bed, my darling. And you've never told me your name."

"It's Genevieve," she answered. "I suppose we've not been *properly* introduced," she giggled.

"No, but we shall be—soon," he said between lazy kisses. He was undoing her shift buttons at a maddeningly slow pace, baring her breasts to candlelight and his gentle hands. She let him lay her down, kisses deepening, then his lips were at her ear, throat, nipples—God. She said it aloud. "God!" His dark head was moving languidly, tongue flicking back and forth across her nipples. Again. Again. Again. Slow fire in her veins. He was using all his mouth now, nipping and sucking at her breasts while her nipples rose to swollen pink points.

"Please," she heard herself say as if from afar. "Please—don't stop—please—please more—" Because the feeling was filling her, she found herself touching him too, not even stopping to think about it. There was only need and gentleness and the desire to have him, all of him. She peeled his clothes away and thought: *He is beautiful. Such a strange thing to think of a man, but he is beautiful. I didn't know a man could be so good to look at, so aesthetically pleasing, so very exciting.*

He was slender, but strong—hard-muscled as they twisted together, learning each other. It was not enough for her alone to be touched. No, she must touch him, learn, seek, find. There was only the need to know him completely and the yearning for something she could not yet define.

His touch was excruciatingly wonderful. Face, shoulders, breasts, then down. Ribs, stomach, hips, thighs—what was he doing? "No, what—Michael, you mustn't—ohhh—" He shifted her in the honeysuckle and hyacinth candlelight, bending her shapely ivory legs so they went over his shoulders. Searing kisses on the insides of her thighs and then—oh, God, it was burning her—tormenting—the long, deliberate licks, the touching, the haze of champagne and unleashed passion. . . .

She opened her eyes wide a minute before the peak. Opened them and stared ahead at the steady golden candle flames through the gauzy bed drapes they'd knocked loose in their amorous struggles. The light was dreamy and unreal, much as she had become this unpredictable evening. She was frightened, she was anxious, she was waiting for something—there it was. There! It gripped her in shuddering waves like a storm at sea. She rose with the tide, fought it, gloried in it. When it sank her, wasted but hungrier than before, she felt him touching her again, kissing his way to her mouth.

His body was on hers, both of them damp with a film of perspiration that gleamed gold in the candlelight. Genevieve held him, thanking him wordlessly with each kiss, each touch she gave him. Why had she never realized what could happen between a man and a woman? Grateful, but chiefly selfish and starved for more, she lost all timidity, took hold of him, guided him into her throbbing flesh. Penetration fed her renewed arousal. She dug her fingernails into his back and buttocks, admiring the sleek, sinewy lines and curves of his body. He filled her, moved her, made her body sing with satiation.

The champagne was thickening on her brain. She was losing track of thoughts and things; losing control; losing forever the clenched fist of reserve she had held herself in for so many years. It had taken Evonne and Xantha, a sister and a friend, to start the process —two strong women to shake her and make her take charge of her life. But it had taken a man to show her it could be sweet, this new self-ownership. She slid away into wanton sensation, gone to all save the searing need that would never again lie dormant. A small voice in the back of her mind cried out warning: *be careful, this man is dangerous.*

But she did not heed it.

7

In the morning Genevieve slipped guiltily from bed and staggered to the wash basin. Her nakedness was strangely comfortable, but after splashing herself with warm, perfumed water she slid into a silk wrapper for tradition's sake. She stretched and arched like a waking cat, then found her ebony-and-boar-bristle brushes and attended to her short tangled curls.

I shouldn't have done what I did, she thought, refusing to look back at Michael in the canopied bed. *I could claim I was drunk and he took advantage of me . . . but that would be a lie. I started it, not him. And . . .* the brushes stroked to a halt. *And I liked it!*

She heard Michael stir and turned to him. He was flat on his back under the covers, sunk down among fluffy satin pillows like a sybaritic mouser. Hands behind his head, he looked lazily comfortable. "Good morning," he purred with a sweet, shiftless feline smile that spoke of utter satiation, yet the willingness to endure more bliss if necessary.

"Good morning," she echoed stupidly, not knowing what etiquette demanded in such a situation.

"You were about to slip out the door, weren't you? You look embarrassed."

Color climbing her cheeks, Genevieve nodded dumbly.

"And I suppose in the morning light the entire evening appears vulgar, obscene, and undignified?" he asked, face illegible, all traces of satisfied cat gone. She shook her head. "Well, Milady, then how *do* things look?"

"Strange," she blurted out. "Good. Bad. I don't know! That wasn't me last night—but neither was the old stiff figurehead with buttons all the way up to her chin."

"The woman last night *could* be you, if you let her. You're years younger this morning, like a fairy princess waking from a thousand years' sleep."

"Not a thousand years. Fifteen. I don't remember the first five," she replied softly, setting her brushes down. "That's a decade and a half of self denial and too much common sense for any one person. Do I really look younger?"

He sat up as if peering for crow's feet on her youthful countenance. "Decidedly. You could be some barely marriageable island girl in that exotic silk thing."

She sat timidly on the foot of the bed, poised for flight. "What would you know about island girls?"

"I was a cabin boy in the Caribbean, anchored just off Port Royal during the quake of '92, in fact."

It was a side she would never have suspected of this grave, polished, dryly humorous young solicitor. "Really? I was on the other side of the island at the time. I know dear old, dripping-hot, fly-infested Jamaica like the back of my hand."

"You may know the backs of your hands but not the rest of your body," he said bluntly. "What happened last night pleased and frightened and surprised you, didn't it?"

Studying those objects of pre-breakfast conversation on the ends of her arms, Genevieve swallowed hard. "What am I supposed to say to that? Is there a proper answer?"

"Yes, of course. It's either 'Leave, cad,' or 'Stay, Michael.'"

He was smiling again. Genevieve knew it even before she glanced up and saw the corners of his smoky eyes crinkle upward in gentle, unmocking amusement. He was not laughing at her—he was laughing at himself in the most benign way she'd ever seen. "What a terrible flirt you are, but in such an awfully nice fashion. Stay, Michael," she surprised herself by saying. He held his arms out. She crawled into them, smiling, and was pulled down in a loose hug. They lay like that awhile, his heart beating steadily beneath her ear. "You're good not to hurry me," she murmured.

"Stop that or I'll feel too humble and Christian to do anything but pray."

"Last night you said the only thing you'd pray for was more," she retorted, feeling desirable and utterly secure in the smug realization of it. She bit lightly on his arm—and neck and ear and wrist until they rolled over, laughing and grappling. He finally pulled her under the covers. Genevieve forgot that he was a potential enemy in her business dealings, forgot that he was a man and she was timid with men. He was friendly as well as attractive. She decided with a start that she trusted him and found him not only desirable but a great deal of fun as well. She surged against him in a lazy, comfortable haze of bliss. There were years to make up for, *lifetimes* to make up for. "Teach me," she whispered in his ear with a damp kiss. "I want to know what you like. I want to know what *I* like. I want to learn how to make it as good as possible."

Lesson Three was in progress when the door banged open. Xantha strolled in with bare brown feet and plopped a gilt scrollwork tray down on the bedside table. "De least some folks can do is quit for food and rest before certain parts of de body fall off. Go all night and half de day and de brain, she rot right out. Beginners—faugh!" she ambled gracefully out, splashy print skirt swaying, and clicked the door shut after herself.

Genevieve and Michael emerged from the quilts and coverlets, gasping and sweaty. They wolfed down breakfast without stopping to see what it was, then settled back in each other's arms. "So that's the secret of the universe. I had *no* idea," Genevieve mumbled dreamily, kissing his fingers. Metal scraped her lip. A ring? She turned his hand over. A ring indeed, a gold signet, the flat surface engraved with a rose and French fleur-de-lis bound by thorns. "What is this? I've never seen anything like it."

"Belonged to my mother, or so I'm told."

"What do you mean, 'told'? Don't you know?"

"No. I was raised by several families before being pressganged into ship service. My presumption is that I'm illegitimate, but that doesn't explain why I was moved around so much."

She nibbled his fingertips. "Maybe someone had you who wasn't supposed to. Like a duke and a servant girl. And there was a jealous wife and a dangerous rightful heir, and—"

He gently tugged her hair. "What a romantic you are! My earliest memory is being jolted on a horse on a cold, rainy night. There was a thin man asking if I still had the ring. The ring was dark then, painted to look worthless. His name . . . his name started with an 'M.' Matthew, I think. I still can recall the smell of the wet wool cloak he hid me under, and the warm horse and creased old saddle. And the sound of thunder shattering the skies."

"Hmm," Genevieve mused, "maybe you've blotted out the rest like I did before I found my sister."

Michael caressed her bare shoulder. "I have a feeling that's as much as I'll hear on the subject from you. Afraid to look back too far?"

"No, I've exorcised those ghosts. They went along with dresses up to the chin and clunky shoes. I wonder if you get those gray eyes from your mother."

"I don't know, my only memories are of living with nice, normal farm families. The last ones were wonderful old people, very kind. Funny you should mention my mother. The man who always moved me from place to place—once when I asked him about her, he said, 'Beautiful as an angel, Jean-Michael. Always remember those exact words. 'Beautiful as an angel.' And then he'd give a weary chuckle as if there were more to it but he couldn't say. And he chucked me under the chin, and the horse kept plodding through the night, taking me away one more time."

He was distant now. Genevieve did not want to see him sad. Although she ached with weariness and unaccustomed soreness, she snuggled closer and kissed him on the ear. "One more time? Please?"

Michael gave a low laugh. "I doubt I'm capable, chérie. At this rate I'll quit praying for more and light candles pleading for a speedy death."

Later, entangled with him in the best of ways, she thought she heard him add, "Ahh . . . but it's the very sweetest death there is!"

After Michael left, Genevieve collapsed back in bed. It was hours later, in the midst of pleasantly repetitive dreams, that rough hands shook her awake. She opened bloodshot brown eyes to see Xantha glaring down at her. "Last of de world's greatest courtesans, you forget de cap'n need to hear old lady Justine's not gonna pay ransom."

"Isn't Henry back yet?" Genevieve asked, coming back suddenly to the real reason she was in London.

"Faugh! Dat Henry not comin' back if you ask Xantha. Found some fat old bawd with a half-acre of ground and a cow and settled down already. Cap'n Meddows probably hoppin' up and down cursin' de three of us. Better get yourself down to Rye fast."

"All right! All right!" Genevieve said, stiffly crawling out of bed. "Get a carriage for us."

"Us?" the beautiful mulatto snorted derisively. "Us? Ho no, white girl. You dug your own grave—you gets to lie in it all by pretty little used-up self. Xantha stay here and fix fingernails and shop for clothes and find some gentlemen friends. I not bust face racing over damn rocky England with news for She-Wolf Meddows. Get dressed, false ladyship. Got business to attend to."

Genevieve found herself hauled out of bed and flung into a tub of steaming water.

* * *

If there was one thing Michael had learned, it was the value of spies. Having been one himself starting at a rather tender age, he was well aware of the ease with which young boys could loiter and eavesdrop without anyone paying any attention to them. He therefore bribed an apple vendor to lurk and catch the scraps of information passing between Lady Faunton-Ffolkes and her "maid" as the former left their lodgings. It bothered him to treat her so badly after what they had shared, but it bothered him more that she might be a partner to the pirates who had kidnapped his best friend.

The ragamuffin apple seller returned soon, munching his own wares. "Rye," he announced between bites. "The Mermaid," he added, naming a tavern notorious as a hangout for smugglers and sailors. "Does I git me other copper now?"

"All that and more if you tell me how soon she's going."

"Leaving soon as she settles some business 'ere. An hour or so. Did I do good?"

"You certainly did. Here's your money, and a bonus."

Michael strode off, deep in thought as he approached the stable. A quick plan formed. He stopped, ducked into the alley, and shed his coat and collar, messing his hair and rolling his sleeves up. He hadn't attended to the stubble on his chin yet, so it should be easy to pass for a servant. He strolled coolly into the stable and called the hosteler over.

"Good day, good fellow. Master's sent me for his horse."

"Which 'orse be that, lad?"

"Why, the famous Bristol Racer, of course. Legs up to here and blood bluer than the Thames in June," Michael blithely rambled on, figuring that in such an expensive hotel there was bound to be at least one expensive race horse lodged at the stables. He was in

luck. There were four. The hosteler said he didn't
know which was which. Michael chose a lean bay
gelding with a baleful eye and was promptly bitten by
the animal. Never mind teethmarks and blood—he
needed a fast horse to beat Her Counterfeit Ladyship
to Rye, and this horse was surely it. He'd already forgotten which animal he'd ridden there the night before.

Rye at noon was a bustling little seaport full of
barking vendors with baskets of fish and hot potatoes,
as well as a hundred illicit wares. Sailors swaggered
up and down the cobblestone streets; doxies paraded
in tawdry finery and feathers; innkeepers bellowed
their prices. What little there was of the law looked
the other way and pocketed discreet bribes.

Michael wasted no time in purchasing a well-worn
seaman's jacket and a disreputable cap from a drunk-
ard who didn't wonder what he wanted with such
shoddy wares. Then he stole a spyglass and set about
scouting the harbor. Only one ship could be the *Black
Angel*. They'd performed a masterful disguise on her
—infamous figurehead replaced by a modest blue-
gowned matron; black sails stowed away in favor of
white; and a plank with the innocuous title *Bonny
Nan* hanging over her true name. The one thing they
had not been able to disguise was her black hide,
gleaming in the sun. Otherwise she looked a normal
enough little trading vessel.

Still no sign of Genevieve nor any clue as to who
would meet her when she arrived. He saw a dozen
likely candidates who might be hard-faced, taut-jawed
pirate captains waiting for news on the sale of their
prey.

Night fell and still no Genevieve. He wasn't surprised. If she wasn't used to riding it would be a long,
hard journey, even with the assistance of that surly
"footman" of hers. Footman, ha. He was probably
another pirate, and both Genevieve and the magnifi-

cent Xantha pirates' women. No, he corrected himself as he reentered The Mermaid. Genevieve was too shy, too new to experiences of all kinds to be some steel-souled brigand's mate. There was an improbable innocence about her.

He shared pitchers of gut-singeing rumfustian with several sailors and gathered gossip as he went. Men were a far better source of it than women, despite popular opinion. Drunk men spilled their hearts and everyone else's. It jolted him to the core when he sat down with a ragtaggle lot and had a new-found friend drop a startling bit of news square in his lap.

"Eh, yew know 'oose strange now, it's that black ship in the 'arbor, the one they call the *Bonny Nan.* I seen her cap'n just last night strutting the decks prideful as a peacock in full bloom, shoutin' orders and makin' thet crew scramble to obey. An' boys, laugh as ye may, that cap'n was a woman!"

Only one man laughed. Another nodded. "I seen her too, a hard-boiled, black-haired bitch with a tongue could flay an elephant from across the road. Handles that crew good as a man and prob'ly scalps them what gits in her way."

"Black-haired?" Michael asked, mouth dry.

"Black-haired all right, boy, wit' a mane down to her pretty, buxom buttocks, and a figure fair to burstin' out a'her trousers and blouse. Meanest damn woman I ever crossed, and fast as Satan Hisself wit' a sword. I damned near qualified fer the priesthood!"

Michael finished his drink and melted through the door with the next roaring drunk bunch. If he didn't know better, he'd have thought they were talking about Sabelle. It wasn't difficult to mingle with a small group from the *Bonny Nan* and, hat low over his eyes, join arms with them and sing THE KEELHAULING OF BLACKJACK BOWERS all the way up the loading ramp.

A trim ship, sleek lines, dainty bowsprit, the gleam of riveted metal on her hull under the glossy black paint. Nicest brigantine he'd ever boarded. The thought made him lurch. He hated the sea and all its memories of beatings, rainy nights in the crow's nest, and standing watch while icy sleet drummed down on his bowed shoulders and stiffened his hair with a crust of ice. Scurvy and dysentery and fever and vomiting two weeks on end, that was the sea. Being on it even while aboard a stationary ship made the dinner and rumfustian sit heavily in his disturbed stomach. He faded behind some rigging and half-mended canvas and tried to figure out where Robert was. He decided to begin his search in the captain's cabin.

Judging by the silence and darkness, there was no one inside. He crept in like a hungry mouse on the trail of a delectable snack, closing the door soundlessly behind himself and groping along the wall for a lamp. He located it and dug flint and tinder from his pockets. A flame was struck, the whale-oil lamp ignited. There was a creak in the bunk that made his skin crawl.

"Is that you, my domineering vixen?" came a sleepy male voice.

"Robert Justine, you jackass, what the hell are you doing in the captain's cabin?" Michael marveled.

Robert sat up so fast he bumped his head on the wall. He rubbed sleep-swollen eyes, the light glinting off wrist shackles. "Michael! What on earth—hey, old man, have you got a pipe on you? I haven't had my eager hands on a tobacco pouch in days."

They shook hands as casually as if they ran across each other on pirate ships every other week. Michael pulled up a chair by the bed. "You inestimable fool, how did you get yourself tangled up with a female buccaneer?"

"Easy, old man," Robert said, sitting and clanking his chains for dramatic effect. "She attacked the ship I was on and threatened to cast us all ashore if we weren't worth ransom. No thanks! I decided Barbados is one of the two most boring places on earth, the other being . . ."

"I know, I know, Eloise LeBeau's boudoir, as you always say. So what happened?"

"So I told the devastatingly attractive lady in knee-pants that she'd lose a large chunk of ransom setting me ashore. I was of a mind to catch a fast ride home to the ladies in my life and, of course, you and your horse stealing, wenching, gambling, and mad government adventures."

"I get the general idea. In short, you gave the address of your family and freely gave your worthless carcass up to be sold into freedom. Just tell me where the keys are and we'll both have a chuckle at the lady's expense. In the desk, maybe?"

Robert crossed defiant arms on his chest. "I'm not telling you. It's only another week before the final transaction is made, and seven days isn't any too long to spend with a woman like that. You wander back later with the cash and two good horses and a case of Château Margaux and maybe I'll ride back to London with you. Until then, son, I'm staying and making the best of things."

"You've lost what few brains you had, my addle-pated friend. Sit right there and nurse your crippled mind while I find those keys.—What's that?" Michael asked, midway through an intense rummage in the desk drawers.

"Sounds like the captain's boots. Better hide under the bed."

"Under the bed? You damned twit, this is a ship-board bunk! It's fastened down! There isn't any 'under the bed'!"

"No *wonder* she always leaves her boots in the middle of the room."

"You jackass! I ought to kick *you* under the bed headfirst!"

Michael sprang for the whale-oil lamp, blew it out, and ducked down next to the wardrobe. A moment later the door whacked sharply open. He gaped in the light glaring from the torches on the deck outside the door. A shock ran through him as the woman entered. She could have been Sabelle twenty years younger, twenty pounds lighter, and twenty times the wrong person! He waited until the door shut behind her, then stepped forward and swung the lamp at her. It clunked on her temple, followed by the thud of a limp body on the floor. "You maniac, what're you doing?" Robert shrilled.

"Shut up before you get both of us killed!" Michael snapped, relighting the lamp with frightened fingers. He knelt and studied the woman. She was uninjured except for a small lump on her forehead. "Good God, it's Sabelle and it isn't Sabelle," he gasped. "I've never seen an eerier sight in my life! The coloring, the build, the swagger—Robert, what's her name."

"Evonne Meddows—or at least it was until you killed her."

"She's breathing fine, quit nagging like an old farm wife. Let's go."

Robert swung his legs over the edge of the bunk. "Knock your brains back into place, Don Quixote—I don't want to be rescued, damn you! Let Grandmother pay the ransom, it's a drop in the bucket to the old biddy and I've been having a regular lark around here. This pirating is marvelous stuff! I haven't had so much fun since the night we kidnapped the Dean and left him and the drunk hussies on his mother-in-law's lawn! Michael, I'm being well treated, I'm on a ship piled high with gorgeous women, and I'll be home in a week. So drag your sorry face back to London and keep on playing family helper til I get back. I'm fine, really I am."

"You haven't a brain in your head," Michael announced.

"You're just a bad loser because I ruined your rescue."

"Just one thing before I go, you ungrateful ass—the

brown-haired woman, the one passing herself off as Lady Faunton-Ffolkes—"

"Gen, the captain's little sister? Lovely girl, that. Like to talk her out of her virtuous ways. Viable working material there, old man, heh heh! Cold but boiling below the surface, dear Genevieve is. I have a fantasy wherein both sisters—"

"I'm writing you out of my will," Michael announced, hand on the doorknob.

"You don't have a will—you don't own anything! You penny-clutching miser, why don't you break down and buy a horse of your own?"

Michael raised shocked eyebrows. "The upkeep, old man. The upkeep!" And he exited with a mockingly sad "tsk-tsk."

Genevieve rode to Rye in a warm pink haze of recent memories. She arrived, lulled and pleasure-sated, to a scene of temper and upheaval. Evonne, an angry blue blush at one temple, was striding about spitting orders like a piece of green wood thrown on a roaring fire. "So! *You've* come back!" she snapped at Genevieve.

"Yes," Genevieve said, confused by this outburst. "I sent Henry here days ago, but he didn't return, so I came down myself. What's wrong? How did you get that bruise?"

"Ask your friend Robert!" Evonne looked about, fingered a pistol at her waist, and glowered at a couple of sailors who were attempting with little subtlety to eavesdrop. They immediately found things to do elsewhere. "As for Henry," Evonne sneered, "he rolled in here drunk as a mallard, curly-tailed and quacking. He's been sobered up—" the malicious glint in her eye made Genevieve shudder at the thought of what measures might have been applied to effect this cure. "You must have passed him on the road. He said Robert's grannie wouldn't fork over the ransom.

She'll have to if she wants to see him again. It's just a bluff."

Genevieve knew better than to contradict her. "You can't kill him if she really won't pay—" she said. It was half question, half plea. "Wouldn't it be better to have the ten thousand she's willing to pay than nothing whatsoever?"

Evonne had begun to pace about the deck, but the movement jarred her throbbing head. She stopped, one well-shaped hand held gingerly to the side of her face. "Oh, very well. Anything to get rid of him. He's worse than useless—he's a liability. I imagine it's too much to expect you to turn right around and go back for the money?" she snarled.

"I *am* tired and hungry—" Genevieve said.

"Then get something to eat, rest a while and get back. I don't want to be at anchor here for much longer. It's not safe."

"Evonne, shouldn't you be resting too? You don't look well."

"Well? I probably look like something a whale threw up. Of course I don't look well! Would you if someone had knocked you in the head?"

"Is that what happened? Who? How?"

"I didn't think to ask at the time," Evonne said dryly. "I just walked into my cabin and the next thing I knew your friend Robert was leaning over me taking off my clothes—loosening them so I could breathe, he said. I nearly loosened his teeth." Genevieve guessed it was the indignity—the temporary loss of control—that was bothering her more than the pain.

"Did Robert see who did it?" Genevieve asked.

"He claims he didn't, but he was right there. Go get something to eat," she said, suddenly tiring of the subject. "I'm lifting anchor at the full moon, with or without you and the St. Justines' money."

Genevieve recognized the dismissal and didn't ask any more questions. But she was troubled and wanted

to know more. Had it been a robbery and a simple act
of vindictiveness? And where did Robert come into
the matter?

She headed for the galley and was pleased that
several of the sailors whistled and made appreciative
if obscene remarks about her appearance. They didn't
recognize this stylish young beauty with the spring in
her step as the weatherbeaten dormouse who had
worked beside them cleaning the decks and sleeping
next to them in hammocks in the stinking hold.

She ran into Kate, the Scotswoman she'd met in the
crow's nest. "If it's not *you*, lass!" she exclaimed.
"What's gone and happened to you? Such clothes!"

"Kate, what happened to the captain?"

"Aye, verrry strange, that. There was much coming
and going and it might 'a been someone who came on
board and left again. Or it might 'a been one of the
crew—hoping somebody else'd be blamed. Who's to
say?"

"You don't think it was Mr. St. Justine then?"

Kate looked at her, smiled and said, "Do you think
he'd do that?"

Genevieve shook her head. "No. I'm sure he
wouldn't."

Kate fingered her short curls. "Do you think my
hair might do that like yours? Did you cut it short
for wigs?"

Genevieve got some bread and ale, talked with
Kate for a bit about fashions, then went in search of
Robert. She finally located him on deck. His clothing
was a little the worse for wear from his weeks on
board ship, but he was freshly shaved, bathed, and
combed and was a picture of unconcerned elegance as
he leaned on the rails, contemplating the view of Rye.

"Mr. St. Justine?" Genevieve said as she approached.

"Ah, Genevieve," he said. Then he turned. "So
you're ba—" His words were choked off as he caught
sight of her. With frank astonishment he looked at
her from head to toe. "My God!" he finally managed

to gasp. "How did you do that? I cannot believe—!"

As flattered as she was at his admiration, she wanted to find out what had happened to Evonne and get back to London. "How was my sister injured?" she asked.

"That dress really suits you—"

"Were you there—?"

"—and the hair, unusual but flattering—"

"Who was it—?"

"—matching shoes, very nice—"

"Robert! Much as I'm enjoying this little critique of my appearance, I'd rather have some answers," Genevieve said sharply.

He turned away, resumed his stance against the rail. "Answers?" he said pleasantly, as if he hadn't noticed questions.

"How was Evonne hurt?"

He frowned, as if in concentration. "I wish I knew. Truly. I was taking a nap, you see, and there was this thud. I awakened to find Captain Meddows on the floor and caught the merest glimpse of a cloaked figure dashing out." When he'd finished his pat recital he smiled as nicely as a child who'd eaten everything on his plate and expected to be rewarded.

"Then you took her clothes off?" Genevieve said.

"Oh, she told you about that, did she?"

She watched his smug profile for a moment. "Robert, you're lying," she said.

She expected him to deny it, but he just looked down at his hands as if something important was written on them. "Am I?" he asked coolly. "Interesting theory, that. You might be right."

It was Genevieve's turn to be surprised. To accept her accusation and all but admit his guilt so blatantly! Who or what might he have seen that he would cover up for? A shred of suspicion wafted through the back of her mind, but she quickly rejected it. No, she'd just left him in London and anyway, he had no way of knowing where the ship was docked. It could have been at any of a score of seacoast towns, and she was sure, no matter what other information she might have indiscreetly let slip, they had not discussed Rye in any context.

Another thought crossed her mind. Another woman —that must be it. If Evonne had come in on Robert and another woman—yes. That would account for everyone's reluctance to discuss the matter with her. Why was she worrying over her sister like a hen over a chick anyway? That was truly absurd! *Evonne managed to take care of herself under extraordinarily dangerous circumstances for many years before she even knew I was alive,* Gen thought.

"What are you smiling about?" Robert asked.

She cast him a sideways glance. "Why, Mr. St. Justine, we must all be allowed our little secrets, mustn't we?"

"Touché," he answered with a charming bow.

Michael rode back to London in so preoccupied a fashion that his latest purloined steed (a sorry nag, all neck and teeth-rattling lurches) had to pick the road himself. There was a fine drizzle crawling down the back of Michael's neck despite upturned collars and an old muffler wound haphazardly about his throat. He sneezed as he rode, wistful noises in the wet morning air.

The going was slow, his thought processes were considerably faster and more melancholy. Robert had ruined a perfectly good rescue, and enchanting Genevieve Ffolkes-Meddows-Faunton-Whoever was a cohort to the pirates. Had all that fresh, unspoiled guilelessness been an act? A ploy to distract him from the business of ransom and from the fact that he plainly knew there was something suspicious about her? All that doe-eyed sincerity—had it been the act of a seasoned extortionist? He liked her far too much to be angry at the thought, so he gave a troubled cough or two and sneezed at a bedraggled tree.

"I fell so easily for that Crude-Insensitive-Husband routine—but I could have sworn, from the way she reacted, that a man had never treated her decently before." He mumbled it almost aloud so that the horse let one fly-nibbled ear flop forward. "I *believed* her. The women I've known have either been fun-loving doxies or cold social beauties. She's both and neither."

And then, of course, there was that fool St. Justine, refusing a flawed but serviceable escape plan—ransom —Genevieve in the candlelight with her curly hair like a flood of cinnamon-spiked cocoa—the sister—a woman with Sabelle's coloring and reportedly, temperament as well—

It couldn't be a coincidence, two women looking so alike. Or could it? *Maybe*. Or had he been made a fool of by a manipulative woman? Manipulative? With that pent-up nervousness so evident in quivering lip and shaking hands as she faced the St. Justines?

She had the damnedest, most oddly attractive way of looking at him, as if she were afraid he'd hurt her and yet trusting him not to.

The horse plodded relentlessly onward. Michael wetly smacked himself on the forehead. "I forgot Sunday dinner with Althea! And my appointment with the Secretary and the Minister!"

He slumped dejectedly in the saddle as the muddy nag nickered chastisement and clopped sloppily onward.

8

Genevieve's thoughts as she unwittingly followed Michael back toward London were slightly less morose, but no less confused. On the way to Rye she had still been under the warm, cozy influence of a night of love. Now, in a dreary May rain that oozed coldly through the carriage door and made her clothes feel clammy, Genevieve was brought back to her normal, sensible self. What had she done, getting involved with the handsome young solicitor who was, after all, on the "other side." He was the legal representative of the people she was conspiring to rob—that was the flat, hard truth of it.

There was another truth that was coming on her as well. She was just a little ashamed of herself. A few weeks earlier on board the *Black Angel* she had deliberately cut herself loose from the clanking chains of Faunton morality that had encircled her all her life. She had become, or meant to become, an independent person making her judgments without the weight of traditional prudery. The chains were indeed gone, but underneath had been a sticky cobweb of inbred ethics that she might never be free of. Certainly such pleasures of the flesh, undreamed of a few days ago, must belong rightly in the marriage bed, must they not? And yet—marriage? That she would not have—not now, not with anyone.

Was she in love with Jean-Michael Clermont? Love was not something she'd been encouraged to expect from life, yet she would have been an unusual girl had she not imagined love striking her like a crackling bolt from heaven. But she had supposed its object would be a handsome prince whose eyes would meet hers and they would both instantly recognize that they were meant to spend eternity gazing lovingly at one another.

More knowledgeable now about life, she had a deep foreboding sense that this dream had been utter, clotted nonsense. Stupid schoolgirl ramblings of an uninformed mind and heart. Evonne's cynicism was rubbing off on her a bit. The "prince" in question was handsome enough, but when she first looked into *his* eyes she had read not romance, but abiding suspicion of her. He did not trust her, nor she him—and yet, she wanted to. She truly wanted to put her heart in his gentle, considerate hands and say, "I am yours." But she could not.

Laced, powdered, perfumed, and properly wigged, Genevieve was back at the St. Justines' mansion for the third time. But she was bone-marrow weary from her trip to Rye and back and was beginning to be desperately afraid of what she was doing. She had refused to surrender her cloak, hoping that she could relay her message quickly without seeing Michael again. But a deep and heartfelt sneeze from one of the dark corners of the St. Justine drawing room alerted her to his presence.

"So the pirates have been back in contact with you, Lady Faunton-Ffolkes?" he said nasally.

She felt a sudden, unaccustomed blush warm her cheeks. Why was she feeling like a schoolgirl in his presence? She caught his knowledgeable gray glance and looked away. "Yes, an hour ago."

"And they have agreed to my conditions," the Dowager said. It was a flat statement of fact, not a query.

"Yes, they have," Genevieve answered.

"I told you that was the way to handle such people," the Dowager exclaimed, primarily for the benefit of her daughter-in-law who was nervously folding and refolding a pleat of her pale tan dress. "Very well.

How are we to get the money to them and when shall
we see Robert?"

Genevieve, concerned with the way Michael's gaze
was burning into the back of her neck, was taken
aback. "What? Oh—they said you are to give me the
money and they will collect it from me at their convenience."

"Michael? Will you take my draft to the bank and
take the ransom in a parcel to Lady Faunton-Ffolkes's
lodgings?" the Dowager demanded. "A transaction of
this magnitude will take hours and we don't wish to
make our guest wait."

"Most assuredly," he answered, then buried his
face in a large linen handkerchief to muffle a sneeze.

Genevieve stood quickly, prepared to take flight,
but the Dowager had become chatty now that the
business was taken care of. "I don't believe we asked
about your family, my dear," she said. "It was most
inconsiderate of us. Who is it these ruffians are holding of yours?"

"My—my brother," Genevieve said, trying desperately to remember the story she had ready to tell them
the first time she'd called. But she was tired and fear-
ful and confused. "My older brother."

"And has your family settled with them?"

"Yes. Yes, they have."

"I'm frankly quite surprised that you are responsible
for this—"

"Responsible?" Genevieve asked, panicked.

"Yes," the Dowager went on, placidly unaware of
the turmoil her words had caused in Genevieve's
mind. "I would have thought your father would be
handling these negotiations."

Genevieve breathed an almost audible sigh of relief.
"My father has passed away, your ladyship, and I
have no other brothers so the task has fallen to me."

"Where are your people from?" the Dowager persisted in what was, so far, an innocent inquiry.

Genevieve drew a complete blank. She had not

counted on this. She knew the names of few cities in England, never having lived here, and feared desperately that whatever she named would be familiar to them. She stared at the Dowager, rummaging wildly in her memories for the name of some obscure village. The seconds seemed to tick by like hours and no name came to her.

"Saltfleetby St. Clement—in Lincolnshire," Michael's voice cut in.

They all turned and stared at him in surprise.

"Isn't that what you told me, Lady Faunton-Ffolkes?" he added cordially.

"Yes, of course," Genevieve said, stumbling over her words. "Please forgive me. I'm so terribly distressed about all this, I can hardly think anymore."

The Dowager regarded her with a placid gaze that betrayed neither sympathy nor suspicion. "Naturally, dear. I can quite understand. We really should allow you to get back to your hotel. Michael, will you see Lady Faunton-Ffolkes to her carriage? Bert—" she signaled to the lurking servant, "after you attend to the door I would like a word with you."

As Michael handed Genevieve into the carriage, he held her trembling hand for a little longer than necessary. "I will come see you later, when I have the ransom money," he said.

She had to say something. He might be able to pretend that awkward moment inside had not happened —but she could not. "Thank you," she said simply, then asked, "Why did you help me?"

He bowed, smiled, and said, "Because you needed help. We will talk later. There are a number of things we have to discuss."

Then he closed the carriage door and the vehicle lurched forward.

"Bert," said the Dowager Duchess St. Justine. The major domo, in his yellow and white livery, stood like an overly attentive canary in front of her.

"Madame?"

"Bert, you are our most trusted of servants and your family has been with ours since the first St. Justines crossed the Channel," she reminded him.

"Madame." There was no tone in the word, only respectful agreement to this simple fact. The Dowager sat forward in her knobby, thronelike chair, and pointed toward the double doors with her walking stick.

"The reputed Lady Faunton-Ffolkes has a footman, I believe, a Henry. I would like you to fraternize with this Henry person and learn what you can about this mysterious young lady."

"Madame," Bert agreed with a bow, still looking alarmingly like a grave-natured if riotously colored bird.

"You will take this money and get this man most heartily intoxicated, despite the disagreeability of the task. And you will report to me anything of the remotest interest."

"Madame," Bert agreed with quietly malicious enthusiasm that in a lesser person would have been marked by hand-rubbing and low, lurid chuckles. On Bert, however, the tone was accompanied by the merest tilt of a feather-hued eyebrow. He bowed and left by way of the double walnut doors with their scrolled griffins and myopic sphinxes. Once out of earshot, he uttered what sounded suspiciously like a deviant chirp, and indeed rubbed his hands together and smiled.

Michael arrived at Genevieve's hotel suite after dark. He carried a nondescript satchel packed with ten thousand pounds and a flask of lemon tea and whiskey with which he was nursing his headcold. Genevieve, uncomfortably back in her role of the bogus Lady Faunton-Ffolkes, admitted him and took the satchel.

"Is Henry back from whatever adventures he got himself into this afternoon?" she inquired of Xantha.

"He back and faugh—sobering up fast. Want Xantha hurry him along?"

"If you would, please. He knows where to deliver this. Make sure he takes all of our trunks, too."

Xantha sashayed gracefully to the door, skirts swaying. "By de way," she tossed back over her shapely shoulder, "you got fire in de eye to talk to solicitor person who not look willing. Pour hot rum in dat man and let him bake his feet at fire before you commence hammering words in de boy's head. Only one thing worse dan lawyer—a *sick* lawyer. You get dis boy in chair front o' fire. He fadin' fast. Man worth nothing when he in dat shape—not even talk."

Genevieve glared at Michael, but he had already obeyed Xantha, settling himself into an overstuffed chair and unstopping his flask. "Make sure keeps his feet off uppolstery. Ain't paying for muddy boot prints. Need help, scream."

"I will," Genevieve replied stiffly.

Xantha laughed. "Did not mean *you*, Ladyship," she said, and closed the door behind herself, exotic, lush Caribbean sounds of amusement fading down the hall with her.

Genevieve whirled to face Michael, her hands nervously clasped. "You extricated me from an unpleasant situation this afternoon and I'm not sure why. We are plainly on opposite sides of the fence."

"More plainly than you think, Genevieve. I caught this devilish cold spying about in Rye yesterday."

She jerked as if the tip of a barbed whip had cruelly kissed her skin. "You—you spied on me? I trusted you. . . ."

"No, Gen, you never trusted me, nor I you. But I thought we could overcome that. Anyway you should not be so indignant. Part of my job is protecting my clients, and part of my personal belief says that a man always helps his friends. I would naturally find out all I could about you. Don't look so shocked and angry— you are the pirate and extortionist, not I."

Resentment smoldered in her but it was a cold blue flame, under stringent control. "I see. And yet you stepped in to help me this afternoon when I was busily bungling the entire transaction. Why? Does it amuse you to have me at your mercy?"

He laughed as if it scraped his throat. "No woman is ever at a man's mercy. Don't try to paint yourself as a victim, you're clever and resourceful and when cornered, you doubtless have fangs and claws—I can vouch for the claws well enough after the other night. No, don't wince, I did not mean to hurt you. But the fact remains that your profession is in the way."

"Of what?" Genevieve snapped.

"Well, of—of us," he fumbled.

"I see. And what does this 'us' consist of? We are rivals and all we have in common is a rather drunken evening in which we were both carried away by lack of judgment."

He stood, gray eyes flaming. "Do you expect me to believe that the only thing we felt was intoxication?"

"It certainly was not love, Mr. Clermont, was it."

"No—but I wish it *had* been."

She caught her breath. No, he couldn't mean it. Could he? She stared at him in surprise and saw that his expression was the same. They tried to glare at each other as if insulted and succeeded for only a minute before Genevieve let a betraying giggle escape. Michael fought the smile that threatened to give him away. Another moment and they were laughing. Michael held his arms out and she went into them, laying her head on his shoulder.

"What are we fighting about?"

"A better question is what we're doing together. Listen to me, Genevieve, I think the Dowager is suspicious of you. There's no telling what that steel-hearted harpy might do should word of your identity leak out."

"My identity?" she drew back.

"Yes—the fact that you're the sister of the *Black Angel*'s captain."

"How on earth could you know that unless—" she began, but Michael interrupted her with a kiss. She pulled away. "You must be the one who hit Evonne over the head and—"

"Hasn't anyone ever told you it's rude to talk in bed?"

"We're not in bed," she replied, kissing him again. He picked her up and casually toed the bedroom door open.

"We will be in three seconds, chérie."

The Dowager St. Justine had lived a rich and full life. The pampered only daughter of a rich, indulgent duke, she had seen the world. She had stood at the ice-rimmed bank of a Norwegian lake and watched the shimmering aurora borealis; she had dangled girlish toes in the stinking canals of Venice; she had sailed blithely past the Pillars of Hercules in a private yacht that could have accommodated an army in comfort; she had seen the sunrise on midsummer morn over the ancient stones of Stonehenge.

But she had never seen anything that quite took her breath away like the sight of Bert when he returned from his revels with Henry.

Her servant, usually seen only in crisp livery, was in a state of positively shocking disrepair. His wig and hat almost parted company, having slipped down opposite sides of his head. His bloodshot eyes had a glazed, aghast look that would remain with him for weeks. His coat, a mottled tweed object, was spotted with wine and something green and he reeked of cheap perfume, bad cheese, and stale tobacco.

"Bert!" she exclaimed.

"Madame?" he moaned, one hand fluttering toward his brow.

"Are you—all right?"

"In a manner of speaking, Madame," he replied dismally.

She looked at the smoking wreck of a ruined servant and decided that strong measures were required. "Pull yourself together, man!" she said crisply. "What were you able to find out about the lady?"

Bert tried to swallow a belch and failed. "Beg pardon, Madame," he grieved. Life would never be quite the same again, he decided. "The object of my questioning," he began, attempting to recapture formality, "is one Henry Neeley, originally from Brighton—"

"Bert! I don't want to know the man's life history—"

"I am aware of that, Madame. It seemed to be all he wanted to discuss, however. I shall, of course, gloss over his background if you desire—"

"I do! What about Lady Faunton-Ffolkes?"

"I'm sorry to inform your ladyship that she is a pirate."

"A pirate!"

"Just so, Madame."

The Dowager levered herself to her feet and paced stiffly before the fireplace. "Then she is not the pitiful young lady she pretends to be. Hmmm. I dislike being toyed with, Bert."

"Yes, Madame," replied Bert, who could not conceive of anyone daring to "toy with" the Dowager St. Justine.

"I dislike parting with money unnecessarily, but I dislike far more being toyed with!"

Bert nodded and wondered desperately when he would be allowed to escape to his own quarters and a proper cup of tea.

"Where is my grandson?" she barked.

Bert almost reeled from the volume of this question. "I'm afraid Henry was disinclined to discuss the matter, Madame, though I judge that the ship is docked somewhere off the south coast."

"Why didn't you ask him where it is?"

"I did, Madame." Bert had found a friendly knife flirting with his jugular vein when he had put this question. "He was unwilling to reveal that information, Madame."

The Dowager resumed her seat, thought for a little longer. The incident that had first made her suspicious was still fresh in her mind—the young woman had not seemed to know where she was from. Jean-Michael had reminded her.

Jean-Michael. Hmmm.

Nice young man. Had always seemed attentive and loyal except for the strange intervals in which he seemed to drop out of sight. Could it be—? No. But then—

"Bert, what did this man know about Master Clermont?"

"Apparently nothing, Madame, except that he is concerned about Master Clermont's curious interest in the lady."

So, Jean-Michael was already investigating the young woman without having been asked. She should not have doubted his loyalty to the family. "Bert, fetch me parchments and inks. I wish to have this young woman arrested just as soon as she has sent the money along to the ship. That way Robert will be safe. I wouldn't think she would serve as carrier herself—"

"No, Madame. I am under the impression that Henry is to serve in that capacity."

"My nephew is a private secretary to the King. I will inform him of the circumstances and he will be able to get the girl arrested and arrange to have someone follow this Henry. I must be sure Master Clermont is not implicated, however. Yes. Get me the ink!"

Deep in the gauze-curtained bed, encircled by candlelight and Michael's arms, Genevieve existed in a state of worried bliss.

She liked this young man a great deal more than she wanted to. Given time, she might come to care for him deeply. But there was no time. The candles were guttering one by one, burning down to tiny, flickering orange glows in dishes awash with beeswax. Some had already gone to cold black flecks, more ash than wick. Morning was spreading across the dirty city sky in low, timid stripes of mauve and tangerine, casting light on the sooty corkscrew chimneys of a reluctant-to-awake-London.

Michael slept uneasily. Genevieve stroked his warm, smooth back. She had slept awhile and once heard him murmur, "Ahh, Jenny, I could learn to love you so easily . . . ." Remembering and wondering about those words made her reluctant to slide from his gentle embrace and face the stark morning and an uncomfortable journey to Rye. Back to the ship and Evonne. Back to trimming sails and scrubbing decks and taking turns at the watch in howling winds and lashing, wet gales.

I could learn to love you. . . . That would be so nice, to be loved and held dear by someone, especially this man. But she had spent so long without a family and now there was Evonne . . . Evonne and the search for their mother. A pipe dream, probably. But to stay here with Michael—as what, his mistress? The thought made her scraps of Faunton morality cringe, and yet marriage made her hesitate. She had been married and disliked it. There was so much left for her to do and see in the world. And yet—and yet having him was so sweet, so right. Had they been in love and ready to make a commitment, even then she would have had difficulty abandoning her new-found sister and the hope of locating their mother. As it was, there was nothing to hold her here, nothing of substance. No future, no promises.

But there was laughter and kindness and honesty and—*and this,* she thought, as he woke and began to touch her lazily. She curved against him, making sleepy kitten sounds of arousal and kissing all the bare skin she could find. His mouth met hers, then she moaned softly, feeling his hands on her breasts. She was sore, but he was gentle, easing her onto her back and slowly sucking her red nipples. Genevieve tangled her fingers in his thick brown hair, seeing the auburn glint in its depths sparkling like garnets.

She steered his head back up to hers, drinking in deep, weary kisses. She gasped with penetration, moved with it, tangled her long legs with his and gripped his muscular shoulders. They arched together in enjoyment before exhaustion dropped them, spent, in the melee of sheets and quilted coverlets.

A scarlet ray of dawn cast a light on the mirror, reflected itself into Genevieve's flushed face. She stirred lazily. Dawn! she realized suddenly. Henry had gone with the money hours and hours ago. Evonne would be furious, having to wait like this or—or *not* wait! Genevieve sat up suddenly. What if Evonne had felt it was too dangerous to tarry any longer and had left her behind? She reached for her shift, but Michael grasped her wrist in a love-light grip. "Where are you going?"

"I must leave. You know that—"

"Wait. There is something we must talk about."

"There's no more time."

"Only a moment. It's about your sister—"

Genevieve stiffened. "What about her?"

"I saw her for a moment—only a fraction of a second really, but she looked just like a woman I know—a woman named Sabelle—"

"Sabelle!" Genevieve echoed in an aching whisper. "You know my mother!"

There was an ominous clatter of hooves in the courtyard below. But neither of them noted it for a moment. "Then it wasn't my imagination," he said, "you and your sister are the children she's been looking for ever since—"

There were sudden shouts, door flying open, boots

on ornate rosewood stairs. Michael sat up, frowning.
"Gen—I—" The door of the suite exploded open.

Genevieve screamed and clutched a sheet to herself
as four armed men burst into the bedroom. "Are you
the woman passing herself off as Lady Faunton-
Ffolkes?" demanded one. "We have a writ for your
arrest on charges of piracy and extortion. Are you
Master Clermont?"

Michael looked wildly into Genevieve's accusing
eyes. "Yes," he admitted.

"There is a horse in back for you, sir, so you won't
be seen leaving," the soldier said respectfully. "You
are free to go. I'm to tell you the Dowager St. Justine
is waiting to see you."

9

Henry staggered up the gangplank and handed the satchel of money to Captain Meddows. "Where are Genevieve and Xantha?" Evonne asked him.

Henry shrugged. "Doan know. Said they'd be along in a bit." He inched away quickly before she could question him any farther.

Evonne went to her cabin, poured a generous crystal goblet full of honeyed rum, and sat down to count the money. Ten thousand pounds exactly. Hardly worth the trouble. Kidnapping Robert St. Justine had been one of the worst moves she'd made, no matter how appealing he might be. She eased off her boots, enjoying the refreshing feel of the cool floor on her tired feet. Tired. Yes, she was tired. She never felt this way on the high seas. She could go for days it seemed on mere naps when she had the roll of ocean swells beneath her and the prospect of open conflict and untold treasure over each new horizon.

But sitting in port like this for days on end, waiting like a church warden's wife to find out what was happening elsewhere—this was not life. Not her kind of life. She had lost control—that was the problem. She should have risked it and gone to Robert's granny herself. If the old harridan had made objections to the ransom, Evonne would simply have stolen the candlesticks and dinnerware on the spot and would be out at sea by now.

She sent for Robert. When he arrived he walked to the wide desk, fingered the bills and remarked, "Odd. I thought they'd be dripping her blood. Granmère doesn't part with money easily."

"Easily or not, I've got it now and we don't need you anymore."

"You mean I'm free to go? What if I don't want to?" he asked sweetly as a glass of warm sherry. "Aren't you and I and your lovely sister going to have a little going-away dinner?"

"You're the one going away and you can get your dinner wherever you like," Evonne answered, handing him a bill of a lower denomination than the one he was trying to tuck into his breeches pocket.

"Perhaps we'll meet again?" he said.

She turned, a smile curving her voluptuous lips. "You never know. Aside from the financial difficulties you've caused, you've been—let us say, entertaining?"

"I strive to please," Robert said, returning her smile and pulling her into his arms.

Evonne laughed, a throaty laugh Jean-Michael would have recognized as a legacy from her mother. "You do, generally."

"I'll make sure I don't get kidnapped by anyone else until I see you again," he said.

Robert stood on the dock, gazing back at the *Black Angel* as she bobbed gently in the pre-dawn tide. He really did hate to leave, he realized to his own astonishment. Especially to leave without seeing Genevieve again. A wonder what a trip to London had done for the girl's looks. The transformation in her since they first met was remarkable.

He decided to stay in Rye for a while. She was not yet back, and he was certainly not in any hurry to get to London and make an accounting of his adventures to his grandmother. There was a tavern just a few steps along the road. He could have a glass or two of ale, keep an eye on travelers, and perhaps get a farewell word or two with Genevieve. What those words would be, he had no idea, but it would come to him. Words had never deserted him before.

But as the hours went by and the empty tankards collected in neat array on his table, Robert's mind began to wander. Cheerfully drunk and loquacious, he endeavored to interest a man at the next table in a discussion of the watch his father had presented to him on his eighteenth birthday. "Aw, lemme look at the damn thing then," the man said in an effort to get the conversation over with.

"Have it right here in my vest po—dear me, what can I have done with it?" Robert said, making something of a spectacle of frisking himself. Next he dumped the contents of his battered portmanteau on the tabletop and went through that. "Now I remember!" he announced to a small audience that had remarkably little interest in the whole topic. "I changed my shirt before I got off the ship. Bet it bell on the fed—" He chuckled. "I mean, fell on the bed. I think I'm drightly slunk—slightly drunk."

"Not by half—" someone muttered from across the room.

"I'll just run back to the ship and get it," he said, stuffing his belongings into the case. "Now, don't go anywhere. I'll return shortly," he assured the patrons of the tavern.

His intention was to walk to the end of the dock and hire a rowboat to take him out to the *Black Angel*, but he unfortunately misjudged just how far the dock extended and quickly found himself floating next to his portmanteau. Ah, well, he reasoned, the purpose of a rowboat was to keep one's feet dry, wasn't it? And since he was already quite wet, he might just as well save a farthing and swim. It wasn't far. Leaning on his luggage, which served nicely as water wings, he began to languidly kick his way toward the ship.

It wasn't that he came on board surreptitiously—not on purpose. He even called out for help climbing the rope ladder up the side, but when no one noticed his calls, he proceeded to haul himself and his belongings up the side of the ship. By luck more than planning, he found himself back in the cabin he had occupied when not with Evonne, a tiny, dark cubicle belowdecks. He started conducting a blind search for the watch, patting the bedclothes gently.

But he couldn't find it. With a flash of drunken intuition, he decided to pull the bedclothes off and shake them. He would hear the watch hit the floor, then be able to find it. But the far corner of the spread was stuck. He leaned over, tugged, tugged again, and fell forward. How comfortable it was—sprawling disjointedly in the bed he'd become so accustomed to these last weeks.

Perhaps just a nap—just a short rest until his head cleared a little. He wouldn't be in anyone's way down here and he was *so* tired.

"The Dowager St. Justine is waiting for you and your horse is out back?" Genevieve shrilled at Michael. The soldiers stepped forward, one gathering her clothes from the floor while the other two seized her arms. "You used me—trapped me into staying here while waiting for these men to arrive and arrest me!"

"That isn't true!" Michael shouted as she clutched at the sheet for modesty with one hand and aimed blows at his face with the other. He made a tentative grab for his trousers only to find them under the boots of the nearest soldier. "Genevieve, believe me, I—"

"Please, Sir, hurry before people begin arriving and asking awkward questions!" urged the soldier.

"I'm a lawyer, damn you, I've heard awkward questions before! Genevieve, listen to me!"

Heartsick, terrified of these rough men dragging her naked from bed, Genevieve fought and twisted. They tried to force her wrist into a shackle. She sank her teeth into the nearest male hand. She knew what arrest meant: incarceration in filthy, squalid Newgate Prison among whores and perverts and murderers;

trial of a sorts before staunch Englishmen who believed piracy worse than any other crime; and death by slow strangulation or, if she was lucky, neck-breaking, depending on how skillful the hangman was. Fear made her strong; the two men could hardly subdue her. In her blind, raging fright she did not see that Michael was in the battle with her, trying to make the men release her half by force, half by persuasion.

In the midst of two men subduing a woman, one woman fighting like a Fury, a lawyer negotiating and punching, and a soldier gathering up a voluminous armful of lady's lingerie, there was an abrupt eruption of light and sound that blew the nearest window into the street.

In the immediate and awed silence everyone lay still where they had flung themselves to avoid probable dismemberment. A cool female voice swathed in Caribe overtones said, "Let go de lady—fast—else I put white men's faces where de winder went!"

Genevieve yanked her head up to see Xantha in the doorway, dressed in men's riding clothes—sapphire damask greatcoat, breeches, and thigh-high boots, hair hidden beneath a flamboyantly printed silk scarf. Hammered silver hoops the size of tea saucers glittered from her ears, matching the dully dangerous gleam of the primed pistols in her ready fists. She wore a sword at each voluptuous hip and a curved Moorish dagger through her embossed belt.

"Grab solicitor's clothes, get in dem fast, Gen—no can straddle horse in dress—or naked like now! Hold right dere, lawyer," Xantha barked as Michael made a move toward Genevieve. "Hurry, white girl, constable surely on way, too, with more men. Dese three I lock in de wardrobe."

Genevieve scrambled into Michael's velvet breeches, cinching them about her narrow waist with another of Xantha's garish silk scarves. She flung on his full-sleeved linen shirt, and had barely tucked it in before Xantha tossed her a sword and pistol.

"Out de back, quick. Three horses dere."

"Three? Why three?"

Her beautiful deliverer replied, "Because hostage help us escape safe. And if slippery solicitor person's head must be blowed off, ah well, so be it. Grab dat sheet, boy. We going."

When Michael protested he suddenly found the tip of a razor-sharp Toledo dueling rapier pushing at the tight skin over his sternum. "Sheets good enough for dressing traitor-sort legal persons, too. Hurry, boy," Xantha ordered crisply.

Another minute and he was being rushed down the back staircase with two rapiers pricking his shoulder blades. Xantha tied his wrists to the saddle and took his horse's reins before mounting her own steed. Genevieve, who had been an excellent horsewoman in Jamaica, swung aboard, reflecting nervously that she had not ridden astride since childhood. She was furious, frightened, and deeply wounded by Michael's presumed treachery, so that when he spoke she turned on him with an animal's crippled snarl-whimper and smacked his horse on the rump with the flat of her hand. The startled animal reared, nearly toppling him, then all three horses wheeled and fled down the narrow alleyway and out into the dirty dawn.

Curs and hotel workers pursued them a short ways. then they rounded a sharp, squalid curve in the slimy streets and found themselves racing straight at the constable's party. There was a startled hauling on the reins so that Xantha's mare collided with Michael's. Genevieve's gelding slid, banging into the greasy brick side of a house. She felt stinging pain and dull thuds on the side of her head. "Good Lord!" cried the constable. "It's two women—and some damned Roman!"

Genevieve regained control of her whinnying horse and leaned to one side, kicking a fruit seller's cart from his grasp and sending it careening into the soldiers. Conscience smote her; she dug in the pockets of the velvet trousers she wore and flung the man one of Michael's gold sovereigns. "For that price," bellowed Michael as they raced back up the alley, "I should've gotten at *least* one apple!"

They slid around the next garbage-carpeted bend in the alley and found themselves confronting another rude shock. The alley ended in a low fence overflowing with rubbish and festering foodstuffs. Behind it grew a straggling yew hedge and before it stood the three soldiers from the hotel—with raised pistols!

There was no time to alter course. Xantha snapped the reins back, forcing the horse to spin on his haunches. He presented belly and flailing forelegs to the nearest soldier, Xantha completely shielded by the action. The soldier tumbled to the ground.

Genevieve dug her bare toes into the gelding's ribs. He had long legs and a bold heart; he took fence and hedge in a single soaring bound. Pegasus-like he landed and she spun him about. Xantha's horse came down, leaving her fighting the double reins of two terrified horses. The flint flew from her hands as she tried to light her pistols. Genevieve clutched horse-mane and pistol as the quickest soldier fired. There was a jerk from Xantha, as if an invisible blow had rocked her, then blood darkened her shirt just above the waistband—a vital area. Genevieve did not watch long enough to see Xantha reel and recover—she aimed and squeezed the trigger.

The soldier spun to the garbage with a low cry, then was still. To the stunned Genevieve there was something ghastly and yet viciously victorious in it. He had wounded, perhaps killed the friend who had risked much to save her—and perhaps Genevieve had killed him.

The third soldier, the only one remaining, ran to the slumped Xantha's horse and grabbed for the reins. To Genevieve's stupefaction, Michael lurched to one side and dealt the man a stunning kick in the head!

Xantha, hand to her side, backed her horse up and
booted him forward. The two mares, Michael's following reluctantly, came clumsily fumbling through
fence and hedge, bruising themselves and nearly un-
seating their riders.

"Xantha!"

"No," the lovely mulatto snapped, "not to stop.
Ride. More coming!"

Genevieve watched her anxiously, but the bleeding
had slowed and Xantha seemed none the less resolute
for the wound. They jabbed desperate toes into their
mounts and clattered down the gnarled brick path.
Dawn was brightly bloody through a yellow haze as
they galloped through sleazy London streets toward
the relative safety of open country.

At mid-morning, Xantha brought them to a sudden
halt. The road was a meandering pair of dirt tracks.
"Dis good place to leave lawyer feller," announced
the exotic gunner's mate.

"I'm innocent, I tell you. Didn't I prove it by
saving your lovely neck back there? I did not send the
soldiers to you. Robert's grandmother must have had
you followed," Michael insisted angrily. "I can see
you're not quite sure. Well, then, go ahead, cut my
bonds and let me head the horse back home."

"Horse?" Xantha echoed, slicing through one bond
so that he had a free hand. "No horse. You head
straight back to constables, send dem to *Black Angel*.
No, legal feller walks."

"In a *sheet*? Genevieve, you know me better than
to think I betrayed you. Listen to me! I'd never hurt
you deliberately, let alone let anyone *hang* you. Genevieve—Gen—"

She faltered, torn both ways. Then she saw Xantha's
withering glare. "Off the horse, Michael darling,"
Genevieve snapped.

Prodded by Xantha's rapier, he gracelessly slid off.
Xantha then freed his other hand. "Maybe not traitor,

but only swine hurt nice girl like Gen—Still, solicitor *did* kick soldier over to help. Nice walk, solicitor. Good weather."

Squinting in the sun, looking like some handsome, perturbed young Roman senator, he cocked an eyebrow at Genevieve. "I meant every word I ever said to you—including the fact that I know Sabelle."

Hooves pounded in the distance, a cloud of dust cresting a distant emerald hill. Genevieve, heart crying out, stared into his face with humiliated, hopeful brown eyes. "If you have been truthful about nothing else, be truthful about her."

He gave her the sad spectre of a smile. "She's raucous and gaudily gorgeous and has a heart wide as the Thames. Black hair, flashing eyes, and a sword arm the King's own guards couldn't match. Swears like a sailor. She was very nearly a mother to me— wiped my nose and boxed my ears when I needed it."

"Where is she now?" Genevieve demanded.

"I'm sorry—I don't know. I really don't," Michael answered.

There was no time for more. More unsure than ever, Genevieve was jolted back to reality as Xantha brought the hilt of her sword down on the rump of Genevieve's gelding. The horses sprang off, darting away into the midst of a flock of befuddled sheep.

The soldiers were a safe distance behind. Michael perched himself on a fence post to await their arrival and a ride back to London. When they finally clopped to a halt at his side, the constable huffed and waved. "So you're safe, young fellow. Which way did those murderous hussies go?"

"Straight away toward Brighton," Michael lied blithely, knowing perfectly well they were racing to Rye.

They left him leaping up and down and shouting in a wake of dust. He kicked a boulder, swore some more, and, as a last resort, began walking.

Several footsore hours later he heard the creak and bounce of buggy wheels. A rambling beetle in the distance grew into an incredible carriage frosted in velvet and ornate gilt appendages. There was a familiar coat of arms on the door. The footman leaped to open the door. Michael accepted the slim white bejeweled hand issuing from within and entered. The driver shouted and clucked to the six strapping white German coach horses. They neighed and turned back to the metropolis at a smart trot.

"Althea Pasteau, you are straight from the halls of Paradise! What on earth are you doing here?"

The slender eccentric blond woman who had ejected him from her home upon her marriage short weeks before made no reply. Another moment and a dusty sheet came sailing from the window flap of the coach. "Althea!" came the male protest. "What the devil are you doing? I've been shot at, stabbed at, arrested, abused, tied to a horse, dragged across half of England, and dumped in the noonday sun for an interminably long walk home. We are old, old friends, Althea, and you know I adore you, but—"

A sudden hush. The chuckling footmen were startled to hear him add, a moment later, "Althea, what the hell—Althea, have you taken leave of your—Althea, why are you putting me in my best suit?"

"The Minister," came a muffled voice, for Althea Pasteau, notorious smoker of long, carved pipes and noxious tobaccos, had her teeth clenched on a smoke-ejecting masterpiece of Venetian walnut, "contacted me this morning to locate you. You have missed another government meeting. I went to the St. Justines' who sent me to the hotel where I witnessed the tail end of that delightful debacle with the troops. You have a four o'clock audience, dear boy, and I must warn you—the King is furious!"

The rain that had darkened and cooled the last few days had lifted and it was the most perfect of

English summer mornings. But Evonne Meddows, watching the dock with a spyglass, was not appreciative. They could not wait much longer mere yards from the shore of the country that thirsted of late for pirates' blood.

If it had been anyone else she would not wait at all. She would simply assume that the tardy crew member had decided to join another ship, or changed his name and had gone into some other branch of thievery. But not Genevieve. Her naïveté, her idealism, her girlish sense of honor were difficult for Evonne to understand. But she could identify them easily enough to know that Genevieve would not stay away without sending a message.

It was nearly noon and the bright English sun was sparkling along the peak of each wave. Evonne called to the quartermaster, "We set sail in half an hour—no matter what."

"Do you want our small boat to stay at the pier until then?" he asked.

"Yes." Evonne snapped.

The crew came to life; fresh supplies of food were packed into the hold and lashed together; the last of the water casks were stowed; the surgeon checked his medicines and locked them into cabinets; new ropes, still clean and golden in the sun, were uncoiled; the bo'sun's mate went about the ship, checking the crew members on his list; final inventory of weapons, instruments, supplies, sails, fuel, and ale were noted. The newest—and therefore most easily cowed—crew members were set to operating the bilge pumps causing the fouled water to run down the side of the ship.

Finally everything was ready. "Bring that boat back and hoist anchor and be fast about it, or I'll have your ears in a stew!" Evonne said to the hovering quartermaster.

Evonne stood on deck and swung the spyglass about for one last look for her missing sister.

There *was* someone riding furiously along the marine parade road. She squinted into the harsh sun. Two people on lathered horses. Men—? Women—?

"Hold!" she shouted to the quartermaster.

She leaned forward, holding the glass tightly against her eye. Closer. Closer yet. A dark person, clad in breeches and a vivid blue coat. Xantha. It had to be. But she was riding strangely, leaning slightly and holding her side. The other—Genevieve—whose short hair, slim figure, and men's clothing made her convincingly boyish looking from a distance, was riding a little ahead, turning back at intervals to urge Xantha's mount. They reached the end of the pier. Genevieve leaped down, slim legs scissoring expertly. She reached up to Xantha, helped her off her horse and into the small boat which she frantically rowed to the *Black Angel.*

Evonne was at the rail, furiously relieved, when they came aboard. She turned Xantha over to the waiting surgeon and asked Genevieve, "Is there someone following you?"

"I don't know," Genevieve gasped. "Probably. But I don't know how far."

"We won't wait to see," Evonne replied, then barked out a series of orders to sail immediately.

Genevieve sank to the deck. She sat cross-legged, head bowed, trying to get her breath while the sails unfurled, caught the wind and billowed. When next she looked up, Rye was a water-colored painting of a seacoast town. Clean and placid in the distance. She got to her feet, knees still weak and shaking, to join Evonne at the rail. "What does the surgeon say?" she asked her sister.

"She'll be all right, he thinks. A bad graze, probably a broken rib, but she'll live through it and be proud of the scar. What happened back there?" Evonne asked, turning from her contemplation of the sea. But before Genevieve could answer, Evonne's black-fringed eyes had opened very wide and she said, "Oh, *hell*!"

Robert St. Justine's voice, slurred but strong, cut through the salt-tanged air. "Has anyone seen my watch?"

Part Two

PERILOUS PASSAGES

10

They were well out of European waters before they slackened their wind-wild pace. Robert St. Justine, happily reunited with his watch, was stuck away in a small cabin where he would not get underfoot until a decision could be made as to his disposal. Genevieve spent the first week at sea nursing Xantha. The gunner's mate's wounds were not severe, but she developed an infection and was in serious danger for several days. Genevieve and the ship's surgeon, hollow-eyed and weary, took turns bathing her fevered forehead and forcing liquids down her.

Genevieve would have been miserable enough in any circumstances, but she was heartsick knowing she was the cause of Xantha's misery. She shouldn't have stayed in London with Michael. That had been pure sensual indulgence on her part, endangering not only Xantha, but the entire crew. Evonne, wearing a golden cloud of rare restraint, had not once mentioned this obvious fact to her sister. It made Genevieve want to grovel with gratitude.

In those sea-slumbering hours when all that could be heard was the morning laughter of gulls and the hypnotic slap of sea against cedar, she held Xantha's damp, clutching hand and tried very hard not to think about Jean-Michael Clermont. Slippery solicitor fella. "More than slippery," she whispered to an unheeding Xantha, "he tried to give us away to the law." He had proved untrustworthy. But that was silly! She had not needed proof—she had known the first time she saw him that they were doomed to be adversaries. But she had thought, with dangerous naïveté, that their delightful intimacies had changed that—neutralized and diluted the conflict between them.

She would not be so foolish again. Not with any man. She might be free of the many conventions which had ringed her with dreary propriety, but she was not free of responsibilities. Quite the opposite, in fact. As the poor little adopted daughter of the Fauntons she'd had no responsibility other than rising in the morning and remaining as much a nonentity as possible until it was time to retire again. No one's life, happiness, or well-being turned and hinged on her.

Now, to her chagrin, she'd spent one night thinking only of herself and very nearly caused the arrest of the men and women aboard the *Black Angel*. They hadn't needed to wait for her. Henry had returned to the ship with the ransom money hours before Genevieve made her appearance.

She thought she would never forget that long ride back to Rye. She had been sick for fear that Xantha would not be able to make it and in a turmoil about Michael and the things he'd said. Like unsecured objects on the ship when seas were high and reckless, her thoughts careened wildly every time she thought of him. She recalled the tender moments, the longing in her to touch the chestnut sheen of his hair and luxuriate in his admiration of her body. She remembered the way he had stepped in and helped her when the Dowager questioned her. She also recalled the way he had denied having any part in her arrest. She could almost believe it. She wanted to believe it and yet—

If he had been entirely innocent, why did the soldier have a horse waiting for him? Why did they know his name and expect to find him there?

The worst of it was, she'd realized from the very beginning she should be careful of him, and had stupidly let her guard down just because he seemed so kind, so considerate. She would learn to be wary of such masquerades. Was this experience the sort of thing that made Evonne as she was—suspicious of protestations of affection and trust? Perhaps so.

Michael rode sulkily through the greenlands of France, reflecting at length on the whims of women and sovereigns. King William had decided he needed a new agent in the French Court of Versailles, and who better than Michael? He had protested that his accent was dissipated by years of English life, and the Minister had practically incarcerated him with three language instructors for a month. He had once worked for the diplomatic corps in Marseilles so his accent had been tailored for that part of the country. A noble native family had promised to claim him, and any number of people would swear to have known him from birth. A fine "cover."

Michael had done a great deal of courier work and espionage in his life, but he had never before been foisted off on a hostile court and told to spend the next few years there. He fully expected to be dead or gray-haired by the end of his mission. Oh, well, when he thought of the good he might be doing, it eased the sting of losing Genevieve and being sent straight to the jaws of the lion. Plans were afoot in Europe, plans hostile to Britain, especially with Louis XIV's grandson on the throne of Spain. It meant two strong adjacent countries were under French rule—and France was growing more belligerent to England over the years.

Though Michael had spent his early years in France, he had considered himself entirely a loyal Englishman for many years. All the people who had loved him, helped him, and respected him were English (or, like Sabelle, of no particular nationality). His higher education had been in English universities. He loved the land, the language, and the people of England with a

fervor it would have embarrassed him to express. Yet
here he was in France, possibly the land of his birth,
certainly the country of his earliest memories, and it
gave him an odd, dislocated feeling—something like
the queasy rootlessness he always felt on the hated
sea.

The horse clopped along. Michael absently patted
the animal on the shoulder, thoughts returning to
Genevieve. He hoped he had made her believe in his
innocence at the end. But even if he hadn't . . . well,
he would never see her again anyway. Pity. He liked
her a great deal more than he first realized. Wouldn't
it be something if she really was Sabelle's daughter?
Sabelle, his oldest and maybe dearest friend. Colorful,
splendidly vulgar Sabelle. . . .

Missing parents and lost children: Genevieve had
innocently reminded him that he had a family to find
too. He could still taste the rain on that stormy night
when an oddly familiar man—Matthew, his name had
been, though he was not sure how he knew that—had
taken him from one family and left him with another.
And the mother he had never seen—"Beautiful as an
angel, boy, don't ever forget that. Beautiful as an
angel." And the feeling that Matthew had meant to
say more but couldn't.

The kindly old couple raised him after that. A cottage in the woods. Making cheese, collecting warm
eggs from under fat speckled hens on dappled summer
mornings. Reading in front of the comforting fire
while winter clawed at the shutters. Whispered con-
versations that stopped when he approached. The
wonderful way the old couple had treated him, not
merely with love, but as if he had been something
special—special beyond all bonds of affection.

He had tried to write to them over the years, tried
to find his way back there without success after being
kidnapped and forced into service aboard a pirate ship
at the age of twelve. He had come out ahead, actually;
been bought by Sabelle and befriended by Captain

Roque. After that, the English ambassador in Marseilles had hired him, thus making connections that eventually led to government work and a reputation as one of the fast-ascending young agents so strenuously trained by the Ministry.

Michael patted the horse again. They had agreed to let him have a week to find the old couple who had raised him. One week to thank them, try to repay them, find out what he could about his parentage and true identity. One week to find himself. Only seven days, nearly over now.

The horse had come to a crossroads. Michael ran a hand through his wind-blown hair, the chestnut highlights darkly bright in the late afternoon sun. The area was familiar, hauntingly so. *You will sail the seas and some day find what you want, Gen. But I am landbound and lost.*

"This way," he told the rangy bay. They took the right fork, following sun-splotched tree shadows down a meandering dirt road. But the trees were straight and tall. That was not right. *I have been lost here before,* he thought excitedly, reining in the attentive horse. "This way, back, it's the other road!"

It was indeed. Once on the other dirt track his every sense came alive. The pines and honeysuckle—he knew their mingled aroma. The old bent evergreens, warped by lightning in their youth—the stunted fruit trees—he had climbed those trees as a boy. Heart pounding, he urged the bay on faster, soaking in sights and scenes from his youth. He did not have to think about where to turn although the trail was by now only a deep, grass-filled rut. He was too eager about nearing the end of his long search to recognize the grass as a sign of desertion. Birds twittered drowsily overhead, old sweet songs he knew from youth.

Familiar sounds. They rounded another turn and he found himself wondering why he heard no goats bleating, no sheep stupidly quibbling over choice bits of grass. Michael dismounted, stepping into deep vegetation instead of wheel-and-hoof smoothed path. This evidence of undisturbed growth at last connected in his mind; he led his horse down the almost nonexistent track, craning for sight of the cottage's cheerful thatched roof.

Michael's heart was hammering so loudly he could no longer hear the birds nor tiny creatures romping in the dense underbrush. Where there had been a neatly tended field he found seedlings and old blackened tree trunks. Above the seedlings loomed cedars and evergreens well into arboreal adolescence—disturbing evidence of long-past damage.

He left the horse and plunged through the brush recklessly, shouting for the old couple who had given him their name. In the face of his charge, birds leaped, fluttering away, and deer took hedges in swooping, graceful bounds. Silence surrounded him, as if the land held its breath. He thrust through a matted lacework of cobwebs, hung like some tawdry tablecloth to dry in specks of tree-barred sun.

"Madame Clermont! Monsieur!" Then, desperately, "Grandmère?" Stillness and immobile greenery answered him. He floundered through the last leafy barrier and found himself staring at the cottage.

It was only a crumbling foundation, rain-faded black stones wired together by wild grape vines. Little needlepoint-delicate leaves and tendrils curled around the hollow shell of his only remembered home. He staggered wildly through the ruins. Fallen building blocks, mortar turning to sand, all lay tumbled and tossed about. He followed them out the rear of the once-house, and saw, in what had formerly been a clearing, three upright rectangular stones, ornately carved and engraved.

Time had begun sinking these tombstones, roughening the scrolled corners and softening the deeply incised letters. Cherubs and saints surrounded the names he knew would be there even before he knelt and gently stroked away the vines: "Madeleine Clermont," "Jacques Clermont," and the same date, 1692. Ostentatious stones for two simple peasants with no living relatives. Suspiciously grand monuments to people who could never have afforded or desired such relics.

Michael shook his head and rose, dusting mud and crushed ferns from his knees. He shoved his hands down in his pockets. He had come too late. They would never know what they had meant to him now. From a purely practical viewpoint, the loss was also one of his identity. He would never know who he was. He kicked at the grass with a booted toe, already turning away before he remembered the third stone. He pivoted back slowly, intrigued, and scraped the vines away from the last marker with the side of his foot.

It did not register for a moment. He stared with blank, uncomprehending eyes for a full moment before the hand of protesting fear eased frigid fingers about his throat. He sank to his knees, fingers braced against the frozen stone. "No," he said. "No. No, no, no! It cannot be! It cannot!"

For the name on the stone was Jean-Michael Clermont.

"Where are we bound for?" Genevieve asked.

"Wherever the wind takes us," Evonne answered. "The wind, and a chance for profit."

"But not back to Europe?"

Evonne just looked at her.

"You see, I think our mother is in England. Or she was not so very long ago."

"You're still thinking about that?" Evonne asked.

"I met—someone—who knows her. He said she'd been looking for us. Evonne, she *wants* to find us—"

"You believe that?"

Genevieve spoke in an almost whisper. "I have to believe it."

Evonne did not reply, but turned away, a vaguely troubled expression on her face.

Genevieve went back to sorting the maps that were laid out on the desk. Evonne thought she was a fool. Was she right? Was Michael's talk of Sabelle only that—talk? Something to hold her back a little longer so that she would be caught and arrested?

She tied a length of cord around a section of crackling parchment and slipped it into its proper pigeon-hole. She gazed unseeing at the leaded glass panes at the back of the captain's cabin and tried to reconstruct the scrap of conversation she'd had with Michael about Sabelle. She closed her eyes. *Concentrate. Concentrate.*

He'd been talking about seeing Evonne and he'd said something about how she looked like a woman he knew, "a woman named Sabelle." Genevieve's forehead crinkled in concentration. Those had been his exact words. She was sure. *Think very hard*, she told herself. She started going back over everything that had passed between them. No. She had never referred to her mother's name. She was quite sure of that.

So it must have been the truth rather than just a trick to delay her. He must actually have known her mother. It was an uncommon name and he'd said Evonne looked just like her. Genevieve remembered enough of her mother to recognize the resemblance.

Dear God, if she'd only had a little longer. A moment more to ask where the woman Sabelle was, where he'd seen her, how she was, what she was like.

But there'd been no time. And now it was too late.

She'd never see Jean-Michael Clermont again and she might have lost touch with the only link to her mother.

Damn! she muttered and went back to work filing away the maps.

Michael sat by his tombstone a long time, head in hands. His mind raced, but uncovered no logical conclusions. He briefly considered exhuming the grave but realized that would accomplish nothing save blisters on his palms. He was here and alive, therefore the grave was empty. Or, if not empty, someone else resided in it. Either way he would learn nothing.

He was suspicious of the too-expensive tombstones, those conspicuously elaborate monuments to two poor old people—as well as his own cenotaph. His date of death matched the others. *I am not in it. There must be another Jean-Michael Clermont. Or I am someone else. Or someone wants the world to think me dead—though who and why is beyond me.*

The government he worked for—there was a possibility. But if the English had decided to cover his past, they would have had him change his name. Besides, this burning and burying showed evidence of being done long ago, fitting the date on the tombstones quite well, in fact. At the time the engraving had been done he had been a cabin boy in the Caribbean, not a skilled English agent. And yet it looked as if someone had wanted to cover up all traces of that insignificant little boy.

Michael spent the afternoon sitting over his "grave" and walking about the ruins of the house searching for clues—any clues. But there was nothing left. Finally, in what had once been a backyard, he found an unfamiliar mound. He pushed aside the sparse vegetation and found everything that should have been in the ruins of the house—a distorted pewter platter, a few coins, fire-charred pieces of ceramic dishes, shards of pottery that had been baked all the harder by the flames, the iron tip of the plow his foster father had used in the fields.

Why were all these things here? Only one reason occurred to him—someone had searched the house after the fire. Searched it with inordinate care, setting aside household effects as they went.

Searching for what?

What could there have been of value in that house?

Had they found it?—whoever "they" were. They must have found the bodies of dear old Monsieur and Madame Clermont. Michael turned and took another look at the inscription on the third thin slab of stone standing forlornly in the weeds and wondered. But they hadn't found his body—yet someone put up a marker with his name.

Could he have been the reason for the search? No one, including the Clermonts and the mysterious Matthew, knew what happened to him when he disappeared. Perhaps someone had searched the smoking ruins of the house for some clue as to his whereabouts. And having done so—they erected a headstone for him?

It made no sense.

Worse yet, he realized that his conjectures led to another terrible thought. Had the fire been set deliberately? Who would want to kill two old people with little money and less property? Chills of guilt engulfed him. *He* was the one with the mysterious past. *He* was the one who had emerged from circumstances so carefully guarded that he himself did not know them. If any fires had been set deliberately, they had been set to get *him*.

"Pointless . . ." he said aloud. The horse raised his dripping muzzle from the brook and whinnied in sympathetic agreement. *I am talking to myself and people who do that are not well,* Michael told himself bitterly. His head hurt from thinking and another part of his anatomy throbbed from sitting so long on the grave marker. He braced himself to stand, pushing off against the back of the stone.

It had been smooth-backed where he'd touched it before; now his fingers met a deliberately rough place. He struck a spark from his pistol flint, lit some tinder, and knelt at the back of the marker. There, sloppily incised in the stone, was a most remarkable thing—the number 9 and the outline of what looked like an arrow, pointing straight up. It had been added to the stone years after the fire, for the marks were light-colored and yet not so light that they could have been done within the last few months. Michael stared, entranced at this newest cipher. A child's aimless etching? No—when he dug at the stone with his knife he found it uncommonly hard and difficult to mark: unlikely that a child would have persevered at so troublesome a task. And yet anyone bumbling across the hieroglyphs would have shrugged them off as juvenile vandalism.

A clue? Was it a clue? Or was he simply tired and seeing signs where there were none? A nine and an arrow. Why would anyone carve an arrow the hard way? Why not simply a line with a cap on it, instead of this solid outline filled in as if the artist had scraped his carving tool back and forth many times? "Nine arrows? Arrownine? Gibberish," Michael whispered.

The horse snorted, as if agreeing it sounded uncommon rubbish. Another moment and the burning tinder met Michael's clutching fingers. He swore quietly and extinguished the flame. The nearest town was none too far; he craved wine, a long bath, and a good night's sleep. He saddled and bridled the bay and aimed him toward the road.

Two hours later he was a good deal more relaxed, due to several tankards of spiced wine and an evening at the bathhouse. His clothes clung to his damp skin as he paid and left, boots and saddlebags flung over his shoulder. The cold brick alley felt good under Michael's bare feet. He walked slowly, head down, stuffed with annoying thoughts and images. Just before he stepped out onto the street where his horse waited, whispering shadows leaped. A bottle crashed against the back of his head.

Well-trained as he was, he should have been able to avoid it. But he was tired and worried and liquor-fuddled; another blow and he sprawled full length on the bricks. "Well," drawled one buccaneer to the other, "thet meks twelve tonight, Jacques. I theenk thet is enough for a full crew. We can set sail now for ze Caribbean."

Pressganged again!

11

Robert had been absolutely immovable on the question of doing hard physical labor on the ship. No manner of threat could persuade him to climb, lift, scrub, paint, or cook, but he *had* been interested in puttering among the treasure in the hold. "That's a mess!" he'd said to Evonne. "How do you even know what you've got?" The next day he'd arrived in the captain's cabin with a neat list of categorized items in his hand. "You've got a crate of cheeses down there that no one even opened and looked at. They've rotted and the velvets next to them stink to high heaven. You'll never get a shilling for those fabrics now. All the bullion is on one side of the hold with nothing to counterbalance the weight. Some of it's on top of crates of porcelain that've been broken up. Four barrels of cloves are sitting in six inches of bilgewater. Have you ever smelled a clove in that condition?"

Evonne stared at him, eyes flashing sparks of resentment. She'd enjoyed his debonair company at first, when he was there at her bidding, but since they'd left England she'd found him a trial. It was this sort of thing that annoyed her, primarily because she knew he was entirely correct, and it implied a well-deserved criticism of the way she ran her ship. He brazenly returned her stares until she snatched the list from his hand and started going over it. Finally she said, "What an extraordinarily tidy little mind you've got!"

Her sarcasm didn't dent his assurance. He lounged in the chair across the desk from her. "When I was fourteen my family had a lovely maid who was in charge of the linens. I spent a good deal of that year in the closet with her—counting sheets, of course. Excellent experience."

Evonne ignored his leer. She waved the hateful list in his face. "What is the point of this?"

He leaned forward, elbows on her desk. "The point, *ma belle Capitaine,* is that we are quick approaching a particularly foul little group of islands, known only for the number and quality of spiders and lizards it produces, upon which you will almost certainly abandon me unless I can prove myself useful—true?"

"Just what I had in mind, now that you mention it."

He took back the list. "This is how I'm going to make myself not only useful but downright indispensable to you. Just because your business is illegal and very possibly immoral, is no reason it should be sinfully inefficient as well. If you'll give me three men and the authority to tell them what to do, I'll have the trash thrown overboard and the rest of it sorted, stacked properly and inventoried in a week."

So it was that Robert managed to remain on the *Black Angel.* In much the same way Genevieve had found her niche on board. She showed a remarkable aptitude for reading maps, gauging distance, and handling the navigational instruments. Evonne had put her in charge of sorting and crossreferencing the hodge-podge of maps she'd accumulated over the years. This clerical work, necessary but regarded as deadly dull by the captain, threw Genevieve and Robert together much of the time. Genevieve seemed to enjoy his company a great deal and looked forward to seeing him.

He asked her once what had happened while she was in London and what had caused her to be so long in returning to the ship. She had answered so curtly and noncommittally that he'd not asked again.

A few days after Robert and Evonne's discussion, they spotted a trading vessel on the horizon. Genevieve was struck with the full force of what was now her place in life. "Evonne, the hold is full of goods already. You don't really need to attack that ship, do you?"

"Change of heart?" Evonne said coldly.

"I just don't want to be party to anyone getting hurt or killed. I've been on the other side of a boarding, you know?"

"—and you think I haven't?" Evonne sneered. "No one will be hurt anyway unless they put up a fight like that fool commanding the ship you were on. That isn't a passenger vessel," she added, pointing to the ship they were closing in on.

"Evonne, we're going to swamp ourselves if we bring anything else on board. Even your cabin is full of bolts of silk. I can hardly get to the maps and navigation instruments as it is."

Evonne hooked her thumbs in the waist of her trousers. "Send Robert to me," she said, "with his lists."

Genevieve hurried to do as she was told. "She's about to attack a ship!" she explained when she'd wakened Robert from a nap he was sneaking in a quiet corner.

"My God! *We* could get hurt that way," he said.

"Go tell her the ship is already too full to hold anything else."

Between them they managed to convince Evonne that it would be a real waste of time, energy, and gunpowder to attack the vessel. Robert took Genevieve aside after they'd talked to her. "I need a word with you," he said, pulling her along toward the galley.

They found Xantha along the way. "I need your advice, too, Xantha," Robert said.

"You need advice more dan you know, fancy mister."

Robert cleared the three of them a tiny corner in the galley and managed to procure some ale. "Xantha, what's going to be done with all this stuff Evonne's been accumulating—the jewels and spice and gold?"

"Sell it, ninny man. No eat de stuff."

"I know, but I mean where and how is it sold?"

"Here and dere, all 'round Caribbean."

"How much of the true value does it go for?" Robert asked.

Genevieve wondered what he was getting at, for it was apparent that he had something in mind.

"Mabbe one tenth, if you lucky."

"Do you ever find anyone in the Caribbean to buy the whole lot?"

Xantha threw back her head and laughed. "Everybody dere doin' just what we doin'—no need to buy from us. Easier to just steal de whole boat."

Robert gazed thoughtfully into the middle distance, tapping the scarred table top with a bent spoon. "Hmmm. Just what I thought," he murmured.

"Robert, what is all this about?" Genevieve asked.

He turned, took her hands, and spoke more seriously than she'd ever heard him speak. "I've done some worthwhile work on this ship and kept myself from being thrown off, but now the holds are neatly arranged, the lists are complete, and I'm unnecessary again. I want to go home, or at least get out of this part of the world, and none of that's going to happen unless I can find a way, as fast as possible, to make myself indispensable and your sister richer than she ever dreamed."

"I see—and you think you can find a way to sell the pirated goods?" Genevieve asked.

"Maybe. Xantha, what would happen to this stuff if we were legitimate?"

"Don't know 'bout you, but my folks—" she bristled.

"I mean, if these goods had been purchased legally, not stolen."

"Oh," she said, only slightly mollified. "Den we be sellin' to American colonies. De fancy gents go dere. But we no can, cause dey know we pirates—"

"But we've *got* a 'fancy gent' on board," Robert said.

Xantha and Genevieve stared at him, uncomprehending.

He flung his arms out in despair. "You're looking at him!"

Genevieve suddenly stood up, starting to leave. "Where are you going?" Robert asked.

She turned back. "I don't trust you when you get ideas. They seem to involve me in ways I'd rather not be involved. You'll recall you're the one that threw me into your grandmother's jaws."

"But nothing can go wrong with this plan," he assured her.

"That's what you said last time," said Genevieve uneasily.

It was high noon in the Bay of Campeche. The loading docks of Veracruz gleamed with sordid flamboyance, slaves wearily loading Spanish treasure galleons in the blistering blaze of the Mexican sun. Sweat, filth, and the stench of rotting mangoes wafted on festering air. Overseers swore, the bare feet of slaves slapped on warped loading docks, cargo clanged and thudded into ships.

Precious woods were packed carelessly into the slimy holds; rosewood from Brazil, tamarind, planks of cinnamon, scented balsam, the fragrant campeche wood that gave the bay its name. Pearls were bagged and loaded by the hundred-pound lot—pearls gathered in three years of tortuous diving off the coast of Venezuela. Native divers had died in droves from depth bubbles in the bloodstream and from pure exhaustion caused by repeated dives with too few pauses in between. The pearl beds of Margarita Island lay all but barren now.

Uncut emeralds, amethysts, and raw opals were dumped aboard in the squalor with no attempt at order or cataloging. Wares from the Orient—exquisite bolts of silk, fragile porcelains, lacquerwork, cinnabar carvings, ivory—all had been shipped to the Isthmus and brought to Veracruz by muletrain through the fever-infested jungles with their slithering reptiles and tropical madnesses.

This was the treasure fleet that the combined forces of Spain and France had been gathering for three years. Phillip V, King of Spain, was the grandson of France's king—therefore the affinity between two normally unfriendly countries. Spanish hustle, bustle, and barbarism had gone into the long and haphazard loading of the fleet. Now innate French fastidiousness stood with senses mortally offended. The Count de Château-Renault, sent by Louis XIV to supervise these last few months, was appalled at the slovenly work and waste involved in readying the fleet.

The loss in slaves was staggering but convenient. Better that none lived to spread word of the phenomenal hoards, largest ever assembled in the Americas. There were none on the docks who had been there when the work began in 1699. There were, however, some who had survived up to six months and one in particular who had been at this backbreaking labor for the better—or worse—part of a year.

At first glance he could have passed for a native—skin burned brown by the scorching midsummer sun, long, unkempt hair caught in a snarled knot at the nape of the neck, lean body naked save for the tattered remnants of what might have once been trousers. But his hair was wrong for a native, a startling, deep mahogany shot through with red. Château-Renault, sweltering in the shade, noted the hair and pointed it out to the nearest Spanish officer. "A crossbreed?" he asked. The Spaniard mumbled something.

His French was so barbarous the Count could scarcely understand it. The Count went back to his tablets, trying to keep a tally of the silver being brought in from the Royal Spanish Mint at Mexico City. When he looked up again he saw the slave in front of him, loading a gold shipment. Their eyes met. To Château-Renault's astonishment, the young man's eyes were a cool, clear gray and his high-boned face held something gravely intelligent, even aristocratic in it. The Count stared, seeing past the dirt, rags, and beard. This was no native—the young man was not only European but well-bred. The Count was so intrigued he did not notice the top tally sheet slip from his tablet.

The slave retrieved it with an understated sweep of his arm, a too-polite gesture. He held it up to the commander. "Monsieur le Comte dropped this," he announced in faultless French, perfect enough for an audience with the King.

The Spanish officer struck the slave in the face with his reed fly-swatter. "Get on with your work and do not annoy the gentleman," he ordered in his native tongue.

"The gentleman would have been far more annoyed had he lost track of the silver tally," the slave replied in Spanish. Château-Renault gave an inarticulate exclamation of pleasure.

"You speak their language? I have been trying to find an interpreter since I arrived! My Spanish is unintelligible and their French, alas, worse. I am in need of someone to translate orders. How did you come to be in this place, someone of your learning?"

"I was pressed into service in France."

"Your accent . . . southern?"

"Marseilles, Monsieur."

"You do not speak like a peasant. What did you do before this?"

A sardonic smile tried to curl the young slave's lip. "I was, Monsieur le Comte, an attorney."

Château-Renault's eyes went wide for a moment before he burst into laughter. "Then you will do quite well, my friend, for who shows more interest in other people's money than a lawyer? You will go to my head steward to be fed and clothed, then you shall report

back to me and assist in this poorly planned operation. I cannot make these Spaniards understand a
damned thing!"

The slave took his directions, gave a stiff, courtly
bow, and walked in the indicated direction. Château-
Renault clapped his hands together and gave the
Spanish officer a demonic chuckle. "A lawyer! Now I
can make some sense out of the muddle you people
have caused! Wait—wait—what is your name?" he
shouted after the departing slave.

The young man turned. "Jean-Michael Clermont,"
he replied.

Michael bore a vague resemblance to himself by the
time he was sent back to the French Count. He was
still as brown as the Indian workers and thin, but he
had bathed, shaved, and cut his hair. The steward
found him some presentable-looking breeches and a
lightweight muslin shirt, garments that rested strangely on skin used to sun and the rasping lick of torrid
winds. Michael tied his newly clipped hair back, refused the offer of shoes and hose, and padded, bare-
foot and well-fed, back to the overseers' shaded wharf.

Count de Château-Renault did not recognize him
when he returned. Once affairs were settled, Michael
was put to work with sums and quill, haranguing the
Spaniards who had beaten and cursed him only hours
before. They still cursed him but dared not raise fist
or whip now. He catalogued jewels, pointed out errors
and inconsistencies to the Count's underlings, and
tried to convince the officials that better treatment of
the slaves would lead to more efficient work.

As days passed in this manner he gained Château-
Renault's total confidence. There was a fervent plan
in his mind, not only to escape, but to alert the British
government to this fantastic and ill-guarded treasure.
There was booty here beyond the wildest imaginings,
galleon after galleon stacked with precious woods,
spices, gems, and bullion. It had been accumulating

for three years, coming from all parts of South America and the Orient to gather here until it could at last sail to Spain and ease the empty royal coffers there. The escort fleet would be a third the size of the British navy—overladen, slow-moving prey for the swift-moving British warships and their calculating captains.

Château-Renault took it for granted that Michael was a loyal Frenchman who would return with the fleet to a family in France. But that could not be. He must escape, find passage back to England before the Spanish-French Armada sailed. It would be impossible to capture the astounding fortune once it had reached the armies of Phillip V on land. It must be stopped before that. They intended to leave Veracruz after another six weeks of loading; he must be in England, alerting the King and his ministers by then so that the Spanish could sail into their hungrily waiting arms.

The only problem was several hundred miles of inpenetrable jungle or the same distance of open sea —oh God, how he hated the idea of the sea voyage between him and the next port open to British shipping. He had not yet taken into account how he would get there, let alone persuade a captain to rush him to England.

It would be too dangerous to copy tally sheets and the proposed route to Spain, so he spent hours memorizing maps and sums. Stretched out on his cot at night (a welcome change from chains in a rat-infested shack), he counted casks of rubies for the King. And sometimes, when sleep would not come, he let more pleasant thoughts lull him. Thoughts of pleasant times and places, thoughts of women and friends. Thoughts of Genevieve.

"Is this the last of the snuff?" Michael inquired of the nearest Spanish captain, pen poised over dull yellowish paper.

"Yes, but only until the three final boats arrive.

They're due in a few weeks with snuff, jalap, tobacco, and spices."

"Yes, that's right, the sugar galleons," Michael said, tabulating slowly. "The last shipments of sugar and indigo and vanilla. We've already got more in the warehouses than the ships can hold. That's all we need, to be overloaded to the point of danger. What was it you said after snuff? Jalap? That's familiar but I can't place it."

"Medicine," the Spaniard said, igniting his noxious pipe. He gave a long, parrotlike laugh. "Purgative. Wring your bowels right out, lad. Makes you feel damned good, like rum, just before it hits you. First you see nice pictures. Then you park yourself on the chamberpot for the next fortnight. It's a powder."

"Make sure it isn't packed with the snuff—we don't want King Phillip getting the two confused and blowing himself across the Pyrenees."

Snuff was highly combustible. Michael made an underlined mental note concerning which ship it would be packed in, then went on with his work. A soldier tapped him on the shoulder. "The French Count wants to see you. He's at the third dock."

Michael made a final calculation and headed for the third loading dock. Château-Renault was indeed there, trying to make some sense of the mad melee of slaves and shipments. "They've sent a soldier to do a damned clerk's job—or a diplomat's job, I don't know which! Jean-Michael, we're missing an important shipment."

"The wood and cocoa from on down the isthmus. I know, it's long overdue."

Château-Renault wiped a weary aristocratic hand across his sopping brow. "The Spanish are getting edgy about it, talking about going off to hunt for it. I can't have them wandering off at a time like this. Do you speak any of their Indian dialects from these parts?"

"I picked up about a dozen words on the slave crew.

I know of a man from the Isthmus and several others from Venezuela—pearl divers, in fact. They speak many of these regional dialects."

Château-Renault regarded him gratefully but with worry. "You've been my most valued assistant and an excellent interpreter. I will not order you to go on such a dangerous mission through hostile territory and diseased swamps. But . . . I need someone who can communicate with both Spanish guards and Indian guides."

The Indians were as bent on escape as he was. Michael looked the troubled Count in the face, swallowed feelings of guilt, and said, "Yes. I will lead this expedition."

Michael's expedition did not quite go as planned. For one thing, there was no need to overpower the Spanish guards. They simply went out hunting one morning and never returned. The Indians, vastly cheered by the freedom speeches Michael had been making all week, huddled for a conference.

When they stood, smiling, he smiled back at them. "Now! If you can just get me to Jamaica or Martinique. . . ."

"No Martinique. Venezuela!" growled the largest native, a tattooed behemoth in a shark's tooth necklace.

"Why Venezuela?"

"Home!"

"It's right on the way to Port Royal—that'll work out just fine for me."

"Mebba take you home, too. Venezuela."

Michael had the distinctly uneasy feeling he was not being handed a hospitable invitation. When someone invited a person to meet the family they did not usually surround him, jab him with sticks, and growl at him to march faster. "I've got to get to England—I've got to get to *my* home, not yours. What are you doing? We worked together—I thought we were friends! I got more food for you, I—"

"Food," echoed two Indians, and began to eye him in a speculative manner, pinching his arms as if to see how much flesh draped his bones. He sucked his breath in, trying to look as gaunt and unappetizing as possible. A fierce argument ensued among the Indians while Michael sat on the nearest rock, fighting utter panic. The debate seemed to be whether he should be considered dinner or a war prize to flaunt back home in the depleted pearl islands.

Three of the Indians wandered off through the woods. He sagged with relief, then he noticed what they were doing—gathering dry wood! He waited until they had all busied themselves, then stealthily crept away into the gnarled jungle. Wild animals and starvation were preferable to providing a Venezuelan repast for six vengeful, hungry divers who had been treated cruelly by white men and could now feed and revenge themselves in one clean blow—to his neck.

The sweating trees had barely closed in on him before he heard a guttural cry of anger and bare feet slapping on fern-padded earth. Fear gave him Mercury's winged heels. The jungle, however, gave him roots to trip over. As he gathered his feet under him and rose, a long, arm-thick viper dropped from the trees and wound itself around his face. The coils clasped him, tail whipping about his throat and squeezing. No air reached his nose or mouth under the hood of writhing snakeskin. Hearing and sight were gone, leaving only the cloyingly sweat taste of rotting fear.

He clutched for the dagger at his belt, but fumbled and dropped it. Michael staggered, smashing his head against a tree. The snake loosened its hold a moment, then caught him tighter. Stifled, slumping, the clamping coils winding patterned death about his life, he fell to the ground and rolled. Again and again he bashed the snake against the ground but it refused to release him. He tore at it with teeth and braced fingers to no avail. Red filled his head. He flung out a hand, clutching at nothing—and finding his knife. He gripped it savagely and seized his viperish executioner by the back of the head. The dagger plunged in again and again. Head all but severed, the snake still fought on. In its crude system there was slow recognition of death.

Blackness and pulsing purple heartbeats, far too slow, filled Michael's bursting brain. He felt a coil slip. Air rushed into his lungs—filthy, fecund jungle air full of dead things, sweeter than marzipan to his starved senses. He hacked at the snake, fought unfeelingly for what seemed like life again.

Still the snake clutched him, strangled him. On one knee Michael struggled, dagger rising and falling repeatedly until he collapsed. The snake, beautiful markings distorted and torn, loosened its grip. Gulping in air, sobbing through strangulation and a torrent of salty serpentine blood, Michael stabbed until he could stab no more.

When the sanguine haze had lifted from his mind, he was aware of the great fleshy coils still roped about his neck and face. They were shuddering but loose. He began to slither out of them. Weariness equaled his repulsion. It took all of his willpower not to simply fall back in that snakely embrace until he had regained his strength.

Alive. Thank God, alive. He sat, head swimming, the thickest coil of quivering python still looped across one arm. His vision wavered, then cleared. Above him towered steaming trees that leaked splotches of blue daylight—and six Indian divers, knives in their hands and hunger in their eyes.

12

Genevieve had halfway expected the American Colonies to be a great deal different than the other places she'd been. She'd expected dour, drably dressed people, barren rocky soil, and wild Indians everywhere. But this port was not so very different from the land in Jamaica, and the people were dressed like proper Englishmen.

"You're thinking of the Northern Colonies," Robert explained, "and these *are* proper Englishmen. Second sons come to seek their own fortune. The more adventuresome types."

They strolled along the docks listening to the shouts of vendors, sailors, auctioneers. Genevieve fanned herself with an elegant ivory and peacock feather fan. It was deadly hot and the air stunk of dead fish and unwashed bodies.

Robert took her arm and helped her over an oily puddle in the street. "You look perfectly exquisite, Gen," he said.

"Thank you," she said with a hint of truculence. She'd been cleaned, buffed, polished, clipped, hennaed, curled, and corseted, and looked like a new woman. It wasn't entirely to her liking, but Evonne hadn't asked her opinion. "Why *am* I here?" she asked.

Robert tipped his hat at a gentleman who stood aside courteously to let them pass. "You are lending credibility to my role. I am a rich young shipping magnate, inexperienced and a bit soft in the head. You are my lovely wife. Bringing along my wife will set the seal on my naïveté. You understand?"

"Yes, but I don't trust your ideas. There's a man

over there regarding you very strangely," she whispered.

Robert glanced in the direction she'd indicated. The corners of his mouth twitched a half smile. "Good Lord," he muttered, "I think it's Piggy Feversham! I'd heard he'd come out here after the scandal."

"You know that man? What scandal?"

"At school," Robert murmured, making his way across the street with Genevieve firmly in tow. "Long story. Tell you later. Buggy whips and blancmange—" he whispered tantalizingly.

By that evening, Genevieve found herself the guest of Piggy Feversham and his wife—a sad little thing called Muffit, who seemed constantly on the verge of tears. Piggy had gone into trade in the Colonies and Robert was busily—and charmingly—robbing him. "You see," Robert was saying as he touched his lips with a linen handkerchief after dessert, "Genevieve's father died quite unexpectedly, leaving the accounts of his shipping line in a complete snarl. I've done the best I could but—" he shrugged expressively.

"But I can't understand it," Feversham said. "How could my firm's name be on one of your invoices? I'm forced to admit, St. Justine, I've never heard of them. And such a large order—such a varied shipment—"

Robert waved away his objections. "Perfectly understandable, old boy. My wife's father had been—well, frankly—he'd been slipping a bit in latter years. I wouldn't dream of expecting you to purchase the shipment, under the circumstances. Of course, it will mean a tremendous loss to me, but a friendship is far more important—don't you think? I was talking about that with my father just before we left. We'd been discussing all the political appointments over which he has control and your name came up—I told him just what I'm saying to you—that our friendship, dating back to those delightful days at school, weighs far more heavily with me than any monetary considerations."

Piggy looked distressed, then hopeful. "Look here, St. Justine—"

"No. You must not worry about it!" Robert insisted. "We'll just haul our goods along the coast, perhaps sail up to New York and sell them for a loss. It won't matter a bit. The important thing is to get rid of that cargo and hurry right home. I want my heir to be born at the family home, you know." He smiled dotingly at Genevieve.

She stared at him in amazement. How audacious could the man be? Now he'd not only invented a marriage but a pregnancy for her as well. She wasn't quite sure whether she should laugh outright or get up and walk out on him, but she was too fascinated to do either. She'd never dreamed he could be so devious. She'd badly misjudged him, taking his easygoing amiability for stupidity. But it was no such thing. He was extremely clever and understood more about how people's minds worked than she could have guessed. Not that he was cheating Piggy. Actually Piggy would get the goods at an extremely fair price—far less than he would pay anyone else. And he would turn a pleasant profit on them.

"An heir! Bless my boots, Robert old boy. I had no idea!" Piggy said heartily. "Well, I do believe this calls for a toast. Fetch the sherry, Muffit."

"If you gentlemen would excuse me—" Genevieve said, using her new pregnancy, "I'm becoming very tired and think perhaps I should retire. My condition—" She smiled a sugary smile at Robert, who had to hastily put his napkin to his mouth to keep from guffawing.

"Of course, my dear," Robert said solicitously.

"Muffit, show Mrs. St. Justine to their room," Piggy said.

Muffit, with a frightened start, leaped to her feet, nearly upsetting her sherry. "Please, Mrs. St. Justine, come this way," she whimpered as she led Genevieve up the stairs. They passed along a paneled, painted hallway. "I hope this will suit you," she said, opening the door to a small, cozy room dominated by one enormous bed.

Genevieve hung back a moment, wondering what to do. She realized that Muffit was staring at her with an injured expression. "I hope you don't mind," Muffit whined. "We have a guest suite, but it's being painted just now and the smell—"

"No, no. This is quite satisfactory. I was just taken back by the beauty of the wallpaper," Genevieve improvised. She would choke Robert at the first opportunity. How did she get into these things? It was bad enough having to pretend to be married to him, to have to share a room with him. But to share a *bed*! It began to occur to her that he hadn't been entirely honest about his reasons for needing her along. She'd watched him tricking Piggy Feversham—even enjoyed the sight—without realizing that he was tricking her, too.

There was only a moment to contemplate the situation between the time Muffit left the room and Robert entered. He stood there, grinning inanely, while Genevieve shut the door and crossed her arms. "You are sleeping on the floor!" she said.

"Pity," he replied pleasantly as he removed his waistcoat and slung it over the back of a chair. He strolled over and bent to poke at the tiny fire in the fireplace. He seemed completely at ease.

Genevieve went to the bed and began yanking covers loose and arranging them in a pallet on the floor. She worked quickly, with angry, jerky movements. Robert, ignoring her, added some kindling and two small logs to the fire. Finally she stopped bustling and he turned to look at her work. "Good Heavens, a nest!" he said in mock horror.

Genevieve looked down at the pile of hastily arranged quilts. It did look like a nest. A smile tugged at the corners of her mouth, she fought it, but the smile won. She began to giggle, then to laugh outright. How stupid it all was, and how well he could puncture her offended dignity.

She kept on laughing until Robert shushed her. "You'll have Piggy and Muffit up here—"

"Piggy and Muffit—!" Genevieve repeated. Suddenly their silly pet names seemed the funniest thing in the world. "P-p-piggy and M-m-m—"

Robert put his arm around her and a hand lightly over her mouth. "Breathe deeply—it will pass," he said and then he began laughing as well.

They collapsed in a heap on the nest, laughing until they were both weak and helpless. Genevieve hiccupped daintily, and Robert tossed the corner of a taffeta quilt over her face. She closed her eyes, took a long, shaky breath.

"Gen, I know you won't believe this, but I really didn't plan things this way," Robert said in a curiously subdued voice.

She opened one eye, looked at him. He was smiling still, but looked so completely guileless she had to believe him. "Oddly enough, you sound honest," she said. "Isn't Piggy going to find out he's getting a bargain rate on stolen goods?" she asked. She'd been wondering about this all evening.

"Probably. Someone will recognize a jewel or set of dishes or something. By that time he'll have made a great deal of money and will claim—rightly—that he had no idea it was stolen merchandise."

"But he'll tell people you sold it to him. What will that do to your name?" she asked, ineffectually trying to straighten her disarranged clothing.

Robert propped himself up on one elbow, his hazel eyes warm in the reflected glow from the fire. "Nothing Piggy can say will damage my name. If things came to that, I'd simply claim he was mistaken or lying and no one would believe him. I'm surprised though, that you'd think of that—or care."

So am I, Genevieve thought. Strangely enough, it had not really occurred to her before how much she did care about Robert St. Justine. She'd been blaming him all along for the difficulties she'd gotten into in London, but after all, that had been her own fault. She had courted disaster and been caught in the consequences of her own doing.

She looked into his velvety eyes and said softly, "I do care about you, Robert." It was no more of a surprise to him than it was to her.

Robert said nothing, merely ran a finger along the line of her jaw and bent to kiss her. Lightly he brushed his lips against hers, and Genevieve felt herself drawing him nearer. "Oh, Robert," she murmured. A small Faunton-voice in the back of her mind was busily scolding her, but she ignored it.

Robert put one arm around her waist, scooped her into a close embrace. She closed her eyes again and felt herself floating freely in a dizzy, dark haze. She felt Robert brush his hand across her hair expertly loosening it. Then, as he dropped light kisses on her temples, her eyelids, and her throat, he began to unbutton the row of mother-of-pearl buttons that ran down the front of her dress.

I should not be doing this, she thought as she reveled in the warmth of his strong body against hers. Was this just another trick of his? But how could she hope to examine his motives when she could not interpret her own. Was the leaping of her heart and the strange weakness of her knees love? Could she suddenly be in love with a man she'd regarded as a friend for so long?

For all her extraordinary experiences in the last year and a half, Genevieve suddenly felt very naïve. She knew about the riggings of a ship, the instruments for determining location, the workings of weapons—but how little she knew of the workings of the human heart. Even her own.

Especially her own.

Robert was kissing the hollow at the base of her throat. He'd undone her dress and his own shirt and she put her arms around him, suddenly aware that the room was cold. And he was very warm. She ran her hands over the smooth, hard muscles of his back. Her breath was coming fast now and his kisses, silky-smooth, were more intense.

He pulled her to a sitting position and without a word, as they stared at each other, he eased her sprigged muslin bodice off. Genevieve shivered a little against the chill of the drafty room, and Robert pulled her closer to the fire. He moved away a moment to put yet another log on the blaze and Genevieve quickly stepped out of her dress and petticoats.

Robert turned back, half silhouetted by the orange blaze. He smiled, sending a liquid ripple of heat through her. "You're very beautiful," he said softly.

She looked away for a moment, suddenly shy. "Robert, is this another 'idea'? A plan of yours?"

He knelt in front of her, cupped her face in his hands. "Oh, Gen, why would you ask?"

Suddenly she didn't want an answer. She just wanted to pretend, to believe for one night that they were in love. She watched as he removed his shirt and helped him pull off his boots, both of them struggling with the scarred leather. He slipped the straps of her shift off her shoulders, gently kissing her neck and the soft rise of her breasts. He eased the loops from the tiny buttons down the front of her chemise. He traced his finger as lightly as a feather around her nipples, then bent his head to kiss them.

Genevieve arched herself against him, eager for more, tantalized by his tender, accomplished touch. She caught her fingers in his thick hair and could smell the scent of his soap. She wriggled the rest of the way out of her shift as he watched. He ran his hand down her side, slowly—appreciatively—before removing the rest of his clothing. How strong and well-proportioned he was, she thought. His skin smooth, stretched tautly over firmly muscled arms, stomach, thighs.

He caught her back into his arms and they rolled over together on the cold, rustling taffeta quilt. The contrast of chill fabric and Robert's warmth made her gasp. She found herself on top of him, looking down into his deep, pleased gaze. He grasped the covers on either side, folded them up over her and cocooned them in a snug embrace.

He entered her and she rocked against him. He gripped her tightly, met her move for move. She drew up her knees, whimpered as the pleasure flowed through her. Robert whispered her name over and over in a low rumble as he crushed her against his chest. Genevieve lost all concept of time and place. It seemed for a moment that all her life, all her being, was one bright, intense pinpoint of light—flaring, pulsing, burning.

Finally they both sank, exhausted, their passion spent and consumed. Genevieve relaxed in the safe, comfortable haven of Robert's arms. A friend, now a lover, confused images floated crazily through her mind. She had thought him a callous rake when they'd first met on board the ill-fated *John Cooke*. She'd considered him clever when he'd taken advantage of Piggy Feversham's ridiculous lust for power and position. She'd suspected him only an hour ago of deceit when she'd found herself fated to spend the night in the same bed with him. Now she was wrapped in a disordered tangle of covers on the floor with him, both of them sated and breathless, and what did she think of him now—? Her thoughts slid from the question. She kissed his shoulder and snuggled closer to him. She would think about it later—

Piggy Feversham purchased a large part of the cargo of the *Black Angel* and persuaded various friends to take the rest. They were smug, their infant sense of nationalism convincing them they'd put something over on an Englishman. Robert cleared the hold of everything and came back with a substantial profit.

Even Evonne was impressed, though she took pains not to say so.

In the midst of it all Genevieve functioned in a confused fog. She'd not been alone with Robert again until they set sail and then she had too much work to do to brood over her situation. They were lying at anchor off Port Royal before she had the leisure to think. She wasn't in love with Robert, at least she didn't think so. But she did feel a certain loyalty toward him. Loyalty, friendship, and respect, laced through with unexpected flashes of passion.

She was standing at the rails gazing unseeing at the skudding tropical clouds when Xantha boomed, "Get into de fancy dress, white girl. We goin' to town. Spend de money, drink de rum, have a good time."

Genevieve smiled brightly at her. "Yes, let's have a good time."

The flames were almost ready. Michael, mottled with bruises and despair, remained where he had been flung, chiefly because two of the divers held him there. The heat of the jungle was stifling. The fire tripled it, sending streams of sweat rushing down bare brown bodies. Michael raised his head only to have a foot smacked into it. He fell back to the sound of knives sharpening against one another.

He must make one last try. He must act stunned, which was not difficult. All the while he gathered strength, trying to summon the calm thinking and swift reflexes of the top government agent he had been. His mind cleared, plans formulating in cool progression. He could not outrun or outfight six men. But if he could—

There was no more time to think. An Indian seized him by the hair. Michael hung as if unconscious although the sight of the gleaming blade made him clammy with fear. He forced himself to relax. The knife raised in the air, coming down in a smooth arc.

He drove his fist into the tattooed giant's stomach as hard as possible. A left uppercut to the jaw, a chop on the side of the neck, and his would-be murderer sprawled senseless in the grass. The nearest man leaped at him. Michael rolled with the impact, gathering momentum. He gained the upper hand and knocked the man out.

He dived, caught the knife, and came up in the position he had been taught. Crouched, knife low so the thrust of it would come up and in, causing the greatest possible damage. Never hold a weapon out so a foe could seize it. Of course, training had not covered being surrounded by four howling, hungry cannibals who were picking up rocks.

They disobeyed the rules of attacking an armed man—they rushed him *en masse*. Their howls and bloodcurdling shrieks rang with his. He shouted and cursed without knowing it, a mad melange of French and English as they hammered him into the ground. He managed to stab one of the divers.

Blood exploded in his head from repeated blows. All at once there was a louder explosion, one that sent brilliantly colored birds screaming away, their plumage indecorous streaks in the somber jungle. Stagnant silence followed. "Sacre Pucelle, Henri, you were right about the shouts—one of them is a white man!" came an excited shout in French.

Another man barked something in one of the Indian dialects. The divers understood, for they all moved away from Michael. The two he had knocked out had recovered enough to stand. Michael staggered to his feet, dully surprised by rescue and the fact that he was only bruised, not torn to pieces. Two men stood staring at him. They were dressed in bulbous-legged breeches and cross-tied, soft boots; the hair of their heads had been shaved and their upper bodies were smeared with a greasy pungent salve to keep insects at bay. Each carried a machete, dagger, short sword, and pistol in his belt. They held loaded arquebuses in their hands. Behind them were four heavily laden mules.

Slavers!

"Another Frenchman in these parts! Tell me boy, what are you doing here?"

Michael weaved unsteadily. "They captured me. I was about to be their dinner."

"Big, strong-looking rascals. They should fetch a good price at Port Royal," drawled one of the men, grinning at the prospect of so much money.

"You're going to Port Royal? I was heading there myself. Your arrival is even more auspicious than I first thought."

One slaver jabbed the other with a sharp elbow in the ribs. "Hear that, Henri? 'Auspicious.' We got ourself an educated one. Hey, boy, that's damned handy. You'll bring good money in the slave market."

Michael sucked his breath in. "I have wealthy friends in England who would pay a fair amount to ransom me—a fairer amount than you could get for me in an auction."

"If you believe that, then you don't know how much they need educated slaves in the Caribe, boy. You were yellin' in two languages, maybe three. Young, healthy slave with a brain will fetch more than we could ransom some accountant for in England. Besides, we want the money now, not in a year. Move, boy."

Michael obeyed, too tired to question. As he achingly began to walk, a gun at his back, he had the wry thought that he was getting to an English shipping port, all right. Only not quite the way he had planned.

Port Royal had not fully recovered from the devastating earthquake of ten years before. In 1692 Genevieve had been a young girl living on the other side of Jamaica. The damage had not been so severe there, but she still remembered the eerie tremors crawling through the earth beneath her feet, and the way the ocean had risen and torn at the shoreline.

Because of he quake and ensuing tidal wave, Port Royal had almost been wiped off the map. It rebuilt steadily, but never regained its dubious title "Sin Capitol of the Caribbean." Pirates and whores still gathered there; some of the tawdry glamour remained; some of the gilt facades and loud music still haunted cobbled streets, but the riotous soul of the place had crumbled in that earth-rending catastrophe.

Genevieve felt an icy thrill grip her as she stepped from the *Black Angel*'s rowboat onto the weathered docks of Port Royal. There was something almost obscene about the city, something that had echoed in her memories of the place, though she had only been there once as a five-year-old child. This was where she had been brought after the raid on Tortuga when her family had been torn asunder. This was where she had been sold as a slave, leaving Gen Meddows behind to be unwillingly reborn as Genevieve Faunton. "Jenna-veeve," most people pronounced it. "Zhawn-vee-ev," someone had whispered in her ear long months ago.

"Penny for your thoughts?" Robert inquired, regarding her with languidly inquisitive hazel eyes.

Xantha gave a loud "faugh. White girl been in de sun too long, dat all."

"Let's get along," Evonne said. She opened her parasol with a pretty flourish, winding her arm through that of a handsome crewman who had accompanied them—Evonne's newest conquest, Genevieve supposed.

Xantha and Genevieve each took one of Robert's arms and they stepped into the busy streets. Hawkers flocked around them, offering wares ranging from hot buttered oysters to sad-eyed, curling-tailed little monkeys on red leashes. Xantha barked the vendors down in guttural Caribe. Genevieve, caught in dust-draped memories, returned to the present when Evonne signaled a taxi drawn by two spanking roan mares with plumes in their headstalls. "I can't wait for real food," Robert announced. "My stomach conjures visions of fresh vegetables, outlandish desserts, and some succulent meats—anything but hardtack biscuits and salt pork! Madeira, rum floating with fruit, old wines—"

Evonne joined in. "—butter sauces, baked crab, saffron rice—"

"—fresh bread!" Genevieve added. "Fresh, steaming bread, bowls of cherries, cold lemonade—"

They climbed into the carriage in high spirits, discussing what to eat and where. Genevieve regarded her companions with pleasure. How different they all looked away from shipboard life. The women were lovely, silk-and-velveted, glossy hair adorned with tortoiseshell combs and seed pearl nets, eyes touched with kohl, mouths and cheeks given a skillful blush. The men were suited and shaved and combed, looking for all the world like the finest English gentlemen on an afternoon jaunt. No wonder—Robert *was* a fine English gentleman. Genevieve settled back against the slick, horsehide seat. *Why does he never allow me inside his thoughts? And why am I so splendidly miserable? Is this love? Or is this the sensation of something missing in my life?*

The horses trotted smartly along, ostrich plumes swaying gracefully between their ears. Genevieve let the background chatter fade away, lulled by the steady clopping of unshod hooves on concave pavement stones. A low buzz began; she paid no attention to it until it swelled and completely overran her thoughts. Voices. Dozens of them. She glanced up to see a great mass of people around a platform to her left.

"What is that over there?" Robert inquired as they drew nearer the crowd. But Genevieve knew the answer before it came, for the fine hairs on the back of her neck stood up like tiny, rigid spines.

"Dat de slave market," the driver answered. "Git along, horses."

"No! Wait!"

Genevieve stood up, hand to her throat as painful old pictures flickered through her memory. Evonne stood also, locking strong fingers on her sister's wrists. "Don't do this to yourself, Gen. Come along to the inn."

"We know what it's like to be in this place, Evonne. What if there's a frightened little girl there right now? Some child who has been torn from her family like we were? Oh, please, Evonne! People bought us! They were good to me and bad to you—can you think of some other child suffering through what you did?"

"You are embarrassing the hell out of me," Evonne announced with acid simplicity. "Sit down!"

Tears of hurt and anger filled Genevieve's eyes. "No," she replied calmly. No hysterics, no surprise at her own strength. "No, Evonne, the rest of you go on to dinner. I have business to attend to. I have money; I'll take a buggy and meet you later. But for now I have something I must do. *Must,* Evonne."

Her magnificent sister gave a defiant toss of her raven head. "You go right ahead."

Genevieve gathered her things and reached for the latch on the low door. To her surprise, Robert was there first. He hopped nimbly down, reached up and swung her gently to the pavement. He returned Evonne's wordless glare with one of his own. They turned to go. "Wait just de littlest minute." Xantha grabbed her shawl and fan and stepped out of the carriage. In reply to Evonne's mute accusation, the gunner's mate scowled and said, "Well, *someone* got to keep an eye on dese ninnies, else dey get cheated."

The three of them linked arms and stalked off. There was a brief, smoldering pause before the much-feared captain of the *Black Angel* spoke. "Goddamn it!" Evonne grumbled. "Slow down, will you? I've got to pay the driver before I can get out of this stupid cart!"

"No children," Genevieve echoed listlessly a few moments later as the auctioneer's assistant returned to his price charts. Robert looped an arm around her slim shoulders.

"Maybe there's some perfectly wretched adult we can buy and fix up."

"We are not talking about used buggies, Robert."

Xantha jabbed her in the ribs. "Fancy gent meant well. Maybe find new cook for ship. Dying from de one we got."

"We can use more deckhands, but I do not intend to purchase them," Evonne informed them.

"Our next category is educated slaves," bellowed the auctioneer.

"We might as well go. This place reeks of sweat and misery," Evonne said in a low voice. Genevieve's entire body felt limp with the awful knowledge of how these slaves felt—people who had no homes or possessions and had become themselves possessions of others. She wished she could buy all of them.

"Look at that," Evonne's escort said. "Wonder what a fellow like that's doing here?"

"Who?" Robert inquired politely.

"Over there, on the stairs behind the auctioneer. The next slave in line. Looks like a real gentleman."

Robert craned his head for a look. There was a long pause, then abruptly, his finger clamped rigidly on Genevieve's arm, making her wince. "You're hurting me," she protested, then stopped. His usually carefree face had gone a deadly ashen color, as if all the blood and warmth had suddenly left his body. His eyes were like old brass, green-over-brown under ice.

"My *God!*" he whispered hoarsely. "No. It can't be. NO!"

There was a pained reverence in his voice that

made Genevieve stand on her toes and strain for a view through the milling crowd. Long moments crawled past before she was able to see the man in question. He stood straight, an aristocrat's unconcerned pose. His hands were tied in front of him, but he acted as if he stood in Parliament instead of a sweltering stair behind an auction block. His clothes were faded and tattered but he wore them like damask. Ugly brown stripes showed through the shoulders of his shirt, evidence of rebellion and punishment.

"He's dark as a native, but look at his hair. It's almost red," Evonne said, on her toes next to Genevieve.

Something churned in Genevieve's mind, something that whirled and danced just out of her reach. The man on the top step looked up as the bidding ended for his predecessor. That did it. Her stomach clenched and clawed. His eyes were too pale against his bronze skin—deepset, intelligent eyes the color of smoke. He glanced up, gray gaze skimming the crowd. For one poignant instant, the merest shard of a second, his eyes met Genevieve's, and she saw her own shock and disbelief reflected in his face. Hand to her mouth, she uttered a cry so stricken that several bystanders turned to observe.

"Christ! It's Michael!" Robert hissed, putting his arm around Genevieve's shoulders almost as if to steady himself.

"It can't be. He's in London!" Genevieve whispered, but Robert was too upset to pay much attention to what she was saying.

"Solicitor? Sassy gent in brown velvet? Same man?" Xantha gasped, then calmed herself. "Serve him right!"

"I don't understand," Robert muttered.

Genevieve tugged furiously at his sleeve. "We've got to buy him. Quick, how much money do you have?"

"I'm not carrying much. Perhaps if we all—"

"Just what is going on here?" Evonne demanded with spiky edges in her sultry voice.

"I've got to buy my best friend—he's practically a brother. How he got here I don't know—but we've got to save him," Robert insisted.

"You never cease to amaze me, Mr. St. Justine. I am not about to pay an exorbitant fee for—"

The auctioneer was saying something about the next slave. His words rushed through Genevieve's ears like the low murmur of an autumn wind, bringing chilly forebodings. Michael Clermont. Here at Port Royal! And in the slave market! It didn't seem possible that something so degrading could happen to such a well-bred, imperturbable person. Especially a man who had lain with her, made love to her, and ultimately hurt her. Perhaps betrayed her. She recognized every line of his slim, strong body—the broad shoulders, thick hair, sensitive mouth, eyes that gave nothing away. "I could learn to love you." Had he really said that, many months and worlds ago? London society, fencing with words, being secure in his arms. It tore at her with wicked, feline claws, to have those buried memories forced unwillingly to the surface.

Michael Clermont with his smooth, polished manners, brought to this humiliating state! But he did not emit the slightest trace of emotion. He bore the same sphinxed expression he would have worn in a ballroom. "They're about to open the bidding," Robert said. "Quick! How much money does everyone have?"

The auctioneer pounded his gavel for silence. In a sonorous voice he called out, "The bidding will open at—"

Another voice rang out, clear and cold as the toll of a bass-voiced golden bell: "Five hundred pounds!"

In the shocked pause that followed, Michael Clermont's head shot up. Genevieve followed the direction of his startled gaze and saw a big, black-haired man, handsome in a rugged, coolly intelligent way. He had wide shoulders, an assured stance, and the icy eyes of an eagle. She felt her blood run cold. He was dressed with expensive simplicity—breeches, shirt, and vest of unadorned but rich fabric and elegant cut. His trousers were tucked into high, soft suede boots with scrolled sterling buckles. There was an unrelenting set to his proud head; he cut as perfect and frosty a profile as some pagan god-king, all power and no pity.

"Six hundred pounds," Robert shouted. Michael's stare swung back to where Genevieve and Robert clung together. His eyes registered a moment of stark astonishment, but he kept the rest of his face expressionless.

"Six-fifty," countered the dark-haired pirate prince (for Genevieve had designated him such in her mind). A scar dissected one of his eyebrows, an old scar that meant deadly affairs in the night with blunderbuss and rapier. He gave Robert a brutally dark look that would have skewered a less determined man's intentions.

Robert returned the stare with a razor-edge resolve few would have credited him with. "Seven hundred," he said and his voice was that of a judge passing a death sentence.

The dark man shot him a lightning look, a bolt of pure concentrated disgust. "One thousand pounds," he enunciated crisply. The entire crowd gasped. Genevieve, hurriedly pooling everyone's money and jewelry, thought she heard Evonne give an inhaled scream.

"Eleven," Robert faltered.

In the awed hush, Michael stepped to the edge of the auction block. "No, it's no use for you to bid, I—"

The auctioneer's assistant dealt him a reeling blow on the side of the mouth. Michael staggered back.

"Twelve hundred," announced the black-haired man. His eyes promised a pauper's funeral to Robert.

"Fifteen hundred!" Robert insisted.

Genevieve yanked at his arm. "Do we have it?"

"Yes, and not a twopence more. Get those jewels together."

The pirate prince put a hand on his hip—a strong hand, knotted with old sword cuts, a hand that could squeeze the life from a man with little effort. Heavy gold rings glittered on his fingers—including a wedding ring. "Damn," Xantha and Evonne said in a single breath.

The man parted the crowd at a prowling lion's pace, mighty shoulders cutting through the mob like a dagger through treacle. He came to a leisurely halt at Robert's side, towering shoulders and head above him. Two shrewd, tough-looking men carrying bulky bags came with him. He stared holes in Robert, turned to the auctioneer and called, "Two thousand pounds —in gold!"

The crowd shrieked. Genevieve crammed the accumulated baubles into Robert's hands, heart hammering so loudly she could scarcely think or hear. "Might I remind you," the regal buccaneer intoned, "that the slave auctioning is on a cash only basis?" He was magnificent and Genevieve hated him with all her heart.

"We're out of the running," Robert said dizzily.

Something seized hold in Genevieve's soul, something so wild and strong it would not let go. She gazed up at her foe with determined brown eyes, a hot wind fluttering her sprigged gown and the delicate tendrils of her chocolate hair. "I will give you fifteen hundred and twelve pounds in gold and silver and—and this jewelry. It's worth at least seven hundred pounds, that's more than you've offered for him so you're making a profit."

"It's not enough."

Bitter bile rose up in her throat so that she had to swallow hard and take a deep breath. "And—"

Genevieve heard herself add in stiletto-sharp tones, "—myself."

He gave her a look, half-pity, half-amusement as his hawklike eyes raked over her. "You must know something about the young man that I don't. Two thousand pounds, auctioneer, the only other bidders cannot match the fee. Call the deal!"

"Sold, Captain!" shouted the auctioneer, driving the gavel down so hard it broke. The assistant slit Michael's bonds as the big man approached the stage to claim his merchandise.

Genevieve, sick and terrified, did not hear Evonne's scalding words nor Robert's laments of self-denunciation. Her eyes were all for Michael, who had begun to act quite strangely. First he rubbed his freed wrists. Then he bent over as if in pain. When he straightened up there were tears in his eyes—tears of laughter.

To the blank bewilderment of the entire crowd, he let out a wild war whoop, crossed the floor of the auction block in one leggy bound, and leaped off the edge—

—straight into the open arms of the pirate prince!

13

They stood, mouths agape, in a stunned silence.

"Michael *knows* that man?" Genevieve asked incredulously.

Robert turned slowly to regard her. "And *you* know Michael?" he said slowly.

"I—I met him—at your grandmother's—"

Robert continued to stare at her, his features slowly taking on a look of understanding. "Well, I never—"

"If you 'never,' it was only because there was no profit to be had by it," Evonne drawled dryly. "Would anyone care to explain to me who that madman is and why that fascinating man bought him?"

"Let's find out," Robert said. Genevieve heard it all through a muddled haze. Robert had to shake her and pull her along after him, as if she were a badly startled child. His eyes probed hers a moment, then she was being led into the center of the action.

Michael saw Robert coming and drew him into a back-pounding embrace. "Robert, you must meet a friend of mine. God, it's good to see you. Robert, this is Captain Roque of *La Doña del Fuego.* He was captain of the ship I was on as a lad. Roque and I were both working for the Ministry at one time. He's settled down now, I hear," Michael said.

Genevieve stood aside, wondering if it was the sun making her feel so dizzy and confused. What 'Ministry'? What were they talking about? Why was Michael pretending not to notice her? Perhaps it wasn't a pretense. No, he had looked directly at them during the auction and certainly recognized her. She hadn't changed so much—not in appearance, anyway, since they last met.

Robert took the captain's hand in a firm grip, not at all his usual cynical self. "I've heard a great deal about you from Michael. I see now why he didn't want me to bid. We just drove the price up and wasted a good deal of money on this no account—"

"Oh, Roque can afford it. He owns half of Martinique and has the biggest shipping business in the Caribbean," Michael said, as proudly as if he were bragging about a family member.

"That doesn't mean you don't have to pay me back," Roque answered with a lazy laugh. Evonne and Xantha purred at the sound and fluttered their fans flirtatiously in front of their faces. Even Genevieve had to admit the formerly imposing Captain Roque was charming indeed when he chose to be.

The men chatted some more, shook hands again, slapped one another on the back in an excess of comradely good feeling. Finally, Xantha cleared her throat loudly. Robert turned and realized they were there. "Let me make some introductions. This is Xantha, gunner's mate on the *Black Angel* and Genevieve Faunton—I think you know each other," he said to Michael.

Michael stepped forward and would have embraced her, but Genevieve, still stunned and hurt by his earlier behavior, turned a cool cheek to his kiss and kept her arms stiffly at her sides.

Michael had indeed noticed her during the auction —noticed her clinging affectionately to the arm of his best friend. What was there between them now? Not wishing to offend either Genevieve or Robert, he took his cue from her action and merely gave her a polite peck and stepped back, glancing quickly at Robert. *Damned awkward situation,* he thought.

"Never seen you get such a cool reception, Freddie," Roque said in a low rumble and bowed graciously over Genevieve's hand. "Delighted to make your acquaintance."

"I've done this all backwards," Robert said. "I

should have introduced captain to captain first, I suppose. This is Captain Evonne Meddows, the charming buccaneer whose ship I've been on."

Evonne had been standing back. Now she took a step forward and lowered her fan. She smiled devastatingly at Roque.

The dark man's handsome face registered complete astonishment, more so even than her beauty customarily caused. "God above!" he said in an awed whisper and stared at her for an uncomfortably long time before turning to Michael. "Freddie, does she look like who I think she does?" Michael nodded. Roque extended his hand, then pumped hers vigorously. "My dear woman, the sight of you takes me back— God! How long? Why, you're Sabelle all over!"

Evonne let her hand drop and turned a startled, black-fringed gaze on Genevieve. "Then this is no idle folly of yours," she said, surprise and something else ringing in her tone.

"Does everyone know our mother but us?" Genevieve asked despairingly.

"What do you know of her," Evonne was saying to Roque. "Tell me, damn you, else I'll—"

The fascinated auction crowd still hung on each savory syllable. "If there is somewhere else we could speak, privately—" Michael said.

"My crew is waiting to go home and my wife is expecting me," Roque said. "Captain Meddows, call in your crew and I'll give them far better fare at Martinique than they'd find here in Jamaica. God, Freddie! Garlanda will be so damned pleased to see you—"

Genevieve was watching Michael as Roque said this and was disturbed at the way his features softened. Suddenly there was a flurry of plans and counterplans swirling about her. Robert was to accompany Roque and Michael. The women would follow on Evonne's ship. Genevieve had the feeling she was in a dream. Nothing made any sense and she had the eerie feeling, as in some dreams, that she was playing two roles. She was the woman who had lain in Michael's arms in London and made that heart-stopping escape when he betrayed her. But she was also the woman who had tumbled, laughing and carefree, into Robert's arms in the Colonies.

Now here she was with both of them. Had she ever envisioned such a circumstance, she would have anticipated having to choose between them. But that wasn't the case at all! Their attention was all for each other. They weren't vying for hers. They didn't even seem to remember that she was there. It was insulting, totally disconcerting.

Everyone was shaking hands and dispersing. "But wait! Please wait," Genevieve said to the dark Captain Roque. "Just tell me how you know our mother."

The man turned to her, laughter lighting smoky fires in his eyes. "Why, she was quartermaster of my ship back in my pirate days," he said.

"She was what?" Genevieve and Evonne echoed together.

"Didn't you know?" he said. "I'll tell you all about her when we meet again at my home," he added, then turned and strode off, arms around Michael and Robert.

The *Black Angel* was anchored in a deep bay and Genevieve and Evonne set out in the small boat. As they approached the island they began to catch a glimpse of an enormous house—a palace, almost. It rested on the peak of a hill with wings and extensions set stair-step fashion on the slope. There were terraces and banks of riotously colored tropical flowers that showed up vividly against the sparkling whitewashed walls. "Are you pleased? About our mother, I mean?" Genevieve asked.

Evonne shaded her eyes against the glare of sun on sea and considered the question. "I'm pleased to know that she survived. And I suppose I'm pleased to know she was quartermaster of a ship. I know how hard that was and it makes me admire her. But it hasn't changed my mind about chasing after her. I've lived my life this far without her, and she without us. I will not believe she has the slightest interest in acquiring a full-grown family she's not known for many years."

Genevieve opened her mouth to object, but thought better of it. If ever Evonne changed her mind, it would be of her own accord and not because of anything Genevieve said. "Look, there they are," she said instead, "on the dock, waiting for us."

Evonne said, "Did that astonishing man mention a wife?"

"Captain Roque? Yes, I think he did. Garlanda, I believe he said her name was."

"Pity, that," Evonne said, laughingly using one of Robert St. Justine's favorite phrases.

Genevieve's first reaction to Garlanda, when they finally met, was pure hatred.

The woman was little and voluptuous and excruciatingly feminine, hardly older than Genevieve. A man could have swept her up in one arm. Roque and Michael both did so by turns. She had burnished copper hair caught atop her perfect head in a pile of ringlets and curls. Her deep violet eyes shone like polished amethysts as she held Michael at arm's length and cried, "Freddie, my dear, how good it is to see you. We have missed you so!" Genevieve was astonished to note that Michael actually appeared to blush. Was he in love with the woman? Genevieve felt an unwarranted wave of jealousy wash over her.

"Garlanda, we have other guests," Captain Roque said goodnaturedly.

The red-haired vision finally released Michael and turned to apologize. Her reaction to Evonne was much the same as her husband's had been. "Pardon me for staring, Captain Meddows, but you look so much like an old friend of mine that it quite took me by surprise."

"These two are Sabelle's daughters," Roque said.

Sudden tears filled Garlanda's eyes. "Does she know? Did she find you?"

"No," Genevieve answered. "Do you know where she is?"

"Please, ladies, I'm starving," Roque interrupted. "Let us have some food first and talk later."

"Yes, yes, you're right. I'm being a terrible hostess," Garlanda said. She summoned servants to show them to their rooms and disappeared to arrange for dinner. While Genevieve soaked in an elegant little porcelain bathtub with clawed feet, she thought about Michael and Robert. Neither of them had been openly insulting to her, but they acted like she was a nice enough girl who just happened to have the plague. What was the matter with them? More to the point, what was the matter with *her*? She was beginning to feel quite clumsy and unattractive around them.

Well, let them be that way, it didn't matter to her, she told herself sternly. She had more important things in her life than pining away over men who had no use for her. She had been fool enough to think they cared for her. It was a stupid mistake to make twice in a row. She would guard against it in the future.

But a few self-pitying tears dropped into the bath water.

After an elegant dinner of fresh tropical fruits and lightly broiled fish—a dinner during which Genevieve might as well have been serving drinks for all the attention anyone paid to her—the ladies retired to an opulently appointed salon while the men stayed behind over port and blustery talk of battles. Michael had been dropping impatient hints all evening about needing to talk privately to Roque and Robert. Garlanda had the servants open a long wall of French doors and the women took their places in the soft breeze on delicate sofas. "Genevieve, I've been admiring your dress. I wish I could wear pastels that well," Garlanda said.

Genevieve was stuck for a reply to such a thoughtfully worded compliment. Was there nothing this woman did badly? But she didn't want to talk about dresses. "Please, tell us about our mother. How do you know her? What is she like? Where is she?"

Garlanda's face glowed with a warm, fond smile. She took a deep breath as if launching into a long story that must be kept short. "Years ago I was on a ship that was wrecked in a storm. My mother perished and I was washed ashore on a small island. The only other survivor was my husband Roque. Of course he wasn't my husband then. The ship that finally found us was his—a pirate ship, or so I believed at the time. His quartermaster was Sabelle. Gen—may I call you that? She was the most wonderful person, though I admit I was slow to recognize her fine qualities under her rough-mannered exterior . . ." Did she cast an anxious glance at Evonne, the living reincarnation of Sabelle, or did Genevieve only imagine it?

"Among the crew members was a boy Sabelle had rescued from the slave block: Freddie—or rather, Michael, since he uses his real name now. Once through circumstance and once through my own error I found myself in grave danger. Freddie and Sabelle helped me out at the risk of their own lives.

"One cannot ask a greater gesture of a friend," she went on, her eyes misting with memories. "I tried to repay them. With Freddie I was somewhat successful. I put him in contact with my Aunt Althea, who took him to England and made certain that he had access to a fine education. But Sabelle—I fear I could do nothing to thank her. She was so independent, so

well able to brawl and swear her way through life
and get what she wanted—all but the one thing she
wanted most."

"And what was that?" Genevieve asked.

"Why, to find the two of you, of course. She was
not a woman who often opened her heart, even to
a friend. But one time, she confided in me about you.
I didn't have children of my own then and I'm
afraid I didn't properly appreciate how she felt."

"Do you know where she is?" Evonne asked from
the corner where she'd been sitting and listening unwillingly. She was trying to sound sharp and unconcerned, but her voice had undertones of the lost child
she'd once been.

"Only vaguely," Garlanda replied. "I saw her about
six months ago. She had taken a rich old French gentleman prisoner to ransom him, but he'd become quite
fond of her and offered her marriage and a ripe in-
heritance instead. When I spoke to her she was planning to accept his offer and go to France with him.
I have his name written down somewhere, I'll give it
to you. You *are* going to France, aren't you? To find
her? She will be so happy. I think she'd almost given
up hope of ever being reunited—"

Genevieve turned to Evonne, a question in her
eyes. Evonne was sitting on the rose-hued sofa, her
skirts spread around her like a flower. She was regarding her fingernails with sullen care. She glanced
up, dark eyes sparking, but said nothing.

She's afraid, Genevieve suddenly realized. Afraid of
being hurt, rejected, disappointed. Her life had held
such full measures of all these, she could not afford
to court failure. Evonne said softly, "Perhaps," in
answer to Garlanda's questions.

Garlanda seemed to know that something silent
and important was being said, and she did not urge
further. Genevieve found herself revising her opinion

of the copper-haired woman. She had more than beauty. She had grace and understanding, and a rare talent for knowing when to keep quiet.

A moment later the men joined them. They were full of port and hearty bonhomie. Genevieve retired to a corner of the room and sat absently brushing her fingertips across the strings of an ornate gilt harp. Imagine! Her mother a quartermaster of a ship. She had believed, with good reason, that Evonne's crew was probably the only crew that included women, certainly the only one with a woman in a position of authority. Now to find out that Evonne had unknowingly followed in their mother's remarkable footsteps.

The news of her mother had made her completely forget about her other concerns and she did not notice Michael and Robert watching her and exchanging puzzled glances. It was an uncomfortable evening for everyone. Evonne was generally sullen, Garlanda watchful, and both Roque and Michael seemed only to be filling the required time with the ladies until they could retire to their secretive discussion of the treasures Michael had been helping to load. Robert made his usual attempt to be charming and amusing, but his heart wasn't in it and he finally gave up and sat moodily, picking at the fringe on a table cover.

Before long everyone gave up the pretense of enjoying one another's company and the women departed to their separate rooms. Genevieve crawled wearily into the high, silk-draped canopy bed and fell soundly asleep. It was much later when she woke, startled and confused. What had she heard? There it was again. A light tap on the door. "Genevieve? Are you awake?" Garlanda's voice came through the darkness. She slipped in, closed the door carefully and perched on the side of Genevieve's bed. "I'm sorry to wake you, but I think we need to talk," she whispered. "I care a great deal for your mother," she said as Genevieve sat up and pushed back her hair. "I want you to find her. It would make her happy and that would make me happy. I think this is what you want as well, but I sense resistance in your sister. Am I correct in thinking she will not willingly cross the Atlantic on the slim hope of finding Sabelle?"

"Yes," Genevieve answered, surprised once again at the young woman's perception.

Garlanda leaned forward conspiratorially. "I have an idea that may be of help to you—and incidentally to me. I've been downstairs, eavesdropping. Do you know what the men are talking about?" Genevieve shook her head. Garlanda explained what she'd heard, that the combined French and Spanish forces had accumulated a vast treasure hoard that was about to be shipped to Spain, and how important it was, financially and politically, for England to intercept it. She'd heard, too, that Michael and Roque, as loyal Englishmen, if only by adoption, intended to race to England and alert the King.

"But I don't quite see—"

"My idea is this," Garlanda continued. "There is almost certainly going to be a massive battle for possession of the treasure. A single ship or even a small fleet could not hope to survive in the midst, but if you were to be close by and wait for the battle to be over, there would be vast spoils—"

Genevieve wrapped her arms around her knees. Her eyes were bright and eager. "Yes! A clean-up operation. No fighting, small risk, and a fortune to be gained. Evonne couldn't turn down the chance. And afterwards, it would be a short trip to France. Then, Evonne might be easier to convince to join my search. But you spoke of a small fleet. We have but the one ship."

"I have ships of my own," Garlanda said. She was no longer a pretty, pleasant hostess, but a business-woman.

"Your husband's, you mean?"

"No. My husband has a shipping line, but I have several vessels that are entirely my own. Three of them are in port now, having just been unloaded. I would send them along to back you up, for a percentage we would discuss later."

Genevieve suspected that the percentage would be quite high—and rightly so. "I think my sister would be interested in this."

"And I think it would come better from you than me. I don't wish to be interfering in your family affairs, although that's precisely what I'm doing," Garlanda added with a wide smile. "I would also suggest this not be mentioned to the men. They would almost surely have opinions in the matter which we would probably rather not know." She laughed lightly, back to being fluffy and sweet.

She handed Genevieve a thin envelope. "Here is the name of the man Sabelle said she was going to marry. I've also given you a letter of introduction to my aunt, Althea Pasteau. Perhaps you met her with Freddie? No? He lived at her home while he was completing his studies. She has returned to France, to rooms at Versailles. I'm sure she would be delighted to take you under her wing while you search for Sabelle. She was recently widowed and would welcome your company. How I wish I could be there to see Sabelle's face when she meets the two of you!" Garlanda said happily.

It didn't occur to either of them that Genevieve might not find Sabelle.

Genevieve had prepared a hundred conflicting things to say upon parting with Michael and Robert, but was not forced to choose which of them to utter. The men had decided to leave immediately; Roque and Michael to aid the British capture of the Spanish fleet; Robert to return to his family at long last. The men's departure was *en masse* and quite public. Roque took his wife's hand, dropped a tender kiss on her forehead and said softly, "Take care, my darling."

The rest of them, touched by the wealth of love

evident even in this restrained statement, took their cue and murmured polite good-byes. Robert took Genevieve's hand as if to shake it, but enfolded it in both of his and whispered, "If you get up the courage to face Grandmother again, I hope you'll visit me in England." The tone was light, typically flip, but there was an undercurrent of injured intensity. Then he was gone, striding off down the front steps to join Roque.

Michael then took her hand and kissed it gallantly. "I know you probably still think badly of me, but you're wrong. I wouldn't have endangered you. I've thought of you often and fondly. Will we meet again?"

Genevieve looked away, willing the tears back. "I don't know." She pulled her hand back.

"I hope so—" she thought she heard him say as she fled to the safe haven of Garlanda's house. She could not look back, nor did she see the way Michael watched her, and Robert quizzically watched his friend Michael.

It was much later in the day before she could emerge from her room, red-eyed and cranky, to suggest Garlanda's plan to Evonne. Evonne agreed almost immediately and fell into animated discussion with Garlanda over specifics.

But Genevieve spent the evening on the veranda, looking out over the moonlit black sea and worrying over a hundred unanswerable questions.

14

It had been a long journey, conducted in haste and heat—first to England where they reported on the treasure ships, then across Europe in search of the commander of the British navy. Now Roque and Michael stood atop a prominent hill outside a Portuguese port. "Too bad St. Justine didn't want to join us," Roque said, shading his eyes with his hand as he stared out to sea. "He's got a good mind, for all that frivolous facade he cultivates."

"I think he wanted to come, but he'd been away for a long time. His family had thought him dead. He didn't want to leave again so soon."

Roque didn't speak again for a while, then said, "Queen Anne," musingly. Michael knew what the older man was thinking. They had brought their surprising news to the English court only to be surprised themselves by what they found. King William had died and his sister-in-law Queen Anne was reigning. She had been all too eager for the English fleet, under the command of Admiral Rooke, to attack the Spanish treasure fleet. But there was "a bit of a problem," as she put it. The fleet had recently suffered a great defeat at Cadiz and she had ordered Rooke not to come back until he had a victory of substantial proportions to report.

So Admiral Rooke was gloomily haunting the Spanish and Portuguese shores and Roque and Michael had to find him and give him his new orders from Queen Anne. "We've got a tailor-made victory if we can just find the man," Michael said, wearily removing the spyglass from his eye. "Surely he must land for supplies sooner or later." He collapsed in the long grass, rubbing the eye that had spent the better part of a fortnight against a spyglass. "They can't land in Spain. They've got to come to a neutral country like Portugal for fresh food and water. But we've been in almost every convenient port in this country now."

"At least your Portuguese is improving. Get your glass back out, son. I think I see masts across the water there."

Michael ran a hand through his windswept chestnut hair and adjusted the glass. "Masts. We shall see what flag she flies."

"That woman," Roque said distantly, "Genevieve. She's sharp as thistles."

"They've had a hard life, she and her sister," Michael said, peering at the almost invisible ships on the horizon. "Neither is over-prone to laughter. Thistles, indeed, but thistles in bloom are lovely to behold."

"You treated her badly. I damned near expected you and St. Justine to elope, the way you paired off and ignored her. I suppose you were being gentlemen, each trying to give the other a chance with her, but all you young jackasses did was hurt her."

"I suppose so," Michael said into the streaming white sunlight, voice uncertain. "But my first sight of her at the marketplace was in Robert's arms. I like her a great deal, Roque, but I wouldn't get in the way of a friend like Robert, not when—Roque! Union Jack! And a man-o'-war, too. She must be from Rooke's fleet."

"Is she coming into the bay?"

"She's turning in the wind, she's waiting—cutting the sails back—Roque! She's coming in. She's going to go in and drop anchor."

Roque pried the spyglass away from Michael. "Let's get into town fast. Can you remember enough Portuguese to get us in and out of a tavern? That's the best place to make contact with someone from the ship."

"I can remember enough Portuguese to *buy* the tavern. I want to get out of this damned sun and dive headfirst into the biggest vat of ale you've ever seen. To hell with the treasure fleet and undying fame—"

Roque gave a dry laugh, not fooled at all. Michael was shrewd and ambitious behind that pleasant little-brother face and the careless words. If he thought it would help, he'd *swim* to Spain looking for the Royal Navy, carrying his orders in his teeth. "Why do you really do this?" he asked.

Michael, already reaching for the reins of his stolen horse and trying to slip the bit back into the obstinate beast's mouth, stopped. He cocked a wary brown eyebrow at Roque. "Why did *you* do it before you retired? And why are you here now?"

Roque smiled. "I could say it's for the glory, which it isn't because no one's ever heard of either of us outside the council chambers. Perhaps I was driven to it by the political situations that made me flee Portugal in the first place. And perhaps you were driven to it by losing everything you ever had in France. But overall, it's probably because we're quixotic fools. What else could it be? It doesn't even pay well."

Michael swung onto his horse and watched Roque reach for his own mount. "It will pay well enough if we can catch Château-Renault—and if I still have all the facts straight about what's in which ships. Ride!"

It took them most of the afternoon to make contact with someone from the ship trustworthy enough and with sufficient authority to help them. Finally they found an Irish priest from the *Pembroke,* the ship they'd seen in the harbor, and managed to convince him that he should take them to the captain of the ship. A few well-phrased code words convinced the captain, John Hardy, that they were indeed bearing a message to Admiral Rooke from his queen.

They were five days finding the rest of the British fleet. Admiral Rooke, aboard his flagship, *Royal Sovereign,* received Michael, Roque, and Captain Hardy aboard immediately. Rooke was not quite what they had expected. Gout had been troubling him, but he was still immaculately outfitted from his spit-and-polish boots to his crisp powdered wig, in the smothering heat of an August afternoon. He was neither young nor truly old yet, and he cast an imposing figure across the navy he ruled. As the men explained their objective, he stood with spyglass to eye, gazing out across the glaring white-hatted waves. "Spanish treasure? Frenchies in league? Château-Renault in charge?" He didn't believe in wasting words, a trait that drove people nearly mad until they adjusted to his terse cadence.

"Yes," Michael replied, wondering how Rooke guessed the latter.

"Damned annoying Frenchy! High water. Waves bad. Clouds? Storm due. Sunset. Rain all night. Vigo Bay?"

"We think that may be where they're headed. We're not sure."

"Big bay. Little neck. Ruined fort on either side. Reinforce it. Blow us clear back to Old Blighty."

"We outnumber them three to one."

Down came the spyglass, showing an intrigued blue eye. "*We?*" inquired the commander-in-chief of all the British seabound forces.

"We're all in this together, Admiral. I can tell you which ship carries what cargo; I can tell you their armament, weight, captains," Michael explained.

"Useful," Rooke agreed, spyglass snapping back up to his face to continue his assessment of the horizon. "You. I know you," he announced in Roque's general direction.

"I was with the Portuguese navy before I joined the British. I did some intelligence work," Roque explained.

"Ahhh. Spy fellow. Remember now. To Vigo. Fetch maps, astrolabe. Clouds?" The glass was adjusted as he stared up at the sky in which there was one distant white cloud. Roque and Michael tapped bewildered foreheads at each other, then stole belowdecks for food and a map of the Spanish coast.

By sunset the sky was bruised with great blue-gray clouds; by the time darkness blotted out the last tatters of daylight, rain was pouring down in needle-sharp torrents that stung the skin and made the sails whine. "He can't be as crazy as he acts. I'd heard he was a brilliant military man, but I didn't expect him to talk like signal flags," Michael muttered into his soup. "He saw that rain coming when I'd have sworn clear sailing for a week."

"Now we know admirals are good for something. I can't get over him knowing me. I'd swear I never saw him before. Acts like his mind and body are an ocean apart, but all the gears are clicking and shifting. Damn!"

"What is it?"

The lantern swung to and fro from its hook, flickering as the walls of their little cabin groaned and sweated all around. "I miss Garlanda and the children. She's at her best in a storm, all that red hair whipping and lashing. She's an incredible woman. She's one of a kind. I think your Gen might be, too," Roque said.

"She hates me. Thinks I turned her over to the law."

"She doesn't hate you. All that remains to be seen is whether you and Robert can straighten it out between yourselves."

"Quit trying to marry me off, Roque. Just because it suits you so well—"

Roque turned the lantern down. "Good night, Freddie."

"God! How I hate the sea!" Michael said in reply. It was something he'd been saying for half his life. And yet, here he was again.

"Spies back. News," Rooke announced to the Dutch and English captains at his table. Everyone was in military best except for Michael, who held no rank. Even Roque had wheedled a uniform out of someone and had it altered to fit his muscular frame. Michael, in a borrowed suit that was far too heavy for August, tried not to sweat too obviously.

Rooke spread the maps out. "At Vigo, indeed. Fortified ruins. Treasure fleet—mounted cannons on land. Shot first British reconnaissance ship full of holes. Second one blew half a boat of Frenchies all the way back to Versailles for it. Armada's cornered. Sitting ducks for us. Weather clear. Good sailing. Take Vigo day after tomorrow. Storms. Plans here."

Michael sprang to his feet. His borrowed boots were too tight, pinching unmercifully as he bent over the table with his charts and discussed the information gleaned from a mad dash into Vigo and back out again. He took the floor, pointing out the barricade that had been built across the neck of the bay, a floating fence of masts, trees, rigging, and mortar connecting the two points of land. On those points squatted the ruins of two ancient forts strengthened by the Spanish and French into formidable arsenals. Behind the barricade, a chilling sight, murderous to any British ships brave or foolish enough to ram it, sat massive French men-o'-war, anchored broadside so that their stationary cannon would meet every intruder in the bay. These ships were in the Spanish crescent formation, the same position they had held over a hundred years ago when they had come to conquer Britain—and had been foiled by England's navy.

He pointed out the positions of the secondary ships behind the men-o'-war, naming the swiftest and best captained, circling in the galleons behind them, holds swollen with riches beyond compare. He sketched in the presumed location of the lightning fast galleasses, intermediate vessels that sailed as smoothly under acres of canvas as they did under the swift oars of their slave crews. These were the ships to fear, with their astounding mobility and dual method of loco-motion. Michael knew their captains to be merciless, shrewd men of maximum experience and ability. When he finished his presentation, Rooke called on the captains for suggestions.

Hobson of the *Torbay* favored direct ramming of the boom. "Otherwise we'll be caught in front of it with those French men-o'-war broadsiding us repeat-edly."

Roque sketched the forts with a quick fingertip. "Admiral Rooke, are we equipped to blow these towers? That will prevent them from firing down into our ships and hitting the powder magazines."

"Thick-based?" Rooke inquired thoughtfully.

"But badly patched," Michael answered.

"Good. Blow caps off towers. Send fireshot into forts. Attack forts by land. Good exercise."

"We have a landing force?" Hobson asked. Rooke gave him a long look of assessment and tapped the gold insignias of rank at his shoulder.

"Army always backs up ships. Blow forts. Send army back through hills. Take towns hiding bullion unloaded for Phillip. Farmers have been evacuated. Blow hell out of Frenchies. Capture towns. Hob-son—"

"I know, Sir. Don't ram the boom."

"Not alone. Line ships up." He extended his spy-glass and shoved the end of it through the nearest porthole. "Clouds? Ahhh. Sun. Clear weather. Rain tomorrow night. Cool toward morning. Cat?"

It was a full half-minute before anyone else heard

one of the ship's cats yowling at a mouse she'd treed in the galley. "Send land commanders in," Rooke barked at an aide. "Spanish fools never learned from Drake. Finish job this time."

"Singeing the King of Spain's beard just like Drake said, eh, Sir?" young Hobson attempted with a laugh.

Rooke withered him with a single glance. "This Phillip *shaves*," he said, and folded up the glass.

Evonne's small flotilla made a safe Atlantic crossing, revictualed in the Azores, and narrowly missed the yellow fever epidemic brought by the Spanish-French treasure fleet. Evonne was able to discover from the few marooned Spanish sailors who had survived that the fleet was heading to Vigo Bay on the western coast of Spain. "Let's hope for a fast discovery of their whereabouts by the British, otherwise we'll have to waste valuable time and risk our necks lurking. I hope the Royal Navy hurries after them. I can almost taste those doubloons. We'll move in the minute the navy has left after the battle. With our divers and—"

Genevieve shook her head. "Don't you ever think about anything but money?"

"Sure. I think about getting arrested," Evonne replied.

"Roque and Michael might be killed. The British navy might be crushed!"

"These things don't matter to me. I'm an outcast, remember? I have no country, no ties. What two damn navies do to each other is of no account to me as long as I come out ahead."

"You believe that?"

"Of course I do. Now go play with your maps and tell me what direction we take to the nearest port off Vigo Bay."

Genevieve stomped off in a fury. How could her own sister talk that way? Certainly it was a bluff, feigned toughness. But perhaps not, she thought.

Why should Evonne love any one country? Why
should I, she wondered. But the fact remained that
she did. Even though she now knew that her mother
was French by birth, Genevieve had always considered herself thoroughly and entirely English to the
core. Nothing would change that.

A week later, moored at the mouth of the Ria de
Arosa, she watched the distant sails of the Royal
Navy inch across the stormy horizon. Evonne shouted
through the hail and wind, "If that damned solicitor
of yours was exaggerating about this fleet, I'll hunt
him down and lash his lungs to the crow's nest."

"And I will help you," Genevieve declared through
chattering teeth.

"I wonder how long it will take the British to finish
the fight so we can get in there."

They eyed each other a moment, pushing at the
sodden hair hanging from under their oilskin cloaks.
"Suppose we don't wait until the fight is over, Gen.
Suppose our own little armada wades in and adds
a little weight to the battle. In the rear, of course.
We might be merchant vessels for all they know—
honest countrymen who have come to the rescue."

"I rather doubt that the navy needs the aid of a
pirate fleet."

"The two merchantmen are heavy, clumsy ships—
but Garlanda's brigantine is remarkably like ours—
lateen-rigged and narrow-prowed for speed and mobility," Evonne mused. "*Black Angel* and the *Nevermore* are two of the swiftest, most maneuverable ships
on the seven seas."

Genevieve regarded her sister with baleful brown
eyes. "And you think we're going to flit in there, wipe
out those towering galleons, and be rewarded by the
British? I'd accuse you of having been in the sun
too long, except that I haven't seen it in three days."

"Or we could simply sail in there among all the
others and pretend we belong there when they're
picking up all that valuable rubble."

"You're forgetting something, Evonne. Suppose the British lose?"

Through flashes of frenetic white light and rolling black bursts of rain, Genevieve saw Evonne's beautiful, water-drenched face alight with an unholy gleam of satisfaction.

"What if the British lose?" echoed the captain. She threw back her pretty head for a laugh that twisted up into the lashing sails. "It doesn't matter a damn. We have Spanish flags on board, too."

15

Morning broke, brutally hot, on a gathering of titans. It was no secret to the Spanish-French Armada that they had been discovered. Ever since they'd traded fire with the scouting vessels they had known this battle was coming. By the night of the twenty-second, British warships were massing. The French galleasses flitted uneasily from place to place beside the five men-o'-war anchored to face the English. Between the two navies lay the massive floating boom connecting the forts; below each fort rested a heavily armed French warship, primed for battle.

Sunrise was slow in coming and never quite completed. Tiger stripes of orange and white marred the night and the Spanish sentries paced the patched walls uneasily, wondering why the sea was so black, water not reflecting the colors of dawn. They had their answer when bands of apricot and bloody pink burst through the night's shroud.

The waves did not reflect because they were covered, as far as the eye could see, with towering British warships. The sentries staggered, gasped, fought for enough presence of mind to cry the alarm.

The sea was black with ships, many with sails painted to give no hint of their proximity during the long night while they had silently slipped into position. Rooke had assembled his highly disciplined English-Dutch fleet into an impenetrable mass. The sight bitterly dazzled the French and Spanish who had labored so long to compose the Armada and bring it to this defensive position. "Look at that formation," said Count de Château-Renault. "Must be George Rooke again."

"Good formation. French Renault," said Admiral Rooke to the gathering clouds.

Michael, aboard the *Torbay* to keep an eye on the impulsive Hobson, spent the waiting time trying to think of the future—it helped make him believe there would *be* a future. First he had to survive Hobson's command and Château-Renault's gunners. After that, he told himself, he would go on to France, just as he had been supposed to do before when he had been pressganged. Yes. He knew who he was to report to. He must get back in the habit of thinking in French.

The only problem was that for some reason he kept thinking of Genevieve. *What if I do live to see her again,* he thought with a wry twist of his mouth. *What then? Robert and I could each grab an arm and make a wish—*

He forced his attention back to the problem at hand. There had been an unsuccessful attempt during the night to sneak to the boom under cover of darkness and sabotage it. Seventeen British ships had nearly reached their goal when the sentries sounded the alarm and lit the cannons.

Michael, under sails the color of fresh blood in the sunrise, shook his head. The floating boom looked impregnable—two thousand feet from fort to fort, nine feet thick and as tall as a man. The anchors holding it still against the tide were as big as drawing rooms.

Lightning blazed, showing high granite cliffs and covering the struggling sunrise with black clouds. Rooke had forecast rain correctly once again. *The man must have prophetic gout,* Michael thought, trying to ease his tension. Rooke was right—there would be no attack this morning under this onslaught of Spanish rain. Thunder boomed deafeningly, loud as cannons.

Michael burrowed deeper into his oilskin slicker and returned to the powder magazine to finish assessing ammunition. The *Torbay* was heavily loaded with

powder and shot, too heavily loaded, in fact. A floating bomb. And *this* was the ship Hobson wanted to
ram the boom with? Suicide. It made him glad that
Roque was safely aboard another ship. He wished *he*
was.

It cleared shortly after noon. All through the blinding storm, Rooke's landing parties had been slipping
through the gloom, taking up positions and waiting
for the opening gambit. It came on time, exactly as
planned. The battle began with a single devastating
cannonade from the British ship *Association,* aimed
at the closest fort. Mortar and stone flew up in an
arc, taking the sentries in an eternal flight through
air and waiting white sea.

As if they were all extensions of one body, the
foremost ships fired at the forts. The gunners worked
like demons, sweating in a bronze-gunned hell, while
powder monkeys raced to fetch water to cool the
simmering metal barrels. The cannon spoke in the
same voice, over and over until there was nothing but
the horrible din. No taste came through the thick
haze of powder, no scent reached senses long numbed
by the scorch of wick and blare of shot.

Michael had long since shed his slicker. Stripped
to the waist, he worked everywhere he was needed—
bandaging an injured gunner, shouting strategies with
Hobson, loading a smoldering metal monster that
spat shrapnel and chainshot into crumbling gray
walls. The repetition was deadening the minds of the
crew as they kept at their tasks, but Michael, shifting
swiftly from job to job, kept a grip on his clarity.

The tension was unbearable—French guns banging
in their faces, their own countrymen behind them firing away with gruesome single-mindedness. And then,
with a whine and a bellow, the first fort exploded.

The flames had touched the bastion's ammunition
and sent rock and mortar spraying for a hundred
yards. The *Torbay* shuddered as fragments of stone
ripped through her sails and pounded her decks.

There was a dazzling glare to the left as smoldering timber struck the *Association* and burst into famished red flames. The leviathan turned away from the wind, crewmen screaming for water.

Her mighty protector having retreated, the *Torbay* was left in the forefront of the raging battle—alone. The full fury of the remaining tower and French warships howled down on her like blood-crazed dervishes. "My God! Do we run or stay to meet certain death?" Hobson shouted, catching Michael by the arm.

"We can't run, the wind's wrong—and we'd all be court-martialed!"

"Better hanged by a court than pounded to splinters by this—"

Another salvo came hurtling from the tower. Michael and Hobson moved as one, flinging themselves on the nearest swivel gun and changing the angle. Volley after volley rang out. The *Torbay* stood it bravely, tattered sails waving defiantly at the Armada. Behind the boom, on the deck of a tower galleon, Château-Renault lowered his spyglass. "I want her shattered, do you hear me? If we take their little leader they'll be demoralized. We'll have time to—"

The fleur-de-lis standard went plummeting from the toppled tower. Another breathless moment and Rooke's first landing party hoisted the defiant stripes of the Union Jack. Michael punched Hobson on the shoulder. "They've taken the tower! Our flank's safe! Why doesn't Rooke send someone else in behind us?"

Hobson cupped smoke-blackened hands to his bleeding mouth. "The wind that's holding us here is doing the same to them—it hits these granite cliffs and twists in a thousand directions."

"It's at our backs now. If we dare—"

"The boom?"

"The wind's right, man! Let it fill the sails!" Michael screeched hoarsely. "It's our only chance."

Hobson bellowed orders, voice cracking and tripping. Sailors stumbled through splintered debris and

fallen rigging, struggling to obey. A broadside hit the
Torbay. One. Two. Then another. Michael, blinded
by acrid smoke, fell to his knees next to a dead gunner. He felt the *Torbay* tremble, then lurch. Her
prow touched the cliff-creased winds. There was a
massive shudder as her sails filled, stretching, seeming
to grow under the force.

She went headlong into the boom. The wall waited,
gnarled tree trunks the size of staircases reaching out
with slimy, chain-bound arms.

And then—impact!

Hull met submerged mast, prow slammed iron-
bound planking. Timbers bent, shrieked, wailed in
the awful crash. Barrels and cannon tore loose from
their moorings and hurtled across the decks of the
Torbay, bouncing off masts or smashing through
flooring into the waterlogged hold. The boom
screamed, strained, stood straight up. Anchors the
size of graveled promenades groaned and saw daylight.
The *Torbay* burst in places, bleeding oils, pitch, bis-
cuit flour, and her precious water supply. The boom
rose higher and higher—

And held.

The force of the impact hauled it up then sent
it back to the black waves with a splash so mammoth
it washed the decks of the impaled *Torbay*. She hung,
hull crucified, full of the macabre colored sounds
of death. The boom lay beneath her, submerged. The
final bombardment began. Merciful fire rained down
on the doomed vessel.

Then, with a roaring crash, the Dutch flagship
rammed the boom! Her ornate cannon answered
broadside with broadside, death spewing from smoking metal muzzles. Billowing sails filled Michael's
hazed eyesight as he fought his way out from under
a buckled gun port. An English vessel was pulling in
next to the Dutch flagship, then another, and two
Dutch men-o'-war.

A low, horrible noise began—iron anchor flutes

being bent by the sheer strain on their ponderous weight, floating trees stretched as if they had been taffy. Chains popped, links coasting through icy black water to join bodies below in the silt. A final ship came blasting in, hitting the snapping boom with all her force.

Then, with a weeping of metal on wood, the boom broke!

Ships burst through her, freed by their own impetus. Before them floated the French ships, anchored help-lessly in place. In a frenzy, the French sailors began sawing through anchor ropes and chains, hoping des-perately to escape the British men-o'-war. Instead of freeing the French ships for flight it sent them drift-ing helplessly in the lazy tide, around and around, while their guns sent bronze shot bouncing off the cliffs and over the tops of British and Dutch masts.

Michael collected himself dizzily. His wounds, he felt, were not severe. He found Hobson, freed him from a heap of rubble, and sent him toward the helm. Michael himself gathered the more coherent of the crewmen to follow him into the hold with bubbling pots of pitch and slabs of splintered ship timbers.

There were many holes, but only one was danger-ous. The sea came pouring in like an ebony flood, wickedly cold despite the heat of the day. Barrels and crates eddied about in the candled murk. The men worked insanely—patching, hammering, reinforcing with tar and nails and wood. Michael had to consider himself satisfied when the frigid flood slowed to a stream.

He manned the bilge pumps for a full hour while they patched, his shoulders knotting and twisting with the effort. The sea was bone-chilling cold on his lacer-ated skin, numbing to the marrow. Blood and dirty water and sweat burned his eyes, filled his nostrils. His band of workers were in equal condition. As they worked, one man died and slipped down from his perch. The corpse whirled in the water, banging

against the legs of the living. They were too busy to
do anything but be sickened by it.

The fight was distant thunder to the men in the
bowels of the crippled *Torbay*. Cloaked in stifling
air and the salty rot of unspeakable things in the
hold, they gasped and fought and won. Michael at
last led them out, blinking, into nonexistent daylight.

Skies once blue were slate with thick, cottony
smoke. Michael had a brief, giddy thought that the
snake had choked him more mercifully than this
thickly padded pain that crawled into his lungs and
squeezed. He blundered his way to Hobson at the
helm. "Three, maybe four feet of water in the hold,
but she'll float and steer. How many gunners are
left?"

"Not enough. The bay's full of our ships. By night-
fall I think we'll have Phillip's Spanish gold in
our—"

The largest of the French men-o'-war, *Le Prudent,*
exploded at that moment. The Dutch had surrounded
her as she whirled in the tide, bringing her down
as relentlessly as wolves did fat, ripe lambs who
strayed too far from their mothers. All around them
debris flew through thick air or swirled in icy waters. Red-hot pieces of metal whistled by, and one
bounced off Michael's hand as he fended it away
from his face. It left a puckered red streak.

He was about to offer himself for the helm to give
Hobson a rest when he saw masts rending the fog
of battle. "Load the cannon!" he shouted through a
smoke-parched throat and cracked lips. "Load your—
HOLD FIRE!"

"Are you mad?" Hobson seized him by the arm,
fingers sliding in blood and sweat. "Man, are you
mad? It—"

Michael wrested free and shook Hobson until his
neck made a dray sharp noise. "Hobson, that's the
French *Le Favori*. I loaded her at Veracruz—she's

packed to the foc'sle with snuff. Snuff, Hobson! As combustible as Satan's own wishes! One good volley and you'd blast us to Hades and back! Hard helm to the right—we don't dare meet her!"

Hobson shrieked orders but *Le Favori* came at them, ghostlike through rolling black and purple smoke clouds. She made Michael's blood run slow and cold. Then, a final horror—little licks of dancing gold light on her decks. Flame barrels.

They were using her as a fireship!

He ran to cut the sails, but *Le Favori* was upon them. Sides scraped, singing sea dirges in the mid-afternoon darkness. Grappling irons on long frayed ropes came slicing through the filthy air. Their metal claws bit into the *Torbay*'s wounded sides, pulling her in like a spider's prey. A fire barrel went rolling across the snuff ship's uppermost deck, striking the mizzenmast and cracking open. Ravenous yellow flames shot up the parched wood.

Le Favori's masts, damaged in the collision, bent into the *Torbay*'s canvas. The thin trickle of orange flames followed, leaping across to the British vessel. Michael found a sword in the melee and hacked desperately at the grappling ropes, elbow-to-elbow with Hobson. Together they rallied the crew, gathering wounded and whole alike in a surge of determination. The grappling irons splashed to sea as the *Torbay* turned her battered head to the wind.

The flames spread aboard both ships, leaping and hopping from sail to rigging to deck and below. The men of the *Torbay* fought with water from the hold, forming bucket brigades and working feverishly.

The fire finally reached *Le Favori*'s highly flammable cargo. The ship blew to an incredible height, planking reaching as far as the cliff tops. With her death throes came a shower of powders, cascading down on the *Torbay* like a smothering blizzard of pepper.

Men's lungs filled and quit. Others went into parox-
ysms of sneezing that sent blood bursting from rup-
tured nasal and throat membranes. Eyes full of the
powder, throats packed so they drowned on the decks
of the ship, the men clawed and fell and died.

One sailor went over the side, then another, each
finding the bitter, killing cold of a Spanish ocean
preferable to this dry death. They jumped by the
dozen, most of them unable to swim. Many were dead
before they hit the water, hemorrhaged by the laugh-
able powder they carried normally in lacquered pocket
boxes. Michael, mouth and nose full of a gruesome
dust-and-blood mud, seized Hobson and tumbled over
the side.

It was higher than he'd thought. The water was
invisible below. He lost hold of Hobson, which saved
his life. Freed, he was able to straighten into a dive.
As a result, his arms hit the wreckage, not his head.
He smashed through wood and rigging, sinking down
into a sea strewn with the flotsam of battle. The rigging imprisoned him with pythonlike coils, but he
knew that trick too well this time. He drew his dagger, quickly sawed through it, and clawed his way up
through debris and corpses.

The water was unearthly cold, as if spring-fed.
Michael felt his muscles knot and cramp, bunching
all over his body from weariness and cold. He felt
warm places at first where blood was oozing from
his body, then the cold sea put an end to his bleeding. He found part of a mast and clung to it, one
eye swollen shut.

Somewhere to his left a ship exploded. He knew
without looking that it was the *Torbay*.

Pain. So much pain. The cold was shutting down
his physical functions, slowing reactions, leading him
deep into a chill, unfeeling death. In the part of his
mind that still worked he knew with cold clarity that
there was nothing more he could do to help himself.
If someone did not pull him out of the water within

a short time he would die. He closed both eyes and let the uncaring wreckage drift around him.

Queen Anne won a fortune that day—and Phillip and Louis, cold red ruin.

16

The pall of smoke over Vigo Bay was flannel-thick and flavored with brimstone. The *Black Angel* and one of Garlanda's merchantmen, *King of Rhye*, sat fastened to a Spanish galleon by grappling hooks, rope ladders, and hastily nailed planks. There had been no battle for the two ships; the English and Dutch had already crippled the treasure ship. She rode low in the water, guns blown to bits, crew dead on the decks or drowned in the chill water far below.

Evonne's men and women poured across her battered sides with wet bandanas tied tightly over mouths and noses. Above these sopping triangles of material showed bloodshot, red-rimmed eyes full of stinging smoke and the odor of charred death. Swords were unnecessary for the boarding—the dead defenders offered no spectral resistance.

"Gen, into the hold. You supervise the unloading— I'll direct the flow of goods onto the other ships. Xantha, put these flames out and ensure that the powder magazine is in no danger. Roger, in the crow's nest, quick. John, Brian, over here—" Evonne stopped for a moment, looked back at her sister. "Gen! Stop standing there looking green. This was *your* idea, remember?"

"Dammit! I remember!" Genevieve said. There were tears in her eyes that had nothing to do with the smoke. She'd heard of battles, studied them in her schoolbooks, but until this moment she'd never known what it meant. Battles weren't feints and flanks and regiments and positions. Battles were a boy, not more than twelve, with half his head blown away, and a man who probably had a family and children somewhere hanging in the rigging, his arms and legs bent in the grotesque angles of death; red seas and smoking ship timbers.

And no one on either side had even pretended that this was for the sake of an ideal—this was a fight for riches. How could men do this to one another for pure gain? It made Evonne's piracy seem almost innocent and girlish by comparison. It would serve all those great political powers right if the whole lot just sunk into the depths of the cold water and was denied to all of them.

"Are you going?" Evonne snapped, "or do I need to get someone else—"

"I'm going!" Genevieve replied sharply, her nerves vibrating with strain. She descended into the hold, candle held high in clammy, quivering hands. Behind her came the burliest crewmen, towering pirates of less intelligence than bulk. At their heels came Kate and the cabin boys, their lanterns casting a lurid glow on the dark passageway. Above them on the first and second decks, Garlanda's men were already tearing into cabins and closets with crowbars.

Downward they crept, closer and closer to their destination. At last Genevieve came to the trapdoor with its heavy iron ring. The men tried to help her, but she felt that as the captain's sister she should show real fortitude and wrested it open herself. She gazed down into the woolen darkness. "Hand me that rope, Kate. Let me down slow, men, I'm not sure what I'll find. She might be so full of water you'll have to yank me back in a hurry."

They lowered her into festering Stygian silence. As she began her descent, her heart seemed to catch and clutch at her ribs. Abruptly, one of the men holding the rope slipped. The rope snaked forward. Hot wax spilled over Genevieve's hands, making her lose hold of the rope. She plummeted down—and landed on a solid platform. Above her, Kate screamed, voice whirling down into the gloom.

"I'm all right. I only fell a few feet. Lower me a lantern on the rope. That's it. I—*God!*"

Genevieve had no words for the things she saw as the lantern settled smoothly in her hands. The gaudy glow staggered her mind. Orange oil light beamed off solid gold ingots, yard-long bars of silver, spilled gems and pearls strewn over shattered shipping chests. Planks of precious woods surrounded her, their heady scent, contained in this cramped place for months, flooding her senses so that she had to lower her bandana to gulp air in.

"Lass?" cried Kate, "be ye safe?"

"Is this galleon seaworthy? Capable of travel?"

"No, lass, she's not."

Genevieve sucked in the spicy air and sat down on an enormous bag of black pearls, some the size of walnuts. "Then g-get some axes and smash the h-hold door in." She took another deep breath, trying to regain her usual control. "Get more men and tell Evonne to get that block and tackle down here and rig me four more like it. Move! I want half this deck torn up—now!"

They ran to obey. Alone in the hold with sloshing waters and an empire's ransom, Genevieve sank to her knees as if drugged. When her head began clearing of the wood's intoxicating aroma, she leaned forward on the nearest stack and accidentally tipped it. A slow flood of color draped her—bundle after bundle of luxurious Oriental silk snaking about her with crisp, proud rustles.

Silver and scarlet dragons twined necks and tails on bolts as big around as a stallion's belly. Icy greens, nubby azures, reds as pure and clear as a thin shaving of garnets. Genevieve held up a piece of silk the color of sunset on the sea and clearly saw the hue and shape of her cabochon emerald ring behind it. Her heart rolled over. *Undergarments of the stuff,* she thought giddily. *Shifts and petticoats with tucks and flounces and ribbons.* She waded through bolts and baskets of material permanently impregnated with the sensual spice of balsam, cinnamon, campeche, and sandalwood.

Some of the fabric was heavier—stiff brocades of white on white, silks shot through with so much gold thread they stood as if starched over wooden frames. How grand a ballgown of the stuff would be! Candlelight shimmering on the full skirts. She forced an armful of folded silver from the pile, silver roses on a silver and white background. How splendidly that would set off Evonne's raven hair! And these waxy pink pearls the size of hazelnuts—she could imagine strand after strand of them around Xantha's slim brown throat. Xantha would have to have new clothes, though—ahh, a billowing cape of this pale pink and a gown of exquisite champagne-colored silk.

And the gems. The gems! An entire trunk full of nothing but sapphires. Tiny ones, medium ones, sapphires so big they looked like chunky handfuls of crude blue glass. A hammock full of opals that sent iridescent twinkles of rainbow colors chasing around the hold. Rubies the size of her fist. Doubloons. Pieces of eight. Francs. Crates of egg-frail porcelains painted with geisha girls in kimonos the hue of bluebells at dusk. Heavy native pots and bowls blazing with bold Mexican patterns. Native fetishes of fat, crude silver. Stone gods from weird, distant islands. Cloisonné vases so large children could hide in them. Demon masks of ivory with amber and ebony eyes. Gold snake bracelets that wound from wrist to elbow and ended in topaz-studded swirls.

A chest of nothing but rings. A tall tricolored basket full of snakeskin for boots and belts and bags. Crates with cinnabar plates, plaques, and beads. Cunningly carved cork villages in green glass bottles. Jars with garden scenes painted on the *inside.* Genevieve numbly looped a string of square jade griffins around

her neck and kept on wrapping until all twelve feet
of the rope were around her, hanging heavily over
breast and waist.

Platters of incised gold from Cathay. Pewter trench-
ers from the Colonies. Gold tableware with etched
crystal handles. Glass goblets with amethysts in their
stems. She was spinning off into the overpowering
scent of sandalwood, cinnamon, and opium when axes
smashed through the floor above and light poured in
on her.

The foul, battle-scented air brought her back to
flat, cold reality. Genevieve clambered out with the
assistance of two crewmen. She had to allow time for
everyone to stare and gasp and stagger. Then, abruptly, the mad rush began. People leaped through the
splintered deck into the hold, wrenching arms and
legs and shoulders. Greedy hands clawed for pear-
sized emeralds, stuffed hunks of turquoise into shirts,
crammed pearls and diamonds and doubloons into
doublets and shoes.

Genevieve cringed against a stout beam as the
crazed rush continued. The orgy of greed peaked in
a welter of babbling voices and shredded silk. This
was what the battle had been for, Genevieve thought
sickly, this obscene lust for *things*. And she was as
susceptible as anyone else.

How was she going to get control? She did not want
to go running to Evonne for help. What would Evonne
do in this situation? She forced herself to think as
coolly as her sister. What would she do with her entire crew gone below in a mutiny of gold lust? She
glanced around quickly. She was the only one on the
shattered deck. The men and women sent to unload
the galleon were all squabbling in the hold.

Genevieve neatly pulled up the ropes and sat cross-
legged on what was left of the floor. In five minutes
it was awkwardly quiet, everyone below staring at
her with bulging pockets. "How do you propose to

get up here with your loot?" she asked casually, voice cutting through the uncomfortable air. "You've all been so anxious to help yourselves and forget your ship, captain, and fellow crew members. What now? Will you sit down there with your loot and starve to death as rich men—or wait a bit and sink with this ship?"

She stood, arms akimbo. "Or will you learn to work together again? Because that's what it will take to get you out of the hold. You'll have to wait for me to lower ropes or you'll have to form human ladders to climb out. Either way you must forget your heavy gold and pearls and work with someone else. I'm not pulling up anyone carrying bullion or thirty pounds of ivory. There's enough treasure for all of us with a queen's ransom left over. It's going to take all of us working together to unload this galleon before she goes down with three-fourths of the treasure. What do you say?" With that, she unwound the long strand of jade griffins from around her neck and dropped them contemptuously down into the hold.

There was a long, belligerent pause, then Kate the Scotswoman stepped to the front, pouring pieces of eight and garnet baubles out of her blouse. "There, lass, I'm rid o' me jewels. Will you be kind enough to fasten the rope to that beam there and toss me an end?"

The mutiny was over. Genevieve complied. "We have to work fast, everyone. We're surrounded by hostile fire, and water as cold as mountaintops. We're also surrounded by the most incredible cache on earth. So let's go!"

They were rescuing people in rowboats. Michael, blue-lipped, almost submerged, and barely conscious, heard oars splashing steadily through killing-cold water. They paused—low voices, a splash, sounds of relief. A bigger splash, that of a body being heaved

overboard. "Too late to help that one, poor beggar,"
he murmured to himself, numb fingers sliding on the
frayed wreckage.

"Hobson? *Hob-son*," came the low call across the
sloshing, rubbish-strewn waves. *I think he's dead,*
Michael thought in reply.

The oars approached. *Over here,* he tried to shout
and could not. Another moment and an oar came
down a foot from his head. He thrust a hand into
the fog and caught it. "Help," he managed feebly.

"Freddie!"

Strong hands found him, hauled him roughly over
the gunwale. "Roque," he mumbled.

The big man shoved Michael's head back, put a
bottle to his lips, and made him drink. Hot spiced
brandy poured down his frozen throat, bringing life,
pain, and fire. He choked, then swallowed until half
the flask was empty. A scratchy blanket was thrown
around him and another half-drowned man. "I
thought you were gone for sure," Roque told him
through a fresh spurt of smoke. They circled a burning hulk, rowers coughing and gagging, searching for
survivors.

After solemn minutes, Michael was able to sit. His
head had cleared; he was cold, battered, bloody, and
indescribably weary, but alive and able to think once
more. "That burning ship—?"

"Yes. It was the *Torbay*. We've only found three
of you who survived the jump."

He closed his eyes. "Ahhh, you saw it then. I
worked on *Le Favori* in Veracruz, clearing her out
for the snuff and jalap shipments. She was to be
staffed with the cream of French aristocracy, young
nobles. When she went she took two full crews, ours
as well as hers."

"That's all over now. We've got to get back to
Rooke."

"We won?" Michael asked, trying to be cheered by
the news.

"Yes, the battle is nearly over and the British and Dutch are the victors. We'll get back to Rooke, then I'm catching a fast brigantine home. What about you?"

"I'm being sent to Versailles. First I'm going to England so the Queen can pat me on the back, tell me I'm indispensable, and turn down my request for a raise. Then I—quiet!"

A ship was slicing through the aftermath of battle and it remained to be seen whether she was friend or foe. The men in the rowboat waited. Towering shadows loomed above them, sour, smoky winds rustling jet black sails. The ebony ship wafted mournfully through the waves like the black barge that ferried the dead across the River Styx. On its proud stern rose a savage winged creature. The rowers cried out and flung themselves down on the bottom of the boat in terror.

Wings the color of midnight blotted out sky and sound. Arched under them was the supple wooden body of a naked female figurehead. "The *Black Angel*! Captain Meddows! Evonne! Evonne!" Roque shouted, leaping to his feet and waving.

The ship swept silently by.

Her passing sent the little rowboat scrambling over swollen waves and spinning about. Michael joined his hoarse voice with Roque's to no avail. It might have been a death ship with Pluto and Persephone at the helm. Behind her came two merchantmen and a slim brigantine with a gilt-leaf figurehead of Mercury.

"That's the *Nevermore*! Garlanda just bought her last winter!" Roque burst out. "And with her *The King of Rhye* and the *White Queen*—what are Garlanda's ships doing here?"

"Passing you by, obviously. The women must have overheard us talking and decided to send a navy of their own after the Armada," Michael said hoarsely. Amazement and warmth brought strength back to him. He knelt and watched as Genevieve sailed out of his life once more.

The rowers recovered their oars and set off into the drowning uproar of after-battle. Soon there was nothing left of the little pirate fleet, not even a wake in the cold sea. The small boat moved on through the haze. A hundred yards on they found themselves in the shadow of a French man-o'-war. Roque began murmuring orders to retreat, but Michael stopped him. "Look, Roque, they're picking people out of the bay. This is my chance for free passage to Ver· sailles and a convincing history as one of their war heroes."

"What are you talking about?"

Michael was already up, shedding the blanket and handing back the brandy flask. "Look, I'm expected to ride God-knows-how-many miles of ocean back to England after this. Just so I can be given orders I already know—orders to go back to France. Waste of time. I'm going with the French now. I'll tell them I was on *Le Favori* with all the other nobles and was knocked overboard before she blew up. The Min-istry has already set up my cover as a younger son of an aristocratic family. I'll go 'home' to France as a hero who shed blood in defense of their flag."

"The only sensible word in all that was 'blood.' You try to swim over there and you'll tear open those cuts. We certainly can't paddle up next to the ship and hand-deliver you," Roque reasoned.

Michael took his hand and swatted him on the back. "I'll write you when I get home and get myself knighted. Give Garlanda my love!" He dove off the side with a smooth motion and began side-stroking through the marrow-freezing water toward the French ship. Every move was agony, sending cramps through legs and arms, rending the cuts that had begun to close. He reached the small boat loading the wounded up a rope ladder to the warship.

His cry for assistance, in excellent French, was im-

mediately heeded. Just as the last precious ounce of
his strength ebbed, an arm reached down, took his
hand and pulled.

When morning came, the man-o'-war was out of
Vigo and creeping up the coast of Spain for France.
Michael, wracked by chills and fever, nevertheless
cast a glad eye at the position of the fading stars.

He was on his way to Versailles.

"But Evonne, I want you to come with me," Genevieve said for what was probably the hundredth time.

"And I keep telling you, if you find her you'll know
where to find me. I've got all I ever wanted—the
money to settle down on that little island I showed
you and live my own life, without having to risk my
neck every day just to survive. Besides, I don't dare
set foot in France any more than I can go to England, and I have to take Garlanda's ships back to
her."

"Look, Gen," she added, her tone softening a little,
"I hope you find her, really I do. But I don't think
you will and I cannot risk hanging or worse for your
pipe-dreams. Go to France. Go with my blessing. God
knows your share of this loot will set you up there
like a princess. If you find her, both of you come
to my island. I'll welcome you. If not—well, come
anyway and I'll try to behave like a lady for your
sake."

Genevieve nodded. She glanced around, making
sure no one was watching them. Assured that they
were alone, she quickly embraced her sister and was
gratified that Evonne held her very tightly for a moment. "Good luck, Evonne," she said.

"Good luck, Gen," she answered, her voice a little
shaky.

Genevieve's crates were lifted over the edge and
she climbed down the rope ladder into the small boat
that would take her ashore.

She was on her way to Versailles.

* * *

"Robert, I want you to marry the girl!" The Dowager Duchess St. Justine said, banging her crystal wineglass down on the walnut table.

"Grandmother, I'm not in the mood to marry, and I don't even know Felicia Phipps. She probably has the appearance and manners of a chow dog," Robert said, absently making pellets of his bread.

"What difference does any of that make? You don't have to love her. Just father her children, otherwise the family money will all go to my brother Randolph's children. Anyway, I hear Felicia is a pretty enough little thing. She's the ward of my French cousins and they are most anxious for the match—as am I. She will bring a substantial dowry and one can't be blind to such things."

"Heaven forfend!" Robert said nastily.

The Dowager took another sip of her wine before replying. "Robert dear, I think you're sickening with something. I've thought so ever since you returned from—wherever you were all that time. No explanations whatsoever—and now these frightful snubs from the likes of the Fevershams. The nerve of them. You just haven't been yourself. I think travel would do you some good. Run along to France for a bit—take the waters, meet new friends, and marry Felicia. It will be quite bracing, I assure you."

Robert stood, dropped his balled-up linen handkerchief on the table. "Oh, very well, Grandmother," he said wearily. "I'll take a look at the girl—but that's *all*."

He was on his way to Versailles.

17

"You're Michael Clermont?" inquired Sir James Hartleigh, surveying the papers with a disbelieving arched eyebrow. He was a bony, twitchy man, trying to cover his unease and not succeeding.

Michael, left arm in a sling, standing awkwardly on a sprained ankle said, "Yes," through bruised lips.

"I was expecting you long ago," Hartleigh complained. "You look like you've been in an abominable university scrape."

"I've been at Vigo Bay." The man regarded him blankly, and Michael went on, "Apparently you haven't heard the news, then. Admiral Rooke and the Dutch intercepted the Armada and are at present sailing home with a phenomenal amount of treasure."

Sir James dropped his mask of reserve for a moment. "What! 'Cloudy' George Rooke found a treasure fleet? Splendid! And you tell me you managed to pass for French after the battle?"

"They patched me back together and accepted my story. You see, as I was on my way here I was kidnapped and put to work on the treasure fleet. King William had set me up with a French family who would claim I was their son in order that I could have a position at Versailles. The Beaumarché family—I believe you know them. They sent a son to Rome for educating years ago; he died and they withheld the news, knowing we needed an opening for agents."

Sir James became nervous and starched once more. "Yes, the young Viscomte Beaumarché—I met him once. You're the proper age and coloring. No chance anyone would question you, the boy was only twelve when he left. Perfect, then. This is all as planned. You may go."

Instead of obeying, Michael sat on a stiff red leather chair and put his one good hand under his chin, "But Sir James—no one, not the late King, not Queen Anne, not all the ministers and the Secretary himself, have told me what it is I'm to do at Versailles! I mean, I know France is spoiling for war with us, that's an open secret—but what am *I* to do?"

"Pass for a devil-may-care rake, chiefly. Nothing overt. Be a social butterfly—get invited to all the right places."

Michael drummed battered fingers on the arm of the chair. "Wouldn't it be faster and easier to work my way into some government board or other? You're making me go at this backwards, eavesdropping and prying on an incredibly simple level."

"That is precisely the point: it is so simple no one will suspect. The Minister says you are to have *carte blanche*. Which means you are to kill anyone who endangers your project."

"So I am to discover troop movements and get myself engaged to every daughter of every war hero from the rank of lieutenant on up?" Michael said angrily.

Hartleigh just shrugged, a tired defeated gesture.

"I do not mean to sound as though I'm blowing my own horn, Sir, but I speak a number of languages, I'm an excellent horseman and swordsman—and you tell me I'm to let these skills go to waste?"

"You have other skills, or so I'm told, that are just as useful in this case. You dance, play cards and instruments. You have a certain reputation for, let us say, successes with the ladies. These, young man, are the skills needed now. I'm surprised that you would complain."

"I've just never pictured myself as a professional fop," Michael said bitterly. "Who is my superior at Versailles?"

"Superior?" Hartleigh asked. "You don't seem to understand, Clermont. You are taking my job. You will be fortunate if you last a year," he added dismally.

Michael tried to overlook the man's pessimism. "I would like to see the list of agents under me," he said in a crisp, businesslike tone.

Sir James Hartleigh gave a lemon twist of a laugh, brightly bitter. "There is only one agent. That one will contact you. The rest—like me—are in too much danger to continue. I will try to take them out of the country with me. Any force you use must be of your own choosing. Agents *will* pass through from time to time, but they will make themselves known to you by means you will recognize when you meet them."

Michael straightened his sling so his injured arm would rest more comfortably. "How am I to know whom to trust? What am I to do with my information? How am I to set up a courier system?"

Sir James stood, eyes glinting, and reached for a hidden knob on a secret door. A panel slid back between the fireplace and bookcases. "They told me you are uncommonly clever about such things. We will soon know. Go swiftly and silently, as you always must from now on, Viscomte Beaumarché. And trust no one. Farewell." He shoved Michael into the black passageway and closed the panel. It was the same way Michael had entered, so he groped along the dark walls confidently. A few minutes later he was swinging into the saddle, patting his latest equine acquisition on the shoulder.

He was only a hundred feet away when suddenly there was an abrupt and horrible light. The earth lurched as glaring yellow light exploded. Sir James Hartleigh's house burst asunder in an arc of shattered tiles, flaming furniture and gunpowder.

Michael fought the horse and won, forcing the panicked beast to wheel and stand still. Distant voices broke through his sorry knowledge that there was nothing to be done for the man. He dug his boot-heels into the horse's ribs and smacked him encouragingly on the flank. "Run!" he hissed. The horse bolted through dark, close trees, flames fading into dull background noise.

The man made no sense, Michael thought to himself as he crouched low to avoid branches. He had said impossible things. How was he to learn anything from open bungling and burglary? How was he to get any news back to England? Whom should he trust? Anyone could be a potential cohort or murderer.

At last he understood. Everything was shrouded in guesswork to keep him alert, to make him shrewd and suspicious. He must do the work of a dozen men and he must do it never knowing who plotted with him—and who sharpened the knife for a swift killing flight on some lonely midnight.

Michael shuddered and rode on through the pine-veiled darkness.

Versailles was bawdy, decadent, and hedonistic behind a painted eggshell veneer of manners and grace. Michael distrusted it heartily, although he enjoyed observing the contradictory behavior of the glittering court: women who acted unapproachable and fainted at the slightest surprise or intimation of vulgarity during the day held extraordinarily intimate salons with select groups after sundown. Gentlemen in foppish lace and lavishly curled wigs stabbed each other to death in disagreements over the depth of a mistress's *décolletage.* Children starved in the streets of Paris as the King's justiciars bled the people of property, money, and livestock. Living conditions in the country were at an all-time ebb. But the Sun King's court danced late into the night, sipping nectar cordials and trailing bejeweled yards of fabric so expensive an army could have been funded by a single sleeve.

Into the midst of this awesome place with its precise codes of unfaltering etiquette came "Viscomte Beaumarché," wounded in the latest battle with the forces of England. He wore his clothes as perfectly as did the rest of the new court followers, tilted his hat at the proper rakish angle, wore a sword with the desired scrollwork, flourished a magnificent cuff trailing the required length of Venetian lace.

Michael acted as pleasantly harmless and dryly witty as all the young nobles at Versailles. He bowed to the same depth, swept his hat off to ladies with the usual overabundant display of false chivalry. And like all the other extravagantly tailored dandies, he was as dangerous as a shark in bloody waters.

He fit in well at the French court—at least as far as the French could see. Viscomte Beaumarché gained a reputation as a man to ask to weekend hunts and fêtes. Perhaps his witticisms were a bit drier and more biting than the average, or it could have been that he wore his splendid clothes with an extra measure of *panache*. Men and women enjoyed his company for similar reasons in the day and different ones at night; the brilliantly dressed ladies wanted romantic wooing and the men, a fearless partner for the gaming tables and brothels.

Michael never failed to appreciate news from "home." His newly acquired family in Marseilles—especially his "mother"—sent long, chatty letters of the exact sort mothers all over the world sent derring-do sons. Some of these letters were sealed off-center, as if they had been steamed and reclosed, but his allowance was always untouched. Mama was extremely generous. He wrote back letters of the sort he guessed a son should send. It was the one part of the Versailles fantasy world he liked.

It was enjoyable, having a family for the first time in his life. He tried to imagine what his mother looked like, just as he had always tried to picture his own mother and father. His real mother must be calm and chestnut-haired, just as it seemed his unknown father must be temperamentally blond for some reason. It would be a long time before he discovered he had the image backwards.

One evening Michael was surprised to meet his "brother" at Versailles. The man hailed him in the doorway, bellowed that mother sent her love, and embraced him so enthusiastically his ribs groaned. This was the first agent he had contact with. It was at this point that Michael realized the true meaning of Sir James's words: "*They* will make themselves known to *you*." He wondered who his next contact would be. It was a great jolt when he found out.

Versailles had begun to pall by the end of the first month. Michael returned from a weekend hunt (which had turned up useful information: a list of commanders) to find his female acquaintances in a flurry of activity. "What is it?" he inquired of one as he fell into step by her in the frescoed halls.

"Why, Athenais de Montespan is visiting—she was the King's mistress ages ago and resorted to magic to keep him," the woman returned, glad of an audience.

"No, Angeline, I don't believe you," he teased. "Magic?"

"Oh, there was the most horrible *scandale*, Jean-Michael! The King immediately ceased his affair with Athenais. He couldn't banish her or anything like that, though, because he had legitimized all her children. She's a dreadful old woman, can't imagine what he saw in her. They say she murdered Madame de Fontanges."

"Fontanges—that's that pretty tiered hat you wear so well."

"Don't flatter me, you devil. You talk that way to every woman between the cradle and the grave. Anyway, Fontanges was this lovely little creature; you must stop by the King's gallery and see her portrait some day. Athenais poisoned her, they say."

He linked arms with Angeline as they started down a winding staircase with sterling cherubs on the balusters. "So the court is in an uproar at wicked Athenais returning. What else has happened in my absence?"

"Well, it's interesting—a woman who was once one of Athenais's ladies-in-waiting showed up the same day! They haven't seen each other in years and years. She's the most madly eccentric thing; people say she and the King once—you know. Why, look, there she is now!"

A splendiferous blond woman was sweeping through the hall at the bottom of the staircase, bizarrely arrayed. Pale hair in a coronet of Valkyrie braids wound around and around her proud head. Over a day gown of respectable maize taffeta she wore the most amazing knee-length Mandarin coat, embroidered in a labyrinth of Samurai swordsmen and flame-belching dragons in yellow, orange, red, and rust, the figures accented in glittering gold thread. There was a blue-tipped paintbrush in her slim, aristocratic hand and a gargoyle-faced walnut pipe between her lovely coral lips.

On her feet were Persian sandals, silver with inlaid amethysts; her toenails were dyed with henna. There were tiny silver bells on her ankles. They left a pale whisper of music as the apparition glided on her preoccupied way.

"Look at those rubies in her ears—big as almonds. She doesn't dress like us during the day, but at night she emerges from her easel crimped, gowned, and smiling like every other woman at Versailles. We've all sat for her sketches during the week. She's quite clever with charcoal cartoons, Michael, but a devil with oil paints. No one can make heads or tails of her paintings."

The tall blonde came to a sudden halt, skirts swirling. Michael gaped into piercingly cool blue eyes, one behind a green glass monocle. "You'll do, young man. I shall sketch you by the window with the sun pouring in," the aristocratic blonde said.

Michael sputtered something at Angeline, who only giggled and pushed him forward. "Don't be alarmed, Jean-Michael," she whispered. "She does it to everyone she finds interesting. Yanked my mother out of a banquet last night to draw her! We're all taking it as a compliment. She's strange but harmless—go ahead."

Michael swept his hat off and bowed to the imperious blonde. "Madame, I would be honored," he said, and meekly followed Althea Pasteau down the corridor.

Michael trailed along in Althea's wake, fifty questions battering around in his head. When they reached her apartments, she grabbed his hand and dragged him in the door unceremoniously. "Jolee, you may go," she informed her maid. "Viscomte Beaumarché and I have things to discuss."

So! She even knew his new name. "Althea, what in the world are you doing here?" he hissed the moment the girl was out of the room. "And in that outfit. Christ! You look like the Taj Mahal during Christmas revels!"

"Do you really think so?" she asked, pleased.

"What are you doing here?" he repeated, not to be distracted by the odd ways in which her ego found nourishment.

"Why, I'm being eccentric!" she explained.

"You have *always* been eccentric."

"Yes, but I've never been paid for it, and I can't tell you what *fun* it all is!" She strolled over to the window where she had an enormous easel set up. She picked up a paintbrush, tapping the dry end against her teeth meditatively for a moment before making a tiny blue line just to the right of center.

Michael leaned on a chairback, took a deep breath and said, "My dear Althea, would you please make some attempt, however incoherent, to explain yourself? What are you being paid *for*?"

A coy smile played about her sensually pink lips and she glanced at him sideways. "My dear Viscomte Beaumarché," she drawled, "can't you really guess?"

There was a long, dry moment of shocked silence. Michael's knuckles on the back of the chair tightened, and the chair made a splintering whisper. "God!" Michael croaked in horror. "No!"

She put down her brush, came to him and planted a distinctly nonmaternal kiss on his lips. "Yes, my darling boy. *I* am your contact!"

Later—much later—when Michael had stopped swearing and abusing the furniture, he was able to ask how this catastrophe had come about. "The last time I saw you, aside from the night in the carriage—"

"Oh, yes, when I found you roaming about in a handkerchief?"

"It was a sheet! As I was saying, the last time we met you had happily hopped into matrimony again."

"Oh, yes. He died. I'll have to start marrying younger men," she said thoughtfully. "I decided to come back to France and when the word got about, certain people asked me to do a few helpful little things. . . ."

"Certain people?" Michael nearly gagged at the euphemism. "How do you happen to know 'certain people'?"

Althea looked at him pityingly. "Darling, did you never question how it was that I was asked to find and return you that night? And it was a very skimpy sheet—"

"Do you mean to tell me you've been working for the government all this time?" Michael asked with astonishment

"They *had* to let me work for them. I read so much

of your mail I was getting dangerous. Chock to the brim with secrets, you know. It is my belief that they thought it would be cheaper to pay me a salary than blackmail. You must not gawk like that, dear. You have an expression like you just stepped in something nasty."

Michael sank into a plump sofa and ran his hands through his hair. "I think I have," he said dispiritedly.

It had taken Genevieve some precious time getting ready to approach the French court. She traveled to a small village just outside Versailles and hired a temporary companion—an elderly spinster. She sent letters to half a dozen solicitors, requesting that they call on her at different times during the first week. To each she explained her desire to invest in some income-producing property and thus converted most of her share of the Vigo Bay spoils into a more conventional form. On shipboard, a rich ruby would as often as not be used as a paperweight or substitute for a missing chess piece until it was needed for trade. But she could not go around civilized society with coffers of jewels to pay for things. She was astonished at just how much property her ill-gotten treasure bought. *I am truly a rich woman,* she thought with awe and some guilt as she locked the accumulating title deeds into a chest.

The rich silks and taffetas from Vigo became outrageously beautiful gowns and some of the priceless jewels, the ones that most struck her fancy, were mounted in appropriate settings. She hired a tutor to help her with the French she had formerly known only as a classroom language. Between solicitors' visits and lessons she noticed that her sea-sun freckles were beginning to fade. She had her wind-whipped hair trimmed, hennaed, and fashionably styled. After a hectic month of lessons, fittings, beauty treatments,

and filing away of documents, she was ready to fling
herself on the court.

Genevieve wondered what sort of reception was in
store for her. Would Garlanda's aunt, Mrs. Pasteau,
welcome her? And what sort of woman might she be?
Elderly, no doubt, and probably as little and sweet
as Garlanda. Genevieve pictured her a little like
Mrs. Faunton, only plumper.

It came as a severe surprise to her when she reached
Mrs. Pasteau's rooms in the labyrinthian sprawl of
opulence known as Versailles. She was shown in by
a pert little maid, to whom she surrendered her letter of introduction. "I shall give this to Madame," the
maid said.

Genevieve had waited only a few moments when
Mrs. Pasteau appeared in the doorway, arms open
wide. "Dear Genevieve!" the woman trilled as if they
were lifelong friends. Genevieve had to concentrate
on keeping her mouth from falling open. Mrs. Pasteau was a tall, stately beauty who could have been
a sophisticated thirty-year-old or a well-preserved
seventy. She had a cascade of thick blond hair falling down her back and was attired in a morning
gown that would be labeled "Empire" in a hundred
years.

"Y-you're Mrs. Pasteau?" Genevieve stuttered.

"Mrs.! Heaven forbid. Althea, my darling girl, Althea! If you're a friend of Garlanda you're going to
be a great friend of mine. Sit down, sweet child, and
tell me absolutely all about yourself. Are you one
of those adorable pirate people Garlanda knows so
much about?" she asked, sweeping Genevieve into
a crushing embrace.

"I—I, well, yes. I suppose I am, but—" *Pull yourself together,* Genevieve thought madly.

"Then you must know that man she married. Man!
He gives new meaning to the word—"

Before Genevieve realized what was happening she

was swept along in a cloud of chatter, exotic scent, and outrageous plans. Her luggage was sent for, unpacked, and stowed away. She found herself living with Althea within an hour of first visiting her. And she wasn't sure how she felt about it. She was charmed and a little frightened of the woman. She was the most fascinating, unconventional person Genevieve had ever met and Genevieve was already acquainted with some very odd people.

"I wouldn't want this known," Althea confided over a luncheon of spiced pineapple and delicately sauteed veal strips, "but I've been feeling the slightest bit lonely here—not that I haven't friends by the bushel load, but I'm delighted to have you here. You are so fresh and unspoiled—like a breath of crisp mountain air."

Unspoiled? Genevieve thought. *She can say that knowing I'm one of "those adorable pirate people" as she calls them?* Still, she was touched by Althea's obviously sincere fondness, and felt instinctively that they would be very good friends.

They had finished their luncheon and were having a sip of wine when the maid announced callers. "The Viscomte Beaumarché and Count de Lieuvienne, Madame."

"Show them in, Jolee. How fortunate," Althea added to Genevieve, "two of the most marvelous men at court. André de Lieuvienne is from one of the oldest families in France. Terribly good-looking and terribly available. Viscomte Beaumarché—" She was cut off by the entry of the most handsome blond god Genevieve had ever seen. He was of above average height and had shoulders that must have been the dream of a hundred women and the nightmare of as many tailors. He was dressed in the height of fashion, chocolate brown surcoat and breeches, peacock blue brocade vest, and silk shirt accented with yards of lace in an eggshell shade. He strode in like a polite lion, all massive grace and carefully restrained power. Genevieve found herself frankly surveying him from the tips of his exquisite leather boots to the mane of glossy gold hair that crowned his head. "Althea, how elegant you look," he was saying in a voice that reminded Genevieve of far-away thunder.

"How dear of you to notice," Althea said. "I understood Viscomte Beaumarché was with you—?"

Count André chuckled, a warm rumble. "He was with me, but got held up in the corridor. Some fool accusing him of stealing a horse. What nonsense."

Althea performed the introductions, and Genevieve managed to respond without fumbling her words. Count André looked Genevieve over as frankly as she had him, and seemed to approve. She suddenly began to feel that the expensive, fashionable gowns, the expert application of kohl and lip rouge, and the many hours of working on her hair had been worth it.

"Oh, here he is now," Althea bubbled. "Genevieve, I want you to meet the Viscomte Michael Beaumarché. Michael this is my new niece—" her voice trailed off.

Genevieve turned from her contemplation of Count André's spectacular visage and took in a sharp breath at the sight of Michael—Michael Clermont! She had thought she would never see him again, certainly not this unexpectedly and under a totally unfamiliar name. She tried to regain her composure.

Althea and André were both staring at her and of one accord shifted their attention to Michael. He, more trained to surprise, had a better grasp of the situation, though he seemed suspended between amusement and shock. "Mademoiselle," he said in a curiously repressed voice. He stepped forward, took her hand and bent over it, brushing a light kiss on her knuckles. When he stood again he looked into her eyes with a wild intensity she could not understand. Was it fright? She thought it might be, but why?

"I am honored to make your acquaintance, Viscomte," she answered and was gratified at the pleased expression that replaced the worried one.

"So you are Althea's 'new niece'?" Michael asked in a detached voice.

"Yes, she is a dear, dear friend of my niece Garlanda," Althea explained.

"A dear, dear friend—I see," Michael said. He walked to an inlaid sideboard and poured some wine from a crystal decanter.

"Are you here to stay with Althea for the winter?" Count André asked, nodding as Michael offered him a glass.

"Your manners have slithered down around your ankles," Althea said sharply to Michael. "What *is* the matter with you?"

"I'm sorry. Ladies, would you care for some wine?" Michael asked.

Genevieve was glad for the interruption. It gave her a moment to compose her reply to Count André. He was still watching her with jungle-bronze eyes. "I have come to visit Althea, and another relative whom I believe to be here—"

"And who might that be?" André asked.

"My mother."

There was a minor crash as the wine decanter struck the table top.

"Michael!" Althea said.

He turned. "Slipped. Sorry. Mademoiselle, did I understand you to say you thought your mother was here at court?"

"Yes. You see, Viscomte, we became separated by tragic circumstances years ago—" *Try not to think of the first time we spoke of this,* she warned herself. But she felt a blush tinge her cheeks. Wrapped in a lover's embrace with this man, wanting nothing to ever change. But things *had* changed. He had betrayed her to the Dowager and at Garlanda's had acted as if they were mere acquaintances. Now he was pretending to be a complete stranger.

"Is there something wrong, my dear?" Althea asked, rising to put an elegantly be-ringed hand to Genevieve's brow.

"No. No, I was just remembering—as I was saying, my mother and I became separated and I have recently learned that she may be here at court, married to a Duc Edouard Serusier," she said, repeating the name Garlanda had told her.

Michael looked stricken; André's left eyebrow rose a fraction of an inch. "Serusier is a friend of my late father's, Mademoiselle. It seems I've heard that he married within the last year. Quite a controversial match, if you don't mind my mentioning it. I don't recall just why it was regarded as such. Beaumarché, what's wrong? Did you make that noise?"

Althea Pasteau, who was not foolish in spite of her determination to seem so, was regarding them all speculatively. "I heard the name mentioned only today," she said, flicking quick glances at Michael and Genevieve. "Monsieur le Duc Serusier and his wife have just departed on a long journey. A trip to see the pyramids, it is said. But only the Duke was at court. His new wife, a subject of much curiosity, remained at their country house during his recent visit. It was a large party that assembled for the journey." She spoke without her usual flamboyance.

Genevieve had paled at the news and now sat down rather quickly, like a rag doll whose stuffing had run out. "I'm sorry, dear. This must be a great disappointment to you," Althea said softly.

"I will follow her," Genevieve said, tears beginning to fill her eyes. She'd never been quite so disappointed.

"You cannot do that. A friend of mine was among the party and told me their plans were to be entirely flexible, without any set itinerary. They were just going to wander about like disoriented gypsies until they stumbled upon a pyramid, it seemed."

Michael watched as Genevieve lowered her eyes and wrung her hands together in her lap. He had an almost overwhelming urge to wrap her in his arms and comfort her, but that would not do. They were supposedly strangers and a great many people's safety and well-being hinged on his maintaining the fiction that he was a social butterfly who had never set eyes on this girl before. He busied himself savagely cramming the silver stopper back on the wine container.

But Althea was under no such strictures. She sat down by Genevieve, enveloped her in the most maternal hug she could manage, and soothed, "Don't worry, sweet. They will be back next summer. You'll see your *maman*."

"No, I'll never see her again. I know it," Genevieve whimpered, giving in to true pessimism for the first time since she began her search. She had obviously forgotten about the two men. Michael touched André on the shoulder and gestured toward the door. A moment later they had discreetly disappeared, leaving a weeping Genevieve to Althea's tender ministrations.

When Genevieve had become calmer, Althea set about briskly getting answers to the many questions that had come to her mind during the initial exchange between Genevieve and Michael. "Now, chérie, tell me all about yourself and Michael," she demanded pleasantly.

Genevieve, somewhat to her own surprise, poured it all out. Her background, her reunion with Evonne, the revelation of her past, even the ransom scheme with the St. Justines and her magically exciting weeks in London with Michael. "And then he betrayed me. The soldiers burst in with orders to arrest me and instructions that he should escape. As it turned out, we escaped, leaving him in a sheet."

"A sheet?" Althea's eyes narrowed knowledgeably. "I *wondered—*"

"Madame?" the maid Jolee inquired from the doorway.

"Yes, yes. What is it, girl?" Althea asked curtly. She hadn't asked all her questions yet.

"The furrier is here, Madame, with the coats to be fitted."

"Oh, very well. Send him in. Genevieve, we will talk more later," Althea threatened sweetly.

Genevieve sat alone for a long while, trying to sort through her thoughts. How was she ever going to endure the long winter until her mother returned? What was Michael doing here with a strange name? And how did he and Althea happen to be on such familiar terms? More important, on what sort of terms was she herself with him?

She had been surprised to see him, so surprised that she hadn't really analyzed the changes. But there were changes. He looked older, of course; and had held one arm a little stiffly. There had been a moment of panic reflected in his usually cool gaze, that had dimmed when she joined in the pretense of not knowing him.

It was not to occur to her until much, much later that her exchange of information with Althea Pasteau had not been mutual.

18

Athenais de Montespan had once been called the most desirable woman in Europe. Artists painted her as Diana, Ceres, and Venus—her children or ladies-in-waiting grouped adoringly about her. Enemies had whispered worriedly that she was the uncrowned Queen of France in the days before her witchcraft scandal with the abortionist Catherine La Voisine. The King had severed his sexual relationship with Athenais at that point but could not exile her because of their many children he had legitimized. La Voisine had said things at the trial about murdered infants and secret aphrodisiacs put in the King's food. Failing to keep him from wandering, she added, Athenais had tried poison. But no one knew whether the witch said this merely to save herself from the stake, or whether it was true.

Athenais, once the most famed of Louis XIV's many mistresses, was now old and fat. She had gout and dropsy as well as an intolerable temper. Beauties of Versailles rarely aged well. Some, like Madame de Fontanges, were remembered chiefly because they had the good timing and poor luck to die young—some said by Athenais's hand.

The children of Athenais and the King were all making splendid marriages these days, which was why the dilapidated former beauty had returned to Versailles. When she huffingly climbed stairs it was seen that her ankles, once the envy of every maiden and matron, were grossly swollen and cross-stitched with varicose veins. Her breasts and eyelids sagged; her hair was an outrageous color and fabric—inferior roasts were held together by less wire and string.

Many considered it a most fitting fate. Michael first beheld her at a ball given in honor of the Duke and Duchess de Chartres—Athenais's daughter and her husband.

Michael had not followed lovely Angeline's advice and visited the King's portrait gallery, so he did not know what a youthful Athenais looked like. He saw only an uncomfortable old woman whose face reminded him of beeswax tapers left on a hot veranda. Her appeal and color had melted and run dismally down a once proud figure, now prodded and stuffed into a girlish gown with ribbons and bows. It was as if a galleon had bedecked itself in a tinseled buggy harness.

He found her regarding him intently during the evening with an expression of faded lechery. It was as if she wanted him, but could not remember what for. He felt the fine hairs on the back of his neck stand up, as if a banshee were coquettishly perched on his tombstone too many years in advance. He remembered he *had* a tombstone behind a ruined cottage in the woods and shuddered.

After one of the slow, stately dances which were in vogue now that King Louis could not do the quick ones, Michael was edged over to Athenais and her suite with a crowd of court newcomers. As he approached the receiving line, he saw that her expression had altered toward him. She suddenly had a face that spoke of brooding curiosity, as if she should know him but did not. When he was introduced as Viscomte Beaumarché her brow furrowed. "You have not your father's coloring," she said frostily.

"Nor my mother's—this year. She said she craved a new shade in her last letter."

"Ah, you write home. My sons should do that more often."

Her eyes had narrowed to slits, an unnerving porcine glare. He forced himself to swallow hard and raise her pudgy hand to his lips. Athenais's fingers

clamped on his like a vise. Her breathing came in
ragged gasps. He feared she was having some kind
of attack and waited to catch her if necessary. Then
he saw the direction of her gaze—his fingers over hers.
His gold signet ring gleamed in the candlelight, the
incised fleur-de-lis and rose clearly outlined by a rope
of thorns.

Athenais continued crushing his hand another moment, then her eyes went wide, searching his. "I am
so glad to meet you, Viscomte," she said in neat,
clipped syllables as if she had only just mastered
the language. "I am so delighted. And this must
be Duchesse de Tassigny . . . ."

Dismissed, he moved away through the line, meeting other people. When the receiving line had finished, Athenais de Montespan gripped the arm of
her nearest male servant. "Jésus, can he be who that
ring says he is? Can he be the owner? It's not possible
and yet my heart says—my heart says—find out all
you can about the young gentleman in blue, the presumed Viscomte." Her servant moved away through
the crowd.

Athenais clasped her hands so tightly they went a
sick, streaky white. "After all these years," she hissed
under her breath while dancers languidly swayed past
in colorful clusters of color and violin music. "After
all these years, can it really be him? Oh, my heart—
how it leaps and races. Too fast, I must rest. Take
me to my rooms!"

Michael was too far away to hear any of this exchange, but saw the once-beauty led away and noted
the looks being directed at him. Because he was so
preoccupied, he did not notice until too late that he
was within a few feet of Genevieve. He had been
attempting to avoid her since their initial meeting
in Althea's rooms. He would eventually have to give
her some sort of explanation of his false name, but
he dared not share the truth with her. The truth was

not his to share with anyone. He would make up some likely-sounding story when he had the leisure to do so.

"You are attracting a good deal of attention, Viscomte Beaumarché," Genevieve said.

Michael stiffened. This was not the time. He had to find out what de Montespan had said, why she had left so suddenly—what she knew about the ring. "I beg your pardon, Mademoiselle, but there is something I must do." He started to move away.

Genevieve stood for a moment as if she'd been slapped. How dare he! Before she could think, she snapped, "Who are you hurrying to betray now?"

Their eyes locked in a blaze of conflict. "Does your own background provide you with a podium from which to condemn treachery, Mademoiselle?"

Furious resentment reddened Genevieve's vision. She could have given away his game, whatever it was, at Althea's but had refrained out of some sort of misguided affection. Loudly she said, "How nice to have seen you, Michael Cl—"

A fierce grip locked onto her elbow before she could complete the word. "Genevieve!" Althea said coldly, not releasing the nerve-shattering grip. "How delightful that I found you. I want to introduce you to someone. Good evening, Viscomte!"

With a curt nod, Michael was gone and Genevieve was left in Althea's iron grasp, feeling like a petulant child who had gone too far and been caught at it.

Michael Clermont, alias Viscomte Beaumarché, sat over a late breakfast. He was still smarting with anger and frustration from the evening before. What was it about the girl that made him want to hold and comfort her one moment and slap her the next? Well, whatever it was, he dared not anger her like that again. She was the only person at court who could destroy his cover—and that would not only endanger him, but endanger his entire mission to acquire vital information. Genevieve herself might even come to harm and *that* he could not bear.

Within an hour, he stood before her with a spray of hothouse flowers in his hand. "I'm sorry," he said simply.

Genevieve looked surprised and contrite. She'd had a long sleepless night thinking over her own behavior. She had acted like a spiteful fishwife, and was annoyed at herself for having so little dignity. Just because he had played her for a fool in London was no reason to go on acting like one. Moreover, as long as she stayed at court she was apparently going to be thrown into his company a great deal. She must not create scenes that accomplished nothing but to make her look like a rejected lover for the whole world to see. She reached out and took the flowers. "Thank you. There was no need. I was to blame." If he wanted to play at being strangers, she would oblige him.

He was surprised at her gentle courtesy and more surprised that she didn't ask any questions. He had expected her to tax him for information about his disguised name. He had even prepared a flimsy assemblage of half-truths to give her. But she asked nothing, merely smiled sweetly as she smelled the flowers. He was more frustrated, he realized later, by her lack of interest than he would have been with questions. "There is to be a ball tomorrow in honor of the Dauphin. Ought to be dull as yesterday's bread. Would you consent to go for a carriage ride with me after we've made appearances?" *Damn it, man, don't you know when to keep quiet?* he thought angrily as soon as the words were out of his mouth, but he was unreasonably pleased when she replied affirmatively.

"That would be lovely," Genevieve answered. She, too, was wondering what made her accept so impetuously.

* * *

Michael was dressing for a ball in honor of Louis's heir, the Dauphin. His servants were fussing over the third cravat he'd refused when André rapped on the door. One of the valets answered it. "The Count André de Lieuvienne and guest," he announced.

"Please come in, André. I am just finishing dressing," Michael called back over his shoulder. Then, to a valet he added, "No, no, man—not enough lace. I won't wear anything this unfashionable, it's at least two weeks out of style! Tell me, André, how does one go about finding servants who keep up with these incessant changes in *la mode*?"

It was done with the proper touch of French pique, not quite flowery but far too fussy for an Englishman. Michael made an exasperated flourish, thoroughly enjoying his role as he pushed a valet off to the wardrobe room for another cravat. His smile stumbled, recovered, and continued at the unexpected shock of seeing that the Count's guest was none other than Robert St. Justine!

It took him unprepared, but he hesitated so briefly that to an observer he might have only been taking stock of the newcomer. Michael had a brief, nauseated thought that it was a good thing he'd smuggled a letter to Robert, telling him no more than that he had survived Vigo and, should their paths cross in France, they must pretend to be strangers. The gleam in Robert's sunny hazel eyes said this was much to his liking.

"Viscomte Jean-Michael Beaumarché, this is Mr. Robert St. Justine," André said. The valet returned with another cravat.

"Viscomte Beaumarché, this is a pleasure," Robert sang out, wringing Michael's hand so enthusiastically he nearly broke it. The valet, trying to adjust Michael's cravat, scowled at Robert.

"Charmed, I'm sure, Mr. St. Justine."

"Viscomte, you speak excellent English."

"And *you,* very good French. Tell me, Mr. St. Justine, what brings you to Versailles at a time when our countries are on rather hostile terms?"

"A potential French bride, Viscomte," Robert replied casually. Michael, standing still long enough to approve the latest cravat, choked.

"Is that valet tying it too tight? Really, Beaumarché, you must borrow my chief valet for the next fête. This fellow is intolerable. You're wearing an inch more of lace than is allowed," André announced drolly as two valets helped Michael into his claret-colored coat, an impressive garment stiff with gold-stitched lining and scrolled sterling buttons.

"Ahh, dear Count," Michael replied, "but you see, I shall act as if it is being done deliberately and it will start a fad." To further the image of deliberate difference he broke off a peacock feather from the maid's duster and pinned the "eye" on his lapel. "You see, Count? Studied eccentricity. It takes the sting out of being unfashionable. Is your new English friend here coming with us?"

The three of them started out the door together. "Yes, I have invited him along. We promised to stop for Madame Pasteau and her lovely niece, too, remember?"

You're going to love this, Michael mouthed at Robert behind the Count's back.

What the hell does all of this mean? came the unspoken reply. They were soon at Althea Pasteau's door. Genevieve answered, unable to keep the surprise from her face as she saw Robert. After all, it was known she had married an Englishman and lived in the country; could she not show she knew Robert?

Robert himself solved the dilemma. He dropped to one knee, kissed her hand, and murmured, "It is Mrs. Faunton, is it not? My dear, dear lady, how are you? What a pleasant surprise!"

She had no recourse but to invite the entire trio in

—one in the wrong place, one with the wrong name, and one with a Mona Lisa smile. André's expression, as he passed, said a calm: *My, my. What* will *these people do next?*

Inside sat Althea at her easel, wielding a green-tipped paintbrush at a canvas of mammoth proportions. Her hair was crimped and spangled with ribbons, pearls, and ostrich feathers for the ball; a watered silk gown of starred sapphire showed from under her gray cheesemaker's smock. She flashed a knee-weakening smile at her guests. "If you will be so kind as to wait a moment, gentlemen, I shall finish this and be right with you. André, you useful, ornamental being, who have you brought me this time?"

Introductions again. Althea and Robert grinned conspiratorially, knowing each other as old names in Michael's vocabulary. "Genevieve," said Althea after Robert had kissed her hand longer than etiquette required, "do be a dear and fetch my fan while I clean up here. We'll be unacceptably late if I tarry much longer."

Fascinated, Genevieve hated to lose a moment's worth of this bizarre situation, but she obeyed nonetheless. She was anxious to take her promised carriage ride down the tree-draped avenues of Versailles with Michael. She could already picture the full winter moon beaming benevolently above prancing carriage horses, their breath silver against the purple December night. *The odd thing is,* she thought as she picked up her voluminous skirts and hurried to find Althea's fan, *his horses are bay this week. I could have sworn they were gray last week—and black the week before!*

Michael leaned around Althea as she unbuttoned her smock. The painting sent a furtive chill creeping up his spine. There, among the usual Pasteau splotches and indefinable squiggles, were the same abstract arrows he had seen on the back of his tombstone! His breath seemed to stop, as if some solid object blocked his windpipe. The numeral "9" and a solid arrow—and now these same triangle-topped lines. "Althea," he whispered. "Althea, what are you painting?"

"Oh, some castle I saw last week. A darling little château with those conical towers—"

Castle towers! Of course! They peered up through the trees all over France. He was about to say more but he caught himself. Was there a castle in France with nine of these towers? Or did the "9" mean it was the ninth castle in a certain area? A ninth-century castle? Were there still any that old? Ninth largest, smallest, fanciest, oldest, newest? Michael was so excited his brain seemed to wheel and dive. Nine, nine . . . castle nine—he was thinking in English again! What was castle nine in French? Château Neuf.

He smacked himself on the forehead. The clue on the tombstone had to mean Châteauneuf—but why, he did not know. He could only presume it had been left him by the one person who knew his identity, the one strange, solitary figure winding through his childhood—the man Matthew. He remembered that last ride in the rain, the questions Matthew had not answered although it was plainly in his power to do so.

He whirled to face his companions. "Madame Pasteau, is that your chestnut hunter beneath the window?"

"No, but that never seems to stop you."

"André, give my regrets to the Dauphin," Michael snapped, flinging the window open. Before anyone could do more than gasp, he had leaped. The next sound was hooves clattering on the perfect paving of the King's drive.

"I *say*," Robert exclaimed cheerfully, whacking André on the back, "I think I'm going to *like* this place!"

Genevieve raced back into the room with Althea's fan. "What was that racket? Where is—"

"He spotted a likely-looking horse and hopped out

the window at it," Robert announced with a pleasant expression.

"He's supposed to take me for a carriage ride after the ball! Why would he leap out a window? What happened? Why did—"

Althea gathered her shawl and fan. "Let's go, dear," she said, as if nothing extraordinary had occurred. Genevieve sputtered, but André courteously held the door open and gave her a leonine smile.

"It was churlish of the Viscomte to desert you so, but he is simply one of those young men who is always dashing off to second someone at a duel. I have a carriage, Mademoiselle Genevieve, and two new horses—perfectly matched Austrian mares. Perhaps you would allow me to give you a carriage tour of Versailles by moonlight? The trees are ghostly in December, and the moon . . . ."

She did not hear him for a while, she was so angry and hurt at Michael's ridiculous defection. Then André's suave words began to make sense. She felt the first tiny licks of mollification at the edges of wounded pride and confusion. When Genevieve gazed up at André she saw his brass-and-topaz eyes reflecting the low glow of subtle candlelight. "Yes," she found herself replying, "I'll go!"

It was bitter cold in the early morning forests of France. Rivers and creeks were frozen so solid that Michael had to chop ice and build a fire in order to water his horse. He was on his fourth one, having traded twice and stolen once, getting himself a threadbare cloak along with this last truculent nag.

The castle was a sullen silhouette above stark white fields. Below it lay the drowsy little village called by the same name as the castle—Châteauneuf. Michael had ridden around the château itself for an hour or so, looking for a way in. He did not know who owned the building nowadays but he had been fired upon, which he bitterly resented. It left a hole in his purloined cloak and gave his favorite suit the disagreeable odor of gunpowder.

This reception led him to believe that perhaps the clue had not meant the castle but the town. So now, perched on the chilly withers of his morose mount, Michael waited for the village to wake and go about its business. He did not have much longer to sit and freeze. Long before the last star faded, townspeople were stirring. Shops were thrown open to the cruel December air, bakers stoked brick ovens and kneaded stiff gray dough, skinny redhaired girls in wolfskin boots milked bleating goats.

Michael dropped his cowl back from his face and lightly prodded the horse with his toes. The beast gave a surly snort and obeyed, starting down the slippery hill to the village. There was no definite plan of action. He simply rode up to the first man he saw and asked if there was anyone thereabouts named Matthew. The man shrugged, said he didn't think so, and strode away quickly. Michael wandered about stopping everyone until someone who appeared to be an official told him he was frightening the townspeople. The man demanded to know what Michael was doing. "Looking for an old friend of mine. Tall, thin man with tawny hair—although it must be gray by now. First name was Matthew. Don't remember his last name. I think he lives around here—or used to. Does the description sound familiar?"

The man scratched his grimy head. "Can't say that it does, I—wait. Madame Mariette had an uncle—"

His heart seemed to hit the ground. *"Had?"*

"Second cottage down that way."

Michael hurried to Madame Mariette's. A plump, cheerful little thrush of a woman answered his rap on the door. "Yes, Sir?"

"I'm looking for a long-lost friend of mine and I've been told he might be your Uncle Matthew."

She gave him a sweet, gap-toothed smile in the glow

of her fireplace and shifted a sleeping baby to her other shoulder. "Bless you, no. Uncle Matthew hasn't lived here in years since he gave us his house. He was in Paris a while, then Rheims. Heaven alone knows where he's off to now. I couldn't even give you an address. Sorry."

She turned away, having brightly dismissed him. He waited in the doorway, snow mantling him unkindly. The plump young woman turned back to him with an inarticulate sound of surprise. "Wait! I remember now —beg pardon, Sir, but it's been so many years! He said, should anyone come knocking for him, bring them in the kitchen and hand them a knife!"

She allowed a bewildered Michael in and put a blunt-edged butter knife in his hand. She made a broad, sweeping gesture toward her kitchen and stepped back.

For the next dim half hour Michael painstakingly searched the room, being careful to put everything back in the same place he'd found it. The woman calmly nursed the baby while her husband went about his cobbler's trade, glancing up from time to time as if to reassure himself that the best cutlery wasn't being pocketed.

As the sun rose higher, there was more light in the cottage. Michael stood, hands to his aching back after a detailed exploration of the hearthstone. He had no idea what he was looking for but finally huffed and puffed to the conclusion that it couldn't be under the huge hearthstone. Nature had probably flung the thing there centuries ago and men built the cottage around it. He could not make it budge.

He was standing, stretching, when the morning light picked out the patterning on the brick wall over the fireplace. Flower patterning. He was about to turn away when he saw that each brick bore a different combination of flowers. He held his hand up to the light, forgetting that Athenais's reaction had made him put the ring on a slim gold chain about his neck. Al-

though he had seen the signet every day of his life, he
still pulled it from the depths of his shirt and stared at
it in rapt fascination: on the inside, a delicately engraved "L.R. à M.A."—on the flat surface of the ring,
a rose and fleur-de-lis bound together by thorns. He
scanned the bricks intently, cool gray eyes missing
nothing. There it was. To the left, up high. A brick
bearing the identical device. He ran taut fingers over
the petals of the rose, traced the fleur-de-lis, gingerly
touched the thorns as if they could draw blood.

Michael hit the brick with the side of his fist. It
sounded solid. He turned to the couple behind him.
"Forgive me; I will pay for the damage," he told them
simply. He slid the edge of the knife between bricks,
as Matthew had known he must, and worked it in,
wiggling it until the brick gave way. It was an exasper-
ating task, for the brick had been set in like all the
others, leaving no clue that it was the one important
one.

Another moment and Michael had it. The brick
came out to rest warm and solid in his hand. Behind it,
in a hollowed-out place, was a rusting metal box. He
withdrew it with clammy hands. There was no mark
of ownership on the box, as if even in this hidden
place there must be an absence of concrete clues. He
forced it open, then started at the slip of parchment
inside, as if despite all this effort, he was unwilling to
learn what the note said.

At long last he unfolded it. The date at the top in
strong, sprawling black letters was 1692, the year after
his kidnapping by pirates—the year of his foster parents' death.

"To Jean-Michael, should he live and rightly read
my clues," it read.

> I saw the Clermonts after your disappearance; we
> concluded that you had been captured and killed
> by that same hand which separated your parents
> and caused the need for your concealment. But

when I returned later and saw their graves and yours, dated a full year after you had vanished, I knew you must have been swept away not by the enemy but by one of those mysterious coincidences that rules men's lives. I exhumed your grave and proved it to be a sham.

I dare not leave information concerning your identity in this place, it would endanger us all. Should you live and return to the Clermonts' home and understand my cipher, you will be more convinced than ever of the mysteries of your circumstances. I can only say you were taken from family to family to protect you. One of your parents is dead and the other has abandoned all hope. I will not abandon you, who were once a small child in need of help.

As long as I live I shall keep a rendezvous in the hope of your arrival. Each winter solstice I shall wait in the sacred woods among those oaks where La Pucelle heard the voice of your patron saint. I will notch the wood that you may know whether I still live and return each year. Death alone is capable of breaking my wait.

Should you be amongst La Pucelle's woods on December solstice, wear a white plume in your cap. If I do not arrive it is because I am dead and with my death you are safe, for no one else knows your identity. Should the wrong persons learn of this meeting, we are both dead men.

God bless and keep you, Fortune's Child.

Matthew

Michael memorized the note, fed it to the flames, and replaced the brick. He emptied his money pouch on the table in front of the staring peasant couple. "A thousand more if you can tell me where Matthew is."

"I don't know. He's always moved around with never an address; it's the way he lives!" the woman exclaimed, wide-eyed.

"When is the winter solstice? Do you know?"

The man puckered his forehead. "Three days before the Nativity."

Something in Michael clenched and burst. "The twenty-second of December? That's tomorrow night!" And he blasted out the door so rapidly that it banged against the cottage walls, snow and wind whistling all about. Then he leaped astride the horse and was gone in the glare of a snowy morning.

La Pucelle's sacred woods, Matthew's note had said. Michael rode northeast to Domrémy, home of Jeanne d'Arc—Joan of Arc, the warrior virgin who led her countrymen in battle against the English and perished at the stake. Her battle instructions, in fact, her very cause, she said, had been dictated to her by Saint Thérèse and Michael, the archangel, in the witch-whispered forests near her home. Here she had tended sheep and perhaps remembered legends of the area dating back to an earlier, un-Christian epoch when strange rites and evil winds blew through these gnarled trees.

Michael spurred onward as if something rode, twisted and shrieking, on his back, talons braced in his soul. He rode out of Châteauneuf into the worst blizzard the region had seen in years—and it kept pace with him clear to Troyes. By that time he had crossed three rivers, one by ferry through congealing waters full of jagged ice floes. The other two had been frozen solid enough to ride across—or so the local boatmen had assured him. When his horse (the second since leaving Châteauneuf) crashed through the ice and into the gut-wrenchingly cold waters of the Seine, Michael had to shoot the animal. It was a merciful death compared to smothering under the ice or struggling, waiting to die in the aching water.

He went on foot after that, until he came to an inn and took two horses. Someone shot him but he did not consider the injury severe; it bled itself clean and he bound it with strips from his once-fine shirt, riding resolutely on despite the pain in his leg.

He rode one horse to exhaustion that night, then set it free. The other dropped under him a few miles from his destination. Michael was a connoisseur of fine horseflesh and a kind master; it said something frightening about his state of mind, this unrelenting way he drove himself and his mounts on through the unpitying hours.

He walked for miles through the snow, striving desperately to find the way to Domrémy while night still remained. When he looked back on where he had been, there was a dark thread of footsteps and blood in the snow. The wound had broken open. He was unable to feel it due to a staggering weariness of body and mind as well as the frostbite settling in feet and fingers.

A new day was breaking with melon and strawberry streaks in the east by the time he reached the twisted oaks of Domrémy. Bare branches loomed menacingly over his head. Michael started to sink to the ground but dared not. Freezing was so seductive a way to die, so painless, so falsely friendly. He dug braced fingers into frost-freckled bark and clung to the tree, trying to clear his head. When he was able to see again, he raised his head and stared wild-eyed around him.

The woods were silent and unholy. "Matthew," he called. "Matthew! I've come at last! Matthew! Answer me! ANSWER ME!"

The trees bent in a breathless wind as if waiting for proof of his identity. He began to flounder through the drifts, branches slashing at his face. "Matthew, it's Michael! I found the note—I found it! *Matthew, why don't you answer me? You promised to wait!*"

He stumbled to a halt, panting and swearing. Matthew's note had said he marked a tree every year —which tree? Michael began to stagger from oak to oak, clawing for proof that the letter had not been some intrigue-spawned nightmare of his overwrought mind. At last he floundered into a dry creek bed and fell heavily, striking both his head and wounded leg. It was soft and forgiving in the snow, so he stayed where he was, gasping. He looked straight up at a deformed giant of an oak with branches twice as long as its trunk—and on that trunk were neatly cut notches.

Michael crawled to the tree and pulled himself up in the red snow. The first few notches were so weathered as to be almost indistinguishable, dull gray marks against the grain of ancient wood. Then the marks grew lighter, contrasting more sharply with the rest of the tree. He counted dizzily. Matthew had written the letter in 1692 . . . eight, nine, ten notches—notches—

And one final one, so fresh the edges were still green and moist with the lifeblood of the oak. A bent aging man had left his mark for one more year —perhaps the last. Between the ground-tapping branches a dark, distant horseman turned against the wind and was lost in the expiring dark of dawn. Michael toppled like a felled sapling in the mottled snows of murdered Jeanne d'Arc's forest. He heard them calling her as he lay dying: "Jeanne? Jeanne! Come home before the witches get you! *Jeanne!*"

Little fairy footsteps in the snow. Something feathery touched his cheek. He opened his eyes and saw it was a long brown braid. Above it was a young girl's sharp, pixied face with pointed chin, snub nose, and slanted elfin eyes. "Jeanne," he gasped, "have you come to take me home?"

"But of course," she said, resting a hand colder than his own on his forehead. Around him the forest spun and jeered. Then mocking night draped him.

Athenais de Montespan sat enthroned in a high-backed rosewood chair, gripping the pierced-work arms as if her fingers would bite through the wood.

She set the letters on her lap and faced the young male servant. "So what else did your visit to Marseilles prove?"

"Nothing else, Madame. His alibi is so complete, he must truly be the Viscomte Beaumarché. I cannot find a single flaw. The family, the schooling—he has it all."

Athenais rolled up the uppermost letter and tapped on her knee with it. "He cannot be who he claims to be—not with that ring. And yet a man does not devise so perfect an alibi without dire motives. There is something sinister in his disguise."

"Or he could really be Viscomte Beaumarché. What then, Milady?"

Athenais crumpled the letter in a vindictive fist. "I am too closely accounted for. I cannot act without proof. If he is who that ring tells me he is—! What better victory than to let those who should love him best destroy him? I would see that happen—I would see my final triumph against his parents who damaged me so badly. My day is not yet done. I will lay out the snare and his own flesh-and-blood will draw it in." She laughed a horrible, dry sound of rage and hatred that had festered for too many years. "I will make them ruin him—and see that they do it before he learns his true identity!"

19

Genevieve was immediately accepted among the professionally idle coterie that was the Sun King's court. Pretty enough to be an ornament but not so beautiful as to represent a threat, she was befriended by women and men alike. Somehow the information that she was fantastically wealthy filtered like an invigorating miasma through circle after circle of gossip. Invitations to balls, hunts, fêtes, and intimate little dinners soon deluged her. She accepted a great many as a way to fill the empty days until spring and her mother's anticipated return. What other young women had to socially slit throats for came to her on a silver platter and her unshackled rise in the *beau monde* was both admired and envied.

For herself, it meant little. Not that she did not enjoy the pretty clothes, the dinner tables adorned with scented boughs of blossoms from the King's *orangerie,* the elaborate and graceful dancing, the handsome men glittering like supernatural butterflies around breathtaking, silken women. She watched, listened, and sometimes participated in their never-ending revels. But it was not an entire existence to her; it was a stage of her life to be observed, savored, then pressed away in a mental memory book.

It was partially her gentle aloofness that attracted Count André de Lieuvienne—that, and other considerations. He saw to it that she was invited where he was invited and urged her to accept in a hypnotic velvet voice she found difficult to refuse.

It was his doing that Genevieve and Althea one night found themselves in an enclosed carriage with a minuscule brazier at their feet to protect them against the bite of the January air. They were on their way, along with a veritable army of the fashionably bored, to an enormous country home for a week long hunt. "Althea, look at the children skating on that frozen pond," she said, pointing gaily. "Althea?" But the older woman was gazing straight ahead deep in some private, perplexed thought. She had been like this for most of a week and Genevieve was becoming concerned. But none of her subtle questioning had elicited any explanation of Althea's subdued mood.

"Who else is coming here for the week?" Genevieve asked, lightly touching Althea's arm.

Althea's automatic smile blazed for a moment. "What? Oh—" she began listing friends and acquaintances.

"What about Viscomte Beaumarché?" Genevieve asked in spite of her earlier resolve not to mention his name—or names! She'd not seen him since the day he had promised her a carriage ride and disappeared instead. She had, by now, passed from anger and wounded dignity to a plateau of vague worry.

"He was invited," Althea answered curtly.

The line of carriages was pulling up in front of massive steps leading up to gargantuan double doors. The two cloaked, befurred women waited until Count André opened the door for them and let down the little iron filigree step. "Thank you, André," Althea said, taking his extended hand and emerging into the snowy cold. Genevieve saw her looking, not at André, but back along the long, swept drive. Suddenly her face seemed to light up and she jammed her hands back into her marten muff in an expression of glee. "There he is," she said, almost triumphantly. "Genevieve, get out. Viscomte Beaumarché has decided to join us, after all."

Genevieve emerged from the carriage feeling a lightening of her heart she had not expected his appearance could have caused. Michael had ridden in behind them. He was on horseback, not in a carriage.

Bundled to his eyebrows in the richest of furs and suedes, he dismounted. But his usual spring was missing, and there was something painfully cautious about the way he dismounted. He blazed a bright social smile at his assembled friends, but Genevieve could not help noting how alabaster pale he was.

"Viscomte! How delightful. We've missed your charming wit," Althea said, rushing to his side. "Where in hell have you been?" she added in a low hiss. "I've already ordered the drinks for your memorial service."

Michael bowed over her hand and whispered bitterly, "I've been out pursuing the years—and they have won."

She locked her fur-clad arm through his. "You're hurt!"

He smiled down on her. "I'm also a bit of a fool, but I wouldn't want you to start writing ballads about it. André! How fit you look in sable."

Later that evening the lords and ladies scrambled out onto the sumptuous lawn bundled in their ermine cloaks, sable muffs, and fox-fur mittens. They set to building snowmen with studied abandon. Michael limpingly approached the hostess, Madame de Coursé, and engaged in weary, flirtatious chatter with her— why had she not been at Versailles lately, why did her husband disappear last Tuesday and leave her so dangerously unchaperoned when she was so lovely?

She only fell for it a little, but that little was enough. "Another of those boring meetings of state at the Minister's palace. He returned laden with paperwork and dark, devious plans."

"All the better for me, Madame—it means he will be too busy to keep an eye on his beautiful wife."

"You rake!" she exclaimed appreciatively, and dumped a snowball down his shirt. A mock battle ensued that ended with Michael in a snowdrift and five triumphant ladies tittering above him.

"The most awful tease, and he never came to *le petit déjeuner* with me last week."

"I warned Angeline but she said—"

—"and it looked suspiciously like my missing horse that he rode up on. You can't believe a word he says, he simply wants to wear our hearts on a string around his neck."

"Not dependable like André. André always arrives on time and never breaks appointments."

"Didn't you hear about André?" another of the giggling ladies gossiped triumphantly. "He left as soon as he saw his room this afternoon." A chorus of excited inquiries sparkled on the cold winter air. "He took offense at the appointments in his room and the distance at which his valet was housed. Just packed his bags and disappeared."

Michael, hauling himself out of the snowbank, said, "There must be more to it than that. No man in his right mind would miss a week surrounded by all this beauty for such a trivial reason." He made a charming gesture indicating that the bevy of ladies around him were the beauty he referred to.

"Count André would," two of them answered in unison and collapsed in giggles at the coincidence.

The ladies thus distracted, Michael slipped away. From the corner of his eye he saw a cloaked female figure picking her way through the yard toward him. The size and shape told him it was Genevieve. She of all people must not intercept him. *No, Gen, don't stop me now,* he thought, walking faster. The cold and exertion shot icicles of pain through his leg.

Trembling, on the edge of exhaustion, he was afraid of what he might reveal if he were to have a confrontation with her. It would be such a relief to confide in her—and yet so impossibly dangerous to both of them.

When he reached a safe distance, he gritted his teeth and began to run, ducking under trees and turning a wide arc until he was coming at the mansion from the other side. He slipped in through an unlit window. He closed his eyes a moment, took a deep breath and willed the waves of pain to ebb. Now there remained only one problem: to figure out which of the sixty-seven rooms housed Monsieur de Coursé's papers. He looked for the room most resembling a fortress and knew he had achieved his desire.

The locks were a triviality; he had picked far more impressive ones. He closed the doors after himself, lit the candle he always carried, and carefully broke into the sandalwood desk with its pine and mother-of-pearl veneered surface. Beautiful desk. Some day if he settled down—if he *lived* long enough to settle down—he wanted a desk like this, full of cubbyholes. But when he settled down he would not have incriminating papers in his desk.

His wounded leg was throbbing again. Hands trembling, he began to whisk through the letters and notes. Among recipes for *pâté de foie gras* and letters from Mother he found nothing of consequence. A hidden drawer, then. He knelt, running sensitive fingertips along the bottom of the fragile desk. Ahh, there it was. He put the rifled papers back in perfect order, locked the desk, and popped the secret panel. It gave him what he wanted, names of commanders and troop figures.

Worry creased Michael's forehead as he read. Some major assault was being planned, but there was no date or place to the attack. For weeks now he had been finding indications of renewed martial activity minus all goals. It made him knot a fist as he scanned the correspondence. All this planning and no conclusion! He had burgled one of the chief minister's mansions the month before, a hair-raising escapade with vicious dogs, and learned little more than he had tonight. So what? In what way were the English helped by learning the name of this general or that commander? He needed times, places, plots. He was risking his life for petty information a chambermaid could have smuggled out of a boudoir. He replaced the papers and found himself doubting the usefulness of his entire mission. It was a waste of an expensive agent—for keeping him in the guise of a wealthy viscomte at Versailles required vast sums of good English money.

Good Spanish money, actually, he told himself with a twisted grin. The entire venture was doubtless being funded by the Vigo haul. Fifty viscomtes and their descendants could live off the Armada's cache for a century before they felt the remotest financial pinch.

Michael straightened his collar and stepped furtively into the corridor, locking the door behind him. "Aha. I knew if I waited long enough I'd find you skulking in some unlikely place. Did you think you fooled me, doubling back like that?" Genevieve asked. "Where did you disappear to for a week and a half? And what were you doing just now, in that—"

Footsteps sounded around the corner. Michael silenced her the best way he knew how—with a kiss. He wrapped her securely in his arms and backed up against the nearest wall.

Genevieve was too stunned to object. She heard the scurrying footsteps and girlish giggle of a chambermaid. Then Michael released her. "She could not have seen your face," he said. His voice was low, razor thin.

"Michael—what is it?" she asked quickly. She'd never heard him sound quite like this.

"Nothing," he said, attempting his usual light tone. "Nothing at all. Please forgive my indiscretion." He bowed over her hand, kissed her fingers lightly, and turned away.

But in that second, in the faded light, she had seen the blood on his thigh and noted that his hand was shaking.

He strode away, trying to conceal the limp and foil the excruciating pain. The bullet had moved in the wound. With a quick swirl of his cape, he stepped through a double door and onto the veranda. He banged a defiant fist against the stone side of the mansion, refusing to voice his pain. Then he stepped into a deep shadow when he heard Genevieve open the door and softly call his name.

She called him twice, afraid for his sake to draw attention to him, then she hurried to Althea's rooms. "He's hurt," she said without preamble.

"I know," Althea said. "Where is he?"

Genevieve told her.

"Go to bed," Althea ordered. But her voice was kind and there was deep concern in her beautiful eyes.

A hasty, feathered tapping on her balcony door woke Genevieve from a restless sleep. She fumbled for a bedside weapon, then saw that the shadow at the lace-curtained windows was female in form and of a height to be none other than Althea.

Genevieve quickly donned a filmy wrapper and unlocked the door-length windows. "Get yourself to my room as quickly and unobtrusively as possible— and wear an old dress," Althea whispered. "You're right—he's hurt. Hurry!" And she vanished. Genevieve struggled into one of her sleeping maid's gray dresses and hurried down the balcony to Althea's quarters.

Inside, a strange tableau met her eyes. Michael was sprawled in Althea's huge, soft bed, with Robert leaning over him. Robert appeared to be making short shrift of his friend's best trousers with a pen- knife. Althea was heating a basin of water at the fireplace while her maid, Jolee, wound strips from a nightshirt for bandages.

"What is it?" Genevieve asked, bending over Mi- chael.

"A musket shell I ran afoul of eight or nine days ago," he croaked from between badly bitten lips.

"Why didn't you do something about it?"

"No time for a doctor—too deep to dig it out myself."

"It's shifted. I think with a little work we can pop it right out." Robert spoke brightly, but the face he turned to Genevieve was grave with doubt. She soaked a sponge in Althea's basin, wrung most of it out, and began to dab at the wound. The puckered edges of flesh were red-streaked around a neat purple hole. Infected. He made no sound as she probed, but his hands clamped on the bedclothes.

"Sterilize the knife, Genevieve, while I pour some more of this brandy into him," Althea said with uncharacteristic competence. The bottle was already half empty, but the aristocratic blonde forced Michael's head up and poured. When she quit, he fell back with a twisted countenance, hair soaked with sweat. Genevieve took his hand and was surprised at the strength there. He was very nearly breaking her bones. "I'm sorry," he said simply.

"For what?"

"For the many terrible ways I've treated you. But I never, ever betrayed you. I—Robert? Don't let Robert do the cutting. You wouldn't believe what he can do to a Christmas ham." His fingers knotted on Genevieve's, but she forced down a cry of pain and painted on a smile she hoped was reassuring. "Jenny —make sure he has that ridiculous little knife sterilized. Gangrene doesn't suit me at all."

She moved up, taking his head in her lap. "Michael Clermont—or whatever your name is this week—quit trying to be brave. Shriek and shout if you have to. Or break my arm. Only don't joke and persist in putting on this stupid, gallant act of yours. I know better."

"I don't," Robert commented coolly, withdrawing the orange blade from the flame and watching it cool to blackened metal. "I don't believe he can cry. He has mathematical equations and horse-thieving notes packed into his tear ducts. Here's the knife, Althea. I'll hold him."

Althea came from the fireplace, smoke-haired, the simmering basin in her cloth-padded hands. She set the pan of hot water on the bedside table and reached in her pocket for her green monocle. It slipped from her wet hands and dashed itself to delicate shards on the icy stone floor. "God *damn* it," she snapped with the first real anger her friends had ever seen from her. "Robert's the only one strong enough to hold him down and now I can't see to operate. Gen—"

Genevieve was already moving, settling Michael more comfortably among the quilts and pillows. She took the knife, dipped it in the brandy, and, with cold-blooded calm, poured the sweet liquor onto the wound. "Hold his legs, Althea. He can kick me all he wants when this is over, but for now—"

When she was sure they had him immobile, she made the first incision. Michael twitched spastically, then was still. She made another cut, across the first. Then she pinched the edges of infected skin together. Foul-colored matter and blood came out. She washed it away with the last of the brandy and slid the knife down into the hole.

The blade was halfway to the hilt before she felt it nudge something solid. Bone or bullet? Genevieve shifted the blade; the solid thing shifted, too. Bullet, then. She called for Althea's maid, Jolee, to bring her a tweezers and more alcohol. "There isn't any liquor, Ma'mselle."

"Then steal me some. And salt, too," Genevieve snapped, remembering the ship's doctor on the *Black Angel* saying briny water helped slow bleeding, in effect burning blood vessels shut. The maid was gone in an instant. Genevieve cut further, hating herself for every jerk and flinch of Michael's straining body. She had held this man, known him in the most intimate of ways, and now she must do worse things to his flesh than he had ever done to her heart.

She had to go deeper to get the knife tip under the musket-shell. Michael was fighting now, still making no noise, but trying to thrash against Robert and Althea's iron grips. There! She could feel it shift, coming up. The knife slid in her sweaty hands. Where was Jolee with the tweezers? Where? Blood, so much blood. Genevieve wiped her streaming forehead on her shoulder and reached for the sponge with her free hand. She took water up in it, squeezed it dry over the wound. It flushed gore and matter away, allowing her a glimpse of dark metal before the wound filled again. "Sit on him, Robert. And clap your hand over his mouth."

Genevieve brought the knife up, edging the bullet toward the surface while the blazing fireplace sent waves of nauseating heat through her trembling body. She clamped her teeth, set her shoulders, and went after the bullet with bare fingers.

Michael screamed against Robert's stifling hand, screamed and screamed again. The bed shook with the force of his struggles but they held him. Genevieve threw the bullet on the dressing table. "Got it. Now I only have to rinse the wound out and sew him together."

The almost-scalding hot water sent him battling again, but it was a weaker battle this time. When Jolee at last arrived with supplies, Genevieve used the tweezers to get the last of the shell splinters, then dissolved salt in the water and used it to flush out the bullet hole. Michael fainted long before she finished. She swabbed the wound clean, took a few neat stitches, and uncorked the bottle.

"What's that for?" Althea inquired as she and a pale Robert climbed off Michael.

"Me. I deserve it," Genevieve announced, and raised the bottle to cold, dry lips. They all had some, then Althea set about straightening all evidence of uncommon activity.

Genevieve pushed her hair back from her face and

collapsed into a deep sofa by the fire. Robert came and joined her, stretching long velvet-clad legs in front of himself. "God! What a night," he said on a long ragged breath.

Genevieve was forcing down the impulse to gag or cry—she wasn't sure which. "Yes," she agreed.

"He'll be all right, you know. I've seen him recover from worse things—"

Genevieve paled, shook her head. "Please. I can't talk about it now. What are you doing here?" she asked in an attempt to switch to a pleasant, non-emotional subject.

"In France, you mean?" Robert asked, correctly interpreting her question. "I came to please one of your favorite people, my grandmother."

Genevieve shuddered delicately, then cast him a weak smile. "Knowing how you and your grandmother get on, I can understand how shipping you off must have been a pleasure to her."

"Actually, it wasn't so much to get rid of me as to get me married," he said. There was a vague note of apology in his voice.

"Married?" Genevieve asked. Why should she feel wounded by that? And yet she did in a small guilty way. "Who's winning? You or your grandmother, the tigress?"

Robert leaned back, ran a still-shaking hand over his forehead. "I'm afraid the tigress is. Do you mind?" he asked hesitantly.

"How should I have the right? No. You and I were friends before—before we visited the Colonies. We've been friends since. Tell me about her—"

Robert quickly obliged, a little too quickly to please Genevieve. "Her name is Felicia. Twenty. An orphan. She's been the ward of a cousin of my grandmother's for years now. They've not treated her very well, I judge. Nothing overt, just little everyday cruelties—"

"And you're going to marry her and take her away

from it all," Genevieve said and was instantly ashamed of the gilt thread of sarcasm in it. "I'm sorry," she said, taking his hand in hers and holding it tightly. "But Robert, are you in love with the girl or sorry for her?"

Robert didn't answer for a long time. Finally he said, "I'm not sure. I think it's love—but I *knew* it was love with you."

Genevieve shook her head. "No, Robert. We just both *needed* to be in love then—and it was lovely, wasn't it?"

He put his arm about her shoulders and she leaned against him staring into the flickering fire and listening to Althea bustle about straightening up the room. Michael's ragged breathing had settled and they were both breathing in unison with him, as if to ease the effort. Eventually, Genevieve spoke again. "When shall I meet her?"

"She's here," Robert said. "May I introduce you to her tomorrow?"

Genevieve nodded. "What has Michael been up to?" she asked.

Robert shook his head. "I'll share any secret of my own you want. I'll tell you my middle name, I'll tell you about losing my virginity, I'll chart how often I clean my teeth—"

"But you won't tell me about Michael?"

"I can't. In the first place, I don't know anything really. He's my friend, as dear to me as my own gorgeous skin. Beyond that, I've never needed to know what he does."

Genevieve listened in silence. Finally she stood and bent to kiss his forehead. "Then I'm glad you're *my* friend, Robert. I can't imagine a better kind."

She went back to Michael's bedside and watched him sleep until the first frost-glittered pink of dawn showed through the leaded windows. Althea laid a be-ringed hand on her arm. "Go back to your rooms now. I can watch him."

"I'll stay with him," Genevieve said.

Althea's voice was steely. "If you are seen coming from this room it will help no one. I shall be putting about the word that Michael became outrageously drunk in the small hours and is spending the day sleeping it off. My reputation can withstand the aftershocks—yours can't. No one is to know the truth."

Truth. That word again. Genevieve knew, looking into the beautiful blond woman's face, that there was no truth there to be shared. She did not even ask. "Very well. I will come back to check on him."

Genevieve crept furtively back to her own room, shed and concealed her bloodstained clothing, and fell into an eerie dawn reverie. When she had been sitting by Michael's bedside most of the long night she had felt strong waves of some emotion she could not afford to put a name to. She told herself it was only a form of sympathy, heightened and heated by the extraordinary circumstances. But she could not truly deceive herself. She could very easily fall in love with Michael Clermont, or Freddie, or Viscomte Beaumarché, or whatever name he might later choose for himself. Perhaps she already had.

She could not allow that. He had hurt her before when he had betrayed her in London—or had he? It had nearly cost her her life and Xantha's. Then in Jamaica she had offered herself to a virtual stranger to save him, and he had subsequently ignored her. Twice, since she had been in France, he had asked for her company and simply failed to keep the appointment, later spouting tissue-transparent excuses.

This man is not good for me, she thought self-mockingly.

Besides, the question was academic and egotistical. He did not want her—that had been made abundantly clear. He had some devilishly intense secret life that left no room for anyone else. Secret—and very, very dangerous.

No, she would help him out of this as she had attempted to help him at the slave docks and as she had helped by keeping his name a secret, but thereafter she would make sure she moved in different circles whenever possible. A woman needed a man to accompany her in this society, but it would not be *him*. She had a man near who was all too eager for her company.

André would be her companion and escort in the future. She, too, had heard about his departure and argument with the host, but she was sure there was simply a misunderstanding of some sort. Unexpected business to attend to, perhaps. But she would see him back at court in a week and would let him know that she welcomed *his* company.

20

Michael heard voices in the other room and knew
there were friends inquiring after him. Althea had
been in earlier to tell him the story she and Robert
had concocted. He'd gotten drunk, come to her rooms,
thought he'd heard a prowler on her balcony and, in
the process of pursuit, accidentally stabbed himself
quite badly in the leg.

Michael had nodded his assent to this tale. It was
precisely the sort of half-witted chivalric thing Viscomte Beaumarché would do. He lay in the comfortable bed thinking about the night before. It wasn't
the wound and the treatment that held his memory;
it was Genevieve.

He'd not found it so difficult as he had anticipated,
being around her. It wasn't until this morning that
he realized why. At Versailles, she was a lady just
like dozens of other pretty, pointless women. She
moved from day to day, from party to party, with
lovely, aimless grace. They all did.

The woman he had feared he was falling in love
with in London had been different. Adventuresome.
Honest—if not about her calling, at least about her
emotions. Capable. Yes, that was it. The London
Genevieve was living her own life, not just letting it
roll over her. The Genevieve in Versailles was like
all the others—sweet, proper, and ornamental.

Until last night . . . .

Not one of the others—the girls he courted in order to steal secrets from their fathers—not one of
them could have done what Genevieve did the night
before. He'd seen such wounds before. He'd helped
treat them and then gone off to be quietly sick in a

corner. But she'd not hesitated, not fainted nor made silly, feminine squeals of horror. Even through his pain he'd been aware that she'd simply done what needed to be done, competently and without any excess fuss.

If only . . . .

But there was no point in thinking of it. Not now. When this was over, when he'd done his job in France and was allowed to be his own person again, perhaps then he could afford to fall in love with her. *If* he survived this and ever was free to order his own life.

And if she wanted him.

What a nerve I've got, he thought bitterly. Assuming that he could put her out of his mind, like a parcel to be reclaimed later, at his leisure. Since that last night in London she'd never done or said anything to indicate that she cared for him. Removing the bullet? No, it was an act of mercy, not an act of love.

There was a tap on the door. "Michael, are you awake?" Robert St. Justine's voice called. "You have visitors."

Michael turned to the door just as Genevieve stepped through. She was a vision in burgundy velvet and an ermine cape. Several ladies were with her. Genevieve inquired prettily about his health, pretending amusement about his accidental stabbing of his own leg. She was being light, pretty, innocent, only the faint weary hint of blue under her eyes giving away the truth.

She was back to being the Versailles lady.

Very well. That was how it was to be. Michael was suddenly very tired, the pain in his leg and head beating counterpoint rhythms. He seemed convincingly hung over, but responded in character with Viscomte Beaumarché, as the ladies chatted about the day's activities and how sorry they would all be that he could not join them.

When they left Genevieve pretended to have

dropped her fan and stepped back into Michael's room for a moment. She wasn't sure why she was doing it. To share one private word with him? But what would the word have been? To touch his brow? To hold his hand for a moment of comfort? But he had turned away and did not know she was standing there in the doorway, staring at him before turning to leave.

Genevieve didn't have another moment alone with Michael that week. His guests, most of them feminine, were always clustered in giggling knots at his bedside offering him candied tidbits and plumping his pillows. It set Genevieve's teeth on edge and after two days she ceased to visit. He did not need one more woman in his ample gallery of admirers.

She met Robert's Felicia and was, to her own surprise, charmed by the girl. She had expected someone rather dismal and waiflike, but Felicia, though of clearly frail health, had the spirit of a bright-eyed forest creature. She was little, bright, cheerful, and totally, madly in love with Robert. *And he with her*, Genevieve thought. He had tried to sound reasonable and level-headed when he had spoken of her, but in her presence he was besotted and bedazzled by this delicate, glossy-haired girl. Genevieve felt happy when she was in the presence of two people so much in love and at the same time suffered a mad jealousy of their good fortune in finding one another and having nothing to stand in their way.

When the house party broke up at the end of the week, Robert invited Genevieve to ride in the carriage with him and Felicia, but Genevieve turned down the invitation. She feared by the end of such a journey she might be biting through her wrists. She wanted so to be in love like they were! It seemed so easy, and exalted an emotion. "Isn't Michael riding with you?" she asked. "He can't ride a horse yet, can he?"

"No. He's staying on for a few days," Robert explained, watching Genevieve rather closely. "He asked me to thank you," he added very softly.

"He has no reason to thank me," Genevieve said and was embarrassed at the crankiness in her own voice.

She rode back to Versailles with Althea. Neither spoke all the way back.

Michael returned briefly to Versailles, but was immediately gone again on his fever-bright round of visits and weekends. Genevieve did not see him except across a ballroom or down the length of a banquet table.

André, in contrast, was a constant companion. The little wounded places in Genevieve's heart could not help but respond to his gallantry, his compliments, his thoughtfulness. Listening to him and knowing she was a fragile, many-petaled blossom of femininity to him, she felt something warm and grateful. He courted her so sweetly, so kindly, yet the sheer masculine power of him awed her.

There was more than just physical and social charm to him. He also proved to be a knowledgeable businessman. Genevieve was having difficulty with some of the legal details of one of the many properties she had purchased with the Vigo Bay money. The lawyer had sent some papers for her signature and they awaited her when she returned from the week at the country house. She puzzled over the document at great length, unwilling to sign until she at least had a thorough understanding of what it meant. She confided her problem in André when he called on her one evening.

He glanced at the paper, nodding and frowning. "It's impossible to tell whether this is reasonable without seeing the original deed. Do you have it at your bank?"

"No, I have it right here," Genevieve answered,

fetching the brass coffer she kept such things in. She unlocked it and rifled through the stacks of deeds and receipts. "Here it is," she said triumphantly.

André was staring at the box. "Do you mean to tell me those are all property deeds?" he said with astonishment.

Genevieve found herself flushing with embarrassment. He must think she was trying to show off her wealth. How gauche of her to have not known better! She had still not completely acquired the habit of thinking how her actions might be misinterpreted before making them. "Well, actually, not quite all of them . . ." she began to say.

"And you just keep them thrown carelessly into a box that way!" André went on, ignoring her remark.

So that was it! She was relieved that he was surprised at her business sense rather than her social expertise. "It's not careless," she said mildly. "I know how to find anything I need and I've learned what most of it means, the legal terms and such."

"But you should have them filed in order and have a ledger to record the income," André said.

"I suppose I should," she admitted. It was not that she couldn't figure out how to keep important records, simply that she'd never felt the need. The various lawyers she'd hired collected and forwarded her rents and since it had always amounted to far more money than she needed, she'd given little thought to keeping close track. She was dimly aware that some of them were probably cheating her, but since she had stolen the money originally from the doomed Spanish ships at Vigo Bay it didn't seem right to complain of someone else getting a share of it. In fact, it assuaged the guilt a little. But she could not explain any of this to André, who believed her to be a fine lady, so when he politely offered to help her put her affairs into better order, she agreed.

He hired a clerk to make a weekly accounting of the monies received and changed banks. "Why are we transferring?" Genevieve asked. "I've always felt Monsieur Legrand was honest and competent."

"Honest, perhaps," André replied. "But I received a letter from him today in which he spelled my name incorrectly."

"A small mistake certainly?"

"A sign of carelessness. A man of business should know that an individual's name is his most important asset and should not be regarded lightly."

He was just as meticulous as this in all aspects of their relationship. If it was cold, he refused to take Genevieve out unless sure she was properly bundled against the elements. He would not allow anything that even hinted of discourtesy to touch Genevieve. A valet who rose too soon after bowing to her was fired on the spot and a former friend who made mildly humorous reference to the mysterious source of Genevieve's wealth was challenged to a duel—a challenge he fortunately didn't accept.

In short, André was the sort of man who could and would stand between her and the world if she wanted him to. But did she? Facing herself with the question, she realized that she liked the padded protection of André's attention—but she did not truly need it, nor did she wish to spend her lifetime being sheltered. Still, it *was* flattering and placid.

As the days lengthened and the temperatures began to rise, Genevieve's worrying and concern over romance began to lessen, for spring was coming and spring meant Sabelle would be back soon. That was, after all, her reason for being here—her reason for everything right now. The dream of her lifetime, to be reunited with her mother, and it might well be any day now.

Michael returned from his round of visits in time for Robert and Felicia's wedding. It was a small, private affair after which the newlyweds retired to a remote estate belonging to Felicia for the remainder

of the spring and summer. They planned in the fall
to go to England. "Perhaps I shall visit you there,"
Michael said significantly to Robert.

Robert sensed what he meant, that his work might
be done by then. "We would be delighted, Viscomte.
My grandmother is half French. You would feel right
at home amongst my family, I feel sure." He winked
at his friend.

"I think it unlikely any of us shall be visiting
England in the near future, Michael," André said.

Michael turned an innocent gaze on the Count.
"Why not?" he asked.

André shrugged. "What a butterfly you are, Beaumarché. Can you be completely unaware of the tension in European politics? We might well be at war
with England by then."

"War?" Michael laughed. "Well, I hope we have
blue uniforms, then. I look so washed out in red,
and it tends to spot too easily." There was a general
ruffle of mirth and no one noticed the blighted look
Genevieve gave Michael before walking away.

Not long after the wedding Michael had another
brief meeting with Athenais de Montespan. He was in
the portrait gallery with Angeline, a witty, vivacious
young woman he had spent a good deal of time with
since his arrival at Versailles. When they had been
there a while, the only people staring at the paintings,
he saw Madame de Montespan and one of her maid-
servants enter by the side door. Her gaze was glassy,
cold, and smooth at the sight of him.

"Over here—this is Anne of Austria, the King's
mother. She certainly was a beauty, wasn't she, Viscomte?" Angeline queried prettily.

"Yes," he agreed, totally aware of Athenais's eyes
drilling pits in his skull. "Who is the tawny-haired
one?"

"That happens to be me."

Athenais's voice sliced through the air like a sword

through a crisp head of lettuce. "Was I the most beautiful, do you think? There was Louise de la Vallière—her picture's on the north wall over there—but when she lost him to me she faded away in a convent somewhere. Her hair was such a delicate shade, the painter caught it exactly. And fragile little Marie-Angélique Fontanges with her blond curls and absurd innocence; I think the portrait of her is masterful. She had that exact look of wide-eyed, breathless surprise that you see in that picture. They say I poisoned her."

"Why would you do that?" Michael managed to ask in blasé tones. "You had children who had been legitimized by the King. You were in power."

"She had a baby but it died. . . . Louise de la Vallière, now, some of *her* children lived. Lovely Louise, not made for the harsh realities of this world. Over there's Richelieu, looking as treacherous as in real life. That equestrian painting of the King doesn't do him justice."

Angeline tugged at Michael's sleeve. "Let's go, please! She frightens me so!"

"Your children are making splendid marriages," he said straight into de Montespan's unwavering gaze.

"Yes, and they are all beauties. Louise and Marie-Angélique were said to be more beautiful than I, but everyone acknowledged me to be the more desirable. Strange to think that now, isn't it, when I look like this."

"No," Michael said frankly. "I can see the reins of power chafing your hands even after all these years. I can see the pride and fury and passion that made you irresistible to kings and dangerous to other women."

Athenais laughed, a mudslide sound of fecund years lost. "How clever you are. You made no reference to my beauty, for that would have been a lie, and yet you handed me compliments wrapped in sharp, colorful foil. You are a very dangerous young

man, Viscomte, aren't you? Don't lie and say no, for
I recognize these things in others. My beauty and
figure may be dust, but my mind is not. I am still a
dangerous woman, Viscomte, for with beauty gone,
what else have I to live for?"

She waved a hand in dismissal, and as Michael and
Angeline hurried away they could hear Athenais's
cynical, gnarled laughter twisting down the gilt-cor-
nered halls in their wake, pursuing them for long,
ugly minutes.

Spring came to France with wild abandon. The
hills were caped with flower-strewn green and the air
was thick with scent, and romance. Young girls tightened their corsets and had the necklines of their
dresses cut down; bachelors made rash proposals
which were accepted; middle-aged women whose husbands had not spoken to them for months found
themselves pregnant, and elderly men with gout were
discovered prancing about in the moonlight with
kitchenmaids. Furs were packed in wardrobes, hunts
gave way to picnics, and well-bred ladies were discovered in compromising positions with delightfully
unsuitable young men.

In the midst of this it was almost possible to forget that France—indeed, most of Europe—stood swaying on the fine edge of war. Louis XIV's grandson
Phillip was on the Spanish throne—a consolidation
of family power that wrought terror in the hearts of
the English and their allies. Troops were being trained
in remote villages, munitions were being stockpiled,
and plans were being discussed in hushed whispers
all over France for the war that would come as inevitably as summer.

In defiance of this reality, Louis's court flirted,
struck seductive poses, and had honeysuckle trysts in
the moonlight.

Genevieve was not immune to the mood which enveloped the world of Versailles. "It's getting dark.

Shouldn't we go in?" she said to André as they stood almost alone in the formal rose gardens at dusk.

"The scent cannot be truly appreciated until dark," he said, putting his hand, warm and strong, at the back of her waist and guiding her gently to a carved stone bench.

Without realizing it she had become used to letting André guide her—had almost become dependent upon his leonine assurance. It seemed so comfortable, so simple to forget for the time being that she needed a life of independence and adventure. André was always so sure what they should do, when they should do it, and was unfailingly, enormously courteous and considerate. His courtship of Genevieve was a stately dance of respect and restraint. There was never a suggestion of impropriety in his words or gestures. He held her hand oftimes, kissed her fingertips, put a protective arm around her shoulders, brushed his lips as lightly as gossamer on hers when he returned her to her rooms after a walk or carriage ride. And if there was a straining of lust against the reins of gentility, it was on Genevieve's part, not his.

Genevieve and André sat on a bench with marble griffins for legs while he commented blithely on her beauty and fragile grace—a frequent enough theme, but one Genevieve never quite tired of hearing nor André of telling. Eventually, however, André turned the topic to other matters. "I've been granted a post with the government, Genevieve," he said, a deep bass rumble she never failed to enjoy hearing.

"You do not sound pleased."

"It will mean a certain amount of traveling—checking on military fortifications and making reports to the Ministry. I will not be here to enjoy your company so much of the time."

She feared that he might be getting ready to propose. Feared or hoped—she was not sure. But she would have to turn him down in any case. Better to change the subject, divert his apparent line of thought. "Then why take the post? Certainly others could do it."

"Why?" He cocked his golden head and regarded her quizzically. "Surely you can guess," he said, but did not explain himself further. It was a remark so light and inconsequential as to almost pass unnoticed, but she was to remember it later and wonder why it had not opened a world of understanding.

While Genevieve chatted brightly and disjointedly about how André would enjoy traveling, the prospect of a mild summer and horticultural theory, other pairs of lovers and would-be lovers were strolling in the acres of formal gardens. Near Genevieve and André and moving ever closer, was Viscomte Beaumarché, with a peach and ivory beauty whose chipped-ice giggles generally canceled out any conquests her appearance might have made.

But Michael had heard worse noises in his time and been intimately acquainted with greater beauty. His interest was not in the girl (though she must never suspect this) but in her heritage—more specifically, her father, a choleric old man who was known to a precious few individuals as the primary repository of information concerning the French national arsenal.

The old man was working in the utmost secrecy, a fact which had only come to Michael's attention by the young giggler's indiscretion. Her father naturally had no official office or quarters and presumably the documentation of his data must be kept at the family's country home. Michael had been applying his considerable charm to getting an invitation to visit there. Only this afternoon the young woman had shriekingly hinted that such an invitation might be forthcoming and Michael had stepped up his efforts to be eligible.

The subject was just about to bob to the surface again as they rounded the corner of a hedge and came upon Count André and Genevieve. "Oh, hello there," Michael said and attempted to courteously steer the girl in another direction. He had found it distinctly and surprisingly uncomfortable to be in Genevieve's presence when she was escorted by the blond Apollo who occupied so much of her time. He became irritated with himself when this reaction came over him. After all, she cared little for him, he told himself; nor did he have the leisure to care for her.

But the cheerful girl who clung so helplessly to his arm was not about to be distracted. She minced closer to Genevieve and André, letting forth a giggle of greeting. "Such a pretty night—so romantic," she said to the group in general and turned an adorable *moue* of pleasure on Michael.

"Yes, very pretty," Genevieve said, unnerved at the sight of Michael and not sure why. "Will you join us? We were about to walk back."

André rose, offered his arm and the two couples began to stroll along the path. There was a moment of sharp awkwardness when they fell into formation and Michael ended up next to Genevieve. The young woman he was with hurriedly crowded between them, all laughter temporarily quelled.

As they approached the palace they noted a subdued knot of their acquaintances, whispering mournfully among themselves. Suddenly one of the group spotted them and broke away, running toward Genevieve, who recognized her as a young woman she'd taken luncheon with several times in the last months, a distant relative of the old Duke Sabelle had married.

"Yvette, what's wrong?" Genevieve asked when she saw the girl's tear-streaked face.

"Oh, Genevieve, it's too terrible! I don't know how to tell you—oh-h-h," she wailed.

"Yvette! Stop this! What's wrong," Genevieve asked,

but another look at the girl's stricken face told her
what it was.

"They're dead," Yvette sobbed. "A messenger just
brought the news. The whole traveling party your
mother was with—dead. Avalanche somewhere crossing from Italy—maybe it was Switzerland—oh, Genevieve, I'm so sorry—"

But Genevieve wasn't really listening anymore. It
wasn't possible. There was a mistake. It was a lie.
Some other party was lost. Some travelers she didn't
know. Not her mother. Not the woman named Sabelle
whom she barely remembered, but loved with all her
heart. No. It was wrong.

She pulled away from Yvette, her eyes full of vengeful horror. "You're lying," she said in a dry rustle
of hope. "Not *my* mother. Not my mother! It's a lie—
a LIE!" Her voice had risen to a reedy scream and
tears were coursing hot and unheeded down her alabaster pale cheeks.

"I'm sorry, Genevieve. Please don't—"

But Genevieve was beyond reason. She reached out
to strike Yvette, to punish her for this cruel error. A
large hand—André's—grabbed her wrist and spun her
about. "Genevieve," he said in his molten-gold voice,
"calm yourself. Let me take you to your rooms."

She cast about wildly, looking for someone to deny
it. Someone to say all was well and she would see
her mother, alive and well, very soon. But Yvette had
her face buried in her hands. Michael was staring
at her with mute, austere shock. For a fraction of
a second it seemed as though he might step forward
to offer comfort, sympathy, or some word of understanding. But the silly girl at his side clutched at his
arm and smiled nervously. He looked down at her a
moment as if trying to remember who she was.

André wrapped Genevieve in his arms, murmured
honeyed assurances, and led her away. Michael stood
rooted for a long time. Sabelle had been a dear old

friend of his, they'd shared dangers and victories and part of his heart died with the word that she was gone. Another part suffered grievous injury at the sight of Genevieve's sorrow.

He almost flung the girl he was with aside, shouting at her how unutterably useless she was, but no, that would not do. He was on the verge of obtaining information that might be the difference between victory and defeat to England. Thousands of lives and the course of history might quite literally depend on his actions in the next few moments. It was too late to save Genevieve's injury; it was not too late for him to complete his appointed job.

He turned to the limpet on his arm, smiled sulfurously and said, "Shall we go in to dinner, my dear?"

"Stop fussing, Jolee," Genevieve said.

The maid laid aside the curling stick on a little marble plate. "Very well, Madame. But it is your wedding day and I thought you would wish—"

Genevieve put a hand over her eyes for a moment. "Yes. Yes, very well. Later. I have to write a letter, then I'll let you do what you will to my hair."

"Your dress is hanging—"

"Please, Jolee! Leave me alone for a bit," Genevieve pleaded.

When the maid had gone, Genevieve pulled open the delicate desk, assembled ink, paper, a quill pen, and a tiny jar of sand.

Dear Evonne, she wrote

No doubt it will be many months before this letter reaches you and I wish I could be speaking to you in person, but that is not possible. It may never be possible, I regret to say. My search for our mother has ended. When I reached France, she had departed on a long tour. I waited all winter for her return. But she did not return, nor will she ever. The party with whom she was traveling met their unhappy fates along a mountain road as they were returning. An avalanche.

I suppose you were right in advising me against this attempt to recapture the past and make it my future. Still, I would not have been content in my own conscience had I not tried to find her.

For many reasons, this has been an exceedingly difficult time for me, but I have hope for the future. You see, this is my wedding day. I am marrying a handsome, considerate man named André.

Genevieve laid aside her pen for a minute. What else should she say about André? What else *was* there to say? she asked herself brutally. That he would wrap her life in cotton wool, pamper her, keep her from danger—and adventure—forever. She felt a twinge of unreasonable longing. How foolish! she chided herself. Her adventures had led her only to heartbreak.

She would have no more.

She signed the letter, sealed it, and wept quietly for the briefest of moments before sending for Jolee to finish her hair.

It was very late that night, almost morning actually, before the newlyweds went to André's rooms. Freshly redecorated in Genevieve's honor, the apartment smelled of tuberoses and cinnamon with the faintest undertone of new paint and lemon oil.

Genevieve had moved, puppetlike, through the long service and longer hours of party and celebration afterwards. She wondered once or twice why everyone seemed to be enjoying themselves more than she was. She supposed that was only natural; none of the guests had made a lifetime commitment. To them it was just an excuse to order new clothes and have a fine dinner at someone else's expense.

André dismissed the servants and helped Genevieve remove her spangled tulle wrap. "I'm sorry Althea and Beaumarché couldn't have been present," he said.

Genevieve sighed. "Yes, it was a pity. I had a letter from Althea. She says she'll be back from Italy soon."

André poured them each a glass of Madeira. "I was surprised that Michael didn't run down for the week. I suppose he's very serious about that girl. Why else would it be so difficult to tear himself away?"

Why indeed? Genevieve wondered. Aloud she said, "I don't know." André need never suspect how relieved she had been when they received the short polite note of congratulation from him with the postscript that he regretted not being able to attend the ceremony.

André gestured toward the door of the bedroom. "There's a lovely view from the balcony."

They sipped their wine in the midsummer moonlight and made light, inconsequential talk about the guests that evening, about the success of the dinner, about the way the flower girl's dress had matched the blossoms she had carried. Finally, they reentered the bedroom and André discreetly disappeared into the adjoining dressing room. Genevieve disrobed and crawled between the whispery silk sheets. She didn't understand why she felt nervous. She was no blushing virgin. She'd been a married woman once—oh, so long ago . . . another lifetime, another Genevieve ago, it seemed. And had made love to Michael Clermont and later Robert St. Justine—she smiled a bit at the memory of that night at Piggy Feversham's. But this was different—so very different.

With Michael and with Robert, it had been a burst of passion. Unplanned, unsanctified, and for the simple unbounded pleasure of the act. This was so formal, almost cold-blooded. She sank into the downy bed, closed her eyes for a moment, tried to convince herself she was in love with André. Really in love. But she knew better.

Even that horrible night when she heard of Sabelle's death and André offered to marry her and protect her from any more hurts, she had known she didn't truly love him. She liked and respected him—a great deal, in fact. He was bright, witty in unexpected bursts, intelligent, superbly good-looking, and, most important, he wanted to take care of her—very good care. And if he was often unyielding, perhaps it merely showed a degree of strength she didn't understand. Quite a fine catalogue of traits. Certainly more than most women could ever expect in a husband. She was very fortunate to have won his heart, and who could tell? In time she might come to love him. She intended to try very hard to. She owed him that.

Tonight, more than ever before, she found herself wondering what he saw in her. What made her a better choice of wife than the many other women he must have known over the years? André was no inexperienced boy, falling headlong for the first girl who took his fancy. *I know his traits,* she thought. *But what are my own? I am courageous—no, I was courageous once. I won't need to be anymore. André will save me from the necessity. I was determined. I took risks to find my mother and help my friends and my sister.*

But she was thinking in the past tense. She *had been* all these things. She was, no longer, brave and determined. But she would be loyal to André. That much remained of the Genevieve she had been.

The moon cast a shimmering blue light on the dressing room door. Genevieve heard the snick of the door and watched as André stepped through. His smooth, hard body seemed almost to gleam in the watery light and Genevieve was struck once again by his powerful grace as he moved toward the bed and got in beside her. Everything about him made her think of a temporarily tamed wild animal of vast jungle beauty.

He kissed her once, very tenderly, then again. It was restrained, almost impersonal. His light touch on her body was cool, careful. He did not speak, did not even seem to quicken his regular breathing. She turned a little toward him, put her hand on his muscled shoulder, and then, before she quite realized what was happening, she found herself being gently pushed back. André rolled his body onto hers. He put his weight on his elbows, buried his face in her neck, and entered her. He began to move—rhythmically, slowly at first, then more quickly.

Still he said nothing. He made no sound. She put her arms around him, traced the muscles of his strong back. Perhaps he had expected her to dislike this and was trying, for her sake, to get it over with quickly. She would have to encourage him, assure him that this was to be an act shared and enjoyed, not just tolerated.

"André," she murmured, moving under him in unison to his movements. "André, wait—" but he moaned slightly and she felt a light dew of perspiration spring up on his skin. He arched his back, held for a moment, then moved away from her.

Genevieve was stunned. "André, what's wrong—?" she began, but he had rolled to his side of the bed. She heard his controlled intake of breath and a second later he had risen and gone back to the dressing room. He did not return for some time and then he was clad in an embroidered silk nightshirt. He said nothing of what had just happened, but got into bed, turned to Genevieve and said, "Good night, darling. Perhaps tomorrow we can go riding if the weather is nice."

Genevieve was awake for a long while. She should be grateful, she knew that. How much worse it would have been if André had demanded that she enjoy their physical relationship and she did not. But this —this was too strange to comprehend.

She recalled the excited whispers of some of the older, more experienced women at court when André's name came up in their gossip sessions. They were discreet enough that they didn't actually admit to having been his lovers, but Genevieve knew that some of them had. These women, high-bosomed peacocks, proud of their sexual prowess, chose their men as ruthlessly as their husbands chose fencing partners. They demanded skill and grace and challenge. They had apparently found it in André.

She had been wondering why he loved her—now she was left to contemplate *whether* he loved her. Could he behave so mechanically, so dutifully, if he felt anything for her? But he *had* married her. He need not have done so unless it was his heart's desire. She had not coerced him. In fact, she had offered him remarkably little encouragement.

She would talk to him frankly in the morning, she decided. But when she awoke, André was not in the bed. She heard him moving about in the dressing room and she hurriedly threw on a light robe and walked in to find him donning his shirt. She hadn't noticed in the pale moonlight that his back was lightly scarred and there were bruises on his shoulder. "André, what happened?" she asked.

He whirled, surprised, and hastily pulled his shirt together. "I didn't hear you," he said, quickly reverted to his cat-calm manner. "What do you mean, what happened?"

"Your back," she explained. "You're bruised."

"It's nothing," he said casually. "Just a fall from a horse the other day. I didn't think it bore mentioning."

But the bruises didn't look to Genevieve like the sort that might be incurred falling from a horse.

As the next days wore into weeks, Genevieve often

noted new signs of injuries. André never mentioned them and when she asked he simply said it was nothing, he bruised easily. They never quite got around to talking about their wedding night and since André remained unfailingly protective and to all other appearances, fond of her, Genevieve decided that she had no right to expect more. He made love to her on a regular basis. It was always the same as it had been the first time.

Sometimes, late at night, she felt a moment of smothering panic and wondered what was to become of her.

Genevieve's letter arrived on a bright Caribbean morning, but Evonne was not there to receive it.

The captain of the merchantman *Sweet Ladey* stood scanning the horizon. "Is the island in sight yet?" he shouted up to the crow's nest. "We've a load of goods and some mail for that lot."

"Not—aye, Sir, there she is. But . . . something appears to be amiss."

In a few minutes it became evident just how amiss things *were* on the island. It had been torched. Nothing green remained. What had once been a fecund paradise of jungle fruit trees and snug, whitewashed cabins was a charred line of stubble from end to end. Masts broke through the emerald water of the harbor. Rubble littered the once creamy sand where bodies and wreckage had washed ashore to lie festering in the tropical sun.

It was impossible to enter the harbor. The wharves were blackened stumps and the tattered white sails of a sunken vessel swayed gracefully beneath the waves of the bay. A sloppily painted sign was tacked to one of the masts that broke, split and charred, through the junk-strewn waters; it read THUS TO ALL PIRATES and was signed by orders of the governor of a nearby island.

A sunken ship, dead men, land burnt and salted.

The captain of the *Sweet Ladey* took the letter from his breast pocket, stared at it a moment, and let it drift down to sullen seas and the fish-festooned graves of forgotten men and women.

21

Michael moved through an interlocking maze of intrigue and espionage. He continued gleaning information from wives and daughters of political and military figures, burglarizing desks and government offices, and cultivating the friendship of men in high places.

He was shot at twice in the dark, but always managed to escape. Despite his stealth, French agents were on his trail and it was only a matter of time before they uncovered him. He was in a dangerous position, but could not quit, for he was close to the news he had sought for so long: Louis was planning a major summer offensive against England's chief ally, Austria. The question was—where and when?

Michael had spent enough months at Versailles to know the French army was in slovenly condition, poorly disciplined, with no one leader to organize efforts. The poor were taxed to starvation to support troops who were cheated by unscrupulous merchants. Supplies were rancid, insect-infested, overpriced. Soldiers came from the cream of nobility or else the depths of poverty—and refused to fraternize with one another. There were no commanders of sufficient power to pull them together.

André was a source of odds and ends of military information that Michael continually traced to other, more useful sources. It was natural that, with France hovering on the precipice of a European war, they should discuss the state of their country and André's minor governmental post.

At times it was difficult to remain civil to André; Michael would think of Genevieve in the blond

Count's arms and feel an unexpected, unreasoning wave of jealousy. He wanted to wreak juvenile cruelties on him, see him lose his frosty cat-composure for even the briefest of moments. His jealousy threatened to interfere with his work. The French agents were breathing combustible air down the back of his neck, always a scant step or two behind.

King Louis took ill in July and for a while the court—indeed, the entire country—waited with bated breath for the death or survival of their King and news of the impending war. During this time, Michael ascertained that troops were massed for the march on Vienna. He sent word to the Queen and ministers but took no chances—he also sent messengers directly to John Churchill, Duke of Marlborough, and head of English forces in Europe. Louis's army would have a searing reception on the banks of the Danube. Britain, Austria, and the Netherlands would be waiting with cavalry, infantry, and the most brilliant tacticians in the hemisphere.

In the shadows, Athenais de Montespan waited. Her spies and those of the defense ministry were circling for the kill, sharks who tasted blood on the waves and yet could not pinpoint the cause. Michael's nerves were frayed, but he continued portraying the same shallow fop as before.

He had no sooner betrayed the attack on Vienna when he uncovered something of equal interest. André passed him in the corridors, a bundle of papers in one hand and a valise in the other. "Taking a vacation, Count?" Michael inquired with forced cheer.

"No, the King's sending me to meet a board of Spanish ambassadors. In the event of a total European war, Spain's naval defenses need to be inspected and strengthened. One of the places I'll visit is Gibraltar. From what I hear, it's a military disaster—poorly garrisoned, badly fortressed, a genuine pushover."

"Yes, but who's going to push it over? Gibraltar's

quite safe. It hasn't fallen in years," Michael said coolly, wondering if André suspected and was trying to trap him. Michael was seeing French agents in everyone these days.

"Well, I shall find out when I arrive there."

"Yes, I suppose so. But your worries are for naught. Oh—enjoy your journey and tell the Countess farewell for me. She *is* traveling with you?"

"No. I don't want her enduring such rough travel."

They shook hands, then André went coasting quietly down the hall. Michael bit his lip, thinking hard. Gibraltar—the gateway to the Mediterranean. Who held the rock held that angry sapphire sea and all her shipping routes. What a prize! And yet—was he being baited? Suppose he followed André's lead only to send the navy into an ambush? Gibraltar could be impregnable with the proper defenses. Her sheer gray cliffs and lashing waves might keep nations at bay forever, if properly manned. But if things were as bad as André suggested . . . . George Rooke was still in charge of the British navy, and Rooke never traveled without a well-disciplined landing force.

By God, he thought tensely, hands in pockets as he strode briskly along. *I'd back Rooke against hell itself, let alone a sloppy garrison at Gibraltar. But if I'm wrong—*

There was only one way to risk an attack without blindly sending Rooke to disaster—he must present the news to Rooke and the Queen in person, lay his news before them, and see for himself what the decision would be. He hurried to his room and penned a note to his "mother," telling her he was coming home because he wanted to see for himself that she was recovering from her recent illness.

He posted the letter, packed, and publicly took off for Marseilles. Down the road twenty miles he changed identities and horses. The well-planned English dispatch service sent him riding hell-bent-for-leather to the coast on a series of racehorses bred for

no other purpose. He rushed aboard a waiting brigantine that hauled anchor and set sail before the captain had even assured himself of his guest's identity.

A few days later, Michael was kneeling before
Queen Anne and receiving the order to aid Admiral
Rooke in his conquest of Gibraltar. When he was
dismissed, he left the audience chamber, silent, at
Rooke's elbow. The old Admiral cocked a weather-
beaten eyebrow at him. "Bad defenses, weak walls,
inferior commanders. Blast rock to pebbles. Wanted
to for years."

"You think it's true, then, that Gibraltar can be
taken without wholesale slaughter on either side?"

"Hm?" Rooke said idly, stopping to peer out a
window. "Clouds?"

"Sir, I know you better than this. You're avoiding
the issue."

Rooke eyed him with what was very nearly a grin
of conspiracy. "Rain Sunday. Good wind. Sail early."

Michael tapped his foot nervously. Small things
were annoying him lately, things he would have once
paid no attention to. He was overwrought and realized it but he persisted anyway. "And what happens
if, due to my instructions, we go sailing into Gibraltar—and the entire fleet is sunk?"

Rooke cranked the window open, screwing his
countenance into a worried pucker as he held his
hand out. "Clouds early. Rain already." He leaned
back inside. Michael started to brush past him, exasperated and weary to the point of insolence, but a
solid object caught him at the waist. Rooke had
thrust out his knotted walking cane and blocked his
path.

"Fleet sinks, hang half-French spy from last remaining yardarm. Leave for crows. Sit with tankard
and pipe. *Watch* you." Their eyes locked, Michael's
wild with strain. Rooke lowered his cane and limped
goutily away like any other harmless gentleman with
his powdered wig swaying genteelly and his shoulders

squared for battle. He was muttering about clouds again.

André changed his mind and allowed Genevieve to accompany him on his travels.

They had only visited three Spanish fortifications when he was recalled by the King. There was a swift ship waiting in the harbor to take him back to Versailles for an intelligence job related to the Austrian attack. Genevieve stopped short in her tracks, arms in the air. "But our clothes and furniture—how can we leave them all behind?"

"You will have to stay here and pack. Catch the next trade vessel back to Versailles, darling. It might come in a month or so. I must run."

He gave her hand a cool, perfunctory kiss, donned his hat, and left. *Just like that,* Genevieve thought angrily. *He's returning to court without a backward glance and leaving me here on this dismal rock. Here I am with two maids and all our luggage—surrounded by soldiers, townspeople, and whores whose language I don't speak. He didn't even kiss me. His aloofness frightens me—I'm alone here and I don't like it. What will I do?*

She threw on her best lace shawl and went to watch the cold copper sun sink into the horizon behind Gibraltar.

Genevieve slept soundly in the big canopied bed. She had discovered, to her surprise, that she hardly missed André next to her in the night. Alone, she sprawled from corner to corner like a well-fed cat and dreamt of England and the Caribbean. Her distant dreams snapped and shattered at urgent hands on her shoulder. She opened sleep-swollen brown eyes to see one of her maids hovering nervously. "What is the matter?" Genevieve asked.

"Madame Comtesse—we are under siege."

"What?" Genevieve sprang from bed, heedless of

modesty, and ran naked to the window in the sweltering August dawn. Sails bobbed, silhouetted in the first gray of dawn. She heard thunder roll through the sullen heavens and thought, for a breathless moment, that the ships had opened fire. Then lightning split the sky and she saw that the tall ships had all they could do to keep upright in the dashing waters. "Who are they?" she cried.

"*Anglais,* Madame la Comtesse."

The Sunday morning bells tolled melancholy dirges as if in expectation of battle. Genevieve crossed herself as the mournful notes drifted down from the Lady of Europa chapel up the cobbled street. *Good God,* Genevieve thought, *I've been raised an Englishwoman but I'm married to a Frenchman—and an ambassadorial assistant at that! Where does that leave me? I'll be fair game just like all the other women.*

There was noise in the streets, stampede sounds of mindless fear and hailstones on clay-tiled roofs. "Gather all the money and sterling. Put that and all my jewelry in a small valise," she heard herself say coldbloodedly. "Fold my best ballgown and linens in that box. Get me a suit of men's clothes to wear—and you would be wise to do the same for yourselves. Women are prizes in a war; dressed as men we stand a chance. Don't stand there fish-eyed and gape-mouthed—move!"

Half an hour later, Genevieve was shepherding her shrill flock onto the street. In a man's black breeches and greatcoat, shapely legs encased in sleek cavalier boots, curls tucked under a scarf and plumed hat, she made a slim, intense young man. Her first idea, long before she stepped into the rain, had been to buy, steal, or simply take horses to get herself and her household to safety. Wearing one of André's swords and brace of duelling pistols, she took her small band of followers to the city paddocks, only to see the last of the horses disappear down the street under two portly dames with the same idea.

The houses stood with doors ajar, women streaming into alleys and lanes with no coherent plans. They clutched their prize possessions—casks of jewels trailing broken strings of pearls, ornate dinnerware with silver tongs and agate handles, bags of gold doubloons, heirloom tablecloths woven by forgotten great-grandmothers, sobbing babies, a hooded hunting falcon, faded gowns with mended gold lace and chipped amber buttons.

They milled, ewelike, while far away their men loaded cannons in the driving rain. Genevieve stopped and shot a hasty gaze about her. The Lady of Europa stood on the promontory above them, arms outstretched from the stone roof. The roof—Genevieve glanced about. The cottages and houses were wooden, with clay-tile roofs or worse yet, thatched tops. But the chapel stood slick and shiny in the downpour, walls and roof of slab stone reinforced inside with monstrous beams. The walls were two feet thick at their narrowest point—and there was a deep cellar behind the altar.

She climbed onto a paddock railing and shouted for silence. Then she told the women to bring swords, pistols, daggers, rocks, anything that would serve as a weapon. And she led them to the chapel.

Inside it was cool and thickly quiet. Genevieve barked orders, once again playing the fervent game of pretending she was Evonne. Only this time she did not need to ask herself how Evonne would act. She simply knew. She herded children and pregnant or old women into the cellar, then dragged carpeting and furniture over the trap door. Cannons were booming in the distance as she swore, cuffed, and ungently coerced her troop into obedience.

They broke out the windows and loaded every musket and pistol they had been able to locate. She showed them how to fire and reload. Then Genevieve led them in, piling pews, statues, and the altar itself against the double doors. Flying metal, cannonballs that blew a wide arc of jagged metal on impact, and chainshot were blasting into the walls of the fortress below. The chainshot, called two-headed angels, made her think of Evonne's ship and gave her a brief tremor of emotion amid her work.

Square-cut stones held by ancient mortar exploded under the shelling and tumbled to the surging sea below. Soldiers who had never seen battle before loaded cannons incorrectly and had them erupt in their faces. Massive bronze guns, heated too abruptly with no water to cool their orange-hot barrels, cracked and spat their metal hearts into the very sentry boxes they were supposed to protect. Genevieve, in the uppermost window of the steeple, saw tiny figures in the Royal Navy's crisply colored coats scaling the rugged face of Gibraltar. The town was all but deserted in the steamy glare of dying rain on smoldering streets.

"The bastards," she said aloud, clenching her fists on the splintery sill. "Those arrogant Spanish bastards, leaving villagers and military wives protected by inexperienced boys! They have signed our death warrants—they have sealed our doom by leaving the most important post in the Mediterranean understaffed and open to the first attack. And the French farmboys and dandies marching off to Austria—they are killing themselves. They are killing *us*!"

Evonne. What would Evonne do? Surrender was out of the question. It would mean women and children given freely to rape and slaughter. Genevieve had no illusions about men in war. Women belonging to the enemy were enemies themselves; rape was not lust but the inflicting of pain and shame on someone smaller, softer, more susceptible to suffering. She climbed back down to the center aisle with sparks of defiance in her once-kind eyes. "I want the chaplain's larder raided and a fire stoked. We are going to boil lard, oil, water, anything to keep them at bay. And we are going to fight, ladies—for our children, ourselves, and our friends. Now get that fireplace stoked and start tearing the pews apart."

They set about their tasks, Genevieve's Spanish maids continuing to translate orders and directions. The women built the fire and fed it, heating liquids, and chopping prayer benches to use for clubs. And then, as suddenly as it began, the battle outside ended. Gibraltar went queerly, clammily quiet but for the muffled tramp of racing feet on mud-cushioned cobblestones. It was the sound of death, the death of both the town and its pitiful defenders. To the hushed women, trembling in their sweaty refuge, a more horrible sound could not have been imagined.

"The town . . . is overrun," someone whispered. "It's only a matter of time before they take note of the—Blessed Mother! They're stopping and staring! They're coming up the hill!"

There was no need or time to say more. Coarse voices split the gaunt anxiety of the terrified women. They came alive to fear and the tense almost-anger of awaiting a fight for their lives. There came scufflings at the door, strainings against the bolted, barricaded wood. "Ho there—the chapel's locked up tight. Bet the women are in there."

"The Admiral said no rape or robbery."

"Where there's women, there's jewels and gold. Get something to batter this door down with. I've a taste for Spanish skirts."

"When more of them gather at the door, overturn that barrel of oil on them. But don't waste it until we have a good many under it," Genevieve ordered sharply. She climbed rapidly up in the steeple, crouching amid cold, door-sized bells and peering at the scene outside through louvered shutters. "They're coming with a cart to batter the door in. Get ready."

Men were pouring up the hill now, forgetting their orders in the lust for gold and victims. Genevieve waited until the cart was thudding against the doors before she shouted for the oil to be dumped. The hiss of it on the pavement was lost in a hellish cacophony of agonized male screams, swearing, the crash of the cart against the walls, and musketfire. Genevieve's shouted order had not gone unheard by the soldiers; they began to fire at the steeple.

Bullets whined off the bells about her with tortured musical notes of forced gaiety. Genevieve crouched and shouted for the women to open fire. Among clouds of powder, tense voices, and the low bark of musketfire, the pounding at the chapel doors began. Genevieve took aim on a soldier below and lit her musket. She cried out for her cohorts to pour the oil and boiling water till there was none left. She fired until her musket jammed, then made do with her long-barreled pistols.

She had enough ammunition left for three shots. Below her, in the insane commotion and blood, the doors were bending inward. Wood was growling and whining, nails popping, great, ragged chunks breaking off. Women in gore-splashed gowns of dainty muslin and satin raised empty muskets to swing as clubs. Swords of dead husbands, sons and fathers glinted in pink-nailed, plump little hands that had never raised anything more dangerous than tweezers. Genevieve felt a swell of hopeless pride choke her. They were beautiful, her doomed, delicate Amazons. She allowed herself the brief luxury of tears.

The barricade was breaking. Genevieve smeared smoke-stung eyes on her sleeve, the silver dragon buttons scraping her face. The doors were almost below her, the men would pour in under her feet. Another shell ricocheted off the nearest bell, sending a falsetto *ping* through her head. She rested a dirty, wet cheek against cold metal and grasped her sword, crouching for the leap that would take her down to defiant death.

The bells. The *bells*.

"Stand back!" she roared in a mighty voice, heaving her sword aloft. With a glint of naked steel she cut an arc through the acrid air, blade descending on the closest bellrope.

The doors gave way with a tormented shriek of burst hinges. Men swarmed into the powder-fogged church. At that precise moment Genevieve's sword bit through the final fibers of rope. The biggest bell plummeted to the flagstone aisles with a reverberating roar and ringing.

Still crying out for the women to keep back, Genevieve slashed the next rope and the next. Bells sang and bellowed as they fell, exploding through stone, timber, and flesh. Their combined voices sent the women screaming to their knees, hands clapped over throbbing ears. Genevieve leaped into the carnage. The deafened women staggered behind her with weapons aloft.

Every lesson taught her by Evonne and Kate rose to the surface, every feint, slash, thrust and parry she had ever seen or used. At first the men fell back from her charge, then, seeing her to be a woman and the most fiery of the band, closed in on her. Through the blistering din she heard two male voices raised against the violence. "Stop it! Orders of the Admiral! Any man persisting will be tried for mutiny," and a second, oddly familiar man's cry of, "Leave them alone! What if they were your own daughters and wives? Orders of the Admiral!"

Two sane voices opposing madness and blood. Hopeless. *Hopeless!* And yet those two men were cutting a swath through the crowd, coming to the aid of the women. Genevieve let them in, covered them, felt the jolts as they aligned themselves on either side of her. Together they held the crowd at bay, swords flashing. "Byng! On the left!" shouted one of them. A bitter chill scurried up Genevieve's spine. She chanced a glance through the uproar and saw that the man on her right was none other than Michael Clermont!

He returned her astonished stare a second, then

gave a whoop of reckless determination and plunged
into the battle, surrounded. She thought she heard
him yell for Commander Byng to find Rooke. There
were desperate men all around him. Genevieve threw
her plumed hat off, echoed Michael's wild cry, and
slashed her way to him. She put her back to his,
heart laughing and crying. Together they fought the
foe, minds and bodies working as one. There was
something savage in it, something brutal and sweet,
very like love and a proud sacrifice to save weaker
beings.

Her movements were slowing. Blood came from a
score of cuts and gouges; her sword arm quivered
spastically from weariness. Yet she fought on, knowing the perfect peace of going to her death with a
glorious, gallant man who felt the same way about
her. She did not know what made her sure of his
heart, she only felt the emotion so strong between
them, there could be no question. He called her his
chérie, his right arm, and killed a man too near her.

Then, with a tumult of cannons and muskets, the
fight was over. Byng and Admiral Rooke blasted
through the frenzied crowd of mutineers, demanding
their immediate surrender. A final sword caught Genevieve in the hip, a glancing blow but painful; she
slid on oil and the blood of others and fell.

Michael caught her and hefted her slender body
across his shoulder. She knew soft blackness and jolting as he took her away from the smoking devastation.
A final jolt. Deep, fragrant grass and solid ground
cushioned her aching body. Sobbing with half-dreams,
she struck him, fought, screamed. Then she collapsed
in his arms.

When she opened her eyes she saw Michael's
blood-and-dirt-streaked face above hers. "Oh, Gen—
Gen, my love—I didn't know you were here! I would
not have risked you, not for all the queens and admirals in England. You're hurt—you're bleeding!"

Without knowing how it happened, she had her arms around his neck and his heart on hers. Genevieve pulled him down and kissed him hungrily. The response was as fervent as her own despite their small, nagging wounds. In the aftermath of fear came crazed relief and desire that swept away all else. They clung together, drowning in an uncontrolled tide. She wanted him; she had been wanting him and fighting it a long time. After André's cool, uninvolved lovemaking, Michael's passion was doubly felt by her.

He was sliding her clothes off, ripping them when they balked, exploring her milky flesh with mouth and fingers. Such passion had not touched her in longer than she remembered. Genevieve ignited again and again, shattering and weeping even before he made love to her. It was violent the first time, then gentle and slow, a cool breeze drying the sweat, blood, and mud on their aching bodies and torn clothes. When they were spent, they said nothing, only relaxed, entwined, in the long, cold grass.

Genevieve had opened her mouth to speak when there was a small explosion in the turf at their sides. They rolled and sat, grabbing for clothes and weapons. Michael gaped at the stony face of Admiral Rooke. "Orders not to molest females. Mutiny. Grounds for shooting. Wife of ambassador. Infuriate Frenchies."

Genevieve, clutching her ripped shirt, flung herself in front of Michael. "No! You mustn't shoot him! It wasn't rape, he didn't force me, I—"

Rooke cocked a puzzled eyebrow at her. "Englishwoman? *English*? No French accent? Pointed out as ambassador's wife!"

"I—I am," she mumbled, crimson-faced as she hurried into some clothing.

"Not have French come screaming for blood. Get you back to women—all under guard now. Whisk you home. Get away, Clermont. Otherwise arrest you."

"But she—"

Soldiers were running up with muskets. "Wife of ambassador," Rooke replied flatly. Genevieve was rushed away under guard. A despairing Michael's last glimpse of her was a lovely, bruised face over a trooper's shoulder. Then Rooke took him back to the ship.

Part Three

FURLED SAILS

22

Genevieve had been alone at Gibraltar for a fort-night before the attack and it was another six weeks before she returned to the palace of Versailles. It was, therefore, going to be difficult to explain to André how she happened to be pregnant.

Eight weeks was too long a time for a woman to miscalculate during pregnancy, wasn't it? She went back to André's cold lovemaking and ground her teeth against the deadness it caused her soul. She was well and truly in love—but not with her husband. Her heart bounded and despaired whenever she thought she had heard Michael's voice.

But it was always a mistake, a trick of the ear, for she didn't hear his voice again after that night at Gibraltar. When Admiral Rooke took him away, he must have immediately taken him out of the country. It was understandable, she told herself in more sen-sible moments. He had been seen aiding the British— seen and recognized by a number of people.

But in the weeks that followed she comforted her-self with the belief that somehow he would get back to her. Even though he would be known now to have been a British sympathizer, probably a British spy, he would get a message to her. Somehow! Once or twice she wondered, ever so briefly, if she was delud-ing herself. *Perhaps,* a small evil voice whispered in the back of her mind, *perhaps it meant nothing to him.* A quick tumble in the grass? *But no,* she would tell the voice. *No, it meant as much to him as to me. That sudden white heat of passion was the manifes-tation of something deep and sincere. To me—and* to him. *Wasn't it?* Now she knew her own heart, but would she ever know his?

She feared that André would immediately sense the change in her. She would tell him, of course, when Michael returned for her or sent a message to meet him. But she dreaded it. She did not want to hurt André. He had been kind to her in his odd, icy way.

But André did not note any difference in his wife. He was too preoccupied with other problems. All of France was preoccupied. Genevieve had left a glittering, sapphire society and returned to find it broken-winged and decimated. Shortly after the British attack on Gibraltar, the French army had been trapped and destroyed at the little village of Blenheim, just outside Vienna. It had been a bloody rout. Michael had wondered why he found so little information about organization of the army. The British and their Allies found out why. There *was* no organization.

Thousands of Frenchmen were killed, regiment by regiment, as they stood awaiting orders that never came from commanders who had no idea what they were supposed to be doing. They were the *crème* of the culture and they were dead now. Young men—farmers, cobblers, lawyers, eldest sons of noble families—all were now dead.

France was on her knees.

Genevieve returned to Versailles only to tell her dearest friends good-bye. Robert was whisking Felicia off to England. A mob of villagers, grief-maddened, had pelted their country home with rocks and threatened to burn it because Robert was English. Felicia's frail health could not endure such a life. Robert would come back later, in the winter sometime, to arrange for the rest of Felicia's belongings to be sent.

The day they left, Althea came to Genevieve's apartments. She was plainly dressed in an unadorned traveling suit of a mournful charcoal and her flamboyant blond hair was confined to a neat bun at the nape of her neck. Missing also was her usual bubbling exuberance. "I'm leaving tonight. I dare not stay. I wanted you to know," she said.

Genevieve pulled the heavy doors shut so that no one could hear them. "You and Michael helped bring this about, didn't you?" she asked.

Althea paled. "It seemed political," she said very softly. "An elaborate game of plans and strategies. I didn't know—" She shook her head, was silent for a moment, then looked at Genevieve with her usual bright smile. "I'm to be arrested tomorrow, if the gossips are to be trusted, and I hear the dressmakers in French prisons are terribly behind the times. It's an appointment I believe I ought to miss. Don't look so alarmed. I can get out safely—I think."

"I will pray for you," Genevieve said. "Althea— what of Michael?"

"I don't know. My communications to England have broken down. Last word I had was that Rooke had hauled him back to England after Gibraltar, though why he'd mind leaving I can't guess," she answered. But there was an odd, questioning look in her eye. When Genevieve said nothing, Althea went on. "Louis's ministers may not be the intellectuals of the age, but they *have* figured out who got the information England needed for the victory at Blenheim. He's a dead man if he ever sets foot in France again. I shall write to you when I get back. I'll let you know if he is safe."

The letter arrived in November. It was chatty, full of fluff and fashion—typically Althea. The last paragraphs said:

> You remember I told you about my sister's boy Angus and all the escapades he was always getting into? Well, he's really done it this time. Has the whole family in a tizzy. He was supposed to have an audience with the Queen. Some school honor or other. But poor dear Anne was suffer-

ing another of those endless female complaints
and he was left to cool his heels for just weeks
and weeks.

Seems the delay just put the silly boy right off
his head. Disappeared. Really! He just went
"poof." His parents are behaving as though it's
the end of the earth, they're *such* worriers. I
keep telling them he's just fallen in love with
some chit of a girl someplace and has run off
to be petted and soothed. I do hope the girl
will have the sense to wrap him up in brown paper and sturdy twine and send him back to his
poor mother. She gets such awful itches, really
quite unbearable, when she's upset.

Genevieve would have known what the letter meant.
She would have instantly understood that Angus was
Michael and his parents were the government.

Unfortunately, *she* did not see the letter.

"You shall, of course, be amply rewarded for this,"
Athenais de Montespan said to André's butler, one
of her private army of spies. "So the Count and his
wife are now living at his Paris home." She folded
Althea's letter and turned to the other men at the
table. "I want the house watched. Take him quietly
when he gets there. I don't want the Count and his
pretty little wife to know when 'Beaumarché' is arrested—not until it's too late."

She hoisted herself, puffing and wheezing, from
her chair and tossed Althea's letter into the fireplace.
More than one of the men at the table felt a shiver
of fear at the sound of her mad, crackling laughter.

Genevieve tied a ribbon around the last package.
In a week it would be Christmas—a joyous time, but
there was so little joy in her life. Only a great, cold
emptiness where her heart ought to be.

She had told André she was with child when it became obvious. He had not seemed to notice yet that she was further advanced than she should be. He had been thrilled with the news of the child and even happier when he got an appointment to England. He was to join the French ambassador's staff there.

Genevieve had felt a brief flame of hope when he told her the news, but it flickered and died quickly. *If* Michael was safely in England, and *if* he had wanted to contact her, surely he could have done so by now. She swung between the belief that he had perished and the belief that he simply didn't care for her as she had thought. Either alternative was unthinkable.

Genevieve put the package in the chest and closed the top just as André came in. He shook the snow off his cape, greeted her with a light kiss, and sat down before the fire, rubbing his hands to warm them. "How was Versailles?" Genevieve asked, mechanically attempting to show interest.

"More like before. The old gaiety is beginning to come back. It will never be the same again, though. Say, I heard something interesting today. You remember Beaumarché?"

Genevieve's heart lurched and she felt herself becoming the slightest bit faint. This would not do. "Beaumarché?" she said as coolly as she could. "Oh, yes. Michael. What about him?"

André poured himself a glass of brandy and took an appreciative sip. It seemed to take days. "Well, it turns out he wasn't French at all. English. He could have fooled me. He *did* fool me, actually," he said coldly. He obviously regarded Michael's treachery as a personal insult.

"Imagine that," Genevieve said, trying to match his tone.

"Well, he won't be fooling anyone else. That's certain."

"Why is that?"

"He's been arrested."

"What!" Genevieve cried.

"Genevieve! What's wrong?" André asked, instantly on his feet.

She sat down quickly in the nearest chair. "Nothing! I—I just—please, I didn't mean to alarm you. I just felt a slight pain. It's passed now."

"Let me call the doctor—your maid—" André was all concern.

"No. I'm fine now. Just a muscle cramp. Please, just sit here with me and tell me about Mi—Vicomte Beaumarché."

André sat, held her hand, and regarded her gravely. "Are you sure you feel all right?"

She nodded, impatience searing her. "Please go on."

"Go on? Oh, yes. Beaumarché. Well, there isn't much more. They'll hang the man, of course. Nasty business. The odd thing is, they arrested him here in Paris, only a block or so from here I think. I wonder why he didn't have the sense to clear out of France."

"Where is he?" Genevieve's throat was so dry she could hardly get the words out.

"In the Bastille. Why do you ask?"

"Just wondering where they had sufficient guards for a spy of that magnitude," Genevieve said.

"Let's talk about something more cheerful. I think this is upsetting you. I'm sorry I brought it up. Come, let's eat and you can get to bed early. You look so pale. Are you sure you feel—"

She wanted to scream, *Leave me alone!* but she bit it back, put on a brave smile, and allowed André to take her arm and escort her to dinner. But her mind was racing and plans were already forming—she knew better than to hope she could save him, but she could at least see him. She had to tell him of her love, for now she knew it was reciprocated. He had been arrested near their Paris home and André thought it merely a coincidence.

But Genevieve knew the truth. Michael had come for her.

Genevieve stepped hesitantly down the slimy, winding stairs of the Bastille. It had taken a great deal of money to bribe the jailers and guards as well as a good deal of sneaking and lying to escape her household. She was half sick with fear and uncomfortable pregnancy as she bundled her bulky cloaks closer about her puffy figure.

The jailer's torch cast flickering, furtive shadows about the clammy walls. Genevieve kept her loaded pistol concealed in the folds of her dress as she followed him. The prison keepers were men of little refinement and she wanted no trouble. Deeper they went, down into the unlit bowels of the feared Bastille, down the cagelike compartments where the most dangerous felons were kept. Above, in the better rooms, a man had lived and died in an iron mask, and a year ago, been taken to Père la Chaise cemetery and entombed forever in the grotesque, face-fettering hood of callous metal. Genevieve shuddered as she thought of that nameless prisoner's uncommon doom. And yet he had known a more merciful end than Michael Clermont would.

"Here you be. I will leave a lit torch with you," the keeper said. He touched his fiery wand to a stick in a wall socket and left. Genevieve peered into stagnant darkness.

"Michael? Michael Clermont? Michael, it's Genevieve Faunton."

In her worry she had forgotten her married name, forgotten André completely. There was a stirring of shackles on stone floors, a rasping cough in the blackness behind the floor-to-ceiling iron bars. "Genevieve?" came a hoarse whisper. Tears started up in her round brown eyes.

"Yes, Michael, it's me. I've brought you food and wine and—I wish I'd thought to bring you candles.

I didn't know it was dark. I knew it would be cold, though—I brought a spare cloak, I'm wearing it—wool socks, too, and a flask of hot tea and brandy."

"You angel."

He said it with a chuckle, almost like his old self. The chains clattered and clanked, then she saw his hands lock about the bars. Beyond that, his face was almost unrecognizable—unshaven, all bones and bruises with scars and scabs. "My God—they've been beating you!" she gasped.

"Torturing, actually. There's a distinction, you know. Beating implies brutal abandon—torture refers to applied cruelty and—"

"Stop it!" she cried, flinging herself against the bars. She took his bony blistered hands in hers and covered them with teary kisses.

"What the devil are you doing here, Gen?"

"Obeying the Bible. Comforting the ill and imprisoned. Sassing the defenseless. It's cold as the Thames in December in this place—here, take this cloak. And the hot tea with brandy—here you are."

"Blessed woman." He managed to shrug into the cape with a semblance of his courtly manners, despite shackles and pain.

In the torchlight she saw the appreciation on his haggard face as he tilted the brandy flask up and let hot, sweet liquid pour down his parched throat. His throat. There were marks there, too. Genevieve made a small choking sound. "Michael. Come here, Michael, put your arms through these bars and hold me as close as you can."

He obeyed, pulling them into a heartfelt, uncomfortable embrace with chains and metal bars biting into their bones. "I love you," he said, face in her hair. "I love you and probably always have. You are the one woman I could have spent forever with—and now I have only a few minutes with you. A few more days and—never mind, chérie, don't cry. I can't bear it when you cry and I'm helpless to comfort you."

"I love you, too, Michael Clermont or Freddie or Viscomte Beaumarché or whoever the hell you really are. Oh, Michael! It was a mistake to marry André, I know that now. You're the one I love, you're the one I can't live without!"

"You don't have much voice in the matter, darling," he replied, twining her curls about his fingers. "Louis is having me executed Saturday and you're Countess de Lieuvienne—you have a husband and a future."

"And you have a chance," she whispered, eyes closed, lips to the pulsing vein at the side of his neck. "Robert's going to the Queen. He's here in Paris, settling some legal matters. I stopped and talked to him on my way here. Perhaps it won't happen Saturday—a postponement?"

He disengaged himself with a jolt. "What? St. Justine's gone to Kensington? Even if there were time, she'd still deny me."

"But you're England's premier agent—"

"Not any longer. My face is known, I'm a marked man—and, as such, am of no further use to Queen Anne. Althea got out safely, then? And the Beaumarché family in Marseilles?"

"Yes, they're all in England, Robert says. The Queen will help you, Michael. I know she will. A king I wouldn't count on—but a woman has more mercy than a man."

He kissed her chin, her eyes, her mouth. "Ahh, darling, you only think that because you've never jilted a woman. They're not always merciful."

"She'll help you, I know. And we'll go away together."

"You'd leave André for me?"

"Yes. Now and forever. We'll get you out and leave Versailles far behind. I love you, Michael!"

He kissed her, deep and gently. "I love you, too, Genevieve, but I know I will die Saturday. I don't believe the Queen will help me. But *you* can."

"How? Anything!" she pledged, kissing him again.

He took her face, glistening with tears between his tormented hands. In the background, green water trickled down cracked walls and a prisoner groaned.

"Gen, I found a clue to my parents. The man named Matthew, I mentioned him long ago when you and I discussed our families—the man who moved me from place to place when I was young." He said it, she thought achingly, as if he were an old, ruined man with no vista but the grave. "He left word that he would wait for me every year. I narrowly missed him last year. If you would go in my stead—Genevieve, a man can't die without knowing his name!"

"Yes, I'll go. Where and when?" she asked, blocking her ears to the stealthy scuttle of rats in the dark.

"Joan of Arc's forest—the woods of Domrémy-La-Pucelle. He waits all night on the winter solstice, that's the twenty-second of December, tomorrow night. He said to wear a white plume in my hat so he'd know me. You could do it, I've seen you in breeches—my own, in fact."

She thought of the new roundness of her stomach, pushing at stays and paniers. She was not heavy yet, but the child was beginning to show. *Our child,* she thought. *I can't tell him or he'll worry too much. He won't want me going to Domrémy, he'll fret and grieve that he's made a child as nameless as himself.* "Yes," she said with forced gaiety, "I make a dashing young rake if I say so myself."

The jailer was returning. Genevieve hurriedly gave Michael all she had smuggled in for him. He refused the pistol, saying it might serve her better than it would him. Escape would be impossible with a *dozen* pistols. She kissed him and reluctantly left at the heels of the taciturn keeper. "Wait," Michael cried. She turned to see him twist something off a bruised finger. "My ring," he said. "Show it to him as proof. Find out what it means."

She promised and was taken away up twisted black stairs.

* * *

It was one of the worst winters France had ever known. It was not enough that France should have been defeated and dispirited at Vigo, Blenheim, and Gibraltar; it seemed as if the weather must join in scourging the country. Too many farmers had been drafted for the attack on Austria, the country was hungry with no one to gather crops now buried under a foot of snow.

Genevieve passed terraced fields with scraggling skeletons of grapevines standing dismally in the crusty snow. Cattle lowed for hay that never came, spindly sheep bleated over dead lambs. France was blindly staggering toward complete catastrophe while the court of Versailles continued fêting their lavish way through a winter that left the peasants lean and diseased.

The roads—the few that existed—were covered with drifters and brigands. Genevieve, in men's woolen underwear topped by the riding clothes of a prosperous rake—velvet suit, suede greatcoat, and fur-lined cape— rode staunchly on through blizzards and highwaymen. She had to fire at a roadside robber whose companions then shot her guide and gave her a heart-straining half-hour chase through the snow.

Once, when a blizzard grew too severe for travel, she dug through three feet of hard-packed snow, scooping out a cave for herself and the two horses. Then she forced the animals to lie down, heaped them with her blankets and cloaks, and crawled in between them. Within a short time, their body heat had warmed a deliciously cozy space. They slept the night like that. In the morning there was another half foot of snow atop them. It had insulated them nicely against the chill.

Cramped, hungry, dizzy, Genevieve clawed her way out and opened her supplies. She fed the animals first, then ravenously devoured dried fruit and strips of highly spiced dried beef. A fire was difficult to build but she managed a small one, heating watery gruel and melting snow for the horses to drink. Then she loaded the packhorse, swung onto her stocky hunter, and guessed her route to the nearest town.

There were no guides willing for employment in such weather. When she inquired, she was guiltily aware of her fine clothes and horses. Townspeople cast covetous looks at her rich, warm garb and fat steeds. She realized with a cold tremor that these hungry villagers would not be above killing her for money, clothing, and horsemeat. She spurred to the wind and rode away at a gallop.

Compass and instinct led her onward. She nearly missed Domrémy. At the last moment, she saw a distant steeple through hand-sized snowflakes and turned. The place was small, silent, bolted against wolves and equally dangerous justiciars who forcibly took crops, livestock, and young men for the army. Genevieve, dull and sick with frost and the strain of travel on her pregnancy, turned her horses toward the twisted trees that showed ghostlike through a veil of snow.

The oaks of Domrémy waited, crouched like deformed old ogres dragged to the ground by age and their own weight. Genevieve hobbled her horse under one, fed them the last of the oats and bran, and pitched her tiny tent. She was too tired to build a fire or worry about whether or not she'd arrive on time. Chills and cramps knotted her up on the floor of her makeshift tent. She bundled up in her marten-lined cloak and fell into a disturbed sleep.

It was dark when Genevieve woke. A horse whinnied—not one of her own, she could hear her hunter and his friend insecurely snuffling about the tent flap in search of food. She rolled to her feet, groping in the saddlebags at her feet for the white ostrich plume she'd brought. It took mere seconds to pin it to her cap and crawl out to face the night.

It was utterly still. Genevieve drew a deep, tense breath and was surprised how loud it sounded. The snow had ceased, there was no wind, no noise—only crisp, ominous silence. She loaded her pistols and turned her cape cowl up to her ears, trying to assume what she considered a masculine stance. She stood, feet apart, shoulders squared, on her toes to look taller. It was difficult to act cocky when four and a half months pregnant.

Brittle snow broke crisply under the weight of neat steel-rimmed hooves. A cloaked roan rider on a lean roan horse was regarding her through the trees. Genevieve set her jaw, forgetting it didn't show through the raised cape collar.

The horse, an old one and used to this journey, picked its way gingerly through the drifts. In another minute it loomed above her, breath forming white clouds in the taut purple air. "I am looking for someone," the thin man said. Genevieve reached in her breeches pocket and took out Michael's ring. She held it up to the gray-and-ginger-haired rider in the palm of a thickly gloved hand.

He took it, regarded it a while, then flipped his cloak open to reveal a pistol aimed at her heart. "You are not the one I seek, your eyes are the wrong color. Tell me what you are doing with the ring and tell me *now*."

She dropped the cowl from her face and heard his sharp intake of breath at the realization of her sex. "You've got to help me," Genevieve blurted out. "Michael's in prison and they're going to execute him Saturday! I've sent someone to the Queen of England on his behalf, but he doesn't think she'll help him. He said to find you so he'd know who he was before he died!"

"Prison? Executed? What crime has he committed?"

"He—" There was no time to fence the issue, even if this man was the most loyal Frenchman on the face of the earth. "He's an English agent. He's been tried and convicted of high treason."

The man doubled up as if in agony. She heard his

incoherent noises of pain and frustration as he pounded a clenched fist on the pommel of his saddle. "No!" he cried, forcing himself upright. "No, I have let this go on far too long! The irony of his work and treason—the irony! Young woman, saddle a horse and leave your belongings, we must ride to prevent an even more horrible crime than treason—a crime so terrible that the penalty is eternal! Hurry!"

The end.

Michael stood on the ebony-draped scaffold, wrists bound behind him, noose resting loosely about his neck. He stood with booted feet slightly apart, well-balanced, steady to all appearances. He alone knew how dizzy, sick, and tired he was. Starved, mistreated —but not afraid. Oddly enough, not afraid at all.

He gazed calmly out at the judges and crowd, wondering with a detached sense of curiosity how he could be so cool about his fate. *Duty, I suppose,* he thought. *Dying for one's country and all. I did what they sent me to accomplish. French power is broken. The lives and futures of far too many people have been affected by my acts. And yet . . . I served my ultimate purpose, as far as the world is concerned.*

Roque, Garlanda, Robert, Althea, Sabelle. His dearest friends; would they ever learn of his end? Genevieve. She twisted his feelings, knotted something inside him. She could have been forever. At least he had the bitter poetic satisfaction of going to his grave knowing she loved him as he loved her. If he'd known earlier! If he'd only known—but then he would have faltered in his work, perhaps abandoned his mission. It would have meant the loss of his integrity, the betrayal of all he believed in and stood for. No. Better to have found her this late. There was a chance for her this way, time for her to heal. And he had done his work, done it far too well.

It was hot in the execution chamber. Darkness rose and fell before his eyes as the sentence was read. His breathing came hard. Yet he still held himself regally, head up, posture unaffected. It was easy for onlookers to believe him a viscomte or better. Princes died with less grace. The audience buzzed and droned like wasps massing at a dying tree, waiting for that final exhalation of life before they moved in to build squalid nests and fell to squabbling. Vultures, jackals, second-hand predators, they waited, eager-eyed for the kill.

Some of the crowd was deeply affected by the sentence. He saw, among the premature mourners, women he had wooed and men he had befriended. He had laughed with these people, amused them, listened to their problems, and counseled them to the best of his ability. The women unashamedly let tears glisten and spill into wadded lace handkerchiefs while the men stood white-fisted and wounded.

Genevieve. Oh, Genevieve! Michael was glad she was not present. Matthew. Had she found Matthew? Was Matthew alive? He felt a dim, pain-blunted sorrow that he would never know his identity, never learn who had given birth to him, perhaps loved him. No origins, no past, only this time, this place.

They had finished reading his list of heinous crimes. Michael agreed with them. Had a French spy affected a similar disaster upon England, Michael would have condemned him with the rest. Politics was a business he understood too well. They were doing the right thing in condemning him. He did not expect the remotest trace of sympathy or clemency, but he had badly wanted Matthew's news before the end.

The end. They were tightening the noose. The chaplain was reading from a tiny, crack-covered Bible with split binding.

The end. The chaplain was finished and glad of it. There was no forgiveness in his patriotic eyes. Michael was not offended by the hypocrisy; he could not believe in the chaplain's promised salvation. He had the wry, giddy thought that it made them even.

The end. The noose was snug, knot resting on the vein behind his ear. The stained black velvet hood was dropped over his head, cushioning him in the stifling darkness and dried sweat of long-dead felons. It was like being smothered. He could not see, could barely breathe or hear or feel. For the first time he was afraid, wanted to shriek, beg, lash out. If they had only left his head uncovered—!

Footsteps. He heard the muffled tread of the masked executioner crossing the scaffold, the slap of leather-gloved hands on the lever that would release the trap door and Jean-Michael Clermont's soul for eternity. He tasted his own sweat in the stale, gagging stuffiness of the velvet hood, counted the remainder of his existence in raw, grasping fractions.

The trap floor creaked beneath him, waiting to open like the maw of a hungry hell. Michael swayed, then straightened, every nerve stretched tortuously taut. He was ready to snap, his courage as fragile and endangered as his neck. The rope was rough—then he could no longer feel it. Oxygen was almost non-existent. Blood. He bit his lip and could feel its warmth but not taste the salty metallic tang. Blood. The end. The *end!*

And then a tumultuous roar. The creak of the trap door lever. A mighty voice rang out, sonorous and terrible: *"Who dares presume to murder my son?"*

He fell into blackness.

23

Aching and trembling with fatigue and wire-tight nerves, Genevieve followed Michael's father and Matthew to the execution chamber. At first she could see nothing but a somber-visaged crowd. Were they too late? She pushed her way between people and saw the black-hooded figure. That had to be him, but what a horrifying travesty of all that was right. The noose rested snakelike around his neck and Genevieve could sense her vision swimming. She felt a sharp pain at the small of her back that seemed to burn its way around her sides and center in her abdomen. She sucked in her breath and gritted her teeth.

It had been only seconds since they stepped through the doors but it had seemed eternities. The old man beside her shouted something, something about his son, but she was so faint she could hardly grasp what it was. There was a shocked silence for a moment, then with the last of her failing sight she saw the hooded figure drop from sight!

They'd been too late!

She felt a trickle of something hot and sticky on her thighs, and the world telescoped into a fine point of light. As she fell, she reached out for support and found none.

When she awakened she was on something soft. She tried to open her eyes, but the light hurt. She heard someone moaning and sensed vaguely that it was herself. A voice. Someone else's. "Keep still. The doctor is on the way," André said.

"What happened?" she mumbled.

His voice was sharp and cold. "I don't know. A friend brought you here, dressed in rags and bleeding. A friend of yours, I might add. She would not say where she had met you. Where were you? Where have you been the last few days?" The question had a cutting edge that seemed to slice through her.

She raised her hands to her temples. "Oh, André—please. Please don't ask. I feel so—so awful. I must know. Did he die?"

"Did *who* die?" André took her hand in a painful grip. "Genevieve! What were you doing? What are you talking about?"

She sensed his fiery anger, could almost understand it, but at the moment it didn't matter. "Did he die?" she asked again.

"You must be out of your head," André said in a tone that was half disgust, half pity. "I think I hear the doctor at the door. Lie perfectly still. He may be able to save the baby."

It took long dark minutes for the meaning of this statement to sink in. Save the baby. *Dear God, I'm losing Michael's child!* Genevieve thought. Suddenly the pains seemed to be shooting through clear to the core of her soul. "No, no, *no!*"she cried out hysterically to the empty room.

For a long while it was a cottony black void. Nothing tumbling over . . . nothing sliding through . . . nothing swimming in nothing slipping against—
Endlessly, endlessly.

And yet, there *were* minute traces of sensation sometimes. A hint of scent. Smoke? The faintest echo of silk against silk. Blacker shadows moving against the infinite black landscape.

The sensations slowly began to cling and grow and form subtle shapes like mineral accretions over eons in dark caves. Gradually, Michael gained the knowledge that he was *somewhere*. Did death, perhaps, feel like being somewhere? But he was breathing. He was aware of the shallow, automatic rhythm of his body. Breathing. Then he was alive. But how?

Someone spoke. A hesitant whisper. "He's waking."

Then careful muffled footsteps, the faint creak of a door opening and closing. Michael opened his eyes slightly. It took all his strength. Cupids, angels, fluffy bits of cloud. Good God! He *was* dead. Then, as his vision began to clear and focus, he realized the truth. He was in a bed. A very grand bed with a vista of heavenly scenes painted on the wooden canopy. Alive. *Alive!*

"Son?" the voice came from his right. "Jean-Michael? Thank God I stopped them in time. Lack of air—the hood—you collapsed—"

He turned his head. Darts of pain exploded in his neck and he had to clench his teeth tightly to keep from crying out. There was a richly dressed old man sitting at the side of the bed. His hair was thin and white and the age freckles on his head showed through.

"Do not fear," the man said in a voice like old parchment. "You will not be harmed here."

Michael's mind was beginning to clear and he had the vague feeling the man was familiar, or would be, if only something was different. But what?

"Who—?" he said through cracked lips, but could get no further.

The old man took his hand, gently patted it. "Don't talk, my son. I will do the talking and you must listen carefully, for you will not be safe for long, even under my protection. Can you understand me?"

Michael nodded. But he didn't understand.

"You are my son. I was in love with your mother, Marie-Angélique Scorailles. I made her the Duchess de Fontanges. Completely in love as never before or since. She was so beautiful, so fine of feature and carriage. Blond, an angel's tread, a saint's frailty. You have her eyes. I should have seen it immediately— you wear the ring I gave her—a personal signet to seal our love letters—"

The man went on about his love and Michael turned his head a little to relieve the pain. Suddenly,

hearing the man instead of seeing him, he knew the
voice. Why hadn't he realized immediately? The wig.
Of course, that was it. He always wore the long, luxuriant curled wig. With it he was truly majestic, powerful, sparkling. But without—without it, without his
court, his armies, Louis XIV, the Sun King was merely
a tired, defeated old man sitting at the bedside of the
son he'd never known. The son who had helped destroy his country!

Michael tried to sit. Of all the men on earth who
might have been his father, why *this* man? He could
not believe it.

"No. No, you must rest a bit more, Jean-Michael.
Let me finish. I've waited years to tell you this, to explain. I had given up hope of ever seeing you. Listen,
please listen—and remember. When you were born
your mother was ill. She was a frail girl, not meant
for childbearing. I feared, and rightly as it turned out,
that she might die. Athenais was jealous—madly, wickedly jealous. I had to get you away somewhere so that
you would be safe until you were older.

"I meant only to protect you," he said, tears for a
long dead past in his voice. "I wanted to save you from
harm, but look what has come of it."

He stopped for a moment, unable to go on. Michael
could hear him taking a long, shaky breath before he
continued. "I asked a man from the stables, one of the
few people I knew I could trust, to take you away. To
hide you and look after your interests until I could
bring you back, but—"

"I know. The fire—" Michael said. His strength was
creeping back in a slow trickle. "Who put up the head-
stones?"

King Louis shrugged. "Athenais, I must assume, just
as I must assume she had the fire set. She must have
thought Matthew would note them and tell me you
were dead; that way I would never look for you. It
would have worked except that Matthew had visited

the family just before the fire and knew you had already disappeared."

Michael had begun to tremble. The true depth of his deeds smote him. "Dear God! What have I done? I've betrayed France—I didn't know—I didn't—"

"Hush now," the man soothed. "You could not have known. It was my fault. I should have plucked Athenais's claws long before you were born. Now it is too late. As for betrayal," King Louis hesitated, fumbling for the words. "It is, I believe, a Divine Justice. I betrayed you—I abandoned you, a mere babe. It was done for the best of reasons, but it was still wrong. You, the son of my most beloved, are the one who led to the destruction of my country. You are not at fault. It is merely some part in the plan of a vengeful God. A vast scale of right and wrong has tilted and you could not help what side you were on. Fate. Cursed Fate!"

"I *am* a traitor to my own country!" Michael said, anguished, fists clenched.

"Yes, you are," the King said sadly. "*I* can excuse. *I* can understand and accept. But—but I cannot live forever. I'm old, son. Others will not be so understanding nor so caring of you. You stand on the precipice of death." He leaned closer. "I could not save you then. I *shall* save you now." It had the sound of a royal decree. "You will rest another hour, then I will have you taken to a place of safety. In a few months, when you are better and the hue and cry has died down, I will arrange for you to be sent back to England."

"No, please. There is someone I must see. I must leave France now with—"

"No!" the old man said. He'd been obeyed for many, many years in everything he said. It had become a habit too deeply ingrained to change. "You will see no one and there is no disguise good enough to allow you to be transported across France right now. You will remain hidden—by force if necessary." His tone softened then, but the determination was still there. "I will save you this time. I failed before. I will not fail now! There is so little time. Let us talk like a father and son for a few minutes. We will never have the chance again, and there is so much I must know about you."

Michael's head was throbbing with pain and the shock of finding out who he was. It seemed too incredible to be true—perhaps he would wake again later and find that this had merely been a dream, a nightmare of a fevered imagination. He looked into Louis's rheumy eyes. This was not, at this moment, a king. This was a sad, defeated old man who had lost, regained, and lost again the child of the woman he loved most. Michael did not intend to let Louis "protect" him, but neither was he going to argue about it. For now he wanted also to talk like a father and a son for the first and only time in his life.

"Tell me, son, where have you been? Who are you now?" Louis asked.

And Michael, weak, shocked, and saddened beyond measure, tried to tell him. He was forever afterward to remember how difficult it was to sort and pick through a lifetime for a way to describe the essence of himself. Finally, the King, with a blue-veined hand over his eyes, said, "So you are familiar with the Caribbean. This is good. I have estates there that virtually no one knows of. I shall arrange to have title to them transferred to you. I shall also have a generous sum deposited in a London bank which you may draw upon—"

"No. I cannot take anything from you—not after what I did—" Michael protested.

"What you did to me was the predestined outcome of my own failure. I shall not abandon you to make your own way in the world again." He took Michael's hand in a gesture of farewell and rose, shakily, to his feet. "We shall not meet again. My regret is unspeakable. Matthew and two guards will take you within the hour to a place where you may recover."

Michael did not intend to follow his father's plan, but there was obviously no point in arguing. "Thank you," he whispered. Before he could say anything more, the old man wiped a tear from the corner of his eye and was gone.

A moment later Matthew entered the room. "We have much to talk about, but there is no time now. We must be off. I will go ahead and make sure the way is safe. These two men," he said, gesturing toward the perplexed guards who had followed him in the door, "will accompany you out of the city where we will meet. I've brought you fresh clothes and a sword. Do not use it unless there is trouble. Draw no attention to yourself." He had spoken with cool efficiency, but before hurrying away, he put his hand on Michael's shoulder with a tenderness greatly touching in so gruff a man and said, "I'm glad to see you."

The soldiers fidgeted uneasily while Michael dressed in the clothing Matthew had brought. He felt drained and pale, but acted even more feeble than he felt. It would not be easy to evade these men and find Genevieve, but it would help if they were off their guard.

They left the building through darkened back halls, went on foot through back lanes, working their way toward the outskirts of Paris. Michael noted with relief that they would soon be near the part of the city where Genevieve lived with André.

They were rounding the corner when a donkey caravan crossed their path. The herd of sad-eyed little beasts with their tasseled bridles and ponderous bundles of silk filled the lane, irritable men in tattered clothing tapping them along with sticks. Michael came to a stop, the hands of his keepers loosening on his arms. He slumped in an attitude of weary waiting, relaxing the soldiers.

A moment later he yanked loose and dove under the nearest donkey. The air exploded with belligerent brays and spilled bolts of silk. The soldiers leaped into the midst of the fray, fumbling through tassels, billowing, snakish ropes of silk, and irate herdsmen. The winter wind blasted men and material against buildings and bystanders. By the time the King's men extricated themselves from the snow-sodden silk, Michael was a blotch of brown homespun shooting past an inn across the street.

"After him!"

He ran with a determination so strong it kept him going long after he should have dropped. His breath came in white-hot stabs, clouds of condensed pain in the bitter clench of December's death. A few more houses—a few more—

Michael flung himself, sobbing for breath, on a green and gilt door. He began to raise the lion's head brass ring to knock, then twisted the malachite doorknob and staggered inside. Valets and maids came running, voices shrill at this breach of etiquette. "Where is she?" he gasped. "Where is the Countess de Lieuvienne?"

"She is not receiving company."

The voice, so stern, so regal, could have come from the brass lion on the magnificent door. Michael spun to see the speaker, gaze traveling up the marble staircase. André stood in leonine topaz, clothes, hair, and skin in coordinating shades of golden tawny, the King of the Jungle eyeing an anxious and ineffectual panther. "Where is she?" Michael repeated, past subterfuge.

"The whereabouts of my Countess is none of your damned business, Sir. You will remove yourself from my presence before I do it for you. How dare you come here! You traitor, you vile, despicable blight upon the face of this nation! What on earth has induced you to come shrieking into *my* abode for *my* wife? I thought they were going to hang you—have you escaped? Not another step!"

André, in a dramatic sweep, caught his scabbard off a hallway table. Metal polishing implements went skittering, rags, jars of paste, gloves. André drew forth the rapier in a gleam of grim steel. Another second and the blade descended upon Michael's head—

—or rather, where Michael's head *had* been. He dove under the blow, colliding with the bulky walnut railing. André lunged at him, both hands on the hilt. Michael stepped away, backing down three stairs in one long stride while he freed his rapier from the scabbard.

André's weapon descended in an arc, tearing a bite of dark wood from the railing. Michael went under his opponent's arm. They were too close for swords; he drove the point of his shoulder into André's stomach. They grappled, precariously balanced on the edge of a stair. Then André brought the engraved pommel of his rapier crashing into Michael's skull.

Little scarlet stars burst in his mind. He threw all his weight backwards, dragging André off balance. Twenty stairsteps unrolled behind them. He could see the blond Count's expression as they fell. Oddly enough, it was fraught not with fear but with fury.

At the last possible second Michael shifted his weight. It snapped the bigger man under him, absorbing the force of their landing and bringing them to a halt after six or seven stairs. They rolled apart, groggy, groping for their rapiers. There was a crippled, swaying moment, then steel rang on steel. The blades met an an angle as both men sprang to action.

Blood flawed André's perfect face, running into his gold lace cravat from an ugly gash in his cheek. He eyed Michael a moment—a cold, killing stare—then came at him with an awakened lion's savagery. Michael began to retreat again. His training flooded back into him despite supreme weariness; he found himself taking the defensive, blows aimed just so, stance proper, rapier whistling and whining against equally tempered steel.

André's size and suavity could not stand up to the superb discipline of an English agent—and a desperate one at that. There was a shriek of tortured steel as Michael's rapier shattered André's. The momentum —physical and emotional—was so strong that Michael drew back his arm for the killing blow, all chivalry and sense of honor dead.

The final thrust never came. The King's two guards blasted through the opened door. Valets and soldiers, two of each, piled on Michael. He was wrestled to the ground, knocked half-unconscious, and disarmed. "Get the horses," shouted one of the guards, passing his military sash around Michael's wrists and knotting it.

Michael was dragged to his feet and hurried outside. The guards bowed to André at the door. "Our apologies, Count."

André took two swift strides forward. His fist crashed into Michael's face, bringing darkness and pain. Something unholy glinted in the Count's eyes. He aimed another brutal blow but a soldier blocked it. "Your pardon, Count, but he is under the King's protection."

A maid rushed into the room. "Excuse me, my lord Count, but the doctor's asking for you. She's waking."

Michael was swept from the house. André watched awhile, then turned and slowly, deliberately strolled to his stricken wife's room.

Genevieve stirred, tried to ease the discomfort of her cramped limbs. How much time had passed since the doctor arrived and had made her drink the foul, bitter liquid? Hours, days? She could not guess. There was no light coming through the window. Night, at least she knew that. But what night?

She closed her eyes again, trying to get her bearings. A door opened and André's voice came through the fog of drugs. "How is she, doctor?"

Another voice, older, muffled. "I'm sorry, Count. We did all we could, but—but it was too late. She will recover, however. She will need rest for a few weeks—"

"Weeks? How many? I am to take my post in England next month. Can she travel?"

"Wel-l-l, that depends. Why don't you go on ahead and leave her here? The servants should be able to care for her adequately."

There was a long silence, then André answered acidly, "No, I shall not leave her. She is going with me."

"If you go slowly, get a good carriage, cushion her from bumping and jolting, I suppose she could go in three weeks. She's basically a healthy young woman. I'd wager in a year she'll be pregnant again, in fact," the doctor said cheerlessly.

Genevieve was gradually waking, making sense of what was being said. Be pregnant *again*? But she was pregnant now. What on earth were they talking about? She moved her hand to her abdomen. Flat. The now-familiar roundness gone. A groggy grief swept over her. Her child—Michael's child—a tear burned its way down the side of her face. She turned away.

"By the way," André said rather more loudly than necessary, "did you hear, doctor, that they finally executed that traitor today?"

"Traitor?" the doctor said, confused by the odd turn of subject.

"Yes, that man who was masquerading as Viscomte Beaumarché," he said, glancing toward the bed.

Genevieve gave a quick gasp of horror.

"Now, Count, that's a strong subject," the doctor fussed. "Be more cheerful, I beg you, what you say in front of the Countess. In her condition such talk is upsetting."

"Yes," André said with languid cruelty, "I suppose it is."

Genevieve received the best of care for the next three weeks, but she was hardly aware of it. Her depression was so deep and slimy-sided that she was numbed to everything outside her fevered mind. Everything that meant anything to her was gone. She'd failed to find her mother; she'd parted ways with her sister, she'd lost Michael and his child. It was more than she could stand. The thinking, feeling part of her shut down, ceased to function. It was easier to feel nothing than to feel the oppressive pain of life.

She was docile, taking her medicine when it was brought to her, eating a few sickening bites of the food that was put before her, rising and walking a few steps when the doctor told her she must. But the essence was gone. It was a mannequin version of Genevieve who inhabited the sickroom. The real woman was gone to some groundless, cloudy sanctuary of peace.

She was vaguely aware that André never came to the room but it did not matter to her at first—nothing mattered to her. Finally, she roused herself enough to ask for him. Even in the depths of her own pit of despair and self-pity she realized that she had done André a great injustice. He came to her room at last, his face set in a stiff mask of hate. "André, please let us talk," she said weakly.

"I have nothing to say to you, Madame. You and that—that abominable traitor misused me, you sullied my name!"

"Please André, listen to me for a moment," she pleaded. "It will never happen again. . . ."

"No. He's dead!"

"I don't mean that. I won't betray you again with anyone." She meant it to the depths of what heart she had left.

"You will not have the opportunity, I assure you," he said, his voice rimmed with frost.

Genevieve sat up slowly, a painful, dizzying act. "You sound as though you hate me," she said. Not a plea now, but a simple assessment.

"How very perceptive of you," he sneered.

"Is there no way I can make it up to you? I know you will never love me again, but—"

"Love you again? You self-centered little bitch! I never loved you at all, but I *did* respect you. It is the respect you can never regain."

Genevieve felt a swirl of nausea overtake her. She fell back against the pillows taking shallow, careful breaths. They did not speak to each other again. Genevieve had tried to make her peace with him. Her offer of loyalty had not been made lightly. Had he shown any willingness to forgive, she would have kept that promise until her dying day. She knew now that she had seriously misjudged him and she understood him less now than when they were first married. But she knew one thing about him with absolute surety. He would never, never forgive nor forget that she had betrayed him. She had seen before what happened to those who dared to cross him in the most minor ways. His good name and his pride meant everything to him. Love, affection, forgiveness—all were as dust motes in his vision of himself.

Knowing that it was now too late to make even a friendship from the parts of her broken marriage, Genevieve slipped back into her morbid lethargy. When, at the end of three weeks, the doctor began to explain apologetically that she must make herself ready to travel, she nodded with abstracted obedience. "Very well," she said, and the doctor wondered if her mental injuries might not be a great deal more severe than her physical condition.

The maid helped her dress bright and early. The head footman carried her gingerly down the steps

and set her in the front hall. A carriage stood outside
in the swirling snow. The maid dropped a heavy ermine cape over her shoulders and fussed over her.
"The wind, Madame, it is strong today. Keep the
cloak fast shut, please," she said.

"I have a jeweled clasp to fasten it," Genevieve answered wearily. "It's in the blue lacquer box."

The girl looked at her, stricken.

"Would you get it please?" Genevieve asked.

"I—I don't know—" the girl sputtered.

At that point André strode into the hall. "What's
this about?"

"The Countess wants a clasp from her jewel box,"
the maid said timidly.

"She doesn't need it," André said and took Genevieve's arm in an iron grip that shot pains through
her.

The footman stepped forward. "Do you wish me
to carry the Countess to the carriage?" he asked.

"No, she can walk," André said, steering her toward the door.

"But the steps are icy, Sir," the man said.

André rounded on him, his eyes full of yellow anger. "I said she can walk. You are dismissed from my
service for your insolence."

"But André—" Genevieve protested.

"Get in the carriage," he ordered, cutting off her
remarks.

The wind-lashed snow struck at her face and billowed her cape wickedly as she stepped outside. For
a moment the cold seemed like an astringent slap
that brought her back to her senses. She almost slipped
on the steep steps and André said nothing. Once inside the warm carriage she ventured, "Where is my
clasp?"

"Gone, my dear Countess. I had a number of debts
that had to be cleared up. The clasp and several of
your other pieces of jewelry took care of it quite
nicely."

"But André—why? I don't understand? Why didn't you pay the debts yourself?"

The carriage was rolling sedately through the snow-shrouded streets of Paris. "You don't understand?" he laughed. "I never counted you exceptionally smart, but I would not have taken you for stupid."

Her head was throbbing and her back was being jolted painfully. Perhaps this was just another of the madly unreasonable dreams she'd been subject to lately. This man hardly seemed like André. Why was he talking this way? She leaned back, closed her eyes a moment, then opened them again. He was still there, it was real. "Please tell me what you're talking about," she said.

Suddenly he leaned forward, his eyes gleaming fiercely. "Why do you think I married you, my dear little slut? For your looks? Ha! I've had beautiful women beg me for a word, a touch. No, not for your looks. For your mind? I've not noted that you have one. What does that leave, Genevieve, what does that leave?"

She averted her eyes, mumbled, "Please, stop—stop."

"It leaves your money, dear Countess. Your beautiful, useful money."

Her mind went reeling and spinning back to the lassitude that had cushioned her against pain. "No, no," she muttered, putting her hands over her ears. The Vigo fortune—it had brought her to this!

But he went on, the bitterness he'd concealed for so long bubbling over. "So now the rest of your jewels are in my cases and your money has been transferred to a London bank—in my name, of course. It was easy enough to convince my banker that in view of your grave illness, it was best to do so."

The mannequin Genevieve, curious but oddly untouched, asked, "But why are you doing this to me?"

"Why? Why! How dare you ask? Were you going to tell me your brat was two months early or two months late? How dare you have taken me for such a fool—and a cuckolded fool at that! Well, they're dead and buried now, the baby and that damned traitor. As for you, my lady wife, you may live a long full life or you may not."

He's threatening to kill me, Genevieve thought. *He thinks this journey will kill me. Perhaps it will.* She heard a woman whimpering. Herself, perhaps, it didn't matter. Nothing mattered.

Nothing.

While the woman's voice wept, Genevieve looked out the window, noted a winter bird, and wondered idly where it spent its summers.

Part Four

ANGEL'S SHROUDS

24

Genevieve survived the journey with a tenacity she hadn't known she possessed. She never really remembered the trip through France, only an unhappy blur of carriages and boats and dull pain. After his bitter and revealing outburst André, too, withdrew to his own corner. They spoke infrequently and with cold courtesy. They had separate rooms on the journey and in the London house André had arranged for.

Genevieve immediately took to the bed in her room, unaware at first of the sunny western exposure and beautiful furnishings. She slept most of the time, alternating between heartpounding nightmares and a deep, comalike void. Inevitably as her body rested and healed, so did her mind. One day she noticed the sounds of children playing below her window and went to watch their game. Then she became vaguely aware that André had hired a very good cook and she noticed for the first time that she had lost a great deal of weight. The next morning she rose early and felt an odd satisfaction in brushing her hair until her scalp hurt. That evening she surprised André by appearing downstairs at dinner instead of having it brought to her room on a tray.

André glanced at her. "I presume you are feeling better?" he asked coolly.

"Yes. Are you sorry to hear it?" she answered, some of her anger finding its way to the surface.

"No. Your health is a matter of supreme indifference to me," he replied and rang for the servants to bring the first course.

"I had the impression you would prefer me dead." Genevieve could not leave the subject alone.

"That's like saying I prefer red to blue. I do, but it doesn't keep me from wearing blue. Don't sit there looking frail and brave. As long as you behave yourself I'm not going to take the trouble to drop stone urns on you or anything so gauche. But if you make any other moves to embarrass me, well—then I'll have to reconsider my policy."

Genevieve felt a shiver of pure terror run down her spine. How could he be so utterly remote? And yet, hadn't he always been? When he wished to get along with her, he had been just as cool, but there was a thin veneer of courtesy over the frost. Now it was a sparkling crust of cruelty. Who or what was the real André? The man behind both facades?

Several months ago, when she felt younger and was full of the spirit of life, she would have defied him, spat out her sudden hatred and walked away proudly. But things were different. Genevieve was different. She was tired, lost, and disillusioned to the core. She merely looked at him, picked up her wine glass, and made a mock toast.

After the long silent dinner André said, "I am expected to entertain and be entertained. You will join me as a loyal wife or I shall give out the word that you are a complete invalid, incapable of going anywhere or receiving any visitors. I'm sure your friend Althea will understand. She's dropped by several times already."

Genevieve placed her elbows on the table, locked her fingers together. She could, and would, be as matter-of-fact as he was about their relationship. "André, why is this? The change, I mean. Is it because of the child I lost?"

"You've been reading schoolgirl romances, my dear. You are still trying to convince yourself that I am raging with unrequited love of you. Don't be a fool. I would not have cared if you bedded an entire regiment, so long as you did not soil my name. No, we had an arrangement, unspoken it's true, but I thought we both understood it. I gave you my good name, my protections, outward loyalty, and respect. You were to do honor to the name and return the loyalty. You failed in your part of the bargain, my Countess, so I'm no longer obligated to maintain my part—not in private anyway."

"You didn't ever care for me then?"

"I liked you well enough. You didn't take up much of my time or emotional energy. You were a satisfactory wife—at first. You will be again."

"Why don't you just divorce me?" she asked.

"I've thought about it, but I want this job for the respect as well as the money it brings. Divorce or annulment would be a scandal and ruin my chances of advancement. Besides, there would be difficulties of keeping control of all your money that way. It's just easier if we get along."

"I shan't share your bed when I'm well."

He laughed, a cruel bark of contempt. "What a punishment! I shall pine away. You really *are* a fool. Did you think I enjoyed the boring ritual? You did not detect the glazed look, the gritted teeth, the quick glances at the clock?"

"You are truly terrible," Genevieve said with astonishment.

"And you are truly boring. You have no idea how to be a real woman. You're a bland little goose-girl."

Suddenly Genevieve laughed. It was the first time in months. "I have the advantage of you now, André. I misunderstood you at first and I have learned what you're really like. But you misunderstood me to begin with and you still don't know what I really am."

"What do you mean by that?" he asked angrily.

"I cannot tell you. If I did, all the romance would be gone, wouldn't it?" She stood abruptly and swept from the room with more strength and grace than she'd had for a very, very long time.

* * *

When Althea called the next day, the message was passed on to Genevieve. She flew to the door and the women embraced, giggled, and cried a little. It was some time before either of them was coherent. They took tea in the drawing room. "My darling, you're so thin!" Althea exclaimed. "Is it deliberate?"

"No, I've been sick. I'll tell you about it later, but tell me—tell me everything first. I've been locked away, it seems. Out of touch with the world. How is Robert? And Felicia? When will I see them."

"Oh, my dear, I thought you knew. Felicia is dead."

"Dead! Oh, no!"

"I'm afraid so. Several weeks ago. Just days after Robert had returned from France. He was crushed, poor man. Roamed around in the house for days, refusing to eat or leave the place. He eventually got a grip on himself and his family has sent him off to Scotland somewhere to recuperate—though God knows, Scotland in winter is the last place I'd have thought of. I can get his address for you to write him. He would love to hear from you—it might be just the thing to get him back to life. Now, you must talk. Tell me—have you seen Michael?"

There was a shocked silence. Genevieve sucked her breath in, but found it impossible to reply.

"How was he when you saw him last?"

"Althea! How can you be so callous?"

"I'm never callous—not unless I mean to be, then I do it quite well. How was he?"

Genevieve was trembling with shock. "He was dead!" she burst out. "I saw him killed."

Althea's eyes widened and her face was suddenly drained of color. "God in Heaven, forgive me. I had no idea. How did it happen?"

"Surely you know. It was the talk of France, probably the talk of Europe. Althea, are you playing some sort of mean game with me? You must know he was hanged for treason in December. Quite a public execution. All the best people were there," she said bitterly.

Althea leaned back. Her mouth was slightly open and there was a look of frenzied wonderment in her heavily fringed eyes. "There is something wrong here. Something terribly wrong. You *saw* him hanged? You actually saw it?"

"Yes, I said I did!" Genevieve felt herself becoming weak and faint. What was the matter with Althea?

"Describe it to me," Althea said.

"Oh, please—" Genevieve whimpered. "Isn't it enough that I saw it, without having to relive those awful moments? I've done nothing else for weeks now." There were tears coursing down her cheeks now. But Althea did not change her expression of determination. "Very well," Genevieve finally said. "I—I entered the room with the King and a man named Matthew. The King shouted something, but it was too late. He—Michael—fell through the trap door and—and—"

"What was next?"

"Next? Oh, God, I cannot bear to think. I did not see. I was very ill and I must have fainted. The next thing I knew I was home."

Althea sat forward. There were tears in her eyes as she took Genevieve's hands in hers. "My dear child, who told you he had died?"

"Who told me?" Genevieve echoed. A sudden cloud of suspicion began to form around her. No. It was too monstrous. She formed the words as if they were obscenities. "André told me. André."

"Is the man mad?" Althea whispered. "Genevieve, Michael did not die on that scaffold. Everyone knows that. I've heard the exact same story from four different people already. The King ordered a halt, the hangman let the rope slacken suddenly and Michael fell to the floor. That was what you saw! He didn't hang, he collapsed. Are you sure André told you—"

"He's alive? Althea, are you truly telling me Michael is alive!"

"Yes, at least he was. The King had him spirited away. No one knows what became of him. Presumably, he is safe. You see, that's why I asked you about him. I assumed that if anyone knew of his whereabouts or had seen him since that day, it would be you."

Genevieve was swept in a rough tide of conflicting emotions: unbounded relief that Michael had escaped the scaffold with his life, and furious anger with André for leading her to believe otherwise. She should have questioned him, guessed that he would have told just such a lie with the deliberate intent to hurt and subdue her. But she had not understood the new turn of their relationship that day. If he said such a thing now, she would know better than to believe him.

And as these thoughts jostled in her mind, another crept in—a tiny, sinister spore of doubt. If Michael was alive, as Althea had said, why *hadn't* she seen him? Why hadn't he come to take her away from André? Suddenly she didn't know anything. She felt her mind slipping toward the deep, dark pit again. It had been so comforting not to think, not to feel. But she would not succumb again.

"Genevieve, you look quite pale. I would have approached this subject more delicately had I but known. Let me call your maid—"

"No. Don't call anyone. I will be fine in a moment. It's just been a shock."

"How could André have done such a thing to you? Could he possibly have failed to hear what really happened?"

"Oh, no. He did it deliberately, quite deliberately. He's not the man we all thought, Althea. He is a fiend, a cruel, despicable man." She took a deep breath, then hastily summed up the past few weeks to an astonished Althea.

"What are you going to say to him about this?" Althea asked, her voice steeped in vicarious vengeance.

"Nothing. Absolutely nothing. I shall not reward him by letting him see that I know, by showing my distress. I am stronger every day. In another week I shall be able to venture out, to visit a solicitor, the banker, some friends. I will find a way to get back what is mine and get away from him somewhere. Then, only then, can I begin to think of a way to balance the scales."

"I believe you will," Althea said.

But she was wrong. Genevieve didn't get the opportunity.

Kensington Palace was ablaze with creamy beeswax tapers in sterling candelabra as Genevieve and André entered. Queen Anne, gouty, dropsical, and insufferably sincere, had announced an audience for all foreign ambassadors at her court, to be followed by dinner and a ball.

Genevieve, in her white moire and damask, delicate flowers and feathers adorning her coiffure to the proper height, felt ill. Her nerves were on edge from André's constant scrutiny and the prospect of meeting so many strangers—among them the Queen and all her ministers, great and small. Perhaps Althea would be there. She thought she had been indispensable in France and did her best to convince the government that they were in dire need of her. Genevieve was surprised they didn't knight Althea simply to get her off the doorstep.

Yes, Althea might be there. That would make the evening tolerable. André presented his card to an immaculate footman who ushered them into an inner room. Ambassadors and ministers abounded, perfectly painted wives on their arms. No one seemed very thrilled by the prospect of meeting the Queen: Genevieve wondered why.

A herald was assigning positions in line, announcing the couples as they entered the audience chamber. André was handing the man his card when Genevieve heard a shockingly familiar voice call out, "André! And the Countess!"

She whirled to see Robert St. Justine, devilishly dapper as ever, shoving his way through the crowd as if his life depended on it. "Gen!" he called out as the hulking Portuguese minister blocked his way, "Gen, don't go in there, you'll come face-to-face with my—"

"Versailles, France. The Count and Countess de Lieuvienne," bawled the herald in chandelier-jangling tones. André, fingers locked on Genevieve's elbow, yanked her into the entrance chamber to meet the Queen. What was the matter? she thought. Why was Robert waving his arms and looking frantic? Who had he tried to warn her against? What—?

There was no more time to think. She was kneeling before the Queen's dais, head bowed, feathers swaying gently. Gaze respectfully lowered, she was able to see little but the stair on which she knelt. And the Queen's feet.

The Queen's feet! She wasn't wearing shoes. Her swollen, discolored toes protruded from grimy bandages reeking with camphor and other medicinal salves. The hem of her once magnificent gown was frayed; the silver threads had been worn to frazzled gray with no lustre or youth left.

Wearied by life, seventeen fruitless pregnancies, and sheer traumatic circumstance, Anne of England was an old woman, old, foolish, and disillusioned. Genevieve chanced a glance up at the sovereign and smiled kindly. To her surprise, Queen Anne smiled back—as shyly as if she, not Genevieve, were the underling.

André stood, drawing Genevieve up with him. As they turned to face the room of ministers, the herald repeated his call. "Count and Countess de Lieuvienne, court of Versailles, France, by special appointment of His Majesty, Louis the—"

"Lies. All lies!"

It was as if Genevieve had swallowed a fist-sized chunk of ice. She choked, swaying, as a vengeful harpy in taffeta ripped loose from the crowd and came at her, pointing a brass-wrapped cane. The Dowager Duchess St. Justine—Robert's grandmother!

The butt of her cane caught Genevieve in the breastbone, sending her wobbling backwards several steps. "Countess de Lieuvienne, my foot! This woman is a pirate and kidnapper and extortionist—took ten thousand pounds from me for the safe return of my worthless grandson. They have warrants for her arrest from London to Rye! Guards, take her! She is a pirate and kidnapper and the penalty for both is death!"

"Madame, this is completely and utterly impossible," André snapped in frosty, officious tones.

Robert's little beige mother emerged from the crowd. "I—I recognize her, too. And my husband—"

"Yes," said Robert's father. "That is the woman who came to us demanding money. Robert?"

Robert came to the front with an insouciant swagger. He looked Genevieve up and down as if sizing up any pretty wench at market. Then he gave a quick laugh and stepped back, "Never seen her before in my life. Pity, too!"

"You lying, ungrateful cad! You're no grandson of mine!" bellowed the Dowager. She spun to the guards, poking them with her cane. "Arrest this woman! Arrest—"

André folded Genevieve's trembling hand over his arm, folding his fingers over hers as if with the deepest of husbandly concern. Only Genevieve knew how he twisted and crushed her fingers so that she saw waves of scarlet and black and yet dared not cry out. "Madame," he addressed the Dowager with feline coolness, "Madame, you are mistaken. My Countess and I grew up together. Our lands adjoined and we were betrothed at a tender age. I know and trust her character as I do my own."

Queen Anne was in a helpless dither, wringing her hands at her counselors, fluttering and squeaking over advice. Genevieve dimly heard André saying how upset his poor Countess was—looked quite faint, in fact—they were going home, away from these brutal accusations, perhaps even back to Versailles. Such a shocking breach of etiquette. Poor little Countess. The King would hear. Come along, my dear, home and some cold compresses. Such a terrible mistake. Terrible.

And such was his presence that he had her out of Kensington without anyone moving to stop them.

André bundled her into the carriage and they rode in steaming silence back to the house. His jaw was set and Genevieve could detect a muscle twitching at the side of his face. She'd seen him cold and reasonable but never seen him truly angry and it frightened her.

As they entered the front hall, Genevieve's maid and André's valet began to fuss over them. André dismissed them curtly, then took Genevieve's arm in a grip that pinched a nerve and made her almost cry out. He marched her up the long curving stairway at a double stride pace that had her tripping and stumbling. He shoved her into his room and slammed the door behind them. Genevieve's heart was pounding so hard she could barely get her breath. She started looking around for anything she could use as a weapon. A pair of brass unicorns whose horns were fire tongs stood next to the maroon-veined marble fireplace. Genevieve inched over and sat down in the chair next to the tools. She would not use them unless she had to, but her experiences in the hard life on shipboard had taught her to be ready for violence.

"I presume this is the secret you were alluding to," André said with repressed fury. "Why didn't you tell me sooner about your past?"

"For the same reason you didn't tell me why you were marrying me, I suppose."

"Is it true? Were you involved with pirates?"

"More than involved, André." She got a perverse pleasure from the look of surprise and disgust on his face. "I was a member of the crew, sister of the captain."

"I have to give you credit for a fine performance. I would never have guessed," André said. "I just hope you can go on fooling others as you've fooled me."

"What if I don't want to fool anyone, André?"

"Oh, but you will. You see, you have no other alternative."

Genevieve took a deep breath. "Yes, I do. I could simply leave you."

André smiled viciously. "Simply? I think not. You are a criminal in this country, my dear. Guilty of a hanging offense. My diplomatic immunity is the only thing between you and the rope. I shall protect you so long as you are the devoted wife. The moment you defy me I shall sadly reveal to the law that I was tricked into marriage and wish to turn you in. You cannot leave me, my dear, without parting with your life as well."

Genevieve squirmed a little in her chair. Of course, he was right—as far as he went. "I wouldn't have to stay in England," she said with a silly burst of defiance.

"No, you could set out for—for where? You seem to have forgotten that I have control over your money, my darling. You can't get very far without a farthing. Not unless you are employable." He walked closer, leaned down, and put his hand on her breast. "You're well enough equipped to get a job of some sort, aren't you, my own dear slut?"

Genevieve shrank back, flushed and furious. "How

dare you! I'm not a piece of property you may handle like that. Don't touch me again."

He pulled her to her feet. "You are exactly that— my property. Soiled goods, at that."

Genevieve drew back her arm and slapped him. The sound of her hand on his face resounded in the quiet room.

"So," he drawled, "you do have some spirit after all." He gazed at her appraisingly, then reached out, grasped the front of her low-cut bodice and was about to yank it loose. But Genevieve had undergone certain unofficial training aboard the *Black Angel*. Kate and the other women had taught her tricks for dealing with the rough men she might meet in port. Genevieve quickly grabbed André's wrist, applied her thumb to a pressure point and savagely twisted.

André immediately sank to his knees, grimacing with pain. But his expression quickly changed. Genevieve stared down at him, horrified beyond words. *He is liking this,* she thought. *He likes being hurt.* His face was becoming flushed and mottled, his lips were parted slightly as if in passion, and his eyes had an odd, unfocused look. He was arching his back, pushing his pelvis against her legs and moving slowly. He seemed impervious to the pain that she must be causing to his hand.

No, she realized, *not impervious. He needs the pain. He has pain and sexual passion mixed up.* She was filled with such horror and disgust that she could taste bile. She dropped his hand, tried to flee. But he clutched at her, wrapped his arms around her in a bone-crushing embrace. His movements became more frenzied and he moaned, "Please, Genevieve, please don't stop."

She brought her arm back again, swung with all her might and dealt him a stunning blow on the side of his head. His grip loosened for just a moment, long enough for her to struggle loose and get across the room. She turned for an instant as she opened the door. André had struggled to his feet. His fevered expression disgusted and terrified her.

She turned, ran to her room, and pushed a chest in front of the door before collapsing, trembling and gagging on the bed. It was some moments before she could begin to think coherently, then things began to fall into place with dizzying rapidity. All the little bruises and cuts. He's always had some excuse, as unlikely as they were. Why had she never questioned, never wondered why such a graceful, leonine man should suffer so many falls and small injuries as he claimed? But it wasn't falls, it was the result of his own special brand of lovemaking. And it had always gone on. He had come to their wedding night with bruises on his shoulder, she recalled, and throughout their marriage he had seldom been without some evidence of injury. So there had been other women all along, and perhaps—God forbid—other men. Even here, in the London house, she had heard furtive noises suggestive of blows and muted cries of pain. She had attributed it to her imagination, but no— André, typically protecting his reputation, had brought his partners home rather than visit houses of prostitution where he might be seen. Dear God, it was like living in some sort of hellish brothel. How could she have failed to see it before?

She had wondered about the real André, what sort of person was behind the cold face and manner. Now, heaven help her, she knew, and the knowledge made her sick. At least he hadn't followed her to her room. She went back to the door, pressed her ear against it. No, there was no sound from the hall.

She went to her window and sat staring out for a long time. What on earth was she to do? André had been right about her not being able to leave him. She dared not stay in England unless she was on good terms with him. She could not leave in any sort of safety without money. She would dare not simply present herself at the docks and offer herself as a sailor on some ship. No one would take on a woman for any moral purpose. As much as she wanted to escape André, she would not deliberately hire herself out as a ship's whore.

Besides, there was another consideration that André did not mention. She had to wait until Michael emerged from whatever hiding he'd gone into. Perhaps he had chosen not to contact her after his near brush with death. In truth, she believed this to be so. But she was not blind or stupid, as André had always assumed. She knew in her heart that there was a slight chance that Michael had been forcibly prevented from coming to her and would do so when he was free. She had to be somewhere he could find her. If she were off to sea, there was no chance. He would look for her under André's questionable care and that's where she must wait for him.

If—if he ever came for her. He might now be dead. He had suffered certain tortures in prison that could well have developed into fatal sickness. His enemies might have caught up with him. But it had not been so very long since that awful day in Paris. It had seemed like an eternity, but had only been a matter of a few short months.

No money, no legal recourse. She must stay with André—at least for a little while longer. What a horrible thought, penned up in this loveless house with a maniac. Genevieve brought her knees up to her chin, hugging herself as a chill night breeze swept her windowsill perch. She heard the front door click down below. A moment later a cloaked man ran from the house. He hesitated at the stable, the street corner's gaslamps picking out bronze and topaz in his fair hair.

André. He was hesitating at the stable door as if measuring his need of a horse against his terrible haste. A moment later he was racing down the street on foot, dashing over the cobblestones like some frenzied marathon runner. Genevieve's hair nearly stood on end. She had never seen André move quickly, never seen an untidy or hurried motion from him. The sight of her imperturbable husband throwing a sexual fit had been horrible in a physically repulsive way. His mad, furtive dash down the street, leaping and darting among shadows, was almost worse. She had been afraid and had mastered her fright—and him, much to his slavering pleasure. To see him take zigzagging flight as if pursued by invisible demons was frightening in a way as unholy as any of his private deviations.

Genevieve had the sudden thought that there might be money or jewels in his room. Her money—*her* jewels. "By God," she whispered, rising and clenching her fists. "I won't let him do this to me. It won't be robbery since I'm only taking my own things. He's got to have money cached away. And jewelry—"

He had emerald cuff-studs as big as the end of her thumb. Diamond cravat pins. And he was constantly waving her own money in her face just before he spent it on himself. A cold, calm fury wrapped its talons about Genevieve's soul. She lit her lamp, took it up, and wrested the clothing chest from in front of her door. Then she went straight to the hallway wardrobe where André kept his guns and rapiers.

She took out a long-handled duelling pistol, blue-black in the lampglow. It curved in her fingers like a lover's hand. She loaded it, took up flint and fuse, and strode boldly down the corridor to André's room. If he returned unexpectedly, if he threatened her, clutched at her, offered his filthy, groping attentions— *I will tell them I thought he was a burglar,* she told herself with a grim sense of pleasure. Then—*No. That won't work. They'll dig and pry and discover the Dowager is right. I'll have to kill him and run. Althea will help me. Althea.*

She had it all neatly figured out, barring mistakes —except that all André's wardrobes and chests were locked. She ransacked his room, gleaning a few sov-

ereigns from sofa cushions. There was a small cloth-
of-gold pouch under his bed. She pounced voraciously,
only to discover it contained one golden louis and
half a dozen francs. That wasn't enough to get her
to Althea's, let alone out of England.

She slumped into a slick horsehide chair, pistol in
her lap. André had not only robbed her, he had hidden and arranged everything to keep her a virtual
prisoner of finance. She hated him, not with flamboyance but with low, cold flames that lay burning on
the wronged hearth of her heart. *I will wait,* Genevieve decided, cocking the pistol.

Long minutes passed, drawing out the suspense to
unbearable lengths. She was tired and depressed and
felt her fire ebbing to crimson embers. Why kill him
if her own life would then be forfeit? Was he really
worth going to the scaffold for? She rested her chin
in her hand, gazing glumly at the room about her.

Murder. She could not do it. She rose, blew out
her lamp, and padded slowly back to her room. The
night was still, her room cold and gloomy around
the unlit fireplace. Genevieve wearily bolted her door
and undressed for bed.

She had given up too early. There was sound in
the street, drunken voices. Genevieve crept to the
window in her shift. André and a shabbily bedizened
slattern were on the doorstep. The woman was slapping him and André was behaving as if her slaps
were the most intimate of caresses. Genevieve drew
the crushed velvet drapes with a hard flick of the
wrist. She then built a fire, not for warmth, but for
the roar and hiss that would drown the vulgar sound.

She crawled under the covers and stared at the blazing fireplace, her gaze rooted to the lick and writhe
of orange flames. She wanted to cry, but there were
no tears left.

25

Genevieve sat alone in the parlor with her embroidery, drapes open, watching the constables outside watch her. The Dowager Duchess St. Justine had plainly been heeded with her accusations of crime. No one dared arrest Genevieve because of her diplomatic immunity, but they continued to keep an open surveillance of her all the same.

André had taken a slithering delight in the entire situation the last time he'd spoken to her. "Of course, my darling, I could always tell them that although we grew up together, there was a period of several years when we were parted. And when I next met you, you seemed vastly changed. At the time I puzzled over it, but accepted you anyway. Now, however, I find more and more things cropping up each day that shake my faith and cause me to believe . . . ."

Genevieve stitched faster, forehead furrowed. Damn him—and damn her for being a fool. Damn Michael, damn the Dowager, damn everybody! What was she going to do? Sometimes at night the strain of worry made her feel her head was bursting. She could almost feel the cracks at the edges as she lay in the dark, hopelessly snarled in André's web of cruelty and cunning.

In the daytime she could shrug at her fancies, but it was dark now. The lamplighters made their rounds, the alleys and byways were black with crime. Soon, very soon, she would have to go upstairs to her dark, cold bed and the waking nightmares that hung with folded wings and talons from the corners of her soul. She was growing afraid of the dark, afraid of the sounds she heard at night, the vulgar, desperate noises of animal beings wreaking pain and perversion in the midnight hours.

Worse than that was her fear of the noose. Prison, starvation, hanging. Death! But wasn't it better than dying in this trap? Sometimes she wanted to provoke André, push him into renouncing her, getting the whole disaster over with. But her sense of survival ran too deep in her being. She clung to hope with a teeth-gritting tenacity that alarmed her and pleased André. He seemed to delight in causing her grief and strain. She had learned to make no reaction to his barbs and jibes. It robbed him of his tawdry joy.

There was a resounding knock on the front door. Genevieve waited for the maid to answer the door, then remembered that André had fired her. Only the kitchen staff remained and they had gone home for the night. André had alienated every servant they'd had, even the faithful valet who had been with him for most of his life.

Genevieve set down her embroidery and went swiftly to the door, her feet in their thin embossed slippers of red Moroccan leather moving silently along the marble floor. She stood on her toes, trying to peer out the azure circle of glass on the door. A woman. That was all she could tell gazing through flawed glass into the night. A woman and it wasn't Althea. Genevieve wrested open the door, shoulders squared. It was bad enough to bring his doxies home but must he send them here ahead of time to await his arrival? Indignation grasped her. Say what they might, she was still the mistress of this house!

The door swung open silently, catching the woman unawares. She had knocked and turned to idly survey the constables across the street under the gaslamp. Genevieve saw only the back of a sumptuous black beaver hat, an emerald gown, and fat black ringlets.

Then the woman turned around, face half-veiled

in the shadow of the door. Her skirts swayed with the fragrant rustle of many layered silk. Peacock feathers adorned her hat, beginning at the jeweled hatband and curving proudly over shoulder and arm in a splendiferous cascade of blue and green eyes.

The gown was expensive beyond words, the latest fashion from Versailles, with a low heart-shaped neckline that made the most of the wearer's magnificent *décolletage*. There was a sapphire the size of a plum resting in the valley of cleavage, surrounded by cherry-sized diamonds and emeralds. Black ringlets, glossy with the exuberance of life, neatly draped the woman's lightly lined ivory throat. She tossed her head, allowing Genevieve a glimpse of ripe coral lips and dangling diamond earrings that danced from lobe to shoulder.

There was something queerly *déjà vu* about the scene. André's women were never this expensively arrayed, this perfect. There was a thread or two of gray in the bouncing curls that flooded from a ribboned bunch at the left of the hat. As Genevieve stared, the woman put a scarlet-nailed finger up, flipping a stray peacock feather into place. "I been waitin' damned near twenty years," the woman announced, hand on hip. "If you make me wait much longer, my patience might get outa control. Now where's the Countess?"

Overly conscious of her demure gray gown and the smooth governesslike braids wound about her head, Genevieve took a step backwards, hand to throat, "I—I'm the Countess de Lieuvienne."

"*Christ! Genevieve!*" the woman whispered hoarsely, stepping forward, arms out. The first sight of her face in the light made Genevieve reel as if struck. It was Evonne and it was not Evonne. Her sister, twenty years older. Twenty years—the eyes, the mouth—

"*They told me you were dead!*" Genevieve sobbed, and threw herself into her mother's arms!

"*Ma petite, ma belle chère petite*—don't they feed you?" Sabelle demanded, holding her close while they cried into each other's hair. "You feel like a parasol, all your ribs sticking out. Oh, Gen, Gen—! What a long search! I didn't even think you'd remember me. There was a snowslide—everyone died but me—I came back to King Louis's court only to find out I got a daughter there lookin' for me, who left for England. Hades gettin' into this country, they meant to hang me a couple years back."

"Now I *know* you're my mother!"

"And you're my own girl. I can tell by the gendarmes outside. I only got a few days, Gen. Then it's back to me ship. She's waitin' down river at Gravesend. I can't stay long or they'll catch on to me. Gen. Me own Gen!"

It was as if something had given Genevieve a new lease on life, renewed her will to live and fight and emerge victorious. As she held Sabelle, the years filled her and scalded the empty holes in her heart, the places she needed love and reassurance. She was so full of pain and joy she couldn't hold it and she wept—gladly, achingly, spilling her hates and fears and loves in the arms of this woman who was very nearly a stranger. She remembered little of Sabelle and yet what she could recall was deep and powerful. A mother who was friend, companion, and parent. A woman who let no one harm her children, allowed no criticism of them even by her own husband. Someone who fought for them like a tigress and would have died rather than see the least harm or distress come to them. A fairy tale princess, a protecting sorceress, a vivid Earth Mother.

Genevieve held her and cried. That night in front of the fire they unfolded the lost years they had known, each opening her heart. They talked through the night, sometimes laughing and hugging one another, sometimes crying on each other's shoulder.

Genevieve recounted her meeting with her sister, told Sabelle what she knew of Evonne's life before they met. "Where is she now?" Sabelle asked, wiping the tears from her eyes.

Genevieve told her the name of the tiny Caribbean island where Evonne had gone. "But I wrote her and never received a reply. Perhaps she didn't get my letter," Genevieve said.

"I'll find her," Sabelle vowed. "Come with me?"

"I—I wish I could," Genevieve said. "But there are reasons—"

Sabelle raised a warning hand. "You don't have to explain nothin' to me. I just thought there might be a wind in that direction. You got yer own life, Gen. I ain't gonna sail into the middle of it flyin' me own flags."

"Tell me about us when we were little," Genevieve begged.

Sabelle's eyes misted. "Oh, you were the most beautiful of children. "I've been askin' round the Caribbean for a lot of years, but I could never find any trace of me girls. Not dead nor alive. But now I've found you and soon I'll find Evonne. Do you remember the island? Them dolls yer father brought—?"

They were still happily discussing the past when dawn began to filter through the windows. The distant past. Of their recent past—both Sabelle's marriage and Genevieve's—they said nothing.

March, defying all precepts, had come in like a lion and persisted in exiting with the same bellow and bluster. The Thames, sluggish but finally free of ice, flowed on its way, the thawing mud trails flanking it alive with travelers once more. The Channel ports were open again for business, bringing in travelers from abroad and spewing them forth on the riverside roads.

Heavily laden carts rolled on their way; horsemen

lazed past; peasants walked with bundles of bread;
lean dogs drove befuddled sheep. All traveled along
the crooked roads, unhurried, unconcerned.

Save for one rider. He had been hunted the length
and breadth of the continent and had grown nervously
accustomed to haste. Ill-fed, ill-clad, hungry, and unshaven, he spurred his stolen horse to the wind and
rode as if all the Furies followed. The steady measured
beat of the horse's hooves seemed to say: *Genevieve,
Genevieve* . . .

The chant of it whispered and thrummed in his
head. He had lost his pursuers in Marseilles, killed
several horses fleeing through Spain, and worked his
way to England on a merchant vessel. The cold British wind tasted like ambrosia, reviving his numbed
senses from the stupor of winter and the hunt. Trees
were budding. Little fragile nubs of green grass nuz-
zled their way up through mud and rotting leaves.
Spring. It was spring and Robert would know where
she was.

Michael Clermont swatted his horse, gave him free
rein to London. London and Genevieve. All he'd
lived for these hard months! Sheep scattered before
him, round-eyed workers cleared the path. They whispered as he blasted past them on the lean black
horse, shared an aghast secret apparent to everyone
but him.

The constant strain had taken its toll. He looked
like a man already dead.

Genevieve and Sabelle had been to a play, a bawdy
comedy which Genevieve had enjoyed somewhat apologetically and Sabelle had thrown herself into with
her whole vulgar enthusiasm. They had hired a fine
carriage and had ridden all the way home laughing
at the memory of the best lines. As they drew up
in front of the house, Genevieve felt the inevitable
pall of depression that came over her whenever she
thought of André.

She glanced up at his window. Brightly lighted. That meant nothing. He could have another of his doxies with him, but at least he was not watching for her, would not be prowling the house waiting to goad her. She wondered again, as she had often in the last three days, what would happen when André and Sabelle finally came face to face. He had been out of the house most of the time since her arrival, and the few occasions he was home Sabelle had been out shopping.

Genevieve had told her mother practically nothing about her husband yet other than to hint at her unhappiness. They had been together constantly since her arrival, but Genevieve had been too enthralled with getting to know this gaudy, aging beauty—miraculously her lost *maman,* to talk about herself at all. But Sabelle was planning to leave early in the morning. If it weren't for the hope of finding Michael, Genevieve would be going with her.

They stepped from the carriage and went up the steps, arms linked in loving gaiety. "I wish I could take meself to another of them plays soon," Sabelle chuckled. "Specially if that same gorgeous man who played George was in any others. He kinda put me in mind of a captain I met once in Lisbon, specially around the shoulders. That man—God Almighty! I keep on forgettin', I'm supposed to be carryin' on like a mother. Don't suppose I ever learned how, exactly. It's been so long ago you were babes."

"I think you know how to be a mother, just fine," Genevieve said, giving Sabelle a quick hug.

She turned to tap at the door to summon a servant, then remembered that there were none here at night. She rummaged in her tiny blue damask purse with the ornate silver clasp for a key. She leaned a little against the door frame and was astonished when the door slid slightly open under the pressure of her elbow. André must have carelessly failed to push it shut tightly.

They entered the hall, still giggling happily, "When am I gonna meet that man of yours?" Sabelle asked. "I hear he's a good-lookin' buck and rich as hell to boot. Why, Gen, what's the matter. Did I say something—oh, I see. You don't much like him, do you?"

"*That* is an understatement."

"Then why do you stay here? I never would of thought any blood of mine would waste their time with a lost cause."

"It's a long story, *maman,* if you really want to hear."

Sabelle put her heavily beringed hands to the sides of Genevieve's face. "I've been waiting nearly twenty years to hear things from you, my treasure. But you look tired. What's that?"

They had started up the steps and a glint of steel had caught her eye. Genevieve saw it and bent to pick it up. "A knife, a dagger. I wonder what—" she turned it over in her hands and noted the stickiness. "There's something all over—oh, dear. I think it's blood!"

Sabelle took it from her. They stared at one another for a long, heavy second, then Sabelle spoke softly. "There's somethin' awful goddamn wrong here, Gen."

Of one accord, they ascended the steps. At the top all was dark. "What's down that way?" Sabelle whispered into the near gloom. There was a door at the end of the hall, open a slit, showing the light.

"That's André's room," she answered.

"I think we'd better take a look, don't you?" Sabelle asked.

Genevieve swallowed hard. She felt sure that something was terribly wrong but she did not want her newly found mother to think her a whimpering ninny. "Yes, we'd better," she replied.

Surprisingly, Sabelle hoisted her skirts and pulled a wicked-looking knife from the embossed leather sheath at her garter. She brought forth another from the bodice of her gown and handed it to Genevieve. Thus armed, they crept silently toward the door. They stood glacier-still outside the room for long moments, listening. But there were no sounds from within.

Genevieve's impulse was to slowly push the door open and peek timidly, but she knew better than that. If there was someone inside, it would alert them to her presence and give them the advantage. She caught Sabelle's eye, signaled, then pushed the door open so violently that it crashed into the wall inside, the engraved brass knob denting the paneling.

The sight that met her eyes was so horrible, so utterly unexpected that the knife in her hand clattered unnoticed to the floor as she stared in disbelief. André, nude and bloodsoaked, lay on the floor next to the bed in a tangle of sheets and spreads. His eyes were open in a horrified dead stare.

Genevieve opened her mouth, a scream stuck in her throat at the sight of André and the pool of blood around him, but Sabelle instantly clamped a hand over her mouth. She held it there until Genevieve closed her eyes and twisted away. "That yer husband?" Sabelle asked.

Genevieve nodded dumbly. "Is he dead?" she asked in a quivering whisper.

"Well, he ain't healthy," Sabelle answered. "Of *course* he's dead!"

"Dear God, I'll go to the gallows!"

"Begging your pardon, Sir."

Robert St. Justine rolled over, stretched, and demanded, "What is it, George? I generally wait until morning to get up. It's still pitch dark out there."

"I'm sorry Sir, it's just after three—"

"In the morning!"

"I'm afraid so, Sir." George was in a shockingly ornate nightshirt himself and looked mortally em-

barrassed about the whole thing. "There's a person at
the door. I tried to turn him away, but he insisted on
seeing you. In fact, he forced his way in."

Robert slung his long legs over the edge of the
bed, stretched hugely, and asked, "Did this person
happen to give a name?"

"Yes, Sir. He *says* he's a barrister named Clermont,
though I'm sure I never—"

But Robert was out of the bed and past him. "Michael! You old son of a bitch!" he was shouting as he
leaped down the stairs. He skidded to a stop at the
door of the sitting room. "My God, man, what's happened to you?" he exclaimed. Michael was slumped
forward in a chair, wringing his hands. When he
looked up at Robert there was a mad, weary dullness
in his eyes. His skin was pale, his whole posture de-
jected and strained to the nerve ends.

"Where is Genevieve?" he asked.

"With her husband, I presume. Michael, have some
sherry? Brandy? Something to eat? Forgive my can-
dor, but you look perfectly awful."

A momentary glint of the old comradeship sparked.
"I suppose I should be dashing about naked, like you
are. You look damn foolish, I'll stick with awful."

"George," Robert bellowed, "bring me my—"
George who'd been standing behind him, handed him
a dressing gown. "Thank you, George. Now be a good
man, don your best armor and wake the cook. Tell
her we need a plate of sandwiches and something to
drink. There's a new Sunday bonnet in it for her.
Now, Michael, you old idiot, where on earth have
you been?"

"Everywhere—nowhere—I don't really know, or
want to remember. It doesn't matter. Is Genevieve in
London? I knew her husband had been appointed
assistant to the new ambassador just before—before
what happened to me."

"Yes, she's in London," Robert answered, the concern he felt for his friend evident in his voice.

Michael stood, crammed on his hat. "Where? Give me the address."

"Now, hold on. You can't go bursting in on anyone at this time of night. Get a grip on yourself. We're going to sit here and eat and talk until the sun comes up."

"I've been through hell getting here. Do you think I'm going to wait any longer for something as empty and useless as social conversation?"

"That's precisely what I had in mind. Sit down." Robert put a hand on Michael's shoulder and forced him back into his chair. "I presume you have in mind rushing in there and grabbing her. Right? Very well, we're going to have to plan things out a bit. You see, Genevieve's in some trouble. Don't leap up like that, you're making me dizzy. She's not in any physical danger, but she's on hot bricks with the law because of my grandmother. There are constables watching the house constantly, and you don't want to tangle with them. You've also got André to think about. I doubt very much that he'll just tie a pink satin ribbon around her neck and hand her out the window to you. Ah, good. There's the cook, the darling, with some sandwiches. Now, Michael, put up your feet, have one of these watercress dainties and I'll explain it all to you. At seven we will clean the cream off our whiskers and go along to Genevieve's."

26

"What do you mean—gallows? You didn't do it, you've been with me for three days straight." Sabelle blasted. Genevieve sank into a chair, throwing her hands up in despair.

"It doesn't matter. I'll be blamed. You see, I hated him and he loathed me. I doubt that it was much of a secret—"

"Then why in hell did you stay with him this long?"

"Because I'm a wanted criminal in England—just as you are and for the same reasons—"

Sabelle grinned broadly. "Blimy, do you mean it, girl? God, I'm proud of you. But how—?"

"I stayed with André because we had a sort of agreement. He had all my money, I couldn't leave. As long as I behaved according to his standards, he allowed me the protection of his diplomatic immunity."

"But certainly you could have found some way of gettin' loose?"

"Yes, but there's something else. I was going to tell you in the morning before you left. I'm in love with the man who just escaped being hanged as a traitor—"

"I bet I know the one you mean. I heard all about it in France, name of Viscomte Beaumarchand or something?"

"Yes, but that wasn't his real name. He's Jean-Michael Clermont. You know him."

"I don't know nobody by that—what did you say?" Sabelle took hold of her arm.

"Yes. It's the man you know as Freddie," Genevieve

said, and was rewarded with the only truly surprised look she'd yet seen on her mother's face.

"Freddie! Christ, Gen, you don't mean it! Where is he?"

"That's just it—I don't know. I stayed with André only because I knew that if Michael—er, Freddie, came looking for me he could find me. I don't know if he wants to find me. I don't even know if he's alive."

"Well, this ain't quite the time to wonder about it," Sabelle said, bringing her back to bloodstained reality with a jolt. She glanced around the room. "It looks like he had a woman in here—a pretty damned rough one."

"Yes, he brought his women home. I heard them sometimes."

"Don't look like robbery though," Sabelle said.

Genevieve gulped uncomfortably. "André's women might have had other reasons than money for killing him. He was—strange. He liked pain."

Sabelle's face clouded. "Oh, one of them. He didn't hurt you, did he?" she spoke in a tone that hinted she might well kill him herself if someone hadn't already done it.

"No, not me. He didn't like me well enough," she said with a bitter laugh.

Sabelle was suddenly all business. "We gotta get our valuable hides out of here before them constables outside get any funny ideas about coming to the door. You got servants?"

"No, only the cook's staff. They live out."

"So we're not gonna get walked in on for a few hours? We better make the best of them and get a good early start. What about the money this deck-swabber took from you?"

"It's in a bank," Genevieve answered. "What difference does it make?"

"Who brought you up for you to ask a question

like that? Seems to me the sort of squibb-spined Jake
who'd steal his wife's money might keep it pretty close
instead of hauling it off to a bank." Sabelle turned,
pulled at a drawer of the desk. It was locked. So
were the others. "See what I mean? Most folks don't
lock up their ink unless it's printed on good paper
money. Get me them tongs," Sabelle said, gesturing
to the fireplace at the other end of the room.

Genevieve hesitated, sickened by the knowledge of
what else was in the room. She averted her eyes, circled as far from André's lifeless body as she could,
and fetched the unicorn fire tools. Sabelle applied
the point of one to the corner of a desk drawer and
wrenched it open. With a splintering shriek the
drawer face ripped and some of Genevieve's jewels
were exposed.

They hastily invaded the other locked cabinets.
Most of them were seemingly locked out of habit,
for they contained little of value. "He must have
sold most of them and spent the money," Genevieve
said.

"One more drawer and we better get movin'. We're
makin' more noise than we ought. Liable to raise
suspicions. There, that one's empty, too. Take the
cases off them pillows and put this stuff in. Now,
let's get out of here."

She doused the light, pulled Genevieve along down
the hall and steps and back through the servants'
door. "Is there a door opens into the stables?" she
asked as they crept through the kitchen and pantry.

"Yes, to your left down that hallway," Genevieve
whispered in response.

"Keep low," Sabelle hissed, dragging Genevieve
down into a crouch at the back door. "Let's cross
your fingers that your stableboy ain't unhitched them
bays yet. C'mon."

They crept furtively to the stable, easing the latch
and sliding inside with their bags of loot. The bays

were still hitched. The boy had doused the carriage lanterns and loosened the traces but that was all. Genevieve called his name but Sabelle was already at work. She slipped between the bays, patting them as she fastened the traces and tightened the yoke bolts. Genevieve thrust twopence in the boy's hand and told him to keep quiet.

Sabelle crammed her lush black hair under her tall beaver hat, threw her bags in the carriage, and climbed onto the coachman's perch. She struggled into the driver's coat and laprobe, purloined from a nearby hook, and shoved a pipe between her teeth. "Hurry," she snapped. Genevieve hurled her bags and herself inside, slamming the doors and drawing the shades. Her mother ordered the boy to open the doors.

And then, to Genevieve's astonishment, they left at a leisurely walk. The bays strolled out onto the street as if on their way to *le petit déjeuner* at a friend's house. The constables, cozy in the front door of the maisonette, paid little attention. When they had calmly clopped around the corner and out of sight, Sabelle stood up in the driver's box. "Now, my beauties!" she sang out, snapping and cracking her whip in the air and giving the spirited bays half a foot of rein. They sprang forward as if shot from the mouths of cannons.

On to Gravesend! Sabelle handled the reins like the devil's own driver, cursing, snapping leather, urging the bays on with abusive endearments. They raced and skidded through the sordid streets of night-time London, tails lashing, hooves glinting off the pavement with steel sparks. Sabelle cursingly called them her darlings and made the whip dance in mid-air above their sleek red necks.

There was pursuit. Genevieve caught glimpses of armed men riding hard behind them from time to time, but Sabelle's expert handling of the horses and her knowledge of London backstreets kept them safe.

At last the bays were lagging from their flight with the heavy carriage. They slowed, chests heaving, coats speckled with foam and sweat. *They'll never get us to Gravesend,* Genevieve thought desperately. *We need fresh horses!*

Sabelle pulled the team to a halt outside the nearest tavern and leaped to the ground. Genevieve already had the carriage door open and was slinging sacks to her. They hurried the bays behind the inn, picked two likely horses, and tied on their bags. A moment later they scrambled astride their new mounts, skirts gathered about their thighs. They galloped away to the cheers of drunken spectators.

They raced through tiny villages and greens, always hearing hoofbeats behind. Another quarter hour and musketfire was whistling through their hair. But the wharves of Gravesend were in sight. "Them bastards damned well better be mannin' the watch tonight!" Sabelle shouted as they clattered onto slick cobblestones. Genevieve silently agreed. From the corner of her eye she saw her mother snatch a crimson petticoat from beneath her voluminous skirts. "No sign of recognition—goddamn!"

They blasted past thatched hovels while sleep-befuddled inhabitants staggered to the doors clutching trousers. One man held a torch. Genevieve did not stop to think. Her mother was brandishing the red petticoat as a signal. Why not make it more visible in the first striped dawn light? She leaned low in the saddle and seized the brand, nearly decapitating herself in the doorway.

Even before she straightened in the saddle, her mother had swept the streak of scarlet through the flame. They clattered and clanged madly toward the wharves, Sabelle whirling the flaming undergarment about her head. Genevieve repeated the gesture with the torch, then noted with horror that her mother was not slackening speed as they bolted up the incline to the ramp. Quite the contrary, she was digging her toes into the horse's ribs and shouting, "Follow me, girl!"

They rode off the wharf. The horses arched wide as Genevieve hurled the torch straight overhead into the bubbling black waves. It left a spangled orange trail. Then she was flying through the air, soaring as her mount made a terrific leap.

They splashed down hard. Genevieve went under, deep under, to escape the flailing legs of both horses. Her saddlebags of jewels sank past her. She had made a clean dive, nearly scraping the barnacle-crusted bottom of a derelict dhow. Then, long, powerful strokes, up and out, took her yards away from where she'd landed. She broke surface, gasping, to see Sabelle's dark head a few feet away. "Swim for it, Gen."

They tore away petticoats as they swam, trying to lighten the load of so many heavy, wet layers. Musketfire rained down like smoldering droplets from an air-bound hell. Floundering, weighted down by their fashionable garments, the two women struggled onward.

A line of princely black ship silhouettes towered in the water just ahead. On one of them a lantern was swinging in circles, just as Sabelle had swung her incendiary underwear. "I told them bastards to weigh anchor if I gave the alarm! What are they waitin' for?" Sabelle soggily growled.

Her answer came with the creak of oars a stone's throw away. "Captain! Where are ye?"

"Here, you blue-eared son of a snake charmer. I told you deckswabbers to run for it when I gave the—"

The night ignited with bronze and yellow death. Cannonfire from the nearest ship shrieked over their heads. When Genevieve looked back over her shoulder, the wharf was a smoking ruin. Rough hands dragged her and Sabelle aboard the ship's small boat, where they sat and hugged each other as the men rowed. "Another pirate lady?" chirped a cabin boy, handing them scratchy warm blankets.

Sabelle fondly cuffed the little urchin on the side of the head. "Me daughter. I found her. She's comin' home with me."

"Where's home?" asked Genevieve eagerly.

Sabelle held her arm up. In the preliminary glow of dawn there bobbed a stately brigantine. Her figure-head was a veiled Arabic beauty with a sinister raven on her shoulder. The wooden woman held one slim finger to her companion's beak as if bidding him be silent. The raised gold lettering about the bow read *Nightbird.*

"My ship, the fairest prize ever took from the land o' pashas and harems. She can outrun the whole Spanish fleet and maneuver like a circus horse. We're headin' to the Caribe to find our Evonne."

Genevieve said nothing, but some of her weariness and disappointment must have shown through. Sabelle lifted her daughter's chin with a brave, wet hand, and said, "It ain't palm trees and white houses but it's me home and now it's yours, too. All of it. We'll get our Evonne and then build us them white houses. There, honey, cry and get it all out. There, Gen, there."

Robert managed to restrain Michael for two hours. By that time it was almost dawn. "Just tell me where her house is," Michael insisted. "Don't worry, I won't do anything rash—not yet. But I have to see her."

"I won't tell you, I'll show you. I'm coming along. Forgive me, old man, but I don't think you're fit to make a decision on how to button your vest without help."

They rode through the almost-morning fog, Robert apprehensive, Michael in a barely submerged frenzy of anticipation. As they rode, London began to wake. Vendors sleepily pushed fruit wagons into the roads; housewives threw open windows with cries of "Gardez-loo" and dumped chamber pots into the street; young boys who made their family's living by begging took up their corners and set up their pitiful laments, the odors of fresh bread seeped under bakery doors.

They rounded the last corner. A street of fine houses, painted iron fences, and tiny front yards with a few early bulbs flinging up gaudy blooms. The third from the corner was the house that had been taken by Count André de Lieuvienne and the small yard was full of soldiers. Robert and Michael exchanged looks of alarm and spurred their horses. Hooves sparking on the cobblestones, they skidded to a stop before the house.

"What's going on here?" Robert shouted to a soldier as they leaped from their mounts.

"Queen's business, Sir," the man replied. "Be along with you. Don't need no more gawkers."

"Who's in charge here?" Michael demanded.

"Captain Westcott, Sir. But you can't see him now. He's inside."

Michael started to push through the gate, but the soldier was well trained and quickly had the point of a bayonet pricking at his chest.

Robert pulled Michael back. "You won't find out much if you get yourself killed or arrested, you ass." He glanced around, fastened his gaze on a wide-eyed servant, leaning over the fence between André's house and the next one. He dragged Michael along to question her. "What is your name, my girl?" he asked.

"Lizzie, Sir," she said, bobbing a curtsey, but keeping her gaze firmly affixed to the front door of André's house.

Robert passed her a coin and spoke in a warm confidential tone. "What's happening here, Lizzie?"

"Auwww, ever such frightful things!" she said. "There's been soldiers standing round for long as long. Not doing nothing, just keeping an eye like on the ambassador's house, you see. Then way late there was noises inside. I heard 'em myself, truly I did. Auwww, it were awful, Sir, crashing and breaking and such—"

This was promising to be a long and fruitless dissertation. "What happened!" Michael burst out.

The girl cringed back. Robert gave Michael a stern look, then tried to soothe the girl. "Now Lizzie, just tell us, what are the soldiers doing there?"

She leaned forward confidentially. "Well, Sir, not that I could say for sure, not having been in the house, but I hear there's somebody dead in there—done to death most wicked, I'll wager—"

"Michael, wait!" Robert shouted and Michael cleared the fence in one mad bound. Robert dashed after him. Soldiers, alerted by the shout, rounded on the running figures, surrounding them at the door. Just then the door opened and everyone's attention was riveted on the soldiers who slowly made their way out, bearing between them a covered litter.

At first it was impossible to guess in the eerie dawn light the size of the figure concealed beneath the improvised shroud. A murmur passed through the onlookers outside the fence. Michael's face drained of all color and he swayed almost imperceptibly. Then, with a quick searing move he reached forward, grasped the sheet covering the body, and flipped it back a few inches. At the sight of the glistening blond hair, he took a deep breath.

"Here, you can't be doing that," one of the soldiers said, pushing him away roughly.

"Where is his wife?" Michael shouted.

They all stared at him as if he'd gone mad—which was, in fact, perilously near the truth.

"Where is his *wife!*" he screamed. But no one answered and he dashed past them into the house.

Three of the soldiers lunged for the door, but Robert was there first. He blocked the way, faced them. "I'm Robert St. Justine, gentlemen. Some of you who have been watching the house were no doubt hired by my family. Tell me," he said, irresistible authority ringing in his voice. "Where is his wife?"

The men exchanged puzzled glances, then soldier-like, obeyed his orders. "She's gone, Sir. She and the other woman. They killed the ambassador and got away."

Robert could hear Michael pounding through the hallways, crashing through doors and shouting for Genevieve. A chill ran down his spine. "No," he warned the soldier, "leave him alone. I'll see to him. What other woman are you talking about?"

"An older woman, quite a looker," one of the soldiers volunteered. "Heard the Countess calling her *'maman'* when they went out yesterday."

"My God, she found her mother?" Robert exclaimed.

Just then Michael came careening down the steps. "Robert, I can't find her. I can't find her!" He tried to struggle past Robert, shouting at the soldiers, "Where have you taken her?"

"What's going on here?" a raspy, belligerent voice called from inside. Captain Westcott strode forward and Michael flung himself at the man. He grabbed his collar in white-knuckled fists and shouted, "Where has the Countess been taken?"

Captain Westcott tried to pull away. The guards at the door surged past Robert and seized Michael. He struggled, fought insanely, lashed out with fists and words. Like the string of some musical instrument that had been tuned higher and higher over a long period of time, his nerves had stretched and stretched and finally frayed to pieces. Screaming, thrashing, he was completely out of control. He was struck by the soldiers and struck again, but he was beyond perception of pain, beyond reason.

Robert leaped into the fray. He and Michael and half a dozen soldiers crashed about in the hallway. The gray marble floor was spotted with flecks of blood, a table with spindle legs and a tortoise-shell top splintered against a mirror, bringing shards raining down and skittering across the marble floor.

Captain Westcott, intent on subduing this unknown maniac, drew back his arms and swung, but Michael ducked and Westcott made contact instead with a large brass vase that bounced, bonging funereally, along the length of the hall.

Robert's motives were at first misunderstood and one of the guards delivered a breathtaking blow to his midsection. Robert gasped, stumbled, elbowed, and chopped his way through the cloud of uniforms. Shouts, grunts of pain, the sour sweat odor of fright. Finally he reached Michael, backhanded off a man who was attempting to choke his friend. He plowed his fist into Michael's stomach, then caught him in a bearlike embrace as he keeled forward. "She's gone, Michael. Escaped. She and Sabelle got away. Can you hear me, you fool? She's safe."

Michael hung over double in Robert's arms, sucking in deep, pained breaths. One by one, the soldiers backed away, aware dimly that this was a moment that could not bear intrusion. Westcott started to step forward, but Robert glared at him silently. Westcott waved an arm at the soldiers, signaling them to go outside. When they had all done so, he followed with one last glance backward. There was a glint of pity and understanding in the look.

Michael still didn't move. "Do you understand what I'm saying to you?" Robert asked softly. "She found her mother and they've gone."

"She couldn't have—have killed him, Robert," Michael whispered painfully.

"No, of course she couldn't. She's safely out of it. We'll find her. I'll help you," he comforted. "Now stand up straight and we'll go home."

Michael unfolded himself slowly, his joints almost creaking with the effort. His face was the color of the underbelly of a fish and there were tear tracks down his cheeks. "Home?" he said bitterly. "Where in bloody hell *is* home?"

"For as long as you want, my home is your home."

Michael looked at him with reddened eyes, took a

deep breath, and began to tremble before collapsing against his friend in dry, choking sobs.

"We'll find her, old man. We'll find her," Robert repeated soothingly as he led Michael quietly toward the back of the house and out into the dismal morning bustle.

A thousand miles of open seas unrolled before the *Nightbird* in an undulating carpet of jade and turquoise and ivory. Genevieve, at the rail, stared, unseeing. André dead. Her mother alive. Michael lost to her, probably forever. And Evonne and Robert and Althea and Xantha . . . .

She felt a reassuring hand on her shoulder. Sabelle had come up behind her and now stood braving the wind with her depressed daughter. "We'll find Evonne and have a reunion the likes o' which the Caribe's never seen, lass. I been looking at the charts and I think I know where her island is."

"Yes, I have a good idea of its location, too."

Porpoises leaped and played about the bow, tails shimmying in the hot copper light of mid-afternoon. Genevieve wished she could be that free, that unfettered by care. "Mother, what about Michael?"

"Oh, hell, I run into that boy every few years. Nothin' to fret over. We cross anchor lines so often we might as well just dock together. He's a good lad, a brave lad. Damned near good enough for my daughter. He'll come to the Caribe, he knows that's where the *Nightbird* usually sails. We'll see him again."

"I wonder," Genevieve replied dismally.

27

Evonne's island was a blackened ruin. The *Nightbird* could not enter the bay because of the weathered masts of a sunken ship peering over the waves at them. "It isn't the *Black Angel*," Genevieve said, both sick and relieved as she squinted down through bright sunlight on blue waves. "This ship's sails are white. It isn't Evonne's ship. She got away."

There were some ragged men fishing in a dilapidated dinghy a short distance away. Sabelle hailed them loudly, shouting for news. "The lady and her black ship was out to sea when the governor's men come," one of the old fishermen replied, hands cupped about his mouth. "We seen them black sails circle the island but she din't never try ter land again. She's feedin' on merchantmen in the Caribe again, the angel lady."

"You hear that? She's safe," Sabelle told Genevieve.

"That ship's been down there a year at the least. That means Evonne's had twelve months at sea again. She wanted to quit piracy. She had a pretty house on the crest of the hill, she said, and fruit trees, and enough money to last a lifetime. Now she's back, living like a vulture on the high seas."

Sabelle turned a piercing gaze on her, one eyebrow cocked. "I know you don't like it, Little One, but maybe it's all Evonne and me got to go on. My search for you children ate up a bunch o' money so I just kept piratin' and lookin'. I got some to run on honestly now—from the old Duke I got hitched to—but it takes a heap to run a ship and pay a crew when you ain't preyin' on fat Spaniards. If we don't find her soon, I'll be back to my thievin' ways. And so will you."

"I'm not right for this work. I hate bloodshed and taking what doesn't belong to me," Genevieve replied quietly, twisting the knot in her bandana and trying to keep her braided hair out of her eyes.

"I know, Gen. You ain't made for blood and thunder like me—and your sister, judgin' from the sound o' her. But what else would you do, girl? Hire out as a governess and raise some pompous old landlubber's brats? Teach school? Mop floors? Or marry another like that Count o' yours and wear rubies big as dog turds?"

"Oh, Mother!" Genevieve marveled disapprovingly.

"Don't 'oh, Mother' me with your ladied ways and all. You seen life close-up, you ain't no silk-swathed fool, much as you try to let on. You're smart as an old racehorse and twice as tricky."

Genevieve, oddly enough, felt a thrill of pride at these rustic assessments of her character. It was infinitely better than syrupy compliments on beauty or virtue. She found herself smiling at her extraordinary mother. "Well, my Captain, where to? Barbados? Martinique? Jamaica? We have an entire ocean to explore."

Sabelle tightened the belt of her velvet knee breeches. "Don't worry. Your doting *maman* knows what she's lookin' for this time—not two nameless babes but a famous captain on a ship you can't miss. Damn. I nigh-on crossed paths with the *Black Angel* half a dozen times. But I didn't know. I just didn't know." She bullied the man in the crow's nest into wary wakefulness, then sent Genevieve to fetch her maps and charts.

"The *Black Angel*?" inquired the jowly, peg-legged sailor. He scratched his bristly head a while, then spat a wad of murky tobacco at his foot. "Ach, yes.

The black brig with the winged figurehead. She billowed outa here nigh an hour ago, all opened up."

"Did she say where she was headed?" Genevieve asked breathlessly.

"The Mediterranean. Her crew talked like they didn't 'spect ter return. You need to reach ship, nein? Goot luck, little lady. She's fast as the devil's own steed."

Genevieve thanked him, threw him a fistful of francs, and turned heel. She raced to the dock where her boatman was just tying up the ship's dhow. "Cast off! Cast off! We're an hour behind the *Angel* and she's gone forever. Hurry!"

They rowed furiously to the *Nightbird*, making the oars squeak with the strain of such speed. At last they banged against the side of the trim brigantine. Genevieve shot up the rope ladder, shouting for her mother. "Cast off! We're an hour behind her and she's all sails in the wind to the Mediterranean! If we don't catch her now—"

Sabelle, shoulders squared against the wheel, gave her daughter a gleaming look. "We'll catch her. All hands. Becker, Fagan, haul anchor! You there, up that rigging! Unfurl the stuns'le, we'll need the speed! Where's my ship's surgeon? Ahh, there you are, Wilma —the sheeting you make bandages from—I need the biggest uncut piece you got."

The decks erupted with color and action. Sailors went scrambling to attend to the sails while Sabelle yelled for them to head out north-northeast. Anchors up, the *Nightbird* swayed indolently, then gave a surprised lurch as the wind found her unfurling sails. Genevieve took the fat bundle of sheeting from Wilma, tucked it in her vest, and began climbing ratlines up to the crow's nest. She wanted to be the lookout who announced success or failure; she needed to be the one who told her mother aye or nay at the climax of their long, difficult search.

The *Nightbird* breasted the waves like a leviathan

sighting prey. Silver foam leaped and sprayed as the sleek Turkish vessel ploughed ahead, acres of canvas glowing ice-white in the blinding noon sun. Genevieve reached the crow's nest and clambered inside, high above the flap and mayhem of sails and crew. She shaded her eyes against the glare of light on lashing sapphire seas.

The horizon was empty of all save a few ramshackle fishing boats. No haughty black predator bore through the windy ocean. *Please,* Genevieve thought, *please!* She wrested a spyglass from the depths of her breeches pocket and hastily scanned the narrow blue vista before her. Nothing.

She sensed, rather than saw, her mother pause down below, straining her neck in wait for word of a sighting. Genevieve, glass still to eye, signaled with her hand—no ship. Sabelle's blasphemous retort was audible from bow to stern. She stormed back to the wheel and maintained her course.

Genevieve, brown hair escaping its pins to lash wickedly about her face, unfolded the sheet and dropped it at her feet. A white flag—the age-old sign of surrender. She'd been ready to run it up the pole so Evonne would see that their intentions were peaceful. Not that Evonne would ever trust anyone else— but perhaps the flag would keep them from being shot to—

A speck in the spyglass. She wiped it off, then put it back to her eye. The speck was still there. A ship! But was it the right one? "SHIP AHOY!" she brayed, hands cupped at mouth. "SHIP AHOY, CAP'N MEDDOWS!" It struck her, for an exhilarated moment, that the last time she'd shouted those words they'd been for her sister Evonne. She folded her sunburnt hands to her heart and closed her eyes. "Please, God, please let it be her or I think I'll—"

"WHAT DIRECTION, YOU NINNY-HEADED SILK-STOCK- INGED SEA COW?" came the unmotherly bellow from below.

"SOUTH-SOUTHWEST, STRAIGHT OUT! LAY ON!"

The speck on the horizon was growing larger. Genevieve gave an ecstatic whoop as she took in the ultimate identifying feature of the other vessel: even at
such a distance she could tell the sails were black!
It was the *Black Angel,* fully rigged and sailing out
of the Caribbean into the Atlantic. Black canvas rip-
pled and slapped in the wind.

They were growing nearer. Evonne's ship was traveling at a moderate pace while *Nightbird* raced so
swiftly in pursuit that she barely seemed to skim
the waves. The whoosh and chop of foamy water
sang to Genevieve as her sister's ship came fully into
sight without benefit of the spyglass.

The *Black Angel* cut her sails and reversed rudder
suddenly. She swung around, presenting herself at
a defiant angle—a practiced posture that would allow
the least damage to her while, at the same time, giving her versatile swivel guns full range at the *Nightbird.* Now was the time for the makeshift flag. Genevieve shook the sheet out, caught the flagline, and
ran the huge square of white material up it, lowering
the skull-and-raven "Jolly Roger" just under it. That
way their pirate identification still showed, flown
under the banner of truce and parley.

She could almost hear her sister shouting, "Those
fools chased me in order to surrender! What the
Devil is going on here?"

At an order from Sabelle, the gunners cranked
their cannon—swivel guns like Evonne's—down, muzzles pointed at the sea. They were still out of firing
range of the other ship. Sabelle ordered a volley—a
deliberate, unmistakable twenty-one gun salute that
went harmlessly to the bottom of the sea. There was
no way Evonne could take it as a gesture of aggres-
sion. Surely by now she was scratching her head in
wonder and guessing that the intent was nonviolent.

But Genevieve knew her sister was a suspicious
woman, and rightly so. She would not come blunder-

ing into their arms. Sun and wind stinging her face,
Genevieve shaded her eyes with her hands and looked
down. The sails went completely and utterly slack.
Sabelle had ordered them furled—thus leaving herself defenseless against attack. She ordered the cannon withdrawn and their muzzle hatches bolted.

The *Nightbird* perched, helpless, on the dark and
rolling sea. Genevieve saw her mother pacing the
deck, hands clasped behind her brightly clad back. A
plan came to her; she threw down her spyglass and
wriggled down the ratlines at a dangerous speed. At
last she dropped, gasping, at her mother's feet.

"She'll never come to us, she's too wary of traps—
every governor in the Caribbean would like her head
on a pike. We've got to go to her; row over in a
ship's boat. I know Evonne. Curiosity isn't as strong
as suspicion to her. She'll sit and wait 'til snakes
grow wings—or she'll turn and race the wind."

"Lower the ship's boat!" Sabelle barked, then shook
Genevieve roughly, fondly by the shoulder. "You and
your sister—ain't neither one o' you a fool. And I
bet she's damned near as pretty as you, too. Sailors,
both you girls, her a captain, all nerve and steel and
legend; you, the best scout, navigator, and subcaptain
I ever had. Flash and color's her style. But you, you
hide in the background quietly doin' all the real
work. You damned near ran my ship these months,
took a load off me, and you never once looked for
praise. Clever as the whole Royal Navy put together
and sharp as daggers. Willie couldn't a' been yer
father—I think me and Mars mated. Me and the
god o' war, we made children of blood an' velvet an'
iron. Sisters of the sword, you are. If she's half as
loyal and brave and bonny as you, I couldn't do no
better for daughters. Now let's go!"

Genevieve swallowed hard, eyes swimming in proud
tears. She gave her mother's riotous, scarf-captured
hair a quick tug, knowing emotional displays would
only slow them at this point. "You have me so swelled

up with praise I can hardly see straight. You've
spoiled me as a seaman; I'll want to lounge around
all day hearing pretty talk. Let's go—we have a family to complete."

"You just wait. I ain't goin' lookin' like this and
neither are you. C'mon. She's gotta be proud o' her
family," Sabelle insisted, then snapped commands to
the crew, leaving her quartermaster in charge.

Genevieve was yanked into the foc'sle cabin. She
and Sabelle slapped the dust off each other, struggled
into knee breeches with diamond buttons, high boots,
silk shirts, and lush velvet coats. There was a hasty
session with hairbrushes and paintpots, then they
fastened on lace cuffs and cravats. Sabelle topped her
luxuriant black curls with a captain's tricornered hat
made magnificent with an emerald studded cockade
and an entire peacock tail crawling down the back.
She then slung on every jewel in her collection.

Genevieve, feeling foolish and yet delighted with
the whole absurd procedure (they were, after all, a
pirate vessel in every danger of having their ship
blasted to splinters), pulled on a modest cap. Sabelle
yanked it off and extracted a treasure from her walnut wardrobe that she had been plainly saving a
long time—the tricorn hat of a naval commandant,
black velvet with silver piping, an egg-sized ruby
brooch, and a single, yard-long white feather.

There was barely time to admire it in the mirror
before Sabelle yanked her out, shouting for the two
best-dressed seamen to get their "slimy, bilge-bloated
carcasses" to the rowboat and man the oars. In mere
minutes they were in the tiny boat, sitting stiffly as
they approached the ominous black ship. Another
few seconds and they passed beneath the winged
figurehead. Sabelle's face was the color of vulnerable
new ivory under her shipboard tan. Her fingers closed
like vises on Genevieve's knee.

A rope ladder slithered down the gleaming ebony
hull and softly splashed into the water a foot away.

Even before the rowboat had stopped, Genevieve was scaling the ladder. "Give me a moment to see her, put her at ease. She must feel like an Indian mystic on his bed of nails, trying to decipher this entire affair. Give me a minute. Please?" she called back over her shoulder.

"Okay, but you'd better hurry. In one minute I'm swoopin' up there with my mouth blazin' away. Tell her—" Sabelle's voice trailed wistfully off. "No, I'll tell her myself."

Ship-calloused hands caught Genevieve at the top, plucked her up and over. She planted a hand firmly on the top of her ornate hat, brown curls fluttering in the wind. The entire crew, armed to the teeth, stood watching her. She recognized more of them than recognized her. "I want to see gunner's mate Xantha and Captain Meddows, if you please. Also Kate, if she's around."

"Lass! Is it you?" came a Scots-thickened cry. Red-haired Kate burst through the onlookers, arms in the air. "Faith, we'd nigh given ye up for lost! We were going to France to find ye!"

"Ninny white girl save us long voyage. She come back all by silly self. How de King, Gen?" Xantha swaggered through the sailors, words unable to conceal the delighted grin lighting up her lovely chocolate face. She was twice as beautiful and twice as outrageously dressed as normal—something red and rustling with silver-hammered bangles as big as astrolabes shimmering at her ears.

Genevieve, laughing, threw herself into their arms. She, Kate, and Xantha laughed, embraced, and shook each other. Then she heard a light, low "ahem" that could belong to no one else. She whirled to see her exquisite sister, arms akimbo, regarding the proceedings with a teasing grin. "The minute that ship began doing those crazy things, I should have guessed. Who else but a Meddows would have done things so spectacularly insane?"

Genevieve went to her slowly, felt the fervent embrace that came willingly, without urging or reproach.
Evonne cared after all. Evonne cared. It was as if
something sweet and too precious halted in her throat,
clouding her eyesight and clogging all sensibilities.
She had to take a deep breath and force back tears.

"Yes, Evonne, yes, it was a Meddows, all right. But
it wasn't me."

Evonne went rigid. She held Genevieve at arm's
length, then her eyes went round, breath coming shallow. She stared straight ahead as if she had seen a
ghost. She very nearly had.

Her double was coming toward her—her twin, her
doppelganger, her mirror image. Then, as the astounding woman drew closer, the age difference was
apparent. The black hair was flawed with a touch of
gray, there were lightly etched lines of living; the
figure was rounder, more voluptuous. Sabelle came
on board the *Black Angel* like Cleopatra boating up
the Nile. She was ablaze with diamonds, emeralds,
sapphires, flashing beams of colored light off her captain's silk and velvet uniform. Genevieve was so proud
it choked her.

Evonne released her and began to walk forward,
slowly, crookedly. She stopped a foot from Sabelle
and put her hands up to her mother's face. "The
nose—the cheekbones—I paint that mouth in the mirror every morning. I brush that hair—I wear those
clothes. You're me and you're *not* me." There was a
quivering pause, then she whispered, *"Oh, Mother!"*

Sabelle took the slim raven head between her hands,
rocked it, cursed, complimented, shook her daughter
by the shoulders, then clasped her close. Genevieve
joined them in utter silence, the only sound that of
hardbitten, unemotional, cool Evonne's stifled sobbing. "My beauties, my treasures," Sabelle murmured
thickly. "I'm rich past all proper due now. Ah, my
treasures!"

* * *

The *Black Angel* swayed gently in the ocean's slow swell. Wicks burned softly in hanging glass pots full of sweet-scented oil, lighting Evonne's cabin with a loving golden glow. Genevieve, Evonne, and Sabelle, attired in freshly washed shifts, sat brushing their hair on the captain's bunk.

Genevieve closed her eyes, smelling the lavender and ginseng perfume of her mother, mingled with sandalwood combs, cinnamon lamp oil, and the rose attar soap they had used on their hair and undergarments. Other scents came creeping seductively under the door, for the cook was preparing a feast with fresh foodstuffs from the island they were anchored by. The *Nightbird* and the *Black Angel* floated bow to stern like loving old horses swatting flies off each other.

She loved to hear their voices; Sabelle's conglomerate patois of a hundred regions, peppered with nautical terms and flamboyant obscenities; Evonne's, better educated, more clipped, less accustomed to frankness and open assessment. They could have been meadowlarks to her glad ears.

There were footsteps outside, then a rap on the marquetry door. "Dinner's smokin' hot and served prompt, Cap'n," came Kate's brogue at the door. Evonne bade her enter. A most sumptuous sight greeted them—Xantha and Kate, attired in their gaudy best, arms full of covered plates emitting mouth-watering aromas. Behind them came two more women with a wheeled table, dishes, silverware, and more food.

The chuckling apparitions deposited their goods upon crisp Irish linen tablecloths, laid out Oriental porcelains, and eating utensils of gold and sterling with bone, crystal, and tortoiseshell handles. Then Xantha, Kate, and their assistants slipped out, giggling, and shut the door.

Genevieve pounced on the table, lifting the silver-plated domes. A rush of stomach-weakening steam came curling about her face, laden with delicious things: roast parrot marinated in oyster sauce and sprinkled with chopped chives, fresh fruit salad bright with chunks of mango, pineapple, apple, nectarine, papaya, guava, cocoanut, fat black grapes with frosty blushes, and sliced bananas.

In the cloisonné tureen she found bouillabaisse, in the next, green onion and mushroom soup, floating with parsley and thin, twisting noodles. Their rum punch was served in hollowed-out cocoanuts and pineapples. Glossy, braided sour-dough bread and saucers of lemon butter surrounded the biggest platter, on which Genevieve uncovered the largest lobster she had ever seen.

The three women laughingly launched a ferocious attack upon the loaded table. Between bites, they continued their joking, talking, and catching up on the missing years. Genevieve looked at her family and felt a warm, kind hurt in her heart. *They're so beautiful, so clever and brave and sensitive. How did I bear life without them? I've never been happier. Almost never. Good company, good food*—she raised her pineapple "goblet." "To us. To the family. *A nous.*"

"To us," came the twin echo, as all three raised rum punch in salute. They drank deeply, smiled, and continued gorging themselves on the culinary excesses of the inspired cook.

"I wish we could stay like this forever," Evonne said.

Sabelle nodded. "Wouldn't it be grand? But we got a livin' to make and two ships to run. Mind you, my quartermaster's a good lad but he can't run that ship forever. The *Nightbird*'s too valuable to let some boy run her to ruin. Taylor's a good lad but . . . maybe I should appoint Deacon or May temporary captain. . . ." She chewed long and thoughtfully on a savory slice of parrot. "No, it won't do no good.

I gotta get back aboard my brig. Ain't no one can run her like me—and Gen."

"Very well then," Evonne agreed, brandishing a mango for effect, "you take the *Nightbird*'s helm again and we'll sail in formation. No one can stand against both of us. No one. I've the most infamous ship in the Caribbean, most merchantmen give up without a battle. And with *two* ships—I'd take on the Queen's own navy!"

"I didn't come all this way to see us separated again—not even so little a distance between us as different ships!" Genevieve cried out. She sat bolt upright, abandoning her food. "And piracy—my God, it's a miracle you two have survived at all, the way you persist in this business. I've been on the other side of it, I know what a horror it is to be on a ship attacked by pirates."

Sabelle and Evonne exchanged knowing looks, infuriating Genevieve. "We know, too," Evonne snapped. "We don't plunder for the joy of it, we do it exactly as you said—as a business. I've never killed unnecessarily, I don't let my crew torture or rape. Better for a ship to fall into my hands than those of some diehard cutthroat. I'm only continuing long enough to accumulate some assets. Then I'm going to try again for a white veranda'd house on a hill full of palm trees."

"Exactly," Sabelle agreed in a flash. "Save some loot, get the ships full—*sacre merde*, Little Ones, the *Nightbird*'s half full already. Then we'll pay off the crews, sell all the jewels and silks and other cargo—and we'll get us a little white house, all right."

Genevieve wanted to trust their sincerity, but after all, she was related to them and knew what sort of women her family bred. Perhaps they were merely trying to mollify her. "Oh, really?" she asked, trying to sound cool and composed and utterly adult. "And what will you do with these two ships you're so insanely fond of?"

Evonne's brow furrowed in thought—*Aha!* Genevieve thought triumphantly. *She has no idea, she hasn't thought of it at all. I've caught them!*

Sabelle gave an idle yawn, stretching her shapely legs. "Got it all figgered out, *mes enfants.* My old shipmate Garlanda is in business in Martinique; she told me she could use some good, fast mail ships to rush between here and Europe. We could go legal, even captain 'em from time to time when the sailin' urge got too strong to fight. What d'me girls say?"

"It's a good idea, but I'm not retiring until I'm rich," Evonne announced. "And then—maybe Garlanda can use my ship. *I* certainly won't need it."

"Why? Where are you going to be?"

"In that white house on the hill, swathed in silks and taffetas, strutting on my veranda with my parasol and a pair of Irish maids saying, 'Aye, Mum,' and 'No, Mum.' I'll be drinking just-squeezed lemonade and swirling my petticoats and listening to half a dozen rich, eligible, handsome men proposing. Not that I think there's a single man on earth interesting enough to hold me for more than a month. I want jewels on my neck and fat, sleek horses on my lawn. I want to rest at night without hearing the ship's bell tolling out the next watch. I want to sleep in a canopied bed on solid ground."

"Do you really?" Genevieve asked, puzzled. Her sister shrugged and said nothing.

"We got pretty near everything we need right here," Sabelle said.

"I agree," Genevieve said curtly, almost bitterly. "Everything—but Michael."

"Are you still thinkin' like that," her mother carefully asked.

"I can't help it. I mean, things with the three of us have turned out better than I ever dared hope— and yet I'll never be content with the mystery of him. I wonder sometimes late at night when I'm alone and sorting things out—I wonder if he's even alive."

"You really loved him," Sabelle said quietly.

"Yes, I did."

"I," announced Evonne, finishing with her food and flopping down on the bed, "have never loved *anyone.*"

"How can you say that? Do you mean just men? Or do you mean—" Genevieve began almost angrily.

Sabelle put a hand on her shoulder. "You let Evonne be. Her way and yours aren't the same. She's like she is for a reason. It's her way of survival. Your way is to be easier, more forgivin'. We just gotta accept each other like we are. Lissen, Gen—I love that boy a whole lot, too. He's just like a son to me. Maybe we'll find him some day. He writes Roque and Garlanda every so often, you know how Garlanda is. Why, if that girl got a letter from him in the middle o' the night, she'd fling on a nightie and come barrelin' over to that white house of ours, wavin' that letter and screamin' the boy's address. I know it ain't easy, not knowin' what become a' him or if he still loves you— don't look like a cow kicked you, you're my daughter, ain't you? O' *course* he loves you—he can't help it."

Sabelle sat up and stretched. "Now rinse that foolishness out of yer heads. There's a whole lot more drinkin' and talkin' left to do before that sun comes up. Pass that rum!"

The first several months after Genevieve's escape had been the worst for Michael. Now, a year later, he resembled the young man he had been before France. There were some lines of strain permanently imprinted on his face, but most of his acquaintances, who didn't know what had caused them, felt that they gave him more character. Occasionally, on damp days, one or another of the injuries he had sustained in the last few years would cause him some pain, and he was still periodically subject to nightmares. But on the whole, he was now healthy—physically.

But there was an abiding core of discontent, a quilted void of loss, that could not be cured, nor much eased. Robert had whisked Michael away to his own retreat in Scotland—the cottage where he had stayed and sought a perspective on life after Felicia's death. It was a remote highland perch where a man could hear nothing but the distant calls of sheep and gulls. The wind mourned over the gentle hills and sometimes carried in it the ghostly lament of bagpipes. A man could think here—or, if thinking proved too much a burden, could simply give himself over to nature, drown in the scent of heather.

Michael's recovery had followed an erratic cycle. At first he was nearly vegetative. Sleeping mostly, waking and eating when Robert told him to, hardly talking. Then suddenly, he was full of frenetic energy. He borrowed some oxen, cleared a field, built a long precise stone wall and spent hours riding his horse madly through the countryside. And all the while he talked—of himself, of King Louis, of his childhood, his opinions on everything from the way to cook herring to the political situation in China. Mostly he talked of Genevieve. He talked to Robert, to himself, to his horse, to the sky, to a passing shepherd.

Then suddenly in September he had stopped talking in the middle of a sentence, stopped building a half-completed stone sheep pen, and had once again taken to his bed. This time, however, he only remained numbed for a matter of two weeks. One morning he appeared, freshly shaven and alert but calm. "Robert," he said. "I've been the worst sort of ass."

Robert smiled. "Yes, you have rather." And that easily the matter of gratitude and acceptance were taken care of.

The next week Robert decided to ride into Inverness to purchase some extra blankets to meet the

coming cold weather. Robert thought Michael understood and said nothing. Shortly afterwards, Michael
himself suggested making the trip again. As they
neared the city, he became quieter and quieter. He
was pale, clenching the reins as if they were his only
hold on sanity.

"You're going to dislocate something if you don't
quit jerking your head around like that to see what's
behind you," Robert warned lightly, then more seriously: "No one is after you. No one."

Michael relaxed slightly. "It's a long habit."

"You've got a lot of habits to break. You aren't
going back to the diplomatic service—are you?"

"No! God, no! But I don't know anything else but
the law. I suppose I'll set up a quiet practice in some
sleepy little seacoast town and spend my evenings
watching ships pass and wonder if Genevieve is on
any of them."

Robert knew the right treatment for self-pitying
remarks like that. "I do hope you don't think I'm
going to visit you often if that's the sort of thing
you regard as entertainment."

Michael actually laughed, the first time in a very
long time. That one day in Inverness seemed, to
Michael, to last for nightmarish weeks, but he returned to the cottage strutting with pride for having
merely endured the day without making a sick fool
of himself.

They went again, and it was more bearable. During Christmas week they ventured clear to Edinburgh
where Michael completed another stage of his recovery by getting into a heated barroom brawl over the
outcome of a golf match. He knocked a few heads
together, suffered a bloody nose and black eye, then
cheerfully treated all the combatants to a round or
six of ale. He sang himself unconscious afterwards.

So, in the early spring when he suggested returning
to London, Robert felt that he was probably ready.
Michael was uneasy by York, plainly nervous by St.

Albans, and practically distraught by the time they
reached the outskirts of London, but a quiet night
at Robert's lodgings restored him somewhat and the
decision, the next morning, to grow a beard, helped.
A man was not so easily recognizable, he reasoned,
with a beard.

He stayed indoors for weeks, watching the busy
throngs pass in the street and when his new beard
was thick enough to look presentable, he ventured out
on a private errand. He hired a coach and had it
stop in front of the house where André and Genevieve had lived. He ordered the coachman to stop,
and sat watching the house as if Genevieve might be
forced to appear by the sheer force of his will. In
a while the door opened, his heart thudded unreasonably at the back of his throat. A woman stepped
out—a plump, pretty bon-bon of a blonde, dressed
in flounces and frills. Escorting her was a pot-bellied
gentleman with thinning hair.

Michael smiled grimly, as a man who has exorcised
one of his demons, and signaled the coachman to return him to Robert's lodgings. When he returned,
he found a note in a familiar handwriting.

Darling boy,
Robert tells me you tried to go right off your
head and he's got you pasted back together. I've
left you alone because I know that I sometimes
unravel *well* people, so I didn't want to inflict
myself upon an invalid. You two must present
yourselves at my house for dinner tonight. I've
laid in *flocks* of the best quail for the occasion.
Do come, my dear.

Love,
Althea

How like her, he thought. *No mincing about, pretending as though nothing untoward has happened.
Good old Althea (be careful about that 'old' business,*

he reminded himself) *just meets the issue head-on, thrashes it out, and moves along to better things.*

That evening, Michael and Robert dined with Althea. She greeted them in a chorus of shrieks and kisses, and led them into a sumptuous dinner, of roast lamb and pungent mint sauce, lightly boiled potatoes sprinkled with tiny snips of parsley, stuffed quail, garden peas in a butter sauce, sweet muffins, a plate of cheeses, and crisp tiny pastries in the shape of diamonds.

They had arrived early and stayed very late, talking frankly in the manner possible only between very good friends. Robert had been corresponding with Althea all along, so she knew the general outline of Michael's troubles and recovery, but she asked caring questions and elicited a full accounting from Michael's viewpoint.

"So you are yourself again?" she said finally.

He smiled half-heartedly. "Whoever that is," he answered.

"Tell her about the seacoast cottage and watching ships?" Robert suggested.

Michael punched him in the arm affectionately. "No, I don't think so. Seriously—if I may use that term in this company—seriously, I don't know where I'm going, what I'm going to do—and it's time to do something. I'm not normally accustomed to doing nothing whatsoever."

"It's not money, is it?" Althea asked.

"Lord, no. My fa—the King has provided nicely, thank you. An odd little character who pretends a very bad Rumanian accent has visited me a couple of times, presenting the numbers of various bank accounts to me and having me sign things about the taxes on an estate somewhere. Apparently I grow sugar cane—"

"On your person?" Robert inquired.

Althea laughed, lifted the lace of Michael's cuff.

"There appears to be some moss here, but nothing in the way of sugar cane—sugar cane? Your estate, I take it, isn't in Norway."

"No. I didn't pay very much attention. Some island in the Caribbean, it seems."

"Why don't you go take a look at it?" Althea suggested.

Michael drew himself up very straight. "Do you know what's involved in getting to the Caribbean? You have to get on a ship and stay on it for a very long time. You know how I feel about that!"

Robert had leaned back, tented his long fingers and said, musingly, "Yes, but think about it, old man. Part of the reason you've never liked the sea was because of how long it took and how anxious you were to be elsewhere—doing something brave and busy. But you were just saying you didn't know what to do—why not while away the time thinking about it on a ship? You might have a nice place there, after all. You know you like the Caribbean—"

Michael regarded him suspiciously. "I can understand your wanting to get me out of your house, but isn't that going a bit far?"

"Actually, I thought I might go with you."

"Grandmama's sending you off to check on the family interests again, eh?"

"Afraid so," Robert admitted, embarrassed that his ploy had been so easily revealed.

"Darlings, you must go," Althea put in. "Much as I adore your company, I don't look forward to having the two of you adorn my table perpetually—"

Neither of them was fooled by this callous remark. Robert added, "You know, Michael, you might just run across Genevieve."

Michael's laughter died on his lips. "Robert, you know better. Looking for someone in the Caribbean isn't like hunting for them in a closed carriage. It's a big place. Besides, she could be anywhere. She went with Sabelle—and that could mean anywhere in the world. Sabelle knows her way around the Atlantic, the Mediterranean, the Gulf—"

He stopped suddenly, set his wine glass down with a crash, opened his mouth, closed it again, and gazed helplessly at Robert. Robert leaned forward, a trace of alarm in his voice. "What is it? What's wrong?"

"Roque and Garlanda," Michael whispered. Suddenly he stood, slapped his forehead and said, "Damn! I must have truly been out of my head! How could I have not realized. Look, Robert, if Sabelle were to make contact with anyone in the world it would be Garlanda! Garlanda! What a stupid, blithering half-wit I've been. I've wasted a year sitting around feeling sorry for myself and trying to deal with the fact that I would never see her again. Never once did I stop and really think!

"Robert, come on," he said, racing for his cloak and hat. "We've got to be going. Do you think we can sail tomorrow?"

28

"A merchantman, Cap'n Meddows, comin' in toward Martinique."

Evonne stood, hands on hips, regarding the almost invisible crow's nest through a lacy veil of mist. "They're heading where we're going ourselves. I say we take them. Quartermaster?"

Her second in command nodded his head vehemently. Evonne then turned to her mother. "Is the *Nightbird* in on the attack?"

"If a pair o' yer boys can row me over to her, sure. Xantha makes a damn fine temporary captain but ain't no one else about to lead me ship into battle."

"You promised!" Genevieve protested, latching onto Sabelle's arm. "You said we wouldn't split up! You said no more attacks! You—"

"We can't pass this up, Gen. Stay an' help yer sister. And send a lantern up to that fool in the crow's nest or else I'll never see his signals."

Sabelle embraced her daughters crushingly, bade them "the luck o' Satan hisself," and turned away. Genevieve heard the creak of winches as a ship's boat was lowered into the water. "Well, I hope you're happy," she spat out spitefully at her sister. "Both of you promised that French ship last week was the end of your piracy. You said you had enough. You said—"

Evonne gave no sign of having heard. Her eyes glinted with battle lust, a true pirate expression. She rang the ship's bell, deafening clangs that seemed to go on into eternity. The sickeningly, too familiar cry rang out: "All hands on deck! Battle stations, battle stations! *Aux armes, aux armes!*"

Everyone scrambled to obey but Genevieve. She stood like an abandoned lamb, sorrowful head down, letting people jostle her in the weeping wet mist of an intolerable morning. She felt betrayed and so old it hurt just to stand. Killing. There was going to be killing again, cannons belching fiery death, robbery, ships sinking, her family endangered. And those people on board the merchantman—those innocent people, women and children, ignorant sailors, servants—

Half a dozen men scrambled up the ratlines with boards and tools. Genevieve glumly peered through the splotchy mist at them. They were lengthening a platform on the mainmast, working furiously. A few minutes later, armed with winches and cables, they began hoisting the *Black Angel*'s best swivel cannon aloft—a long bronze beauty with inexplicable Scottish lions on the barrel and the coat-of-arms of some long-forgotten warrior king. From this perch the cannon would hurl two-headed angels (chainshot heated red-hot) and grapeshot through the other vessel's sails and rigging, crippling her.

Powder monkeys, fleet young urchins in ragged clothes scuttled from the powder magazine to the gunners, arms full of supplies. Another powder monkey was flinging buckets of water on the canvas "doors" of the ammunition room to keep sparks from reaching it during the heat of battle. Cannon loading was going on with remarkable calm, as if the sweating gunners were setting the table for lunch. Genevieve could see that Xantha was sorely missed. The mulatto's tongue could flay the sea-thickened hide off the dullest seaman. When she was in charge of the guns, everyone leaped to obey. Maybe Evonne could—

She caught a fleeting glimpse of her sister's ivory-and-ebony head disappearing down the trap door of

the hold. Off to secure goods, then. No good chasing
her. Genevieve planted her feet half-a-yard apart, put
fists on her hips, and roared with an enthusiasm that
would have done her mother credit.

"Step it up, you barnacle-brained louts. What the
bloody hell do you think this is, a goddamned Re-
formist picnic? Get those fifteen pounders loaded and
get 'em loaded NOW! I want those two-headed angels
heated 'til they're less orange than white! I want 'em
smoking and I'll put you landlubbers in the same
condition if you don't hurry! Get those ramrods lined
up! Stack your ammo! Take the figurehead down and
put her away! Powder monkeys! What's taking so
long? You up there—get the tarred netting up to repel boarding parties!"

Everyone scrambled to obey. Genevieve felt sadly
proud. Before, when she'd needed to be rough and
efficient—Gibraltar sprang to mind—she'd had to pretend she was Evonne. She no longer did. In fact, it
no longer felt like play-acting so much as releasing
a side of her she was finally adult enough to cope
with. She was a Meddows woman, all right. She could
drink, brawl, swear, and fight with the rest of them.
Where was the dainty lady in England? The society
coquette at Versailles? The ambassador's wife? The
meek, bleak little daughter-in-law in Jamaica? The
Meddows in her had overridden the Faunton's acquisition as well as the Countess de Lieuvienne. And,
surprisingly, she felt a thrill of defiant pride at the
realization!

The gray stuff clambering the sides of the *Black
Angel* was no longer lacy mist. It was fog now, crawl-
ing thick and snakily across the freshly painted decks.
Evonne had ordered them lacquered a bright red after
Sabelle had pointed out her own decks in that color.
"Crew don't panic that way. They can't tell how
much blood bin spilt on no red deck. All the same
color so they can pretend no one bin hurt."

Genevieve stared at the decks awhile, wondering

how true that was. Liquid on a red deck could be blood or merely seaspray—or even this clinging, viperish condensation trying to crawl into her lungs. The fog thickened, intensified, and then the sky burst. The swollen clouds released dreary, needlelike splinters of rain, falling fast and hard and thin. It drove through shirts and coats and breeches, mercilessly stung unprotected skin, tormented naked faces and the bare feet of the crew, for they had all stripped off shoes to better walk on the damp decks. It would give them better traction in the bloody midst of battle, too.

The rain hurt. Genevieve sought refuge in the captain's cabin only to find it being dismantled for protection in the upcoming battle. Furniture was being taken apart, rugs rolled up, small objects rolled and padded in sheeting and tucked away. Genevieve turned back to the gunners with a harpy's tongue, shouting over the storm for them to keep the powder dry at all costs. When they appeared befuddled at the meaning, she whipped off her snug, warm coat and began tearing it apart to cover the opened kegs.

From there on she held no specific job. She went wherever needed, assisting the agile little boys carrying ammunition, packing powder and cannonballs into the long, cold muzzles of the waiting guns, filling buckets and placing them at strategic points all about the ship to extinguish fires. She spent several swift minutes ripping and rolling bandages with the surgeon, setting out surgical and amputatory tools, and laying out pallets to place the sick and wounded upon.

Somewhere through the struggling storm the same things were happening aboard her mother's ship. That thought frightened Genevieve, brought the full gravity of the situation back to her with a queasy jolt. As she rolled her sleeves up and stepped, sweaty and thirsty, out into the cold rain, she could hear the lookout. "Merchantman approaching two degrees south of last sighting. English flag. Almost within range."

Evonne materialized like some lithesome wraith from the bowels of the brigantine. She galvanized the crew with her cold-blooded commands, using her voice like an uncoiled cat-o'-nine-tails. The *Nightbird* lurked at starboard now, awaiting plans. "Captain Meddows!" Evonne shouted, hands cupped around her mouth, "what is your strategy?"

"To catch her between us. One vessel to block and engage her while the other takes the rear offensive. Me ship's swifter, lass—I'll swivel in behind her. We'll all drink rumfustian when this's over. By your leave, Captain Meddows," came Sabelle's shout.

The *Nightbird* slipped off through the gray chill un-light of day. Genevieve swallowed down a fist-size lump in her throat and returned to gauging the wind's speed and direction. She made her report to Evonne, who then planned the attack based on the wind and the sea's action.

The *Black Angel* slid into position, midnight sails slapping stealthily like leathery bat wings in the increasing downpour. The crew crouched with bated breath, swords and pistols drawn. "Strike flint," Evonne hissed in sultry viper tones. Sparks flew and took flaming root. "Hold, hold—shelter them from that rain, boys. Hold it, hold it—"

They were so close to the merchantman they could hear her sails in the sodden fog. Evonne prowled the blood-red deck on panther-light bare feet, pacing like a big cat on a night hunt. Genevieve stared at her sister, saw the queerly pale fervor, the flint-spark gleam of her eyes, the elated, unbearable tension she was tautly fraught with. Evonne looked like a woman in love—in love with this treacherous excitement, the scent of powder, the clench of fist on sword. It nearly made Genevieve ill.

A gray, ghostly shape broke through the copious rain and cotton-thick fog. Then a pinpoint of light appeared far beyond the English merchantman—the lookout on board the *Nightbird* signaling the attack.

"Light fuses," Evonne announced in a snow-cold, spring-clear voice. Sixty hands held miniature red flames to expectant fuses. Genevieve watched, terrified and entranced, as the twisted strips of fiber burnt lower. The merchantman wafted into range so benignly, so guilelessly—

The voice of guns was that of a thousand warring ogres. Sound rang, rang again, reverberated through the sullen Caribbean storm as if all the thunderstorms on earth had let loose their lightning at once. Rigging blasted skyward in a shower of orange sparks. They looked like dazzling fireworks through the awesome shroud of loathsome weather.

Unexpectedly, the merchantman replied almost before the *Black Angel's* volley reached its goal. Two rows of gun hatches flew open. Green-brown cannon muzzles spat smoldering, shrieking defiance into the gleaming black brigantine. They had attacked one of the Queen's double-decked war merchantmen instead of a harmless trading vessel!

It was as if a kitten had turned on a tigress and slashed full-grown talons across the savage animal's eyes. The *Black Angel* shuddered and cried with the impact, lady-smooth hull splintering in an arc of orange and ebony specks. She fired back, one volley, two—through the fog the merchantman loomed larger and larger. Genevieve reeled back in horror. Her impression of double decking had been false. It was a three-decker, an armed transport fully the size of a Spanish galleon from the age of Phillip II. It dwarfed the two sleek little brigantines snapping at its flanks like hounds at a bull.

Evonne leaped on the wheel, a woman possessed. She gave it a wrench so savage it tore both sleeves halfway out of her shirt. "Swivel guns cranked to the rear! NOW!"

The *Black Angel* spun, presenting her less vulnerable stern to the massive English ship. Evonne cried the order to reload and fire with deadly monotony, keeping the guns barking with simultaneous accuracy. Genevieve fought her way through racing sailors to her sister's side. "Evonne! Pull out! Retreat! They'll pound us to splinters! Pull out! *Pull out!*"

Evonne's mouth tightened as if a drawstring had been pulled through it. Her savage eyes went fright-filled, then widened. Her mouth hung open. She pointed with a quivering forefinger.

Sabelle's *Nightbird* was on fire.

Genevieve took the helm. "Load! Fire! Water the cannons before they crack! Load, fire—"

"Yes," Evonne agreed, benumbed. "Ram the bastards. Run out the spikes."

"Spikes astern! We're going to ram!" Genevieve shouted.

Sailors grasped ropes, masts, anything solid. The quicker witted worked frantically to tie themselves to the more immovable objects so that they would not be thrown about like tinder with the inevitable impact.

"Tighten that mainsail," Evonne shouted above a momentary hush.

"Lash down that gun and the weapons' chest," Genevieve added. She watched with stupefied horror as the merchantman loomed up, larger and larger. She was unaware of the movement of their own ship and it seemed that the other vessel was actually swelling and expanding like an evil fairy-tale monster in a childish dream.

"Brace for ramming!" the shout went up. At the last instant Genevieve lunged for the mainmast, wrapped her arms about the wood, and hung on as if it were a lover saving her from final destruction.

The merchantman was now a huge fire-belching shadow hanging over them. Closer, impossibly closer. Genevieve closed her eyes, hid her face against her shoulder, and uttered the words of a prayer. Suddenly gravity and direction were gone, replaced by the booming, shrieking, splintering impact. Her feet were yanked out from under her. She felt the mast biting into her arms and her head struck the wood. She struggled for balance. The world was tilted, gone madly, deafeningly awry.

The *Black Angel* kept her forward motion long after the spikes had pierced the oak hull of the merchantman. Genevieve felt something crash against her legs, looked for a second, and was sickened at the sight of the once human form at her feet. She turned away, gagging and feeling hot tears of shame and outrage burn her eyes. Suddenly the *Black Angel* sagged to a shuddering halt.

Sailors on both ships were picking themselves up, searching for weapons that had been plucked from their grasp by the force of collision. Genevieve, her attention split into a dozen shards of consciousness, made her way to the forward deck where there was a sturdy chest of extra weapons: cutlasses, scimitars, daggers, muskets, all the spoils of a half-dozen other attacks.

"Soak that gun!" she shouted to a pair of young sailors who were preparing to load an overheated swivel gun. One of the boys took a leather bucket of sea water from a hook nearby and flung it at the hulking, smoldering metal death engine. The water hissed on the gun barrel, throwing up a cloud of greasy steam. The boys began again to load the gun. Genevieve turned back, saw what they were doing, and shouted again, "No, you fools, I said *soak* it, not spit on it!"

The bolder boy protested, "We got her lined up to blow a great hole in her hull!"

"All you'll do is blow holes in yourselves and the rest of us, you dolts! Better to miss your shot."

"Goddamn women," the boy said, just loudly enough to be heard over the noise of battle.

Something ripped through the sails over Genevieve's head and a large piece of black canvas, flaming and sputtering in the rain, fell to the deck. Gene-

vieve kicked it aside, oblivious to the burns it made
on her feet. She struggled forward, avoiding the searing metal of the gun barrel. She grasped the boy by
the shoulder, spun him around, and said in an omi-
nously quiet voice that managed, nevertheless, to
carry through the searing, dripping air, "Our lives
all depend on one another. If you can't follow orders,
you can try swimming home from here. Now *soak—
that—gun—*!"

"Yes, ma'am," the boy said, terrified by the feroc-
ity of her tone.

She made her way forward, aware that behind her
the crew was being engaged in hand-to-hand combat
now with the crew of the merchantman. "Kate! Help
me distribute these," she screamed as she hauled open
the lid of the weapons' chest. She dug wildly, trying,
not always successfully, to avoid cutting her hands on
the knives and sabers in the chest. She handed them
out to Kate, who passed them on through an im-
promptu bucket-brigade of crewmen in need of protection.

Finally she scrabbled her knuckles against the rough
bottom of the chest. Two more swords, one for her,
one for Kate. She stood, slammed the lid shut, and
tried to get her bearings. She must help, but God!—
where? While Evonne's men were boarding the merchantman, the crew of that ship were laying down
planks and were swarming onto the decks of the
Black Angel. As she looked about, trying to guess
where she could be of most use, she noted that the
Nightbird had caught an errant wind and was moving closer. The tier of sails that had been blazing a
short while before had been cut down and were a
flaming heap on the deck of the ship. Several dozen
ropes with buckets at the end were being lowered and
raised to the sea, bringing up water to extinguish
the flames. Genevieve could see her mother partway
up the rigging shouting out orders.

Genevieve felt her heart race at the sight—Sabelle

in loose, practical trousers, raven hair captured by a scarf, linen shirt clinging to her still voluptuous figure, silky tanned arms showing beneath rolled-up sleeves. As Genevieve stood, transfixed at the sight of her unlikely mother, there was a roar from the merchantman. A fresh volley sent a cannonball shearing through the mast that supported Sabelle's perch.

Genevieve screamed counterpoint to her mother's cry as Sabelle fell. Genevieve raced for the rail, intent on getting to her mother. Sabelle had not been terribly high and might have survived, but Genevieve had to know. She shouted across to the *Nightbird* and watched helplessly as Sabelle's crew rushed to the point where she had fallen. They could not hear, or would not spare her their attention.

She *had* to get to the ship!

"Evonne!" she screamed. "Evonne!—Kate, get the captain."

She stayed at her place, saber hanging useless at her side, afraid to let her eyes stray from the place where Sabelle had disappeared from her view.

"What in hell is so important!" Evonne barked.

Genevieve turned, saw her sister coming toward her. Evonne was cursing, striding, dodging through the mayhem of humanity, both friend and foe, on the deck of the *Black Angel*. A hulking sailor came bounding behind her. "Evonne! Look out!" Genevieve screamed. She remembered the sword in her hand and leaped forward.

Evonne heard her warning, turned, and engaged the man in a quick, brutal duel. She ducked, spun, and came up fast, her sword burying itself hilt-deep in the man's abdomen. Genevieve, tripping and struggling through snaking lines and fierce spots of fire, had almost reached Evonne when it happened—

"Evonne! It's the *Nightbird*. Mother—"

The earth and sea seemed suddenly to explode. The gun behind Evonne, insufficiently cooled in spite of Genevieve's warnings, had been reloaded and had

ignited, blowing itself into a thousand red-hot pieces.
Evonne, her face a mask of pain and horror, was
thrown forward into Genevieve's arms and they were
both flung to the other side of the ship. Ribbons and
arcs of gunpowder, shot, and deadly metal sections
of the cannon filled the air, filling the atmosphere
with the odor of seared blood.

Genevieve struck her head on something, felt her
vision getting hazy and tried to get up, but there was
a weight across her. Evonne! She sat up, gently lifted
her sister, sucked in a terrible groan at the sight of
blood pouring from a fist-sized hole in the side of
Evonne's shirt. There was a gleam of broken metal
buried in the flesh.

"Oh, my God!" Genevieve whispered.

"Gen?" Evonne said in a curiously calm voice.

"Don't talk! I'll get the surgeon. You'll be all
right. Hold very still, Evonne."

Evonne clutched at her hand with amazing strength.
"No, Gen, I *won't* be all right. Stay—" She took a
long, shuddering breath and repeated pitifully, "Stay,
please stay."

Genevieve bowed her head over her sister's raven-
hued hair and wept unashamedly. "Don't die, Evonne.
Please don't, not now, not when we've found our
family and—"

"Shh . . . Gen? Gen!" There was urgency in the
voice, fright and pain and the desperate need to speak.
Evonne clutched the frilled, strained front of Genevieve's tunic. "Mother . . . don't tell Mother we
stayed in to save her. I don't want her bearing that
guilt. Promise you won't tell her, won't hurt her.
Promise!"

The image of Sabelle's fiery fall ripped at Genevieve's heart as deeply as did her sister's noble plea.
She forced down scorching tears, held herself calm
and erect. Evonne must not be told Sabelle was probably dead. She must not! "Yes, Evonne, I promise. I

won't breathe a word to Mother. I'll let her think we were so carried away by the excitement we did foolish things. She won't know of the sacrifice. She will carry no burden of guilt."

Evonne rested a bloody hand against Genevieve's cheek. "You'll take care of her? A woman her age has no . . . no business . . . carrying on like a girl of nineteen. You'll take care of her?"

Take care of a woman she mustn't suspect to be dying, even dead. "Of course, Evonne. Anything. I'll wrestle her off the high seas and tie her to a plantation if I have to. Now quit talking silly. The ship's surgeon is coming, we'll get you into your cabin and—"

A spasm shook Evonne, tightened her graceful, painstricken body into a parody of itself. Genevieve rocked her gently, smoothing the snarled raven tresses. "Hurts, Gen. God, it hurts!"

From somewhere in the fog Kate emerged with a bottle of rum and bandages. Genevieve uncorked the rum, held it to her sister's cracked lips, pressed snowy white muslin to her heaving side and saw the fabric turn the color of the sanguine decks. Again she fought and mastered her tears. Evonne mustn't know she was terrified. Evonne must think she rested in strong, able arms, a refuge amidst the howling insanity of battle.

"Gen?" came a feeble whisper. She raised her head from the smoke-laced black curls, etched on a loving smile that nearly succeeded in veiling her great grief.

"Yes, darling. What is it?"

"Our white house on the hill—" Agony clenched and unclenched the tortured body, then rum and suffering began to seep, entwined, through Evonne's pouring veins. Kitten-weak fingers fastened on Genevieve's bloodied brown hair. "Genevieve, Gen . . . Little Gen. We had a puppy. He bit me once and you cried . . . pain . . . oh, Genevieve! The white house was a fairy tale! I never could have stood silk

dresses and suitors on a veranda! I was born to take
what I wanted and pay for it. No regrets, Gen. Oh,
Gen, I'm so happy!"

"Happy, you fool? Whatever for?" Genevieve asked
brokenly, unable to stop the tears now. Evonne's face
was growing peaceful, their combined tears and the
rain rinsing away dirt and blood, exposing the perfect, porcelain pallor of her exquisite face.

"I'm happy because I've had everything. I controlled
my own fate. I mastered a crew and a ship. I had
adventures and riches . . . ." The little white fist,
bones standing up like ridges, loosened. Genevieve
took it in her own hand, kissed it, warmed it, blew
breath and life into it, and pressed it to her heart.

Evonne's face was beautiful. She beamed with a
virgin martyr's doomed, radiant joy. "Genevieve . . .
it doesn't hurt very much anymore . . . I had so
much. I was rich and wild and carefree—and I had
love, so much love!"

Genevieve held her closer, kissed her sister's cheek.
It was cool now, cool and translucent as fine marble.
"Love, Evonne? Tell me about your love," she soothed,
imagining some tall, dashing sailor.

"Oh, Gen—it was the purest, noblest thing I ever
knew—it was brave and true and asked nothing in
return—oh, Gen! It was you!"

Genevieve collapsed, weeping and bundling Evonne
closer as if she, alone and unarmed, could stand between her sister and the hooded shadow of death.

"Genevieve? *The Black Angel*—"

She smeared a powder-burnt hand across her eyes.
"I'll send her with you, Evonne."

"Good . . . I'm so afraid to go into the ground
where it's cold and slimy and things turn ugly. Fire,
Gen . . . fire . . . lovely fire. . . ."

"I love you, Evonne. Close your eyes and go to
sleep now."

"It's so lovely and cool here, I—"

Evonne went limp in her loving arms.

Lightning cracked overhead, casting a blue flash of light over the three ships. A second later they were assaulted by the reverberating blow of thunder. Kate sank to her knees beside Genevieve and put her arm around her. "Lass, you're in charge now. I'll see to it she's taken belowdecks."

Genevieve held Evonne all the tighter. "I can't leave her."

"But lass, she's left *you*," Kate spoke softly. "Would you sacrifice all of us to prove your loyalty?"

"Gen," a man's voice called somewhere, but it was only an unimportant echo in the back of Genevieve's mind.

"We have to get both ships out of here," Kate urged again. "The wind's right, but you'll have to take the command."

"Gen!" the voice, a man's, cracked and urgent, was near her now.

Someone touched her arm. She looked up and through a blur of tears and rain and blood saw him—bearded, bedraggled, a cut over his eye weeping red. He said something and started to reach for Evonne.

Genevieve knew nothing, thought nothing, only recognized in some feral way that he was a stranger and meant harm to her sister. She transferred Evonne's limp weight to Kate's waiting arms and was instantly on her feet.

She had the sword in her hand again and her muscles were coiling to spring. The man, the wet, bearded stranger, started to speak again. He put his hand out as if to grab her. She lunged and he, though surprised, was instantly aware of what she was doing. He dodged, parried her fierce slashes. She gritted her teeth, a grieving moan filled her throat as she attacked. She swung her sword in wide, explosive arcs. No dainty sword play, this, but a deadly display of raging sorrow. Like superb dancers at a ball, they soon had all eyes. A space on the blood-slimed deck was cleared as if by a mystical force. Those still able to move backed away and gazed as the woman forced the man ever backwards.

His use of the sword was as expert as hers, certainly more graceful and controlled, but he was on the defensive. Where he could have plunged the cold blade into her flesh, he used the opportunity rather to try to knock her weapon out of her hands. But she was holding it with a grip harder than the steel from which it was made. "You goddamn coward," she screamed at him, her voice cracked and raw, "Fight! Fight! Damn you."

She leaped forward again. The bearded stranger ducked sideways saying, "Gen?"

It almost stopped her, the sheer absurdity of this man using her name as if he had the right to do so. Her heartbeat pounded in her ears. She wheeled around, slashed at him again and felt the tip of her blade brush his sodden sleeve and slip away harmlessly.

The man took another cautious step back—but not cautious enough. His foot caught in a rope. For the barest instant he allowed his gaze to slip downward and Genevieve darted forward. He saw her coming and was forced to step farther back. But his booted foot was hopelessly tangled in the movement and he fell backwards, trying, before he even landed, to turn and roll away.

As he rolled, he came up to find her standing over him, the tip of her sword nestled nastily at the hollow of his throat. There was only a moment left to him.

"Genevieve! Don't! It's me, Michael!" he shouted.

The sword point trembled, pricked delicately at his skin. She stood above him, frozen into an attitude of hope and disbelief. With her free hand she made the oddly girlish gesture of pushing her soaked hair out of her eyes. "Michael?" she mouthed silently. Her fingers on the sword clutched once, then it clattered to the deck. "Michael?" she asked again, still not sure she'd heard right.

She drew back a little. Slowly he rose, careful not to further alarm her. "Genevieve, are you hurt?" he asked, moving ever closer.

She shook her head dumbly. "I—I don't—think so," she said slowly. "Evonne's dead," she said bluntly, purging her grief somewhat by the cold shock of the words. "She's dead—and I think Mother is too."

His blanched reply was lost in the sudden babble that broke out around them at that instant. "She's turning tail—!"

Genevieve numbly looked astern. The merchant-man was moving away, the gaping hole in her hull taking on water.

"Robert!" Michael said, and looked around wildly.

Genevieve was dizzy with incomprehension. "Robert is with you?"

"He was right behind me—there—is that him? Yes!" He took hold of her shoulders. "Gen, is the *Black Angel* seaworthy?"

"I think so," she mumbled distantly, mechanically.

"Can you command her?"

Her pride, stung by the question, reasserted itself. "Yes, of course, I can."

He smiled a little at that. "I'm sure you can. Then do so. The captain of the vessel I was on is retreating, but I shouldn't be too surprised if he fires another volley just before losing range. You better be ready. Sabelle's crew will know that even if Sabelle— if she can't tell them. Give your orders. You're the captain of the *Black Angel* now."

She shook her head, unfeeling, far away. "No, Michael. No one but Evonne will *ever* be captain of this ship." She turned, signaled to the gunners to load and prime, her gaze slipping past the blackened hole in the deck where the deadly cannon that killed Evonne had once been.

Michael took her hand and they turned to see if the *Nightbird* was safe. She spotted a familiar brown face at the near rail—Xantha, waving a large square of cloth and shouting something unintelligible. "What is she saying?" Genevieve asked numbly.

Xantha stopped, lifted something. A figure in a white, blood-spattered shirt, Sabelle! It had to be— the dark hair, the clothing. Then, miracle of miracles, Sabelle waved! It was a feeble gesture, but she was alive!

"Set course for Martinique! We'll take her to Roque and Garlanda's to recover," Genevieve weakly shouted to her quartermaster and heard the order echoed mournfully from the *Nightbird.*

29

On a cool Caribbean evening Genevieve gave Evonne her funeral. Michael rowed her and Xantha from Roque and Garlanda's shipping docks out to the *Black Angel* and remained in the small boat while they climbed aboard the black brigantine.

Early that morning the crew, in various stages of injury, had unloaded the majestic ship. Genevieve, with Sabelle's permission, had seen to it that certain things were left behind. Now, in the black, splashing silence, she and Xantha collected those things.

They had already cleansed all signs of battle from their magnificent captain and arrayed her in her best silks and rubies. Her hands were neatly folded over her flamboyant captain's hat, just below her heart. Genevieve and Xantha entered the cabin by torch-light now, draped the bunk with unfolded swathes of material—gorgeous, stiff moires, rustley soft silks, jewel-bright satin, cloth-of-gold. Over this bier they poured casks of gems. And on top of this splendid display, they sprinkled the costliest of essences: frank-incense, ambergris, civet, attar of black roses, sandal-wood, cinnamon bark. Genevieve flung a bag of gold dust over it all.

It looked magnificent. Evonne was entombed as royally as any queen. Genevieve and Xantha put swords and muskets on the Persian carpet at her feet —the most sumptuous carpet they had found in the hold, lush with topaz, crimson, sapphire, and tourma-line shades. It would have brought a prince's ransom in any port.

They hung up her pretty oil lamps with their float-ing wicks and exotic scents. And then they poured

hot sweet oil all around her. Xantha returned to the
small boat while Genevieve knelt and prayed fer-
vently. She could hear the lulling slosh of the friendly
waves, waiting, waiting to take her sister home. There
was everything on board a dead warrior needed. Like
mourning savages, Sabelle, Genevieve, Kate, and Xantha had cut locks of their hair and twined them together, locking the braid in a small bronze cask with
ornate serpent handles that held Evonne's delicate
paint pots and scrollwork combs—symbols of the femininity she had never entirely conquered.

Genevieve placed the cask with Evonne's swords,
adding a small bag of powder and shot. She uncorked
an onion-shaped bottle of Madeira and set it on the
desk next to an upside-down frosted goblet. Then
she crossed her sister's freshly polished hip boots and
thin kidskin gloves, leaving them on the desk with
the maps and navigational instruments as Evonne had
been prone to do.

There was one last thing—Robert made her promise. She took his etched heirloom watch from her
pocket and smiled, remembering how it had brought
him back to them when they'd thought him long gone:
Has anyone seen my watch? How they'd laughed!
Evonne had thrown back her perfect cream-and-mid-
night head and made the deck rock with good-natured
hilarity. It was Robert's small, heartfelt tribute to
the remarkable woman he had been friend and lover
to—as well as chief stolen goods organizer and unofficial fellow thief.

Genevieve laid the watch on the unrolled parchment maps, lamplight showing fragile and gold
through the paper. Set up like a queen. Yes. The food
the cook had slaved over, the weapons, the offerings—
every member of the crew had left a possession they
treasured in the overflowing weapons' chest at the
door. Rings, favored articles of clothing, jewels, daggers—just like in the books, just like Genevieve had
always read about the way Viking chieftains were

sent to their fiery ends. No human sacrifice—not externally, at least. Only the death of something inside of everyone who had known and admired the unlikely, valiant Captain Meddows.

"Good-bye Evonne. I suppose you were your ship to me—a black angel bursting through the gloom and monotony of my life, grudgingly giving me love, gladly making me into a new and stronger person. Sail on, *ma soeur*. Sail on forever with your hand alone at the helm—the way you want it, with no master over you. Good-bye. I wish you sunshine and smooth waters."

She took down the nearest lamp and flung it against the wall. It caught the oil, burning brilliantly. Genevieve strode away quickly, climbing back to the small boat. Michael helped her in and wordlessly began to row them away.

Brave, dauntless Xantha sat staring straight ahead, soundless tears coursing down her perfect face. But Genevieve sat facing the *Black Angel*, watching the maize and copper flames spreading, climbing the masts, embracing slack sails, licking blood-red decks. Michael rested at the oars as the *Black Angel* drifted through sedate indigo waves. He and Genevieve sat silently waiting through harsh hours as the funeral progressed.

The last thing ablaze was the haughty figurehead. Flames crept inside furtively, then all at once scarlet tongues of molten gold shot from her eyes and the tip of her sword. For a full minute the figurehead stared at them with sudden hephaestion'd life, then her eyes went dead and the fire leaped down her sword. Her wings seemed to stretch and move in the intense heat, great black feathers alight with bronze and orange and yellow.

With a sudden rush and whoosh of water on flames, the ship's backbone broke. She listed regally, not hurrying but sliding gracefully beneath the kind, cool waters. The only intact section of the mighty brigantine was the *Black Angel* herself. Sword aloft, eyes empty and seared by carnage and grief, she slid slowly away from the smoking light of night. Down to the underworld, down into Stygian, eternal midnight. The tip of the blazing sword remained visible for some minutes, then smoldered out and disappeared into the sea that sweetly quenched all pain.

Michael rowed them back to shore. Xantha crept away to grieve in solitude. Kate approached on swift, bare feet. "Your mother, lass. When the first flames shot up she woke and sat screaming in bed for her bairns. It took a moment or twain to subdue her, then she collapsed. The fever of her wound broke as clean and clear—as clear as those stars."

Genevieve looked up. Amid the drifting smoke and sparks there were indeed stars, twinkling white dots of brilliance in velvet shrouds. *Shrouds,* she thought ironically. *I remember climbing and mending the Black Angel's 'shrouds', as they call them. Tonight they played the real role.*

She turned to Michael suddenly. "I laid her out like a queen."

"I know you did, chérie. Come away now, it's over."

"Over?" she echoed. Could it be over, this heart-breaking chapter of her life? Were action, risk, sorrow, deception all safely relegated to memory? Tired, aching inside and out, she could feel the sting and throb of every blow during the battle, could feel all the weight of age and responsibility dragging her heart down. "Michael," she murmured. "I'm going to sit with Mother now—let her know it's all right, hold her hand while she sleeps and heals. And I must heal, too. There's nothing of me that's healthy and intact right now."

He took her face tenderly in his hands. "I understand, Gen." He linked his arm through hers and led her back to Roque and Garlanda's house at the top of the hill. They did not speak all the way. When they reached the door, he finally said, "I was coming to the Caribbean to look at the estate the King gave me and Robert was handling some family business. Should he and I go away and attend to our duties? Leave you alone?"

She nodded. "There are things I must master, wounds inside I must treat."

He kissed her, not as a lover, but lightly on the forehead, a friend. "Go to your mother, Gen. She needs you."

She stood and watched as he walked away, his long easy stride putting distance between them. "Michael," she called softly. He turned, waited. "Don't be gone too long."

It was the first night Sabelle had come downstairs to Roque and Garlanda's elegant dining room for dinner. During the previous two months while her leg healed, meals had been brought up to her, as often as not by Garlanda herself. The two women had spent long hours closeted together talking, at first, of old times, and then of the future. Now it was all arranged—the *Nightbird* would become part of Garlanda's fleet and Sabelle would become full partner to the legitimate shipping line Garlanda was building. "Gen, I wish you would reconsider joining us," Garlanda said again.

Genevieve folded her embroidered linen napkin, touched her lips, and laid it beside her plate. "Thank you both, but I'm finished with sailing. Truly finished."

"Garlanda, stop nagging the girl. Just because you and Belle are buccaneers to the core doesn't mean everyone has to be," Roque said, smiling. He raised his glass. "I propose a toast to the new partner and to Gen for having the good sense to stay firmly on dry land."

They drank the sweet wine and basked contentedly

in the glow of spirits and friendship. "I have some new wines I want to try," Roque said. "Join me, ladies?"

Three new bottles, tiny glasses, and a tray of cheese to clear the palate were brought to the table. Genevieve declined to join them, saying she wanted to take a breath of fresh air.

The other three exchanged knowing glances, smiling. "My lookouts will tell us when his ship is spotted," Roque said.

"I know," Genevieve said, a little embarrassed that they had all seen through her so easily. She wrapped a light silk shawl around her shoulders and went out on the darkened veranda. The heady tropical night fragrance clouded around her, almost taking her very breath away. How could she have ever wanted to be anywhere but here? She sat looking out at the moon-washed sea and thought about the wine tasting. Cheese to clear the palate. Just as she'd needed time to separate the parts of her life. Now, after two months, she'd lost the scent of sulphur and blood. The cannon crack and screams of battle were gone. She'd almost forgotten the feel of sand-dusted oak decks under her bare feet and her rope-roughened hands were soft again.

She sensed the ship's presence before she could actually see or hear anything. Somehow she knew it was out there. She squinted into the heavy, aromatic darkness for a long while before the lights of the vessel, bobbing on the tranquil sea, became visible. She was on her feet, then, picking up her ivory taffeta skirts, running down flight after flight of flagstone steps.

She reached the wharves just as the ship's ropes were being thrown over. The plank crashed down and she had to restrain herself from dashing aboard to find him. But Michael was the first off, dressed as a gentleman, his beard gone now. Lean, tan, laughing. "You're out of breath," he said as he gave her a quick hug.

"I ran all the way," she admitted.

"I'm glad."

He put his arm around her shoulders and they walked away from the bustle of unloading the ship. He chatted about his cane plantation—acreage, crops' production, the overseer's competence, the size and elegance of the house, the horses. "You ought to see the view from the house," he said as they reached the foot of the long flights of steps to Roque's home.

"I *ought* to see the view?" Genevieve asked, turning to face him.

He smiled broadly and wrapped her in his strong embrace. His lips brushed hers lightly, then with more passion. Her response was hungry, eager, and yet a little shy. "Aren't you going to ask me?" she finally said, timid of meeting his gaze.

He put a finger under her chin, lifted her face. "Are you ready for questions now?"

"Only one."

"Will you marry me?"

"Yes. Oh yes, yes, *yes!* I thought somehow, in all our adventuring, we'd never get around to that. Sometimes I was afraid we'd play buccaneers and government agents the rest of our lives, like children gone awry. And sometimes—sometimes it was all I ever wanted, the adventures, the excitement."

He kissed her again, the breeze twining their hair. "And what, chérie, do you want now?" Michael asked.

There was a catch in her throat, as if the words should cause pain but no longer held that sway over her. She gripped his velvet lapels and looked deep into his smoky eyes. "I want a white house on a hill with palm trees and a veranda. I want horses on the lawn. And I want to spend forever and ever with you."

"Horses, a house, and me—I think I can arrange that."

Genevieve rested her head on his shoulder, a smile of deep contentment playing about her soft lips.

"Horses, a white house on the hill, and you—and my sword."

He gave a start, then laughed in bewildered admiration. "What an astonishing woman you are—sailor, navigator, pirate, countess, society blue-blood—but that's all behind us now. We're going to live like real people and never set foot on another rolling deck as long as we live. What do you need a sword for?"

She gave a low molasses laugh that at an earlier time could have been Sabelle or Evonne, but was now totally Genevieve. And she put a hand on her hip.

"I want to be ready just in case someone tries to take you away from me again!"

AUTHOR'S NOTE

Three battles in the early eighteenth century engineered by the intricate British spy system (of which the fictional Michael is a member) crushed France as a world power.

Vigo's Armada, the richest prize in marine history, has been depicted factually, including Hobson versus the snuff ship and pirates making off with the unclaimed spoils. A large portion of the treasure still litters the bottom of the bay.

Byng's rescue of the Gibraltar women in Our Lady of Europa and Rooke's gout are facts, as is the monumental military disaster of the Battle of Blenheim.

The social and economic upheaval caused by the triple loss smoldered the rest of the century and then exploded into the French Revolution.

Class Reunion

RONA JAFFE

author of
The Best of Everything

"Reading Rona Jaffe
is like being presented
with a Cartier watch;
you know exactly
what you're getting
and it's just what you
want."—*Cosmopolitan*

Annabel, Chris, Emily and Daphne left Radcliffe in '57 wanting the best of everything. They meet again 20 years later and discover what they actually got. Their story is about love, friendship and secrets that span three decades. It will make you laugh and cry and remember all the things that shaped our lives.

"It will bring back those joyous and miserable memories."
—*The Philadelphia Bulletin*
"Keeps you up all night reading."—*Los Angeles Times*
"Rona Jaffe is in a class by herself."—*The Cleveland Press*

A Dell Book $2.75 (11408-X)

California Woman

Daniel Knapp

The first novel in a new series

A sweeping saga of the American West

Esther left New England a radiant bride, her future as bright as the majestic frontiers. But before she could reach California, she had lost everything but her indomitable courage and will to survive. Against the rich tapestry of California history, she lived for love—and vengeance!

A Dell Book $2.50 (11035-1)

MADELEINE A. POLLAND

SABRINA

Beautiful Sabrina was only 15 when her blue eyes first met the dark, dashing gaze of Gerrard Moynihan and she fell madly in love—unaware that she was already promised to the church.

As the Great War and the struggle for independence convulsed all Ireland, Sabrina also did battle. She rose from crushing defeat to shatter the iron bonds of tradition . . . to leap the convent walls and seize love—triumphant, enduring love—in a world that could never be the same.

A Dell Book $2.50 (17633-6)

At your local bookstore or use this handy coupon for ordering:

Once you've tasted joy and passion, do you dare dream of

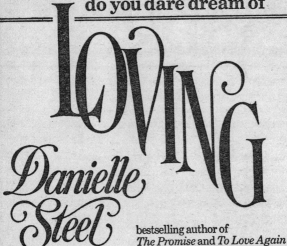

LOVING

Danielle Steel

bestselling author of
The Promise and *To Love Again*

Bettina Daniels lived in a gilded world—pampered, adored, ador-ing. She had youth, beauty and a glamorous life that circled the globe—everything her father's love, fame and money could buy. Suddenly, Justin Daniels was gone. Bettina stood alone before a mountain of debts and a world of strangers—men who promised her many things, who tempted her with words of love. But Bettina had to live her own life, seize her own dreams and take her own chances. But could she pay the bittersweet price?

A Dell Book ═══════════════ **$2.75 (14684-4)**

Second Generation
Howard Fast

**THE SECOND TRIUMPHANT
NOVEL IN THE TOWERING
EPIC LAUNCHED BY**

THE IMMIGRANTS

Barbara Lavette, the beautiful daughter of rugged Dan Lavette and his aristocratic first wife, stands at the center of *Second Generation*. Determined to build a life of her own, Barbara finds danger, unforgettable romance, and shattering tragedy. Sweeping from the depths of the Depression, through the darkest hours of World War II, to the exultant certainty of victory, *Second Generation* continues the unbelievable saga of the Lavettes.

A Dell Book $2.75   (17892-4)